THE AFTERPARTY

Leo Benedictus is a features writer with the *Guardian*. He lives in London with his wife and two sons.

www.leobenedictus.co.uk

LEO BENEDICTUS

The Afterparty

VINTAGE BOOKS

London

Published by Vintage 2012

2 4 6 8 10 9 7 5 3 1

Copyright © Leo Benedictus 2011
Deleted scenes copyright © Leo Benedictus 2012

Lyrics from 'Losing My Edge' reproduced with permission.
Written by James Murphy.
Published by Guy with Head and Arms Music (ASCAP)

First published in Great Britain in 2011 by
Jonathan Cape

Vintage
Random House, 20 Vauxhall Bridge Road,
London SW1V 2SA

www.vintage-books.co.uk

Addresses for companies within The Random House Group Limited
can be found at: www.randomhouse.co.uk/offices.htm

The Random House Group Limited Reg. No. 954009

A CIP catalogue record for this book
is available from the British Library

ISBN 9780099552567

Penguin Random House is committed to a sustainable future for
our business, our readers and our planet. This book is made from
Forest Stewardship Council® certified paper.

Printed and bound in Great Britain by Clays Ltd, St Ives plc

for Sarah

Dear Valerie

My name is William Mendez. I'm a freelance journalist from London, and in my spare time I've been working on a novel called *Publicity*, which tells the story of one night at a decadent celebrity party in 2005. Please find the opening chapter enclosed with this email. At the moment I have no literary agent, so if you think the book has promise I would be delighted if you would agree to represent me in selling it to a publisher.

Before you begin, however, I feel I ought to warn you briefly about the opening scene. Speaking as a reader myself, I must say I've never abandoned anything because of a bad first page, and I doubt that many others have. Nevertheless, I do find many novels quite difficult to ease into. What's going on? Where am I? Who are you? I'm so busy asking all these questions that I often can't absorb the answers. This, no doubt, is why it is 'a truth universally acknowledged' by novelists that the first few lines are crucially important. (Though actually, I'd say one should think more carefully about how a book can engage readers *before* they even pick it up – otherwise, why would they?) To grab people's attention, therefore, *Publicity* begins with something bold, blunt and moderately shocking: a graphic description of its hero Michael defecating. Please understand that I don't mean this to seem confrontational – to you, or any other reader. Although if you do feel confronted by it, I'm sure we can find a way of softening the blow. The scene could easily be relocated later in the book, for instance. Or we could add some kind of preface in front of it?

But you'll be keen to get on. Please email me if you want to see chapter two.

Regards

William Mendez

Publicity

A novel
by William Mendez

Friday, April 1 2005

21:44

They would hate him if they knew he was afraid, all those easy people out there. So he must not let them know. Michael pulled the toilet door shut with his trailing hand and dialled home the bolt. He heard its quiet click declare his safety. Time to be alone.

Yet he was diverted by the sudden beauty of the lavatory. It was an old found thing, with a delicately fluted pan and painted cistern, no doubt a grubby scavenge from the carcass of a wonder pub. It was certainly Victorian, at any rate; no craftsmen since those patriotic days had ever tried so hard. (Or all had learned, at least, to hide their trying.) And look at all that depth and width! How gloriously inaccurate the Empire's drinkers must have been! Although, ahem, the nudging in his entrails had not brought him here to look. So, unbuckling his belt, Michael lowered himself on to the seat. The trousers of his suit, united with his underpants, slopped into a fabric puddle on the tiles. He stirred them with a foot, and the spoon in his pocket clinked in a limestone groove. Finally, he relaxed.

And straight away, a premonition rose within him. Some warm dark power was gathering its mass. His body clenched. Forgotten fibres twanged and snapped. Jaws shook, knees shook, teeth shook, until at last, when surely all must shatter, a knobbled cosh declared its independence and set forth, stately and momentous as an ocean liner, through the last elastic inches to the pool below.

Lightened, eyelids flickering with ecstasy, Michael peed like a king.

It was hard to say how much time had passed when a noise

5

in the adjacent cubicle brought him back into the world. Rising dizzily, he twitched out half a dozen sheets of tissue from the roll, and wiped himself. Wad: immaculate. Then he turned to see what he had done.

It was the stool of his dreams.

Plump, gently curled, and quite comically vast, the thing reared a good three inches through the waterline as though in mockery of its home. For a moment, Michael felt so proud he almost wanted witnesses. He had to fight away an impulse to unlock his stall and usher people in.

But then he heard the whispering. A gleeful sibilance next door. A voice, fast and skilful, and a tapping sound. Discarding his tissue, he crouched down to peer under the partition. The spoon in his pocket clinked quietly again.

He saw four feet. Two were male, in leather boots, creased forward at the toes, as if the owner were leaning on the toilet to be sick. The other pair was female, tanned and painted, grown from lissom ankles on to show-off shoes. These ones seemed to straddle the boots, as though this glamorous woman was stood above her vomiting companion to protect his haircut from the stream. But no retching could be heard.

Then: 'Oh come *aaahn*!' the woman's voice said, American and now not whispered.

Michael stood up suddenly as if he had been spotted, grabbing pants and trousers by the waistband, zipping fast.

'Keep your hair on, love,' the man replied, in loud London. Tap tap. 'There you go.' Tap tap.

Someone flushed, and Michael felt safe again behind the sound. And happier. Fascinating as his neighbours were, it belittled him to spy on them.

The flush had reached its cruise.

So what else was he going to do?

The turd said nothing.

He took out his phone. *21:46.* Too early to leave the party, and too shameful, without having even spoken to another guest.

No, tonight he must be bold. He must be bolder than himself, or take his slow fears home. *Do it!* he almost shouted. Strike back into the scene and *speak!* Ten minutes' fortitude, then outside to Chinatown, to subside into a bowl of noodles. He would eat a hero's dinner if his courage could be brave.

He looked back at the toilet, at his splendid waste, at the painted garden scene upon the handle of the chain. A drop of Doulton, strung up for admiring. He pulled, and left the roaring mechanism to unwind.

Michael sat in traffic. And he was already late.

21:03, said the driver's display.

No movement, said the road. Just a clotted thread of transport working up a smoke. The constant *coitus interruptus* of confinement and release.

If this went on, Michael wondered hopefully, perhaps he might not make it at all? The thought was childish, so he let it drop.

21:04.

Michael sat in traffic.

The taxi nibbled up another metre. Stopped again. The contained compartment air grew warm beneath the driver's rage.

And Michael had not even been invited.

Hugo Marks is thirty-one

said the card in his pocket,

Cuzco, 12 Malt Street W1
8pm, Friday, April 1 2005

On the back was a picture of a bunch of flowers, and in the corner had been written, *Camille McLeish*, the name of his boss. Actually, not his boss. But still someone he was frightened of. She was a gossip columnist on the *Standard*, and a fairly celebrated one, a regular at these kinds of things. Whereas Michael just subedited her column, and subeditors were never celebrated, so he had no experience at all of stars like Hugo Marks. Even so, he was surprised that Camille herself had been invited. With witty little chisellings in her column, she had made it clear what her opinion was of Marks's reclusiveness (affected and self-indulgent, typical of an actor) and his creaking marriage (finished). So perhaps, suspecting hidden vengeance, she had not trusted the invitation to his party? This would be why she had got rid of it, on the pretext that her son was ill. But why then give the card to Michael? Because he had once said that Marks's films were good? Because he was desperate for the opportunity to write something for the paper, and the party might afford it? Both motives seemed too considerate to be hers. And at first, trying to understand the offer, Michael had merely stared back dumbly.

Then Sally had intervened. Lovely Sally.

Oh Michael, you'll never get this chance again! You must go! she had exclaimed, handing back the invitation.

And looking at her face, he had known that he must.

Free drinks, famous faces, and the longed-for chance to see his words in print: the offer was so unarguably good that it would only advertise his timidity if he refused.

So now Michael sat in traffic, and he worried.

21:07.

He would know absolutely no one there. Worse: he would know half of them from TV and have to hide how impressed he was. Worse still: he was supposed to make friends and pick up indiscretions.

£8.60, said the driver's screen. *£8.80.*

And the radio was on.

. . . me coming out of the show, Will Young was saying. *But to be honest, you can't have everything, you know, at once. I mean I had a very quick rise to being very well known as a singer with actually no material behind me. And I got a record contract and paid off my student loan. And I don't think life works like that. You can't have everything.*

The driver listened with interest. Tight mown grey hair sprouting densely from a roll of neck stodge. Michael would not have picked him as a Will Young fan.

£9.40.

At last the road was clearing. The cab accelerated to a red-cheeked British clatter.

As long as he had something to report to Sally. That was all that mattered. As long as he went home with *something*, he might escape disgrace. No need to impress her any more – that adolescent wound had healed over. Just the safe disposal of the night would do.

£11.20.

It was time for the news and sport.

. . . condition of His Holiness John Paul II, said the female newsreader, at full seriousness, *is reported to be grave.*

Michael listened. He had spent the whole day laying out a suite of commentaries and encomiums on the dying Pope, which the senior editors, bored of waiting, had decided to run in the Saturday paper. It had been his flippant guess, in a discreetly organised office sweepstake, that death would occur at 13:13 tomorrow. Which was looking good. Laughing when he asked her, Sally had said *08:12.*

£14.00.

The taxi rattled into Malt Street through drifts of Soho drinkers. Loose-limbed and dressed up, out on a Friday night.

Michael sat forward on his seat. He did definitely need the loo.

Now, through the windscreen, a flash of colour caught his eye. Drawing near, he saw it was a length of carpet – mauve carpet, the colour of the flowers on his invitation – that someone had unfurled across the pavement, over the kerb, and out on to the street. At its edge was a chain of crowd-control barriers, battered and grey. And behind them . . . Michael's body tightened. He had not considered this. Behind the barriers were paparazzi. They leaned against the rail in various attitudes, listlessly equipped. Nobody was leaving or entering the club at that moment, and many of them had taken the opportunity to smoke cigarettes or talk on mobile phones. Seeing the cab arrive, to Michael's horror, first one of them, then two, then three, slapped their embers to the ground, readied cameras, and dug in for his approach.

'£14.80, mate,' the cab driver said, stopping six feet from the carpet's edge.

The door mechanism bounced open.

'Right.'

Michael unzipped the pouch in his wallet to investigate its coins. Arriving by taxi had been Sally's idea too – *to puff you up*, she had said. It had also proved expensive. He straightened, and a brisk volley of flashes caught him through the window. In clownish synchronisation, three photographers all checked their screens.

'There you go,' Michael said, handing the driver a £20 note still flat from its withdrawal.

'Ta. Big party, is it?'

'Yes. Hugo Marks's birthday.'

'Hugo Marks the actor?'

'Yes.'

'Right.' The driver slithered out a metal handful into the tray between them. 'Are you in movies too, then?'

'No,' Michael said. 'I'm a journalist.' Which sounded good.

'OK . . . Here to write about what they all get up to, is it?'

'Yes. I hope so.'

'All right then. Good luck.' He grinned enthusiastically, revealing a network of wrinkles baked deep into his skin. Then he added, 'I could tell you some stories about that lot, no problem.'

Yes please, Michael wanted to say. *Tell me your stories. Just drive me somewhere else and I'll write it all down.*

But, 'I bet,' he said instead. And, 'Thanks a lot,' as he stepped out of the cab.

The photographers seemed calmer now, studying him without interest. Even so, Michael trembled as he hurried up the carpet. Each step he took, each swing of arm and knee, felt counterfeit. Like a marionette's.

Sorry, this is a private party, he kept expecting somebody to say.

He must reek of fraud.

But the photographers just watched.

Michael reached the door and pulled.

Then he pushed, and went in.

A beautiful young woman, draped with elegance in black, stood behind a distressed lectern.

'Good evening,' she said pleasantly. Behind her, a large man nodded in support. He guarded a thick mauve curtain, through which the overlapping clinks and bickers of a party could be heard. Music too.

'Hi,' Michael said.

He handed her the card.

The woman smiled and consulted her list.

She looked at him, and the invitation, and him.

'Thank you, sir,' she said, smiling once again.

And Michael found that he was smiling too.

Now the big man was pulling the curtain back, heavy on its rings. Michael nodded and stepped through. After three paces, he stopped. He collected himself. For the moment, it was all too much.

The room was large, its walls crazy-paved with mirrors – deco, baroque, rear-view, shaving – scattering each a separate snippet of the scene below. On every table stood a vase of flowers, ungathering their colours in a spurt. And rolling in between: the human lake. In Michael's eyes, it seemed actually to pitch and yaw as teams of costumed waitresses worked tributaries of glass around the room.

I'm losing my edge, sang-spoke an amplified voice above a pumping beat. *I'm losing my edge. To the kids from France and from London.*

He felt giddy.

But I was there! A crass bassline split the room.

That was Gordon Ramsay, sipping at a cocktail, listening to a woman's views, desperate for his turn. And there: a younger woman having her picture taken with Tracey Emin. Their faces frozen in defiling light. And there: another kind of camera, making film or television from the conversation of two men. And there: was that Mark Wahlberg? Marky Mark? Michael waded closer.

'This other guy over here keeps talking about Gary Glitter,' Wahlberg, unmistakably, was chuckling to a man, whose hand was on his shoulder. 'I don't know what that means.' The next sentence was inaudible. Then: 'But we didn't think that the entourage fighting amongst themselves – like hitting each other with bottles and shit was going to, like, work.'

Was that gossip, Michael wondered? Should he write it down?

A waitress was standing in front of him, speaking words.

They were: 'Care for some champagne, sir?'

She was dressed as Goldilocks.

'Thanks,' Michael said, and swept a glass up from her tray.

Sip.

She left.

The crowd was thick. Sip.

'Scuse me, sorry,' he said to a gate of jackets and bare backs.

They opened without interest, and he slipped through to explore.

Down one wall stood a line of generous booths, each filled with the disporting limbs of Marks's guests like dolls rush-jumbled in a toy box. A young man even sat cross-legged on the surface of the final table, his fingers strolling idly among the paths of his laboriously landscaped facial hair. Distracted by the sight, Michael missed a plate of morsels that circulated past him on the other side. They were china spoons, containing some brown liquid of great deliciousness to judge from the transcendent grins on the faces of the people tasting it. And doors. There were doors everywhere, surreptitiously recessed into the perimeter. Behind the glass in one, the DJ bobbed above his lights. Through another flowed the Goldilockses with full or empty trays. Michael sidled up and loitered with intent. He was hungry.

Sip.

And very nervous, yes, despite the room's prevailing ease. That Cuzco people felt so comfortable in one another's company only served to magnify his oddness. They dressed well, but casually, and as they liked. They did not smoke, for the most part, but neither did they protest. Guests seemed required only to relax and enjoy themselves. To Michael, this was the very strictest rule.

I'm losing my edge. I'm losing my edge.

And there were so many beautiful girls. They made a sad ache hum in Michael's chest. He wondered what it would be like to take one of them to dinner. It didn't matter which. He wanted to ask her about herself, and he would really want to know. Did she realise how beautiful she was? Did guys bother

her all the time? Had she been born to high society? Or grown up the darling of a little town? Hacking out her path to privilege through the overgrown feelings of men. And did she realise that she was nothing here? Ripe fruit in a glut. Destined soon to rot or be devoured.

Sip.

And the toilets were marked LOOS.

'Scuse me, sorry.' Michael was hurrying past a grand piano to the end of the room. He felt dizzier than ever, and longed for a wall to put his back against. But mirrors, tables, people, doors conspired to prevent him. At last, he found a slot, and stopped there, noticing for the first time a large iron balcony that hung above the entrance. There was a bar up there, accessed by a spiral staircase. How had he not seen that before? And there!

Hugo Marks.

He was standing by the balustrade, chatting animatedly to a large woman and a man in a business suit. He looked somehow different from the man Michael had watched perform *Arcadia* on stage. Smaller, but perhaps a little heavier too. Even so, he was still a very good-looking guy. Wholemeal hair, elegantly plumped above the brow. Aristocratic cheekbones, neat mouth, sturdy spadeish chin, not completely unshaven. In his suit of blazing blue sat a birthday twist of flowers. There was no sign of Mellody, his wife.

I've never been wrong.

In his reverie, Michael had missed another tray. This time pipettes containing green and white had passed him, laid out in a line, as if for surgery.

Did one need permission, he wondered, to climb up to the balcony? Perhaps some people had a special invitation, printed on a different colour card?

Sip.

Not that he was going to try. Hugo Marks would be so busy.

'Best fucking live act?' A London voice, very near him. 'Fuck off! Since when has lip-syncing been live?' Michael turned, and found that he was looking at Elton John, in peach sunglasses, addressing a group of people. 'I think everybody who lip-syncs in public on stage, when you pay like seventy-five quid to see them, should be shot.'

That was gossip.

Excited, Michael took out his phone and began to transfer the fast-disintegrating quote from his memory into its.

Everybody . . . who . . . lip-syncs . . .

'Canapé, sir?'

. . . should . . . be . . . shot.

He finished typing and looked up.

It was the porcelain spoons, five of them. Goldilocks waited, her unused hand tucked, in accordance with its training, into the small of her back, as if it were the rule that all non-serving parts of her body must be tidied deferentially from view. Perhaps it was.

Michael peered at the lumps, heat-edged with brown, in their drip of soup.

'What are they?' he asked.

'Foie gras, sautéed in oloroso sherry.'

'Mmm, foie gras,' he enthused, making a hash of the *r*.

He picked up one of the spoons and tipped it into his mouth. The liver deliquesced.

'Wow, that's fabulous!' He nodded with vigorous sincerity, and a gentle swirly drunken feeling lingered in the movement's echo. He closed his eyes to steady himself.

When he opened them, Goldilocks had gone.

He still held his phone in one hand, and the spoon in the other. The spoon went in his pocket. On the phone, he saved his note, grateful for the pretext to look busy.

I hear that you and your band have sold your guitars and bought turntables.

He wanted more to eat.

I hear that you and your band have sold your turntables and bought guitars.

'Oh I'm sure that's true!'

A sprightly voice was saying this beside him. Turning, as if without interest, he saw a dark-haired woman. Fairly young and almost pocketably small, she was talking to a suited older man. He looked smart and serious, but also, with his back against the wall, a little cornered.

'So you guys are going big on Hugo's movie, are you?' he said.

'Oh definitely. Absolutely. There's been huge interest nationwide.'

Enthusiasm sprang out of her in leaks, as though her tininess had pressurised it.

'When's it out?'

'This month. It comes out later this month. It's definitely going to be the biggest opening of the year so far.'

She was a publicist, surely? Working for a cinema distributor, by the sound of it. The man would be a journalist, or some other person worth impressing. And his interest seemed to have been caught, because next he said:

'Sorry, remind me of your name again?'

'Rosanna. Rosanna Neophytou. Blue Box Comunications. That's my company.'

She tried to shake his hand, realised that hers had a champagne cocktail in it, laughed, placed the glass on the floor, wiped a palm on her dress, tried again, accomplished it.

Who the man was clearly did not need saying.

'Got any time with Hugo to give away?'

He was a journalist then, probably an editor on another paper.

'We'll see. I'm pushing for it. It would be easier, of course,' here the woman's cheeks bunched, 'if I could say there was a paper out there that I knew would treat him fairly.'

'We'll see,' the man said back, with the decision to smile.

This seemed to conclude something. They stood in silence, drinking.

Michael loitered, being ignored.

He was going to have to start a conversation of his own.

But fear. A little pouch of anxiousness, some enemy gland, was squeezing hesitation through his blood. Who would he talk to? And who would talk to him? There had never been a time in Michael's life when he felt good at this. Those friends he possessed, a loyal unit, had been acquired only through the circumstantial engineering of work, education or mutual acquaintance. Out in society, he was a sterile node. Humanity's appendix.

Sip.

Even these self-recriminations were preferable to action. It was all delay.

Sip.

Sip.

And now his champagne was gone.

A fresh tray appeared immediately beside him, waving in a flap of kitchen noise.

He took another glass.

Sip.

So. It was time to talk to someone.

So. Keep moving. It was a strategy he had used before, when alone at parties.

1. Walk, without appearing aimless.
2. Prepare an opening line, but be ready to improvise.
3. Make decisive eye-contact.
4. Pretend not to be doing 1–3.

Sip.

So. Walk. Michael decided he would walk to the DJ booth.

He leaned sideways into Elton John's group. It yawned him through.

'Ever since then I've watched him,' Elton John was saying. 'He's chosen his roles. And he's dedicated himself to not being that teen star that he could have been.'

Michael felt a flicker of temptation to stop and listen further, but he did not dare appear conspicuous. Instead, he pressed deeper into the throng, sorrying and scusemeing a channel to the DJ's lights, scanning for unattended guests, the young, the old, the weak.

On arrival at the booth, he idled, glancing casually inside as if assessing the equipment.

Eye-contact status: no eye contact.

Swig.

Giving himself no time to brood, he selected his next waypoint – the piano – and launched off.

'Phew, lots of people, eh?' was to be his opening line, to a lone drinker, friendly but conspiratorial. Who after all, at parties, did not welcome the companionship of complaint? Michael knew he did.

Sip.

He tocked his glass on to the piano polish, beside the cocktails of an old couple who did not look up.

You don't know what you really want.
You don't know what you really want.
You don't know what you really want.

On the ceiling, a large unlit glitterball revolved without a reason on its wire. Most of Hugo Marks was visible behind it. He was talking on a phone.

'Canapé, sir?'

A different waitress had appeared, in the same wig and pinafore, the same arm tucked back fencer-wise into its securing strings. And on her slate was something new: three tiny crabs, gridded out like Victorian examples, the remnants of a six-corpse display. In the corner sat a white ceramic ramekin with bitty liquid in it.

'They're softshell crabs,' the waitress told him. 'And that's a Vietnamese dipping sauce.'

She was pretty. Perhaps part-Indian.

'Are they good?' Michael asked, in a nice voice, that came out louder than he planned.

'Mmm, delicious. I hadn't tried it before tonight, but they're really yummy.'

'You've been eating them yourself?'

'Of course.' Prettily. 'We taste all the food before service.'

'And you just eat the whole thing?'

'Absolutely.'

Michael stared at the sequence of sandy-brown bodies. They looked exactly as three small deep-fried crabs might be expected to look. It was too late to withdraw. He grasped the nearest by one of its legs, squashed it in the sauce, and tucked the dripping package into his mouth without hesitating, chomping rapidly to disperse the shape. It was soft indeed, and very good.

A new song had begun. Another thumper, so far without words.

Michael continued to chew, looking at the waitress's expectant face.

Though the animals were small, there was quite a lot of food involved. Two bites, next time, would be the method.

Still she watched politely, awaiting his reaction.

'Thraaf,' he said hurriedly through his crab, a little of which escaped.

What must she make of him, he wondered? Might he be a rumpled but powerful newspaper editor? An Internet millionaire? A young literary curmudgeon?

With his tongue, he stored the second half of the food in his cheek, and tried again.

'Nice,' he managed. 'Yooer right.'

The waitress laughed and left.

Michael finished his mouthful alone.

Up on the balcony, Hugo Marks had gone. Below, some people had started dancing, including Tracey Emin. Their movements must have driven others away, because the space had now opened up enough for Michael to see himself reflected in the mirrors on the other side.

And then he realised something bad. It was obvious now.

He had dressed appallingly.

At home, the choice seemed simple. Jeans, trainers and so on clearly would not do. (Though here they were many.) So this left just his charcoal suit, a present from his parents years ago on the occasion of his first job interview, and two possible shirts, for reasons of hygiene, which could combine with it. The white one made him look like he was going to a job interview, so the navy was the only option – tieless, as he had seen done. Looking into the upper mirror now, however, its ornate gold plasterwork twisting lavishly around his torso, there was no doubt that he had made a mistake. Navy and charcoal! Michael could not understand how he had overlooked such an incompetent blend. Footballers wore dark suits with dark shirts, it was true, but usually a matching dark. And their clothes were expensive, and fitted well. Unlike Michael's double-breasted jacket, which flapped like bunting round his middle, and overshot his shoulders with a rueful droop.

There probably were people, he imagined, who had the beauty or the confidence to survive such an outfit. Or even posture it with brio into a design. But he was not one of them. He had not been a pretty baby or a good-looking boy, and he was not now a handsome man. At twenty-nine, time had not yet done its scuffing up; he still had tolerable teeth, only a very mild slouch, black hair of no consequence with, it was true, one or two infiltrating fila-ments of white. But even while he kept his youth, it would never be enough. Not with his low brow and rubberish complexion, which invited pinches and jocundity, and seemed to swaddle any hope of handsomeness beneath a blurring gauze. His body always gave the impression, Michael thought, that it had been made with slightly too much skin, as if waiting to be fat. (Which, no doubt, would come. The thought of that slack capsule ageing empty was not a thing he cared to contemplate, much less bring about by doing exercise.)

Yet somehow, tonight, he had left the flat believing that he looked OK. If only he had worn the white shirt. That would have been better. Or attempted jeans . . . Or he could have just not *fucking come*.

Michael felt himself reddening, and saw it too.

What was he *doing* here?

Nobody was going to talk to him. What did they know, or care, about his life? With their post-production and their golden globes?

He picked his champagne up, and finished it.

The dancers danced, without attracting any more.

Michael needed a dump. Then home.

He had come; he had a quote. Sally, Camille and the rest of them could be satisfied with that.

He went directly to the LOOS door. It led into a large and elegant bathroom that made no mention of gents or ladies. A young woman, slim and dark, was standing in front of the mirror. A shining stripe of hair slipped down her back like the first wet stroke of a brush.

'My look is very much girl-next-door,' she said into her mobile phone, 'just with tanned olive skin.'

She was looking at herself, and her words slapped the empty room, all its cubicles ajar. Nobody but Michael then, not one other person in this gathering, had craved escape. He felt weak, and a little wild. He hurried to the nearest stall.

From: **valerie.morrell@nortonmorrell.co.uk**

To: **williammendez75@gmail.com**

Subject: **Publicity**

Date: **Tuesday, 18 August 2009 15:41:20**

Dear William,

Thank you very much for your chapter. I'm enjoying it. Do you have any more?

Regards,

Valerie

From: williammendez75@gmail.com

To: valerie.morrell@nortonmorrell.co.uk

Subject: Re: Publicity

Date: Tuesday, 18 August 2009 22:08:09

▶ 🖉 Chapter 2 – Calvin

Hi Valerie – Wow! That's great to hear! I thought you'd forgotten about it, to be honest. I'm still doing a final polish on the rest of the book, but you can certainly have chapter 2.

All the best

William

Without warning, a thick forearm swung around Calvin's shoulders. The dial of a Tag Heuer lolled beneath his chin.

'Hey Calvin! How're you doing?'

He turned his head to see a smiling face he recognised. He had met the man recently, at another party. But his name . . . The name was taking a little longer to come back to him.

'Hi. Yeah. Good thanks. You?' Calvin's forehead glistened with a light cocaine dew, and he was buzzing gently, though the acceleration phase had passed.

'Yeah, not bad,' the man replied, nodding in tanned agreement with himself. 'Not bad at all.' He wore a ruffle-chested cyan dress shirt from the Seventies, older perhaps than he was, and open to the hair.

That's right, thought Calvin. They had met at that Puma launch party in the stately home. A music video director. Or was it advertising? Whichever it was, the man had the coolest little car that he had ever seen, a grey Jaguar XKR. The pair of them had split some MDMA on the dash and taken it for a roar around the dark blue morning lanes. Calvin could recall the twisting flume of lit-up hedgerows. The veering flashes of the man's reflected face, concentrating viciously.

But what was his *name*?

'This is Rich,' Calvin said, playing for time, and introducing the Jaguar guy a little reluctantly to his colleague. 'He works with me at Warehouse Records.'

Rich looked relaxed, but Calvin could tell. He was an office man, Rich was, with kids. Sort of dry and cool when he wanted. But you know, not young any more. Parties were not where he belonged. Not in his suit and shoes. Calvin's green and orange trainers, on the other hand, they were prototypes from Japan, humbly submitted with wearing instructions. And clinging to his torso was a couture vest of butter-coloured silk by Alexander McQueen. Around his head the scent of toffee putty curled, used tonight to tweak his haircut to a slant. Yes, Calvin, unlike Rich, was young. And he looked fabulous.

'Hi,' Rich said, with a friendly smile.

'Hi Rich,' said the man. 'Caspar Rose. So what's your beat over at Warehouse?'

Caspar! That's right! Calvin knew it was something weird.

'Talent management.' Rich presented Calvin with bracketing hands. 'I'm babysitting this talent for the label tonight.'

Everybody laughed, but the joke stung Calvin with reminding pain. Because it was true. Babysat was how he felt. He itched to free himself, to circulate, to have another line if possible. Though he would need to find a well-stocked friend now his own stash was finished. His brown eyes shone like wet little chocolates, and he offered them around the room.

'So Calvin,' Caspar said excitedly. 'I'm making a film of the party for Hugo's people. Want to say a few words for the camera?' And without waiting for an answer, he was calling his companion over. 'Hey Clive! Come here!'

A lanky character began to sift towards them through the crowd.

'He's not called Clive,' Caspar explained with a wink. 'But I call him Clive for the film.'

'Why?' Calvin asked.

But Caspar did not hear him. He had turned away to do something to the lens.

'It's from Keith Floyd,' Rich explained quietly. 'An old TV chef, who was always drunk.'

'So!' Caspar was back. 'Why don't you tell us a bit about yourself?'

The lens was in Calvin's face. The little red light was on.

Rich nodded his approval.

'OK, well, my name's Calvin Vance,' Calvin said. 'I'm twenty years old, from Leeds, and I'm a singer. My first single, "Smoothly", reached number

24

three in the charts in January. And, erm, what else would you like to know?'

'That's great, Calvin. And I like that you put your age in there. Very nice. Close-up of the handsome young man, please Clive. So what brings you to Cuzco tonight? Just wandered in for a drink?'

'No. It's Hugo's thirty-first, and we're here to celebrate!' Calvin stretched the last three words into a whoop.

'I see. And are you having a good time?'

'Yay! Tip-top, man. Rich introduced me to Elton John, which was pretty cool.'

'Ah! The big EJ! How was he hanging?'

'Oh he was great. A really good bloke, actually. He said how he was always rooting for me on *X-Factor*.'

'Is that so? Well we all were, Calvin. Weren't we, Clive?'

The cameraman nodded the lens up and down.

'And tell me, dear boy,' Caspar continued. 'How do you know Mr Marks?'

'We were on *The Paul O'Grady Show* together. They made us try Morris dancing.'

'Morris dancing, eh?'

'That's right.'

And it was true. But besides complimenting him on his performance, Hugo Marks had barely spoken to him that day, climbing instead into his car as soon as the recording had finished. Calvin's invitation owed more to the persistence of the people at Warehouse, in fact, than to any imagined friendship. As the people at Warehouse had often reminded him.

'So you waved your hankies at each other?'

'Pardon?'

'Morris dancing. That is what you do, isn't it? With bells and beards.'

'Oh right. Yeah, we did. With sticks, actually.'

Calvin laughed. Mum always said he could be a bit 'slow on the uptake'.

'Can you show me some of this Morris dancing then?'

'What, now?'

'Absolutely. Clive, have you got a hankie?'

The camera shook from side to side.

'OK,' Calvin said. 'Well, I can't remember much, and this music isn't right, but we link arms like this, then we spin round together. That's it. Then I face you and hit your stick on both sides.' He tapped Caspar on the arm. 'Then you hit mine on both sides.' Caspar cheered as he did so. 'And erm, I can't remember what happens next.' Calvin laughed loudly at himself. 'Sorry, LCD Soundsystem isn't really the right music.'

'No, that's great. I'm craving cider already. Calvin Vance, thank you very much.'

'Thanks.'

The little red light went off.

'Thanks Calvin. That was great.' Caspar swigged at his beer. 'So do you guys want to come and meet some people?'

Rich was studying his phone. 'I can't, thanks,' he said. 'It sounds like there's a bit of a meltdown going on at home. You'll be all right without me, won't you Calvin?' He was smiling.

'Yeah, I'll be fine,' Calvin said, secretly exultant. 'I'll just stick around for a bit longer if that's OK?'

'Fine by me. But look after your voice. And no controversy, OK?'

Calvin sighed. 'Controversy' at Warehouse meant 'drugs', and he was supposed to be the only person there who didn't take any. Or the only person not to get seen. Either way, he resented being told what to do. Especially now that he was famous and had his own flat.

Rich held his smile still. Then he left.

'He been keeping an eye on you?' Caspar asked.

'Fuck yeah.' Calvin sighed with relief. 'I got this tour of the Far East coming up – you know, Korea and that. Everyone at Warehouse is being really manic about it.'

'Course they are. Course they are. They depend on you. You could do their job if you really had to, remember, but they know they could never do yours. It makes them nervous.'

Calvin had never thought of it that way before.

'You're right,' he said.

'Mmm. Want a line?'

'You fucking bet.'

Caspar laughed. And the raucous confidence of the sound dislodged more memories: that his dad was an earl, that he had been to Oxford University. It was incredible really, thought Calvin, that he, a lad from east Leeds, a media and communications student who worked in Top Man on Briggate, had become the playmate of these types . . . But then, just four months after his rejection from *The X-Factor*, incredible things had now become routine. The celebrated people, their fabulous parties, the happy obligations of his fame; it exhilarated him almost into numbness. He had actually received the life that he auditioned for, queuing hours last summer with his number in the Yorkshire grey, sucking in his nerves as drizzle tiptoed on his zipped-up mac. Simon Cowell had given him a chance, and he had taken it. He had taken it with 'Smoothly'. He had taken it *despite* his televised defeat. And now he lived among the winners. A life so wonderful that sometimes it did not feel like his. Which must be the reason, he supposed, that still, when he slept, he dreamed in Leeds.

'Hey Calvin! Mate!'

They had reached the door to the toilets. But Caspar was walking past it.

'This way!' he shouted, pointing.

Calvin's brow crumpled in confusion, but he followed, treading lightly on his trainers' puffy tips, as if this might make him less visible.

The next door was marked PRIVATE, and Calvin hesitated. He had never been to Cuzco before, and he wanted to be careful.

'It's fine,' Caspar insisted, in answer to his face.

They pushed through together.

On the other side, the lights were brighter, stripping out the comfort from a corridor that was white and undecorated, with a waft of coolness in its air. At the far end, a couple stood connected by some quiet drama.

'I don't like interesting stories,' the woman was protesting. 'Boring is good!'

Caspar was paying no attention. With a complete smile, he was pointing to another door.

They went in.

There was smoke. Smoke and people making smoke. Perhaps twenty or thirty people, thick and noisy in the room. They gathered, most of them, around a large trestle table by the tiled wall, on which sat glasses and ashtrays and bottles. Mike Skinner – was that Mike Skinner? – was holding forth, with what would be a brandy in his hand. While opposite, along the other wall, some kind of counter ran, stitched with stripes of powder, variously prepared. Above one hovered a girl, attempting both to sniff and keep her balance as she leant in from her position on a metal sink. Below, her shins swung in the void. If you knew parties (and Calvin thought he knew parties) then you knew when you had reached the core.

Boldly, Caspar put his wallet on the counter by the girl. She shifted three polite inches, and he went to work beside her thigh.

'How did you know about this place?' It was lame to ask, but Calvin needed to know.

'My brother's a member,' Caspar said. 'Everybody comes in here. It's like a kind of rule.'

'Oh right.'

The room was hot and windowless. And really very loud, with conversations escalating over one another to the point where Calvin's hearing range began to falter at a yard. And he was glad, or else the others surely would have heard the happy stompings of his heart.

'Skunk is the worst,' the girl next to him was saying to a man. 'Three of my friends have been sectioned. One of them forever. He tried to rape his sister, and then they put him in this home, and then he did rape two girls. I've known him since he was six.'

She was wasted, but still pretty tidy. There were a few nice girls in here.

'But skunk can't make you do that,' said the man after a pause, plainly reluctant to contradict someone so attractive.

The girl lifted a hand to her face and stroked away a panel of hair.

'It's Peruvian flake this stuff,' Caspar remarked loudly. He was tipping a little heap of powder from an oblong packet on to the countertop.

'Mmm, yeah,' said Calvin, appraising every granule with a wanton eye. He did not know that there were *kinds* of coke. No one had ever mentioned that at college, or when he used to score a weekend gramme to work through with his brother Jason.

Caspar set about the pile with his credit card, crunching little boulders into mist, talking quickly about the lovely Jaguar, which now, it seemed, lay wounded in a French garage. Expertly, his hand coaxed a pair of snowy eyebrows from the debris, then offered up a shortened drinking straw for use. Calvin took it, and chose what he guessed to be the smaller helping, vacuuming its length into a nostril. The powder whistled pleasantly through his head.

'Thanks,' he said, with a connoisseur's frown. 'Nice.'

Caspar took back the straw, paused mid-sentence, and traced his own three-inch slug from crumb to crumb.

Sssshhhnift.

Getting out his Marlboro Lights, Calvin offered one to Caspar, and both men drifted momentarily through the pleasure of their virgin puff. A zipper trail of satisfaction. The anxious anticipation of an approaching good time.

'You seen these?' Calvin said at last, slipping out his phone.

'What's that?'

'Sony Ericsson K750i. It's not out until the summer, but they sent me one this week. Two megapixel camera and tons of other stuff. Fucking sweet.'

'Very nice,' Caspar said, smiling at the lens. 'Best not take any pictures in here though, mate.'

Calvin seethed. 'No, sure,' he said. 'I'm just saying.'

How stupid did people think he was? Just because he was young, and they said he was attractive. He blamed it on the way that Warehouse chose to market him, with boy-band dance routines and bubblegum pop tracks, though he had proved his range on *X-Factor* – as even Cowell agreed. In some ways, it had been almost grimly pleasing when 'I Wanna B With U', the silly follow-up to 'Smoothly', bombed. That had made his point. (Except in the Far Eastern territories, where Calvin's tween appeal remained strong enough to take him back to number one.)

He sucked on his cigarette.

They had even tried him on the gay scene, but he wasn't having that. Not that he was homophobic or anything; he just liked girls. And being ogled made him feel like one.

Then he saw Susie. In here. Small, dark hair. Susie Farstein.

'Susie!' he shouted.

But she did not notice.

'Susie!' again.

Now she did, and pinned him with an amused stare.

'I don't believe it,' he explained to Caspar as she walked their way. 'It's my old stylist.'

'Really?' Caspar said. He didn't sound very interested.

The first cold droplets of cocaine began to flow in Calvin's throat.

'Cal-vin. Vance.' Susie, it seemed, was still getting used to the idea.

'Hi Susie,' he said, and kissed her on both cheeks as he had learned to. 'How's it going?'

'Great, Calvin. Great. You're looking fabulous, of course.'

'Of course. Well I've got a great new stylist these days. So much better than my last one.' It was Susie who had left him to go and work full-time on Kylie Minogue's *Showgirl* tour, otherwise he would not have dared to joke about it.

'Oh do you?' She pressed four fingers of mock-reproach into his yummy tummy. 'Well it's nice to see you're in good hands.'

'This is Caspar,' Calvin said. 'He's a director.'

'Yeah, hi,' said Caspar, shaking hands. 'Just videos and commercials so far, but we hope to start shooting on a feature in September.'

'How do you do.' Susie nodded, asking no further questions. Instead she leaned in close to Calvin and said, 'Thank *God* you turned up.'

He gazed back pleased.

'I was stuck with some awful bloody comedy man, but here you are: to the rescue!'

'No problem.' Calvin did not feel much like a rescuer, but it was nice that Susie thought him one. She looked up with admiration, wriggling in her punkish ballgown. Very rescuable indeed.

'I can't remember the guy's name,' she said, 'but he started doing his bloody act right there in the middle of the fucking party. Thought I'd got rid of him by coming in here. And there he is again! Don't *look*!' A meaningful twitch of Susie's eyebrows indicated that the person to ignore was behind her back. 'And I had to fucking *laugh* at his jokes, of course. You can't not, can you? Very not funny. Very tedious. *Very* embarrassing.' She flicked a grateful kiss through the smoke of his cigarette. 'They're all dreadfully insecure, aren't they, comedians? That's why they do it. Real me-me-me-artists.'

'Yeah,' Calvin said, although he did not think he'd ever met one.

There had been a time when Susie still fussed daily round his seams that he had thought he had a chance with her. She was twenty-eight – perhaps now twenty-nine – but Calvin did not mind that. And there was always something in her eyes, as if they shared a little secret. Then suddenly she left to work for Kylie, and became a *could-have* never once converted to a *did*. It might just be the Charlie, but seeing her had instantly brought back the warmth of that erotic thwarting. A second chance to tick her box.

'Time for a line?' Susie said.

Calvin was not going to say no.

'Sure,' he grinned. 'Sorry, mine's run out.'

'No, no. Mine's fine.'

Caspar had now begun a conversation with the people at the sink, so they left him to it.

Susie snapped open a mirror from her clutchbag and placed it on the central table. A dainty wrap appeared, cut from *Wallpaper**. Calvin recognised the *. Inside sat a pallid slab, moulded to a pillow by the paper's swell, and whiskery with cracks. Slicing off a third, Susie chopped it with her gym card.

'So how are things at Warehouse?' she asked.

'Not bad. Not bad. The new single's nearly out.'

'Mmm. I heard.'

'And we finished recording the album last week, which was great. Then there's just the final mixes before I go on tour.'

'Wow! When's that?'

'Two months, I think. It's all happened really quickly, so they're still setting a few dates up. It's in several different countries, so it's quite complicated.'

'Fantastic. Where?'

'Erm . . . Korea, Singapore . . . Philippines . . .' Calvin could never remember them all.

'That's terrific!' She fetched back two pieces of escaping rubble. 'They'll love you out there.'

'Yeah,' Calvin said. 'I hope so.'

He could feel the first line's energy begin to rise. A flickerish awakening in his limbs.

'After you,' said Susie.

A rolled-up twenty was in his hand. Calvin aimed himself, left nostril this time, at the nearer portion on her upstretched palm. It vanished, piece by piece.

'Thanks,' he said, handing back the note and lighting up again.

'So how long will you be away for?' Susie asked, poised above the loaded mirror.

'Maybe three months or so, they reckon. Depends on ticket sales.'

'OK.' She sniffed her share, then mopped the remnant particles with a moistened finger. 'So quite a while?'

'Mmm.'

It *was* quite a while. Just as he was starting to feel settled too. Not as a Londoner – that would never be – but as a customary little groove, perhaps, in London's stone. And now he was to be displaced again, to be recast as the outsider, and in an even stranger land. As though Leeds had not been hard enough to leave, and then revisit, seeing how the place had changed without him. Watching as it shrank and darkened, its sights familiar from memory, no longer from habit. Even Mum and Jason seemed a little different when he saw them up there. Nervous of him, maybe? Maybe proud. They had eaten Sunday lunch at Mum's house several weeks ago, and later watched the football live on Sky. And as he boarded his departing taxi in the dark, Calvin wondered whether either of the pair had noticed when he said that he would call 'when I get home'.

'So how do you know Hugo?' Susie asked.

'Oh, we did some TV together.' He made it sound like no big thing. 'How about you?'

'Well I don't really. I designed the outfits for the serving staff tonight.'

'Those cartoon girls?'

'Spring milkmaids, yes.'

'They're great!'

'Thanks.' She sniffed. 'No, so Hugo was at the meeting when I presented the designs, but we never really got a chance to talk.'

'Shame. He's a nice guy. I should introduce you some time.' A spike of boldness rolled the words spontaneously out.

'Really?'

'Sure,' Calvin had to say,

'I mean I've got some ideas I'd *love* to talk to him and Mellody about.'

'Uh-huh?'

'I think I saw him up in the mezzanine bar a minute ago.'

'Oh yes?'

'Would you really give me a quick intro? That would be supercalifragilistically kind.'

He had meant some time *soon*. Like maybe one day next year. It was just a thing to say.

'No problem,' he said.

And in an instant, Susie had packed up all her things and faced him with a perky grin that said, 'Let's go.'

So he grinned strenuously back, and led her out.

In the corridor, the distant leak of music rose into a flow. And then became a gush, as Calvin heaved them through the final door, piercing a shell of sound and temperature. The sudden warmth made him shiver. Good, though. It felt good. Skin tingling with successfulness. He blinked, and sent his eyes, refreshed, to sweep the scene. Faces registered, such as Mike Skinner's again, talking eagerly to Damon Albarn's. And yes, there, upstairs, was Hugo Marks. He was standing by the railing on the balcony sipping beer and talking to an old man whose sour face was clipped to a cigar. Calvin's gaze swooped back to Susie's upturned hope. The music was 'Mr Brightside' by The Killers. He swallowed and his ears popped. Fuck, he was so coked up.

'Excuse me.'

It was a young girl, younger than him. Standing in a pose of narrow best behaviour.

'Are you Calvin Vance?'

'Yes,' he said, grasping the distraction.

'From *The X-Factor*?'

'That's me.' His intense relief hid behind a practised tone. Lazy good-humour, killing off his cigarette beneath his shoe.

Two other nearby girls, he noticed, were trying to hide behind their hands, squirmingly embarrassed by their failed secrecy, secretly delighted by their failed embarrassment. His saviours. And one was very tidy.

'I *knew* it!' The first girl released a flash of teeth. 'My friend didn't believe me.' She pointed at the pretty one, who immediately lowered her eyes to the ground. 'Would you mind just telling her I was right?'

'Bring her over,' Calvin said, with a smiling 'Sorry, just a minute' to Susie before she could protest. He was growing accustomed to – though by no means tired of – this.

The friends edged forward. Shop-bought girls, taut and freshly packaged. Calvin's favourite came in blonde, her small breasts harnessed in a sequin crop-top, her wide blue eyes delicately outlined, lips still wet with glaze.

'Hi,' he said to her. 'What's your name?'

'Kelly-Marie.'

He shook her little hand and turned to the others.

'I'm Briony,' came next. Briony was American.

And, 'Alissa,' said the one who had approached him, when it was her turn.

'Hi,' Calvin said, taking a look at them in general, and at Kelly-Marie in particular. 'So yeah, um, your friend's right. I am Calvin Vance.'

'Yesss!' Alissa cheered. The others laughed.

'I never said you weren't,' his favourite tried to justify herself. 'I just thought you were maybe a bit taller than you seemed on TV, and you know how they always say people look shorter in real life, so I thought it couldn't be you.'

Calvin noticed that his jaw was clenched tight closed.

'Well it is me,' he said. 'Sorry if I'm too tall.'

'That's OK,' said Kelly-Marie.

'So what are you girls doing here?'

Susie did not look happy.

'We're . . .' and 'My . . .' said two of them, in collision, before Briony took over. 'My dad makes movies,' she said. 'We all study in London, so he brought us along.'

'We don't really know anyone,' Kelly-Marie admitted, giggling, with a shrug.

'But we got our picture taken with Elton John!' Alissa interrupted in a hurry. They all wanted to speak at once.

'Yeah, Elton's pretty cool,' Calvin said. 'This is Susie. She designed the waitresses' costumes.'

'Hi.' Susie waved.

'Oh they're beautiful,' said Briony.

'Thanks. Calvin and I were just on our way to talk to Hugo about them, actually.'

'You know *Hugo*?!' Alissa could not hide her excitement.

'Not really. Calvin does.'

'What's he like?' Briony took over.

'Oh he's great,' said Calvin. 'We only worked together for a while, but he was really cool. All that stuff they say about him in the papers being really grumpy and that, it's a load of rubbish, but then you can't believe what you read in the press, I remember they said me and Kate Thornton had a thing going on, even though she's, like, more than ten years older than me and we weren't even in the same country at the time!'

The girls laughed again.

'So all that stuff about Hugo's drinking and not going out and problems with Mellody and everything's a load of paper talk. They'll say anything they can to sell copies, believe me. Hugo's got his head screwed on proper. And he's a fun guy and all. We had to do this dance together . . .'

There was so much to say. A thrilling slope of words.

'. . . And he was all laughing and joking about it, having a great time. And he didn't mind or anything. I asked him about all the press and that, and he said he just ignored it . . .'

He felt sure it was what Hugo would have said.

'. . . I think if you're famous you've got to keep your feet on the ground, like. And listen to the people you can trust. Because it's the people who know you best who you need to listen to, because they're the ones who really know you. It's like, when you're in the bubble – it's like being in a bubble being famous . . .'

A sudden crash distracted his listeners, the dropping of a nearby tray of drinks. Male voices sent up a shambolic cheer. But Calvin carried on. He understood things. He was sensitivity.

'. . . and when you're in the bubble, there's loads of people giving you advice. Do this, do that, and everything. But I think you need to get to the point, OK, where you give your own advice to yourself, like Hugo does, and that takes practice because . . .'

An ugly man, older than himself, had stopped beside the group. Calvin watched him slide surreptitiously inwards.

'. . . you know, it takes practice. You need a lot of people around you to get everything done. It's like you're a business . . .'

The man was looking back at him, listening.

'. . . You are like a business. And all these people you work with have opinions, and they need to be hired so you can all make money, but, you know, there's a whole world outside the bubble that you never even think about. And I think what people forget is, you know, that money can't buy happiness.'

'Yes it can,' the ugly man said.

Michael whisked himself a glass and halved it with a gulp. The bubbles burned his nose, but he did not flinch.

Already, a more disordered ambiance had come to rule the room. Conversations now seemed coarser, their supporting gestures raggedly flamboyant. Dancing continued on a modest scale, more ironic than expressive, but no less expertly performed. And the occupants of one packed booth were even swaying through a sing-song.

'Get outta my dreams,' they sang together, 'get into my car!'

Michael walked past the piano, looking around. The room had become younger too, and a little emptier, drained perhaps of the stabilising presence of the older guests. One group seemed scarcely more than teenagers. They probably were teenagers, in fact. (These days he was shamingly unsure.) Four girls, listening in silence to the views of a boy. A very beautiful boy, with dark eyes and muscular arms, wearing a vest of point-blank ridiculousness. To Michael, it looked as if someone had taken a yellow scarf of little more than normal width, ripped a hole in the middle, placed it over the young man's head and then sewn the sides up to his armpits.

As he studied the group, he began to wonder. Would they do? He had been searching for a solitary figure, but there were fewer of those around now, and these young people – children, really – well, he was not frightened of talking to *them*.

There was a tremendous crash behind him. Then the dull collapsing gong of a metal sheet. Because everybody else looked round, Michael did not. Goldilocks, he presumed, had dropped her tray; and a yobboid cry confirmed it. He smiled a smile of indulgent good-humour, hoping one of the young people might notice.

But the boy pressed on. Michael dawdled closer. A young guy on his own like that with an audience of four attentive women: it seemed a rare configuration. Was he someone famous? A model? A *Hollyoaks* hunk? He would have to be. Michael was sure that four women had never listened simultaneously to him.

He edged nearer still, loitering on the fringe of things, gradually releasing all pretence of distance until the interest lay plain upon his face. No one challenged him, and soon he felt established. Only then did he pay attention.

The young man was speaking, in a passionate Yorkshire accent, about the pressures of fame. And he was an idiot.

'. . . you to get everything done. Slike you're a business. You are like a business . . .'

Michael sipped his champagne.

'. . . An all these people you work with have opinions, an they need to be hired so you can all make money, but, you know, there's a whole world outside the bubble that you never even think about . . .'

The boy sniffed, and took out a packet of cigarettes.

'. . . An I think what people forget is, you know, that money can't buy happiness.'

'Yes it can,' Michael heard himself saying.

And then there was a moment.

Five noses swung in his direction, snapping the division

between their universe and his. To delay, Michael raised his champagne for a sip. A cloud of quietness stewed around him.

It was time to say something else. He opened his mouth to find out what it would be.

'I mean very little unhappiness, globally, can be fixed without money,' he said.

That pious 'globally' he regretted. But the ball, he felt, had been more or less batted back.

'Oh yeah,' the boy pleasantly agreed. 'Money is so important.'

Michael was outraged. Why was the boy *agreeing* with him? They did *not* agree!

'But you just said it couldn't buy happiness,' he protested. Though he had to be careful. He could win any debating contest with this teenage peacock, so he must not be seen to start one.

'No. Definitely. It can't. You ask people with a lot of money. Snot that what makes them happy.'

'No. Sure,' Michael said, opening his palms in a display of gentle patience, 'but it is very difficult to be happy without any money.'

'Definitely.'

'So you could say that money is a tool with which one's chances of happiness – of freedom from poverty – are improved. Would any of us be able to feed and clothe ourselves without money to pay farmers and, er, seamstresses . . .'

(*Seamstresses?*)

'. . . let alone do any of the more interesting things in life that make most people happy? Although that doesn't mean that happiness is for sale, as such . . .'

He was panicking a little now. All the girls were looking at him – and one, in a strangely tousled little dress, was doing so with open hostility. None of them knew who he was, or what he was talking about. *He* did not know what he was talking about. He felt as if he were sinking, weighted, into limitless sea. Light fading. Pressure squeezing. Air gone. Panting off the seconds till his fatal inhalation.

'. . . so you're right, I suppose,' he said. And resolutely stopped.

They looked at him in silence like he had stabbed a dog.

A tray of drinks arrived, and someone's phone rang. Just a plain *bring bring*.

'Fuck,' the woman in the funny frock said, fumbling in her bag.

'No, you've got a point,' observed the boy at last over the rim of his new glass. 'I mean there's a lot of poor people in the world.'

'Hello?' The woman spoke impatiently, muffling her spare ear.

'Absolutely,' Michael agreed. 'There are.'

'Good to meet you, mate. Am Calvin.'

The boy's eyes shone deep and black. In his jaw, the muscles flexed like working rope.

'Michael.' He was so proud of himself. 'Hi.' He had done it.

The elbow of the woman's phone arm slumped irascibly on the platform of her other wrist.

'And that needs doing now, does it?' she said.

'No, you've got a point. I mean there's a lot of poor people in the world.'

It was true. There were. And Calvin thought that everyone should stop for a moment to remember them.

'Absolutely,' said the ugly man. 'There are.' And smiled.

Here at last was someone who could join him in intelligent discussion.

'Good to meet you, mate,' said Calvin. 'I'm Calvin.'

'Michael. Hi.'

And they shook hands. The man looked very pleased, but gave no sign of recognising him.

'This is Kelly-Marie,' Calvin continued. 'And . . .' Shit. What were the other two called?

'Alissa,' said Alissa, before anybody noticed his pause. Probably before anybody noticed.

'Briony,' said Briony.

And Susie was on the phone. Calvin had forgotten about her.

'How do you know Hugo?' Michael asked, kind of generally.

'They worked together.' Alissa stepped in.

'Oh yes? Are you an actor?'

'No,' said Calvin. 'Musician.'

He enjoyed this, being asked what he did. The man's ignorance did not aggrieve him. Indeed it made him strong. As if Calvin was a Roman emperor – some young, popular Roman emperor – turning up his thumb.

'Calvin, I've got to deal with something for a minute.' Susie's face was pink with self-control. 'Some fat waitress has spilled drinks down her pinafore and can't get into the replacement. We'll catch up in a minute and go see Hugo, OK?'

'Sure.' Calvin nodded to her leaving back.

'What sort of musician?' Michael pressed.

'Singer.' Deadpan, just like that.

'Oh yeah? Have you sung anything I know?'

'Maybe.' Sigh. 'I'm Calvin Vance.'

A glance at Kelly-Marie.

Quickly, Michael tried to produce a noise and compose a facial expression that might, between them, suggest both that he recognised the young man's name and that perhaps he didn't.

'I see,' he said.

And Calvin Vance, whoever he was, looked happy to leave it at that. His busy eyes patrolled their orbits, fiercely interested, it seemed, and yet also perfectly detached, like the boy could actually be a little mad. Or might suddenly go mad at any moment.

If Calvin Vance went mad, Michael wondered, would that be gossip?

The girls' faces shimmered glassily with unconcern.

'How about you,' he asked them, in the interests of fairness and continuance, 'are you musicians too?'

'We're at college together,' said one of them. God only knew which one.

'My dad makes films,' added an American other. 'He's here someplace.'

'And how do you know Hugo?' asked the first.

'Ah, yes,' Michael laughed. 'I sort of don't, really. I don't at all, in fact. A friend just gave me her invitation, and . . .'

'No way! You mean you blagged your way in here?'

Manifest upon the blonde girl's face was her opinion that, if he had, this would be the best thing he could possibly have done.

'I suppose so,' Michael said. 'In a way.'

'Wow! And you don't know anyone here?'

'No, not really.'

'So you came on your own? You didn't bring any mates with you?'

'No.'

'No way! I couldn't do that. We don't know anyone here at all.'

Well I'm a pretty brave guy. Was that what Michael was supposed to think? The instinct twitched to deprecate himself, but the girl had made him reconsider. *I'm a pretty brave guy?* Perhaps he was. He had thought that no one but himself could be so cowardly as to fear this party. But the girl would not have come alone, knowing no one. And he had. He had talked to people, too, and he could go home proud, after noodles, to Google 'Calvin Vance'.

'Well . . .' he murmured bashfully, sipping at his empty glass.

Calvin was lighting a cigarette, between thoughts, cross-eyed in guidance of the flame.

The girl had made Michael reconsider. He was almost emotional.

'Look!' The American gasped, and some of her suppressed excitement leaped into a little hop.

But Michael had already seen.

'So you came on your own? You didn't bring any mates with you?'

'No.'

'No way! I couldn't do that. We don't know anyone here at all.'

'Well . . .' Michael began, and left it at that.

Alissa and Briony were looking at the ugly guy too, transfixed by what? By his ordinariness? It made no sense, and was becoming inconvenient. Calvin was impatient to get back to business. To hook up again with Caspar. To escape Susie. To involve the girls. To phone around for other parties. To start to make a mess.

He lit a cigarette and thought about it.

'Look!'

A startled hiss from Briony. She was staring, in a happy emergency, at something behind him. Calvin swivelled through his puff.

And there he was. Striding neatly towards them. Perfect posture, beautiful blue suit.

Hugo Marks. Alone.

And now everyone was looking at Calvin. Kelly-Marie was looking at Calvin. Brain cramp. A cold spasm. He was supposed to do something. Obviously, he was supposed to do something. So he pressed one foot forward on the floor. It felt nice, distant flesh squidging in his shoe. Then the other foot, on a course to intercept. And straight away he shouted, leaping from the instinct's brink.

'Hey Hugo!' was what he shouted.

The face stopped and turned and looked at him.

'Calvin!'

The face dived in for a hug.

There was a moment of confusion. And then a special batch of celebration burst in Calvin's breast. He hugged Hugo hard. He was remembered! Publicly and joyfully *remembered!*

'How are you doing?' Hugo asked as their bodies disengaged. 'It's . . . been . . . ages.' The words were elongated to describe the span of separating time. Their shared apartness recognised at last and healed.

'Grand, mate,' Calvin said, hot. And, 'Yeah, totally . . . it's all good.' Stumbling over his own happiness like scatterings on his bedroom floor. Then finally, forgetfully, 'Happy birthday!'

'Thank you,' said Hugo with a humble dip of the head.

'Hugo, mate, I've just promised these young ladies that I'd introduce them to you.' Had he? Calvin could not remember.

'Have you now?' Hugo raised a famous eyebrow. 'And I don't suppose one of you would be Miss Briony Warshak?'

'That's me!' she said, stepping forward, almost curtseying, to put her hand in his. 'I lo-oved you in *Little Steve*.'

'Thank you very much. It was a great part. I was very lucky.'

Calvin decided to wear suits more often.

'You were just great.'

'Oh, now you're embarrassing me.'

The girls laughed together, in a shrill release of tension.

Hugo leaned across to speak to a waiter as they did so.

'Could you take a selection of your best malts over to that group of people at the bottom of the stairs please?' he said.

The waiter nodded and disappeared.

There was a moment of silence.

'Hi,' said Michael. 'I'm such a big fan.'

'Oh, now you're embarrassing me.'

She liked this, Warshak's daughter did, and led her friends in a cascade of glittery laughter, to which Calvin Vance breathlessly chipped in. He looked truly wasted, staring wildly out of a patina of sweat.

From a passing waiter, Hugo ordered his intended round of scotches. Another guy queued silently for his turn. He was unattractive, and older than the others, though not old. Strangely dressed as well, like an ambitious chemistry teacher.

'Hi,' the man said, stepping forward. 'I'm such a big fan.'

No one had briefed Hugo about him.

From: **valerie.morrell@nortonmorrell.co.uk**
To: **williammendez75@gmail.com**
Subject: **Publicity**
Date: **Wednesday, 26 August 2009 09:05:11**

Dear William,

Thanks for this. From what I have seen of it so far, I think the book is very promising. I enjoy your style, and the introduction of Calvin adds a valuable extra dimension. You say you are still polishing the rest, so I was wondering if there might be any more I could have a look at, perhaps with a synopsis? Let me rephrase that: I'm desperate to know what happens next!

And another thing: what more can you tell me about yourself? Is this your first novel? And what kind of journalism do you do? Perhaps we could meet up at some point? This week's bad for me, but any day next (except Friday) would be fine.

Regards,

Val

From: williammendez75@gmail.com
To: valerie.morrell@nortonmorrell.co.uk
Subject: Re: Publicity
Date: Wednesday, 26 August 2009 17:12:42

Thanks Val – I'm delighted you're enjoying it. I've been working on the novel for years and you are the first agent I've shown it to, so this really does mean a lot to me. I can't tell you how many times I imagined something like this happening!

As for a synopsis, well, the book is virtually finished now, so if you can bear to wait, I think I'd rather let it unfold at its own pace. I did sit down to write a basic summary after reading your email, but it just felt wrong. Sorry if that's frustrating for you. It won't be long before you can see the whole thing. If it helps, I will say that the finished version is shaping up to be about 85,000 words, and it turns on one central event roughly halfway through. When you get there, you'll know.

What do you think of the names of Warshak's daughter and her friends, by the way? I'm suddenly having my doubts about Briony as an American name – and Alissa and Kelly-Marie sound a bit council-house for such exalted company. In my first draft they were friends of the DJ, but then I wrote him out, and now I'm not sure they belong. Hmmm . . .

As for me, yes this is my first novel. And I, like Michael, am mostly a freelance subeditor, usually at *The Times*. It pays the bills (just about) and leaves enough space for writing. On Sunday I'm off to Sicily for a fortnight, but I could come in to see you on the Friday after I get back? That's Sept 18. Any good?

All the best,

William

From: **valerie.morrell@nortonmorrell.co.uk**
To: **williammendez75@gmail.com**
Subject: **Re. Publicity**
Date: **Thursday, 27 August 2009 08:50:10**

Perfect. Fri Sept 18 is in my diary. Shall we say 4pm at the Norton Morrell offices? And by all means bin the synopsis if you feel it spoils things. Just don't lose interest and leave me hanging!

Vx

PS Girls' names don't bother me, by the way. But then you're the author . . .

From: williammendez75@gmail.com
To: valerie.morrell@nortonmorrell.co.uk
Subject: Chapter 3!
Date: Sunday, 30 August 2009 04:51:09
▶ 🖉 Chapter 3 – Hugo/Mellody

Hi Val – I've worked extra hard to get this to you before I go away. I also hope to do some more work out there, so you won't be waiting long for the next one. All feedback gratefully received – especially on Mellody sections, which are meant to sound/look consistently like US English, but probably don't. And I did decide to change the girls' names in the end. Hope you approve...

William

Flick flick. Fli-ick.

A freelance strand of sinew typed a little overtime in Hugo's eye.

Flick fli-ick fli-ick flick.

It was usually higher up, the feeling. In his brow. He sensed its movements like the rustle of a caterpillar busying itself among the hairs. Painless, and unpleasant only in his inability to govern it. Today this rebel twitch, however, had migrated down into the apron of his eye. It was visible, he knew from bathroom surveillance, as a minute activation in the filmy skin. Though whether others noticed was impossible to tell.

'Anyway, we appreciate that your time is less than limited, so I'll cut to the chase,' said Edie, '*Princess Pam*: *Green Card* meets *The Princess Diaries*.'

The chase. Hugo thought there would be a chase.

'A girl.' With hands, Edie set the scene. 'A law student working pro bono in New York, marries a mysterious European guy to get him citizenship. But at their wedding she discovers his secret: back home he is a prince – and now she is a princess. So together, they must return to the old country to face what he was trying to run away from. You would play that man.'

'Which man?'

He had stopped listening.

'Who are we kidding here? You're Hugo Marks, you play Prince Dmitri. When I heard this idea, I called Brian and I said, "Hugo Marks. No one else."'

She was one of those very Californian women, Edie was. Moderately old. And large, one suspected, beneath her patterned smock. Not Chicken Cottage large, not outlandish, not a largeness that restricts one's choice of chairs. Hers was more the dwindled bulk that might result from being rapidly inflated once (by disease? by grief?) and then let down again, leaving her body grooved with tawny corrugations, like a sundried Mama Cass. Edie was a powerful producer, though. And her husband Brian's hedge fund had a taste for financing her films.

'Well, you know,' Hugo said, 'as ever it's script-dependent.'

'Well, we've got a sensational writer.' Brian joined in. 'Chloe Green.'

'I'm embarrassed. I haven't heard of her.'

'She's from TV.' Old blond Brian looked happy in his money suit. White shirt, red tie. No lapel flag tonight, though doubtless he kept several spares.

'So there's a script?'

'We wanted to surmise your interest.' Edie reassumed control. 'And then tailor the part to your specificities. No one plays an a-wrist-o-crat like you do.'

'You've got it down. Trust me.' Brian grinned like he had swindled a few.

'I take that as quite a compliment,' Hugo said, though there was none he liked less to receive. Ever since the success of his first film, *Little Steve* (attributed to his effortlessly debonair performance as Lord Mayle), it was as if some edict had been passed through Hollywood that nobody should offer him a role outside the aristocracy. Through doggedness, he had found more outré options, playing a drug dealer, a strung-out executive, a hit man and a writer – all with immaculate American accents. And yet even now, as *Sinbad*, the biggest film of his career, was finally on the point of release, three quarters of the scripts he received still contained some suave young nobleman, his dry wit highlighted in yellow streaks.

'So look: directors,' Edie said. 'Chris Columbus is interested. I met with him on Tuesday . . .'

Hugo swigged his drink and stared out across the casserole of names and faces on the floor below. Such energy, such frightening life. Mellody would be in there, of course, folded gracefully into a booth, laughing with her friends, that Pete Sheen character among them. It made Hugo glad to be elsewhere. Though now the mezzanine was growing crowded too.

'. . . could not agree with me more passionately. He was effusive, Hugo, to tell you the truth. And with the two of you on board, I think we have a good chance of getting on set by the fall of next year. If your schedule permits . . .'

He looked around for an escape route.

There was Gareth Morse, a senior British screenwriter and amiably sozzled cove. But Morse had already floridly unloaded his 'Many happy returns of the day', and might be just as difficult to shake off. Or there was Carlotta Bossi, a model friend of Mellody's, whom Hugo also had already spoken to – and then abandoned with the excuse that he was going to get a drink, only to see, on looking down, that his glass was full. Near Carlotta, however, was Don Scarlett. Don Scarlett: fashion designer, diminutive and neatly grizzled, hair black the colour of suspicion, in progressive specs and a clean-lined suit. He was battering another man with cockney repartee. Don would do.

'Excuse me Edie, sorry.' Hugo called out: 'Don! Don!'

The little man grinned through his cigar, and blithely forced his way over.

'Hugo, you old cunt!' he roared, startling the Americans a little.

'Don, this is Edie and Brian,' Hugo said, and everyone shook hands. 'Guys, this is Don Scarlett, an old friend. Mellody's been modelling for him for, ooh, absolutely ages.'

'Don't say that, son,' Don said. 'You'll make her sound old.'

'You're right.' Hugo nodded. 'She wouldn't like that.' And she wouldn't. 'Don's always had a bit of a soft spot for Mell,' he explained helpfully, to keep things running. 'Haven't you Don?'

'Are you joking?' Don was incredulous. 'I could fuck her in half!' Three hacks of laughter followed, before the intervention of a rich tobacco cough, fibrous and long-lasting.

Brian and Edie joined in for politeness.

'Well that's nice to know,' Hugo said.

For years, to please Mellody, he had simulated an affection for Don. And, a good actor, he sometimes convinced himself. Recently, though, as his wife began to weary him, the final wisps of this illusion had evaporated. Don, in Hugo's now concrete opinion, was a misogynist, an ego thug, and a consummate charlatan. He had become notorious in the early punk period for including customers' own blood in his designs, among other fluids; but now he was a public monument, the useful idiot of the avant-garde, though no less pugnacious for it. Badgered by the media after a derided show in Milan the previous year, Don had wrenched a microphone from the hand of an importunate Rai Uno reporter and told him in faithfully recorded Italian to go and fuck his sister with it.

'Don is an institution over here,' Hugo explained to Edie. 'He single-handedly invented drainpipe trousers, and is "the

living embodiment of all that is wrong with British fashion".
The *Independent* called you that, didn't they?'

'*Guardian* . . .' Don growled, through a smile of smoke, like
some predatory beast caught in a digesting lull.

'In fact,' Hugo soothed, 'you just had a show in America,
didn't you?'

'Paris. It was fashion week.'

'Of course! Sorry. Mellody said. How did you go down?'

'Fucking stormed it, didn't I.'

This was not what Hugo had heard.

'Cool,' Brian said, with every appearance of meaning it.

'You not see the pictures, Hugo?' Don and his cigar
looked serious. Prepared.

Hugo had to be careful. Not noticing Don's work was a far
from trivial insult. But being caught in the act of pretending
that he had . . . He must be vague, and fulsome, much as
he would usually be. A designer's new collection, in his
experience, was at least as precious as a baby, and equally
unavailable for review.

'Sorry, yes, Mellody did show me. It was great, totally you,'
he said, committing to the lie. 'Mell absolutely loved it too.'

'Course she did.' The cigar glowed happily. 'Listen.' A
note of earnestness entered Don's voice. Whatever came next
was what he really wanted to talk about. 'You've got to get her
back on the runway, mate. The stuff I'm doing right now, I'm
telling you, she is going to love it. Seriously, she's . . .'

'I'm sure you're right, Don,' Hugo interrupted. 'But
you'll never get her on a catwalk again. Believe me. Too much
temptation, and too much waiting around. It's commercial
work only these days, plus endorsements. And she's got this
fragrance coming out.'

'Bollocks, Hugo. Perfume's for wankers.'

'Yeah, well . . .'

Hugo's phone was ringing. It would be Renée.

'. . . The thing is . . .'

He fumbled in his pocket.

'. . . Sorry Don. I'd better take this . . . Hello?'

'Still sober?' Renée's voice seemed to be asking, above the din.

Hugo pressed a hand over his left ear and offered an apologising face to Don, Brian and Edie.

'Just about,' he said, squeezing through a pore in the crowd and shuffling towards a barside corner.

'Good. And you're upstairs, yeah?'

'Yes.'

'OK. Two things.'

Renée liked to be organised. Appointed chief publicist on *Little Steve*, she had impressed him on sight. Her pragmatic wits, sealed in a box of Chicago toughness, seemed absolutely to embody the professionalism of the upper industry. So casually, informally, he had begun to ask for her advice on other matters. Would it be good for him to do a coffee commercial? ('Sure, yes.') How about a cerebral palsy benefit? ('Definitely not.') Next he was consulting her about Mellody, too, asking how to handle the unrelenting scrutiny that their relationship had brought upon his life. Finally, when he called her to discuss whom he should approach to be his manager, Renée just said, 'Well you might as well start paying me,' and quit her job that day. Since then, she and her assistant Theresa had worked for him unstintingly and indispensably, thriving in the fastidious panic that they whisked into his affairs. No one but Renée could have convinced him to throw this party.

'First thing,' Renée said. 'Rick Warshak's here. Have you seen him yet?'

Shit. He had forgotten about Warshak. Besides re-burnishing his image, tonight was also meant to thaw relations with the chief executive of Pantheon Studios, who had perceived a slight, quite accurately, in Hugo's refusal of a three-picture deal. Indeed the party's date, and designation, had been purposefully set to capture Warshak's visit to his teenage daughter, who was a student in London and, Renée's intelligence suggested, a loyal Hugo Marks fan.

'*Hugo?* Have you seen Warshak?'

'Sorry. No, not yet.' Hugo swallowed. 'But I've . . .'

'OK, well he arrived around a half-hour ago and he's here to see you, so don't keep him waiting.'

'Sure. Obviously. I just got stuck with . . .'

'Thing two. And for now this is more important. You need to go find Mellody.'

'No I don't. She's downstairs.'

'No she's not.'

On tiptoes, Hugo peered above the heads. He could not see Mellody anywhere. Or Pete Sheen.

'She was there a minute ago,' he said, gulping.

'Well she's not there now.'

'Yes, I can see th—'

'OK, look. It doesn't matter. She's with her friends from that stupid band, OK? They just arrived, and it's best they don't monopolise her. So just go and spend a little time together. Be seen. Can you do that?'

Hugo said nothing.

'Then go talk to Warshak.'

'He-ey!'

Pete's denim-coated shins danced towards her through the crush, his arms Italian-wide.

Malcolm, drummer, tall and frizzy-headed, shuffled in behind.

'Mwah, darling, mwah,' said Pete, pecking her cheeks theatrically. His closeness brought a hobo cloud of masculinity, the sour-savoury accumulation of lived-in skin. 'Have you put on a couple of quid?' he added, looking her over, making fun of her profession as he liked to do.

Mellody laughed.

'All right Mell,' said Malcolm. Glum, as was his custom.

'Pete, you smell horrible.' She pitched the cheerful insult at him.

'I think you'll find,' said Pete, head rotated to the fact position, 'that brother Malcolm is the smelly one in this band. Drummers never wash, I tells you. The man is a walking dreadlock.'

And Mellody laughed again. Thank *God* the boys had arrived. She had been so *bored*.

'Malcolm?' she began, as he stepped into the light. 'Malcolm, is there something wrong with your eyes?'

'My eyes?'

'They look kind of weird.'

Pete was laughing now. His eyes were the same: a green iris in one side, an inhuman shade of indigo in the other.

'Fook,' Malcolm said, in his funny accent from the north. 'Have I still got them in? We went home with these two girls last night oo both had colored contact lenses. So this morning we borrowed one each.'

Mellody prevented herself from stiffening.

'It's an *homage* to Bowie,' Pete airily remarked, opening his mouth and plopping in a canapé.

'I can't see shit out me right.' Malcolm winked to check. 'That one were blind as fook.'

'OK,' Mellody said, and left it at that.

Because in her relationship with Pete, no actual terms had ever been contracted. Fun was all she wanted – fun at *last* – after so long watching Hugo sit and drink away their days. And fun meant nothing obligated, an avoidance of the weight of life. *The world's a crashing plane*, Pete had summed it up the night they got together. *Let's all fuck in first class.* So now they both had license. But it was something that she could not get comfortable with. Not like he did, going back with nameless other girls in threes or fours, not even offering a token furtiveness. His wit, his speedy cleverness, his thin-boned looks and gathering success: he made the most of those. She did not particularly care, of course. But, well, she felt at least as though she could have not cared *first*.

A waitress, in that idiotic costume, placed three champagnes in front of them.

'Sean's here,' Mellody said as they drank. 'He's looking for you two.'

In fact, the bassist from Pete and Malcolm's band, The French, had already been sniffing around when Mellody herself arrived. Networking, no doubt, and passing phone numbers to his drippy girlfriend.

'Oh right. Well, he'll find us.' Pete shrugged. 'Do you want a little snifter?'

The world's a crashing plane. She had heard the line recently in one of his songs.

'Sure,' she said.

'I'll come with you.' He rose, an eagerness easy to read upon his limbs. 'Isn't there somewhere in this place that we're supposed to go?'

'There *is*.' Mellody tarried on the word. There simply was no *way* that she was going to line up with the little weekend cokeists in their special snorting room. 'But let's go someplace else, OK?'

As ever, Pete counseled simplicity. 'Just do it here,' he said, gesturing casually at the table. 'Just do it, Mell! Swoosh!' He drew a tick in the air, his finger two inches from her eyes.

Mellody looked at him.

'Seriously,' he insisted. 'I'll rack up behind the flowers and stand in front of you while you tuck in. No one's watching.'

And once she might have done it too. Even now, yes, the fiery little impulse leapt within her. She had discharged her duty, after all, striking faithful shapes on the carpet with her husband, politely flattering his guests. Her agent Karl would say (as he frequently did) that she had done enough for Hugo Marks already. But then there was her own position, and its vile truths: she was a woman of thirty-three, with employees and a brand. Frolicking did not become her anymore, and it never would again. Karl would second that.

'No thanks,' she said, rising like a lady in her shoes. 'Let's just use the bathroom. That's what they're there for, right?'

'Pussy.'

But already Pete was walking with her to the door marked LOOS.

And already in her, rising, was the thrill of secrecy. The coded proposal, those clandestine texts ('mensroom, 2nd on left'), the dirty, locked-in intimacy: coke was so much *fun*. She was not supposed to take it anymore, of course, after all her other problems. But then coke was not about the coke. It never was. It was about the in and out.

Half a dozen toilet doors were open in the bathroom; just one was closed. Mellody led Pete into the stall beside it.

'Come on then,' she whispered, with eyebrows.

He set to work.

'This is totally stupid,' he said.

'*This* is stupid, is it?' She was gleeful. '*This* is stupid? And just racking up out there in the middle of the party, that would be intelligent, I guess?'

'Too right. I mean, if one is going to muck about – and one *should* muck about – then at least have some fucking balls.

No balls, Mell. That's your trouble. Ball-less. With a triple L.'

It was a joke, but it irritated her, so she said nothing.

'Are you allowed to leave this knees-up when you like?' Pete whispered after a while.

'Somewhere between no and maybe,' she said.

'I mean we could skive off, right? After a bit?'

'Well, there's an afterparty set for back at the house. I guess as long as I show up at that later . . .'

With a deft swipe across the wood, he collected the dust into a heap, bit the blade of his card in crosswise, and began another pass of stripes.

'Oh, come *on*!' Mellody said impatiently.

'Keep your hair on, love!' Pete administered some final touches. 'There you go.'

She pulled the flush, and bent down.

Then he took his.

She patted him on the ass. A nice ass. In tight black pants.

'Don't touch what you can't afford, love,' he muttered through the echo of his sniff, swivelling to fix her with a grin. A face of life and wires. Hot. Admittedly. Despite the mismatched eyes. A talent he had: to look good wasted. As did she indeed. Sexier than ever, she would have said she was these days. Not as *fresh* as once, no, but taut still where it mattered. Good blonde hair, shorter now and not too dry. A gently pointed calf, hinting at musculature. And still healthy at her weight, without that equine model look, like a big girl thinned, the will of giantess's genes frustrated outwards into oar-sized hands and feet. Uh-uh, not her. Mellody was in proportion, and she ate well. Heartily even. It was on the other side of the ledger, in her expenditure of energy, that the explanation for her slimness lay. And moreover now, with age, some wry sophistication too had slid into the picture. You could watch it grow in phases through her work. From the playful stringy body of the adolescent, almost ancient in its purity; into glaring glamor next, the territorial strut, staking claim upon the age; and on, on into the now of womanhood. Mellody's was a face these days, no longer a complexion.

With a cleansing pinch, she dusted off her septum and opened up the toilet door. Strode out. Left Pete behind. And through: wading back into the thickness. Her feet, soft and polished, framed by dear Manolo, darted through the dance like companion matadors. Some thigh, only just too much, whispered in and out of the split in her dress. Toe. Heel. Toe. Heel. Her hips flicked the air. Mellody had been looked at all her life, and had learned to put on a show.

'Oh hi, Sean,' she said, lighting a cigarette. He was sitting in her seat, with the girlfriend next to him.

A waiter was mopping wet fragments of glass from off the fizzing floor.

As he descended the staircase, Hugo looked out through its old iron helix, turn by turn, to check if Mellody was there. She wasn't. And it made him anxious. Not jealous. Not exactly. (That species of anxiety was self-correcting. Whatever pleasures Sheen or anybody else had borrowed from his wife, he knew, would in the end be multiply repaid with pain.) Instead her absence made him anxious in a dreading way, as if there was an assumption in his life now that something terrible was about to happen, though he had missed, or just forgotten, the reason for assuming it. Then this – that he had forgotten why he was so anxious – this made him anxious too. And ashamed. He, after all, had been the strong one when Mellody and he had met, back when her wild ways were beginning to outgrow their joyfulness and wilt into despair. Both of them then had needed Hugo's strength, as he stood guard beside her Arizonan rehab, watching his funny, famous girlfriend shiver strings of spit into an orange bucket. He had been strong then, and proud of it. But now he weakened frequently when she was missing, and for other stupid reasons. Especially in crowds, where he found he could be gripped by sudden, unsourced fear, and have to scurry home. Or when, in company at home, he would feel forced to dismiss his guests and drink himself calm. Yet the new quirk, the dread when Mellody was out of sight, was looming almost daily at the moment. He often nuzzled her, annoyingly he knew, with pretext calls and messages, beseeching reassurance that, if it came, was never reassuring enough. Often it was wrought with irritation too. And recently, more worryingly, without.

'It's the birthday boy!'

It was Warshak. He waited at the outflow of the stairs, positioned in a power stance.

'Rick, hi,' said Hugo with a hasty grin, and supplied his hand for pumping.

Warshak was a big man in all directions, and he smiled with everything he had. Legs, nose, ears, even hair, it seemed, were pressed into the effort. A supporting cast of Pantheon executives gathered behind him, with smiles they had made themselves.

'How the hell are you doing?' Warshak said, encircling Hugo with an arm. 'I haven't seen you since . . . well it's been a long time. How's Mellody? You treating her right?'

'She's never been treated better, Rick,' Hugo said. 'And she's been treated pretty well.'

The Pantheon executives laughed heartily at this, and Warshak contributed his own odd puffing sound, like he was surreptitiously deflating a beach ball behind his back.

'And how are you, Rick?'

'Oh I'm great, thanks. I'm super-dooper. Have you met the guys? This is Curtis. Gloria. Ruth.'

'Hi,' said Hugo generally. He recognised them all from Renée's briefing sheet.

'We're really looking forward to *Sinbad*, I can tell you,' Warshak said.

'Oh, you're going to hate it, Rick. Believe me, you're going to hate how good this movie is.'

Warshak did his puffy laugh again, and this time Hugo heard the cruelty in it. Since the movie's earliest days, *Sinbad the Sailor: Voyage of Vengeance* had been a banquet for the LA gossips, who had gleefully dismembered it beneath the nickname *Sinbad the Failure*. Unfair at first, the designation soon fulfilled itself when a dispute between producers had spilled into the courts, delaying principal photography until late 2002, by which time questions had begun to surface about the wisdom of making an expensive movie with an Iraqi hero. After consultation, the studio, Independence, had decided to continue. This news, however, was swiftly followed by the surprise success of two other boat movies, *Pirates of the Caribbean* and *Master and Commander*. Back in India for reshoots as the latter's Oscar nominations were announced, Hugo straight away caught giardia, to the undisguised amusement of the crew. Actually, the patched-up film was not too bad, he thought, and might do well. More than its success, however, he had started looking forward to people shutting up about it.

'Well it's been a long wait.' Warshak stretched the words lazily from his mouth like gum. 'We going to see you in LA for the premiere?'

'Absolutely. My flight is booked.'

Hugo hazarded another glance beyond him. Two guys from Pete Sheen's band were installed at a table, taking fresh drinks from a waitress.

'Great. Well, you must drop by my office when you're

there. Curtis has something in development I'd like you to take a look at.'

'Oh yes? What might that be?' Renée would be thrilled.

'Ahh . . . Well, I don't think I'm supposed to tell you yet. Can I tell him yet, Curtis?'

'No Rick, you can't.' Curtis grinned. 'We're still getting a last polish on the script. You're going to love it though, Hugo. Trust me on this.'

The guys from the band had turned their attention to the waitress's wig. One of them inserted his finger into a ringlet, pulled it out, inserted it again. The waitress smiled bravely. Bending down to inspect her petticoats, the other clipped the edge of her tray with his head. Glass, metal, dregs of drink clanged about him on the floor. His friend cheered, and most of the party turned round to look. The waitress left quickly, trying to prevent the drips from falling off her clothes.

'So . . .' Hugo wanted to move on. 'Listen Rick, I'm so glad you guys could make it. Are you in town long? It would be good to catch up properly some time.'

'Ah, well I'm seeing my daughter for lunch tomorrow –'

'Of *course*,' Hugo cut in. 'And she's with us tonight, is that right?'

'That is right.'

'Coral, yes?'

'That's her. She's studying in London, and I said I'd take her out while I was here. She's a fan of yours too, Hugo. That's for sure. I told her you're taken, but she likes the whole British thing. When you get bored of Mellody, you be sure to look her up, OK?'

'First thing I do, Rick.'

'But you'll give me Mellody's number too, right? Ha ha ha ha . . .' Warshak's wheezing laugh was loud enough that Hugo did not have to make a noise with his. 'So anyway,' the big man continued, 'after Coral tomorrow, I think Gloria has plans for me in Germany . . .?'

'I do, I'm afraid, Rick,' Gloria said. 'All our sales guys are going to be there. Plus there's that thing in Budapest. And I know you need to be back for Monday.'

'Gloria's our head of European operations,' Warshak explained. 'She's trying to get me to see all twenty-eight countries before I die, aren't you Gloria?'

And there was Mellody at last! She was back at her table, looking pleased about something.

'Well, look, I'll see you in LA for sure,' Hugo said. 'And you'll be back for Cannes, right?'

'Never miss it.'

'Fantastic. It's been great seeing you.'

'You too, Hugo. And *really* good luck with *Sinbad*, OK?'

The enthusiasm of Rick Warshak attacked his hand.

'Thanks. Enjoy the party, guys and,' flapping out a wave as he set off towards his wife, 'you must try the whiskies here. They have some fantastic rare malts. I'll get someone to bring a few over.' Then, deflecting several wayside *Hi's* and *Happy Birthdays*, he burrowed off towards his wife. Music hummed through the bodies around him. 'Let's Push Things Forward' by The Streets. The air was curly with the heat of people. A glitterball danced gently in their turbulence. The party was getting stronger.

'Hey Hugo!'

A young man was suddenly in his way. A very handsome young man, smoking a cigarette. Face familiar from Renée's notes. Vince? No, Vance. Calvin Vance, the singer from that chat show. And next to him, he recognised Coral Warshak.

'Calvin!' Hugo said, leaning for a hug into his smokey shoulder. 'How are you doing? It's been ages.'

'Grand, mate,' Calvin said. He looked a little wasted. 'Yeah . . . totally. It's all good. Happy birthday!'

'Thank you.'

'Hugo, mate.' The boy was chewing hard, gathering his courage up for something. 'I've just promised these young ladies I'd introduce them to you.'

'Have you now?' said Hugo. 'I don't suppose one of you would be Miss Coral Warshak?' He sounded like a shopping centre Father Christmas.

'That's me!' she chirped. 'I loved you in *Little Steve*.'

'Thank you very much. It was a great part. I was very lucky.'

'You were awesome!' There was a shine in her eyes.

Mellody was talking on the phone, just a few feet away.

'Oh now you're embarrassing me!' Hugo said.

'Hi Mell,' said Sean. He was wearing a hat.

'Hi Mell,' said Sean's girlfriend.

Mellody expelled a jet of smoke.

'What happened here?' she said.

'Malcolm had an altercation with a tray of drinks,' Sean explained. 'Made a bit of a mess.' He formulated a grin of pastiche embarrassment, teeth lined up neatly in their lip-slot.

Mellody did not like Sean. He was always *thinking*. You could tell.

'I never touched it,' Malcolm said.

'Never touched what?' This was Pete. He had swaggered over and almost put an arm around her, before obviously remembering where they were and lifting it to his hair instead.

'Malcolm never touched the tray of drinks that he knocked over with his head,' Sean explained.

'Pillock,' said Pete.

Through the crowd, Mellody could see her husband. He was standing just a few paces away. Then he disappeared again. Had their eyes met? She decided that they hadn't. Hugo seemed always to be checking up on her for something.

'Listen,' Sean said quietly to Pete. 'I'm hooking up with Giles later. He's . . .'

The conversation drifted out of earshot as Mellody sat down on the booth's opposing bank. She did not need to hear it, though, to know what was being said. Giles was her former dealer, a man worth knowing, whom she had introduced the band to. And now, scarcely six weeks later, Sean already acted like the connection was his. Which was pretty typical of Sean.

Wiping down his hair, Malcolm slid in stickily beside her.

Sean was already on the phone now, talking. The girlfriend Sasha sitting silent in her high-school indie gear, hands in lap. You forgot that she was there. Then when finally she did say something it was always 'we' and 'us' she spoke for, like she and Sean had formally been merged. They had argued badly once, Mellody and Sasha, about Janis Joplin, in an underlit recording studio dizzy with the stink of days. Since then no word of it had been resolved.

Mellody blew out more smoke. She could feel that line now. A subtle, egotising lightness in her thoughts, a feeling you could nibble at for days. And the desire for more.

Sean was laughing, at a joke of Giles's, or one of his own.

'Is that Giles?' she shouted over to him. And again, louder, when he looked back dumbly: 'Is that *Giles*?'

Sean nodded.

She motioned for him to pass her the phone, and he did as he was told.

'Giles,' Mellody said.

'Mellody darling.' That lovely voice.

'How the hell are you, sugar-pop?'

Giles said something, but Mellody could not hear it.

'And we're seeing you later, yes?' she said.

'I hope so . . .' . . . something something . . . '. . . o'clock.'

Fucking DJ. The music was *way* too loud.

'Sorry, Giles. Could you say that again?'

'I have to leave at eleven o'clock – paternal duties. So you'll need to be here by then. I'm on the third floor.'

He spoke precisely. Loud, but not a trace of impatience.

'Sure. We'll be there . . . Where?'

'. . . in . . .' Something something.

'Sorry Giles. Where are you?'

Frustration was threatening to rasp away her mood.

'Sean knows,' said Giles. '. . . later.'

'OK. See you later Giles. I'll be there.'

And why shouldn't she? Why *shouldn't* she be there? And score a little for herself. Why not? To say yes please, and afterwards no thank you. That was true recovery. The thing addiction counselors never understood. And she was so *past* those problems now. Why shouldn't she enjoy herself? It wasn't like she did it all the time. She tossed back the snapped-shut phone.

'You coming then?' Pete asked eagerly.

'Sure. When we're done here.'

'We can't be long,' Sean said, looking at his watch. 'He's leaving at eleven.'

'Don't worry. He'll be there.'

Don Scarlett slid into focus at the table's edge.

'Don!' Mellody yelped, climbing over Malcolm to get to him.

'Mell, love!'

At last someone she really *wanted* to see. He embraced her with his smell of suitcases.

'How the hell are *you*? It's been so *long*.' She was excited, thoughts overlapping. 'How was Paris?'

'Great, great,' said Don. 'I di'n't see you there.'

'Nah, I couldn't make it this year. I've been tied up with this fragrance thing.'

'Yeah, Hugo said. What's it called?'

'"Me". It's just called "Me".'

'OK. And it smells of you, does it?'

A bus-wide cockney beam. He actually leaned toward her for a sniff.

'Jesus, Don!'

She laughed.

'Is that it you're wearing?'

'Yes it is, as a matter of fact.'

'Mm. So Mell . . .' This again. She could see it coming. 'Hugo says you've chucked it in with the runway. Is that right?'

'Yeah. I think so. I've got too much other shit going on.'

'Well look.' He grabbed a passing champagne glass and she followed his example. 'I'm going to change your mind.'

'No you're not.'

'Listen: I'm gonna give you some clothes. From my spring range, but autumn's even better. Try 'em on, then call me. And I'll send some to give to Hugo as a birthday present.'

'I already gave him a present.'

'Oh yeah? What you get him that's better than my suits?'

'A Japanese kitchen knife. He's very particular about his knives.'

Pete and Sean were mocking Malcolm's hair. Sasha was laughing.

'A *kitchen knife*?'

'Yes.'

'What, to cut his cake?'

'He didn't get a cake.' She did this in a sad little voice.

'No cake?' Don was such a pussycat. 'D'you sing him "Happy Birthday"?'

Hugo was talking to some guy, with that courteous look

on his face. He still took such trouble for the opinion of strangers.

'No, I didn't,' Mellody said. 'But we could sing it now if you like?'

'Hi,' the man said, stepping forward. 'I'm such a big fan.'

No one had briefed Hugo about him.

'Hi,' Hugo said, shaking hands. 'That's really nice of you. Thanks. I don't think we've met before, have we?'

'No. We haven't.' The chemistry teacher was nervous and dared not meet his eyes, except by furtive accident. He was leaning so steeply away from the junction of their hands, that it felt like Hugo's grip was all that held him up. 'I'm Michael,' he said.

'Hi Michael.' Hugo was intrigued. He seemed an unlikely friend of Calvin's. 'So how do you know these guys?'

'Um . . .' Michael looked at the girls, and then at Calvin. 'Well, I don't really,' he said eventually. 'We just met.'

'I see. But you're in music, too, right?'

'No, no!' Laughing. 'No, actually . . .'

'What's your surname?'

'Knight,' said Michael. 'But I'm not a musician. I'm a kind of journalist.'

The music faded suddenly, grasping everyone's attention with a jolt of absence.

Hugo looked around, instinctively and anxiously, for explanations. Whatever was about to happen was about to happen to him. He saw his wife, and the sight was followed immediately by a broad cheer. She was getting up on to a table, whooping with delight as her trailing ankle skipped across the surface.

'Gentlemen and ladies!' she called to the room. It cheered again, and paid attention.

Had Renée put her up to this, Hugo wondered? Was that why he had been sent downstairs?

'Gentlemen and ladies, I just wanted to say–' Mellody stumbled slightly against a margarita glass and looked down, crossly, to see what the matter was. It was a margarita glass. With princess poise, she closed her eyes and backheeled the offending object precisely into someone's lap. The room blared with laughter. Cameraflash sequins twinkled on her little *who, me?* smile.

'I just wanted to say,' she continued, 'that my darling husband, Mr Hugo Marks, is thirty-one today – sorry, not today, last week. Oh, you know what I *mean!*'

Laughter, general and synchronised.

'Anyway, he's thirty-one,' she cut it off, 'and I think we should sing him a song.'

There were agreeing cheers.

'Now what sort of a song should we sing?'

The words tumbled out, bruising at the edges. And the crowd responded with a mottled batch of shouts, most of them demanding 'Happy Birthday'. From her vantage point, Mellody could see Hugo clearly. Everyone nearby was looking at him too.

'Was that "Happy Birthday"?' she asked, cupping a hand to her ear.

Yes!! the room shouted back, and *Happy Birthday!* until the words became a chant. *Ha-ppy! Birth-day! Ha-ppy! Birth-day!*

'All right, all right, all right!' Mellody yelled above it. 'We'll sing "Happy Birthday"!'

Somewhere behind her the piano had been opened. A lush

ribbon of introducing notes was bubbling up. Mellody turned to see Elton John announcing the first line. He smiled. Good old Elton. He always got into the spirit of things.

'Ready everyone?' she said.

The music trembled on the brink.

'Happy Birthday'. A holy obligation for the dead at heart. Hugo hated it. As Mellody surely knew.

'Ready everyone?' she asked. 'One, two, three, four . . .'

Ha-ppy bir-thday to yooooo!

The congregated loudness rocked Cuzco with a wallop.

Happy birthday to you!

Even the serving staff were joining in. Coral Warshak with especial gusto, sincerity ripening her cheeks.

Happy birthday dear Hhhyooo-goh! . . .

He alone was not singing. He alone.

Happy birthday to you!

Elton's fingers twiddled a departing scamper up the keys as whoops, cheers, whistles and stamps rumbled all around.

'Enjoy the evening, everyone!' Mellody shouted.

No way had this been Renée's idea.

'Enjoy the evening, everyone!' Mellody shouted, before placing a hand on Don's shoulder and beginning her descent.

Hugo folded himself into a bow and raised his drink in her direction.

Speech! shouted one or two bold voices. *Speech!*

Reluctance creased her husband's face, though a merry glint of weakness leaked out, too. Just enough to bait the calls to a crescendo. At the crest, he relented, raising his hands in surrender. He was so good at this, so comfortable in control. No one, seeing it, would realise the rest.

'Friends . . .' Hugo cried theatrically . . .

'. . . agents . . .' He got a laugh . . .

'. . . tax lawyers.' He got a bigger one.

'Thank you all so much for coming. I hope you've been enjoying yourselves?'

There was a rowdy affirmation.

'I'll take that as a yes,' he barked. 'Thank you for your exquisite singing. And Elton, for your contribution.'

More riotous applause. Elton looked pleased, and glanced acknowledgement at Mellody.

'One take,' Hugo noted drily, 'and without sheet music too. The boy's got a big future, trust me.'

Even she found this funny. Pete's face, too, was lit up with the glee of a child.

'Anyway, listen. I really am so grateful to you all for coming. Everyone at Cuzco has been superb in planning this.' He paused to make way for more polite applause. 'But there really is no such thing as a party unless people turn up to make it happen. So thanks again, to all of you. And if you're having half as good a time as I am, then . . . erm . . . I'm having twice as good a time as you. Cheers! Thank you very much!' he shouted, raising his glass again above the noise.

Peering out at Mellody, the DJ raised his thumb and formed his face into a question. She nodded, and the music resumed.

'Right,' she said to Pete. 'I'm going to go say goodbye.'

And in response, a throng of other glasses turned to Hugo. There was a tender pause as everybody sipped. It cheered him. Surprisingly. Those anxious little gnawings of five minutes ago, what had become of those? Quite forgotten. But he was starting to think about them now. So leaning towards the chemistry teacher, he said: 'Is your name *really* Michael Knight?'

And the music resumed.

Calvin had seen photographs of Mellody, of course. Hundreds. And, in common with the general view, he held her beautiful. But never before had he felt the oddly painful joy that her actual presence had provoked in him just now. It was a sudden sense of certainty, both immediate and total, from the moment that she climbed on to the table, that she was the most attractive woman he had ever seen.

He sang as instructed, but robotically, and with little sense of why.

He simply could not stop looking at her.

Hugo was a lucky guy. Guys like Hugo always were.

And now she was coming over. Fucking hell, she was actually *coming over*. Cornering sideways through the crowd like a breeze-caught wisp of cloth.

And looking at him. Was she looking at *him*?

Calvin battled to control himself. Even above the pulsing rhythm of The Streets again, it felt as if the beat of his own blood might still be heard. This would be a very good time not to do something thick.

'Hey darling, happy birthday,' she said to Hugo, kissing him on the cheek.

Another look, this time unmistakably at Calvin. There was eye contact . . .

The moment was so strong it made ghosts in his head. They walked through walls.

Hugo and she were talking.

Then, 'Hi Calvin.' She was offering him her hand. It was pale and soft and slim. And there was significance in the way she said his name, he was sure of it. Something intended. That soft American voice had taken the sound of who he was, wrapped it in a silk-lined box, and returned it with a big red bow marked 'Pull'.

'Hi,' Calvin said back, prolonging the contact with her skin.

Beep.

What had he been thinking of with Venetia? A tasty little thing for sure – and his – but really, what was the point in having what he had already?

Mellody: she was the prize.

She had stopped talking. She was looking at him again.

He was looking back.

Pete Sheen was standing behind her, bouncing on his heels. His eyes were different colours.

In defiance of her industry, Mellody had never let herself become a snob about clothes. Some people were interested, and some people were not. Yet still it was a serious surprise to see her husband talk to *anybody* who would come to *anything* in a suit like *that*. She felt sorry for the man, and wondered who he was. That he lacked the cocksure calm of influence was clear. And certainly he was not rich. If something in his life had brought him fame, then she could only suppose that it was not the kind of fame where people took your picture.

The man disappeared from view again as Mellody jinked around a knot of media people she had spoken to before: Andy Coulson, Elisabeth Murdoch, Matthew Freud. Coulson acknowledged her in passing with a burst of silent applause tapped out on the stem of his glass. Mellody gave him a smile in return. After *Sinbad*, when she could at last admit that her marriage was over, Karl had warned her many times that she would be needing friends in the press. And it was a friendship often offered, with gifts with notes, and valuable information indiscreetly shared. It tempted her at times. And she could see its sense. Still, more friends she didn't like? She already had enough of those.

Aiming now at Hugo's group, she noticed another figure,

standing slightly to one side. It was a young man. Boy, some would say. And he was just totally *gorgeous*. Slimly muscular, with shining eye-whites and cappuccino skin, a study in fine-boned masculinity, with none of the preening seriousness that emanated from so many male models of Mellody's acquaintance. His was the magic beauty of an innocent, a piece of the divine. Beside him, three young girls stood also, saying nothing. (One of them had a kind of jailbait prettiness, not the kind that lasts.) But the boy . . . oh, yes please. Oh yes fucking *please*!

'Hey darling,' Mellody said to Hugo, bringing her lips briefly into contact with his cheek. 'Happy birthday.'

She looked at the boy again, and he gazed right back. A warm craving shuddered through her abdomen, something primal that twisted and strummed against her nerves. An urgent need. Not a need that could wait, or cared for consequences, or meant well. *Jesus*. Sex with this boy just had to be had.

'This is Michael,' Hugo said, introducing the badly dressed man. 'This is Coral Warshak, and her friends Poppy and Venetia.' He waved at the girls. 'And this is Calvin Vance.'

Calvin Vance. It was not a name she knew.

'Hi,' said Mellody all round. 'Hi Calvin.'

'Hi,' he replied, still holding her hand.

Beep.

'Thanks for that, Mell,' Hugo said. 'Very spontaneous.'

It took her a moment to realise that he was talking about her song.

'Oh . . . no problem, sweetheart. Actually I just came over to say toodle-oo. I'm shooting off to this thing for a little bit. But I'll see you back at the house later, OK? Things kind of seem to be winding down anyway.'

Calvin was watching her. She caught him at it.

'Oh, OK,' Hugo said. And attempting to be casual: 'Where are you off to?'

Mellody was ready for the question.

'Just this music industry thing in north London. There's some people in town from Boston I haven't seen in years. I won't be long.'

'All right Calvin!' Pete's voice at her shoulder made her jump. 'How're you doing?'

'Hi Pete,' Calvin replied. 'Yeah, not bad.' He had a cute northern voice, a bit like Malcolm's.

'You guys know each other?' Mellody asked this very casually indeed.

'Yeah, we met at the Brits, didn't we?' said Calvin.

'You were fucking sizzled, mate,' said Pete.

Hugo could not believe that she was doing this. And she seemed to think that it was no big thing. Like it was just a trifle to leave him – publicly to leave him – and go somewhere else. What could he say? He said nothing.

Pete and Calvin were emitting barrowboy banter. The imbeciles, obviously, were friends.

'So you're a musician too, are you Calvin?'

Was that flirtation in his wife's voice, Hugo wondered, or mockery?

'Yeah,' Calvin said. 'I'm a singer, and I write songs.'

'Come on, Mell, you know Calvin Vance!' Pete jabbed her reproachfully in the ribs.

It was the first time that Hugo had seen something physical pass between them.

'Oh of course!' Mellody pressed her hand in shame to her décolletage. 'I am *so* sorry, Calvin. Of *course* I know your work. Listen, I have to run, but why don't you come along? I'm just going to make an appearance, but you guys can catch up in the car.'

'All right,' Calvin said instantly.

'Hi,' Mellody said to Michael kindly, looking directly at him for a moment before she moved on to the others.

Beep.

His phone vibrated twice in his pocket. A text.

Instinctively, he pulled it out. But what was he *thinking*? To check a text *now*? He slid it back. Yet it was too late; he had produced it. To retreat looked indecisive. So out it came again. No, no, no, no. Put it back. Put it back. What an idiot he was. He must look deranged if anyone (they weren't) was watching.

'Oh, OK. Where are you off to?' Hugo Marks sounded disappointed.

'Just this music industry thing in north London. There's some people in town from Boston I haven't seen in years. I won't be long.'

This music industry thing . . . People from Boston . . . What a world he was witnessing! Here in front of him, right now: the domestic transactions of Mellody and Hugo Marks. Incredible. He did not know if it was gossip. In his life it was news.

'Hi Pete,' Calvin said to a young man in a leather jacket. 'Yeah, not bad.'

Michael looked shamefully at his shoes. What could he say? He said nothing.

He wanted to disappear, but he did not want to leave.

He reached for his phone.

1 new message

His favourite screen.

How's it going with hugo m? said Sally's text. *Got me a signed pic yet?*

From: valerie.morrell@nortonmorrell.co.uk
To: williammendez75@gmail.com
Subject: **Buon Giorno**
Date: **Thursday, 3 September 2009 09:33:40**

Dear William

Sorry to bother you on holiday, but I want to put my cards on the table without delay: I think this is marvellous. Stylish, funny, inventive, and I feel sure that the story is going somewhere. I would be honoured, therefore, to represent you. I thought I should let you know.

You also asked for any early impressions, so here is what I've jotted down. Idle musings all. Disregard at your leisure.

- Pete Sheen/Pete Doherty comparison intended? Change name if not?
- Clash of styles/characters? Sophisticated literary register perfect for Michael and Hugo, but wrong for Calvin/Mell? First-person better maybe?
- Song lyrics, except titles, will need permission from rights holders, and can be expensive, just so you know.
- Yes: girls' new names better. (You were right.)

This aside, I'm loving it. Very few first novels of this quality arrive on my desk, or in such a (so far) finished state. Well done, and see you on your return.

Val x

From: williammendez75@gmail.com

To: valerie.morrell@nortonmorrell.co.uk

Subject: Re: Buon Giorno

Date: Monday, 7 September 2009 23:01:22

Dear Valerie

Just saw your email. I didn't know I might have to pay for quoting songs, so thanks for mentioning. I do take issue with the other points, however.

Of course Pete Sheen is *like* Pete Doherty, but that hardly means he's supposed to be a cipher for him. I called him Pete because it suits the character, and if people see a Doherty comparison then that's fine too. I want them to think about the novel's similarities to the real world, after all, so resonances like that can only help. I find it odd that you would question this, in fact, since there are so many other celebrities in the book who *do* appear as themselves, with their real names. Surely this demonstrates that I welcome comparisons with real life? If you are worried about libel, consider Brett Easton Ellis, whose books are full of real (and non-suing) celebrities. Unlike Ellis, I have given some of my cameos significant dialogue, it is true, but these instances have either been taken from real interviews, which makes them legally acceptable, or they are simply not defamatory. As far as I know, for what it's worth, I am the first novelist ever to do this. (And there are also at least two passages of hidden quotation for readers to find for themselves. One from The Sopranos, actually.) Obviously I couldn't use the same tactic to the extent of casting Doherty himself as a major character. But I wouldn't want to anyway, because it is actually very important that some of my characters remain fictional in order that they remind us not of specific people, but of the archetypes we see everywhere. Without lecturing them about it, I want the reader to consider the stock characters in our media: the self-destructive rock star, the drug-loving supermodel, the talent show wannabe. We all feel we know plenty of these people. But do we? When a private individual becomes a public figure, it is not *he* who is suddenly well known – instead a new version of 'him' is concocted by all the news reports and photographs and interviews. And usually this new version is based less on who the person really is, and more on what we, as consumers of media, want to see. Are all cancer patients really 'brave', for instance? Are all paedophiles 'evil'? Must every debut novelist be 'an exciting new voice' or 'up-and-coming'? This is just a crass simplification of real people into familiar *characters* to help us shape the chaos of the world into satisfying stories. We want to see those who strive rewarded; those who seem too lucky, on the other hand, must fall. The world *is* a novel.

And if I'm honest, I don't understand your objections to my prose style either. Yes, I do drift in and out of the heads of my characters, but I think I subtly adjust the core style as I go. Michael is more verbose, Hugo is posher, Mellody is American, and Calvin is young and ignorant. This has its limits, of course, which I try to be relaxed about. Perhaps you would prefer it if I wrote four different novels and spliced them together like David Mitchell or Wilkie Collins or some other virtuoso one-man-band? Well I'm not going to. And your suggestion of the first person does not appeal either. The first person is a cop-out, used by writers who prefer to shove their typing hand inside a puppet so it can take the blame for their own intolerant opinions and deficiencies of style. (There are a few exceptions to this rule, but you could buy them all on Amazon and still not get the postage free.) Remember: the greatest realisation in fiction of a human being's inner life is *Crime and Punishment*. And that is all 'Raskolnikov', not 'I' and 'me'.

Now I'm off for a gelato.

W

From: williammendez75@gmail.com
To: valerie.morrell@nortonmorrell.co.uk
Subject: Sorry, sorry, sorry
Date: Tuesday, 8 September 2009 04:15:08

Dear Val – just want to say how sorry I am about that last email. I was in a Sicilian cybercafé, slightly smashed and with credit to burn, which always makes me take things personally. I hope this won't put you off sharing your opinions in future?

I also wanted to add that I don't think the next chapter will be quite finished before I return, which means I probably won't get it to you before we meet either. Very sorry about that too. Sorry all round, really.

Yours,

William

From: valerie.morrell@nortonmorrell.co.uk
To: williammendez75@gmail.com
Subject: Re: Sorry, sorry, sorry
Date: Tuesday, 8 September 2009 10:59:00

You are a lamb. Take all the time you need, and don't worry about my feelings. Am sure you're right, in any case. Just idle thoughts is all they were. Take my opinions to the beach and toss them in the sea.
Val x

From: williammendez75@gmail.com
To: valerie.morrell@nortonmorrell.co.uk
Subject: Rescheduling...
Date: Monday, 14 September 2009 12:11:53

Hi Val – just got back, and landed in a pile of work. Any chance we could reschedule Friday for another time?

William

PS I'm having second thoughts about *Publicity* as a title. There seem to be a lot of novels with one-word abstract-noun titles these days, especially from debut authors. (*Disobedience*, *Tourism*, *Politics* and *Electricity* off the top of my head...) So how about adjusting ours slightly by adding five stars, thus:

Publicity*****

It's different, which is always good. And it stands out more on the page. (Perhaps also implying that the book has had a rave review...) What do you think?

From: **valerie.morrell@nortonmorrell.co.uk**
To: **williammendez75@gmail.com**
Subject: **Re: Rescheduling...**
Date: **Monday, 14 September 2009 16:35:03**

Don't worry, old thing. Next Tue any good?
And yes, I love *Publicity******
Vx

From: williammendez75@gmail.com
To: valerie.morrell@nortonmorrell.co.uk
Subject: Re: Rescheduling
Date: Monday, 14 September 2009 21:08:31
▶ 📎 Chapter 4 – Squat

Sorry, the next fortnight is all a bit rubbish now. Can I let you know when things have cleared? Here's the next chapter to make up for it.

W

Michael safely locked and pocketed his phone.

'I am *so* sorry, Calvin. Of *course* I know your work,' Mellody was saying. 'Listen, I have to run, but why don't you come along? I'm just going to make an appearance, but you guys can catch up in the car.'

Her face smiled. It was so familiar to Michael from photographs that the real thing looked wrong. Like footage recovered from another age and digitally blended into his.

'All right,' said Calvin.

'Great. Well we'd better go. See you guys later, yeah?'

'See ya, Hugo,' the leather lout replied. 'Great party, mate.'

And they were gone.

Hugo Marks offered Michael a look of amused perplexity, and seemed about to say something when Poppy, who had been nudging the American girl to speak, spoke up herself.

'Would it be OK to get a picture with you?' she asked. 'Just one?'

'Of course! No problem! Take as many as you need!'

Hugo looked relieved.

'Could you, um . . .'

The girl was offering Michael her camera.

'Oh,' he said finally. 'Yes . . . of course.'

'You press the button on the top.'

He nodded. Even though there were two buttons. And arguably two tops.

The girls gathered smiles around their host, and waited hard.

Holding the camera out awkwardly in front of him, Michael

stepped back, composed the group into the screen, and pressed something. A menu and nine small pictures appeared, showing two of the girls getting dressed to go out.

Still they held their pose.

'Erm,' Michael said. 'I think I've pressed the wrong button.'

'Is the car ready?'

Pete nodded, but Mellody had already turned away, leading them across the thinning room. At the edge of his vision, Calvin could see that Susie had reappeared and was looking around. For him, he guessed.

'So are you guys not playing tonight?' he asked Pete quickly.

'Not tonight, Josephine,' Pete said, in a voice like he was quoting something. 'Maybe for a laugh, but no gigs. Praps you could give us a little warble yourself, Cal? My voice is dogged.'

'I'd love to, man! That'd be brilliant!'

'Nice one.'

They were swishing down the corridor again, this time past the disused kitchen, which remained a little den of occupation. As he walked, Calvin noticed that the white paint on the walls was peeling. That would be damp, he knew, or heat. He reached out to touch it, and watched a leisured trail of flakes tumble from his fingers, looking up only when they butted up against the frame of another door. This one was the entrance to a real kitchen, which Mellody herself was holding open for him with a special gaze. He returned it boldly, without breaking stride, and walked through to where a swarm of staff was packing plates and glasses into travel boxes, fitting every item to its white compartment. No one looked surprised, or even interested, by his or Mellody's appearance.

'Ready?' asked a man's voice from beside a fire exit across the rubber mats. Calvin saw that it was Sean, Pete's mate from the Brits. And a smiling stare from Sean acknowledged this. Beside him stood a man and a woman that Calvin did not know.

'The cars are here,' Sean said. 'And there's just a couple of paps ouside. Sasha and me'll make a break for it first, OK?'

Mellody signalled her agreement with a scooping gesture, as if trying to push him through the door.

'OK.' Sean wrenched flat the exit bar and left, the woman with him.

Calvin, Mellody, Pete and the other man waited together for a moment in a twist of chilly air.

'A'right, mate,' the other man said. 'Malcolm.'

'A'right,' said Calvin. 'Calvin.'

'Scuse me.'

A waiter was trying to reach behind him for an empty box.

'Sorry,' Calvin said, and moved.

Mellody laughed at something secret. She was so beautiful.

Then, 'OK guys?' And she pushed open the door.

The street was still. Sean had vanished. Two van-size bins stood guard, sour with the metallic death of fruit. Strewn across their lamplit surface was a history of stickers, the paper long since rained away to leave just grimy clouds of glue.

Silently, Mellody pointed across the road towards a big black car. Its exhaust pipe shuddered crimson fumes into the brake lights' glow.

Calvin set off, and almost immediately he heard a man's loud voice.

'Mell! Mell!'

The shout clapped wet and hopeful on the cobbles.

There was a push in his back, and everybody started running. Pete opened the passenger door and jumped in as flashes bounced around. Malcolm followed, diving sideways at the seat. Without thinking, Calvin did the same, and felt Mellody land immediately on top of him.

'Go!' she shouted, laughing, 'Go!'

The door was slammed.

And somewhere in the pile of bodies, Calvin was laughing too.

Her breasts were on his neck.

And he had left his jacket behind.

'So, Mike,' said Hugo, 'You said you were a "kind of journalist". What kind of journalist?'

The girls had gaggled off to debrief, and the men were now alone.

'Oh, I'm just a subeditor.'

'I see. Which paper?'

'The *Standard*.'

'So you write their headlines?' Hugo knew what a subeditor was, though he could not for the moment guess why one was at his birthday party.

'Some of them, yeah,' Mike said, 'and I make sure everything's spelled correctly. It's a day job,' he shrugged.

'That implies that you do something else the rest of the time?'

'Sort of. I like to write things.'

The words were said with quiet purpose, though no eye contact, as if the man were ashamed of his pride.

'Articles for the paper and stuff?' Hugo asked, doubting it. He shuffled over to a vacant armchair and lowered himself into its clutches.

'Not really. Just . . .' Mike hesitated. 'You know, little stories and descriptions and things. Bits of fiction. Nothing special.'

'I see.'

Hugo was intrigued. Humility had been somehow shouldered out of almost all the characters he met these days. Did he know anyone who had not already proven themselves professionally, or thought so?

'I used to love writing things when I was younger,' he was surprised to hear himself saying. 'I thought I might be a writer when I was at school.' And it was true. He had even written a play, never performed, about the internal rivalries of a football team. But why was he talking about it now? And why had he *ceased* talking about it before?

'Yeah? What sort of things did you write?' Mike asked with interest, contemplating the chair next door.

'Oh, you know . . .' This was bizarre. 'Plays, I think . . . Or books or films. I wasn't really sure.'

Mike nodded and finally sat down, but said nothing.

'You get distracted,' Hugo felt the need to explain. 'Other things. You know.'

'Mmm . . .'

'Maybe I should get back to it, actually. It might be fun.'

'It's fucking miserable,' Mike said. And they both laughed.

It was nice, thought Hugo, that the man now felt comfortable enough to swear.

Beep.

'Who keeps texting you?' he asked.

'Oh, erm . . .' Mike fumbled the phone out of his pocket and looked. 'It's my friend Sally.'

'Sally, eh? There aren't enough Sallies around these days.'

'You're right. There aren't.'

'And is Sally your significant other?' Hugo had begun to feel almost jovial again.

'Oh no, no, no!' Mike's denial frothed tellingly with fervour. 'She's just someone I work with.'

'I see. At the *Standard*?'

'Yes.'

'Checking up on things here, perhaps?' Hugo said this grinning, to show he didn't mind.

'Yes . . . Well, no.' Mike jumped in to contradict himself. 'Not for work.' He had one of those pale, porridgy faces, and lank black hair, through which he dragged a hand.

'Scuse me!' Hugo stopped a waitress by the arm. 'Could I get a large Macallan 25, please. Two pieces of ice, one squirt of water. Do you like scotch, Mike?'

'Sure. Yes.'

'Make that two then. Actually, just bring the ice and water on the side. Thanks.'

The waitress nodded and left.

'So let's see this text!' Hugo resumed the tease.

'She's just a friend at work,' Mike said meekly, passing on his phone. 'She knew I was coming tonight and wanted to know what you were like. I just told her I had met you.'

'*From: Saz,*' said the top of the screen.

'*Liar,*' was the only word beneath it.

Hugo laughed like a brigand, banged the table – why not? – with his hand.

'Tell her it's true!' he cried, handing back the phone. 'Tell her I'm a self-indulgent pain in the arse, I've been getting pissed all night, and now I'm boring on about how I'm really a frustrated writer and no one understands me.' It felt good to mock his own neurotic nature, to fight it back.

Mike giggled shrilly. 'All right,' he said, beginning to type with his thumb. 'He says . . . to tell you . . .' he commentated as he wrote, '. . . he's a self . . . indul-gent . . . bore . . . And that he's drunk . . . and going . . . on . . . about how no one . . . understands him. There. Send?'

'Send.'

They were still laughing when the waitress returned. She began to unload her tray on to the table, item by item.

'So, tell me more about these things you write,' Hugo said, as he composed his drink.

They were north, but Calvin knew no more than that. He felt fabulously free of knowing, as the car cut decisively through dark, wet night. Going to a party was always more exciting when you could not find your way back home.

He sucked on the cigarette that Mellody had passed him, lit, from her seat behind. Takeaways and pubs jinked yellowly through raindrop lenses on his window, their illuminated signage raising brief electric dawns that sighed across the vehicle's interior. And London went on unknown. He loved this city. Not as you love a friend, but as a hero.

'We just passed that,' Pete said to Sean by mobile phone. Then, 'OK. Yes, I see it.'

The boys were sat with Calvin in a line of three. He and they had not, in fact, had much to say, other than exchanging news.

'Left before or left after?' Pete's temper now was rubbing raw.

In her seat, Mellody was silent. Calvin could hear her smoking.

'Right,' Pete said. 'Take a left after this church, Paul.'

The driver did as he was told, and they swung into a wide residential road.

'OK. I see you.' Pete clapped flat his phone. 'Just here, Paul. Nice one.'

The car pulled in, spotlighting Sean and Sasha on the kerb.

Calvin stepped out first, and held his door for the others. The air was fresh with recent rain, and chilly on his skin. Away in one direction stretched a row of large and pointy houses. Some traffic lights, and perhaps a park, were all that he could see the other way.

'Stay local, Paul,' said Mellody, climbing out last. 'We shouldn't be too long.'

And as she stepped into the municipal orange of the overhead lamp, Calvin realised, not quite believing it, that she had changed her clothes. Gone now were the dress and heels. Here was blouse and skinny jeans. Short ones, with little roll-top boots. She must have taken off her clothes while he was looking out the window!

She trapped his stare.

'Are you not cold, Calvin?' Smiling.

'I'm all right,' he lied.

'Well, it'll be warm inside.'

She clasped his arms in her hands and rubbed them up and down.

'Come on then,' Sean said, and set off at the head of the group.

After just a few yards, they turned into what appeared to be a car park. (Gravel, puddles, cars.) In front of them was a large office building, sagging with age, and so completely unremarkable that Calvin had not noticed it from the street. A British Telecom logo – the old British Telecom logo – still hung on the front, but clearly the place had been deserted for some time.

As they got nearer, however, music could be heard. The walls trembled with a patterned hum, a deep and awesome sound. Cracks of lights were visible around the windows too, and an overweight, middle-aged man was standing by the door. This was no industry event, Calvin realised. This was a squat.

'Ten pounds, folks,' said the man.

Sean whipped three twenties from a wad and handed them to a woman with a nose ring who was sitting at a trestle table. She put his money in an old ice-cream tub and stamped everybody's hands. It was too dark to see what with.

Calvin had never been to a squat party before. Though he had heard about them often. A secret mobile number used to go round college on Friday afternoons. Just dirty binges, he assumed, filled with trance freaks sweating off their body paint for days. That Mellody herself might go to one astounded him.

And already she was walking calmly up the litter-covered stairs. Calvin followed, with the others. The music swelled. The handrail rattled in its fixings. Fell silent when he touched it. Rattled when he let it go. An unempty beer can skittered through his legs and struck the wall with a looping fairground clank. On the first floor, they passed through a cloud of weed that drifted from three women who were leaning through the window. If they recognised him, they gave no sign. Calvin lit another cigarette, and tried offering the packet around as his friends climbed further. But it was dark, and no one saw. Too loud as well, as they approached the second level, where a rise in volume introduced the dancefloor. And still the group did not change course, spiralling left and up and onwards as a set of scarred wood doors swung open, sending out a weary male silhouette and an assault of techno. Hi-hat, bass-thump, hi-hat, bass-thump, unsafe and merciless and urgent. So loud was the sound that it tickled the hairs on Calvin's arms and sent a warming shiver through his trunk. On the third floor, Sean at last turned right and led them through into a large, low-ceilinged hall. There were fewer people here, and it was quieter than Calvin would have expected. Tables and chairs, some upright, were scattered in clusters. Graffiti of all abilities covered the walls.

'There he is,' said Mellody, out of breath and sexy, pointing. She set off across the centre of the room, past the serving rail of an ancient cafeteria. Behind its Perspex hood, where the hotplates used to be, were now just holes, round-cornered oblong openings, filled with cans of beer and bottled water. On the wall hung an old felt noticeboard, still studded with the kind of plastic letters that the chip shops used where Calvin had grown up. And there, beside an empty four-tiered cake display, stood a man of almost superhuman height, picked out against a bank of UV tubes. He seemed to be waving, and tapped his watch in a mime of impatience.

Sean reached him first and shook his hand. Then Mellody.

'Giles,' she said, proffering a cheek as well, which the man bent low to kiss.

'Mellody, mwah,' said Giles. 'You do realise what you've done to my schedule?'

He was well spoken, and wore one of those upper-class waxed jackets, extra large to contain his stupendous limbs. The look of someone who has eaten well for generations.

'You haven't been waiting *ages*, have you?' Mellody was concerned.

'Oh no,' sighed Giles gently. 'Mrs Giles is on the warpath again, but she knows what Fridays can be like.'

'Of course. How's the little boy?'

'Horribly healthy!' he snorted. 'A bloody tyrant. I'll be on fatigues all night when I get home.'

Calvin had never met a posh drug dealer before. The lads in Leeds that he and Jason used were usually young rude boys. Party lovers blessed with business brains. Always in a rush. Paranoid too, they were – or not nearly paranoid enough. But then it must be difficult being a dealer, he always thought, trying to tell one's customers from friends.

'Hello Peter,' Giles said.

'All right mate,' said Pete. 'Sorry about the wait.'

Malcolm and Sasha just waved hi.

'Giles, this is Calvin.' Mellody stepped aside so he could be seen.

Giles extended a large soft hand.

'How do you do?' he said pleasantly.

Calvin shook it and said, 'Yeah great, thanks.'

'Business good?' Sean asked.

The question felt embarrassing, but Giles did not seem to mind.

'Oh, you know . . .' he said, and left the rest to slide.

'Mustn't grumble, eh?' Sean was jokey. 'So, er, do you have what we talked about?'

'Ah yes, you'll need to talk to Rasta Phil about that.'

'Rasta Phil?'

'He's in the kitchen behind the cafeteria.'

'OK great,' Sean said. He paused. 'And he's a Rasta, is he?'

'Yes, he is.'

Sean waited, as if he was expecting more information. 'Nice one, thanks,' he said when he didn't get it, and led everybody back towards the little bar.

But Mellody did not go with him.

Calvin panicked. To follow or to stay?

He looked at Mellody for guidance, and she asked him immediately: 'Have you got a cigarette?'

Suddenly, and unexpectedly, Michael understood that he had become relaxed. It was just so good to talk about his writing when a person was sincerely interested like this. And somewhere, as the conversation detoured through the territories of Style and Story and (his own favourite) the Crisis in Fiction, he had forgotten that the person he was talking to was Hugo Marks. Indeed it felt now – almost – as if this movie star and he just naturally belonged in one another's company. He tried to recall the time, just hours before, when he and Sally had discussed the guy as if he were a mythic being, something conjured by the folk imagination, like a cyclops or a sasquatch. And now: here he was. Now. Here. And basically a normal bloke – a *nice* bloke too, intelligent and tolerably read.

Looking up, he saw that Gordon Ramsay was towering over them with a big blond grin.

'Those canapés were shit,' he sniggered. 'Did you make them?'

'Gordon, hi!' Hugo stood to embrace him. 'No I didn't, as a matter of fact. We don't all have two kitchens in our house. How are you? This is Michael Knight from the *Standard*. Actually, is it Michael or Mike?'

It was always Michael. But standing up he said, 'Either's fine.'

'The *Standard*? Shit.' Ramsay gripped his hand. 'Not the *Evening Standard*? I'm suing you lot at the moment.'

'No, that's the other one,' said Michael, and with a rush of confidence: 'You've got two kitchens in your house?'

'Yeah, I've got the most amazing, beautiful lower-ground-floor kitchen for my wife. And I've got this lovely, stunning, 1,500 square-foot kitchen upstairs. With a code lock on the door.'

'My God!'

Michael laughed. Surely this was gossip, too? But fearing that the thought was written on his face, he raised his glass and chased the whisky down into the meltwater.

'Well,' Ramsay continued, 'I don't want to come in at 12.30 or one o'clock in the morning finding an overcooked, charcoaled cottage pie. I like my kitchen at home. It's my play area . . .'

'Do you think up new recipes there? I've always wondered'. Hugo had an eager fan face of his own.

'Yeah, I do all sorts of things at bizarre times of the night. It's amazing.' The man's rough energy was uncontainable. His whole body bounced on its heels as if anticipating second serve. 'It's like having a Bentley parked in your kitchen. This stove, it's three and a half metres long; it's all stainless steel; it's got five ovens; it's got an induction wok; it's got a charcoal grill . . .' He planned it out with methodical, even architectural gestures, building the thing all over again. His hands could not help smoothing down the counter, angling the pipes, setting up the knife rack high.

Michael focused hard, straining to impress each detail into his memory for later use.

'Listen, I came over because I've got to go,' Ramsay said suddenly, inflicting a double handshake, a post-match handshake, on them both.

'You're not coming back for the afterparty?' Hugo asked, jerking his head towards the door.

'Sorry, I can't. I've got a plane at stupid o'clock. But look: happy birthday, fuckface. Don't go to bed sober. And I want to see you and the missus in my new restaurant soon, OK?'

Michael watched the chef's departing back light-headedly. He felt high and silly. Helium-filled. How was this night happening to him? *Was* it happening to him? It bore all the distinguishing marks of a night that never would.

'So . . . you and Sally. Is it on the cards?'

Hugo sprung this with a twinkle, as he waved another waitress down.

'No,' Michael said, too late.

'But she is single, right? Two more good Macallans, please.'

'Yes.'

'Oh come on then! Get in there while it lasts! Not that it's any of my business, of course. But me and Mellody, you know, it very nearly never happened. I cancelled quite a big screen test to see her the week after we met, and I always think about how easy it would have been just not to do that.'

He looked sympathetic, and Michael was touched. Though he did not see how his puny little love life could be compared to the celebrated union, the genetic jackpot, of Mellody and Hugo Marks.

'I know. You're right,' he said in the end, and glanced up gratefully to see another group of guests steering themselves into their view.

'F-fantastic party, Hugo,' a girl said, bending down so rapidly for a kiss that Hugo had no choice but to stay in his seat. 'I've had . . . such a wonderful time.' She spoke unsteadily, and made no attempt to acknowledge anyone else as she straightened up.

'You're welcome, Natalie,' Hugo replied, with what Michael had begun to recognise was his customary grace.

'No, seriously. It was wonderful . . . We've all had . . . such a wonderful time at your birthday.'

The words were too fast, her eyes the unblinking bright of a fanatic. Even so, you could see she was an exceptional beauty, thin as rain, with long black hair, pale skin and rouge-ripened cheekbones. Her friends, quite young, said nothing. One of them wore a ragged T-shirt that said *LA Whore*. They seemed to be hanging back, as if to make it clear that Natalie – who continued to speak excitedly of 'atmosphere', 'occasion' and 'amazing' – did not represent them. At times Michael thought he detected a wafting sourness on her words, something cabbagey half-masked with mint. He had heard that bulimics got bad breath. Was that what he read in the air? He hoped, for some reason, that it was.

'Excuse me, sorry,' Hugo said suddenly, rising from his seat and producing a ringing phone from his pocket.

At last the girl stopped talking.

'Renée, hi!' Hugo hid the handset momentarily between his palms. 'I'd better take this. It's been great to see you.' He began to walk away.

'OK, bye then,' said Natalie.

And Michael watched him leave, a little stunned. This then, so abruptly, was how his night with Hugo Marks would end.

Following a loose group wave, the young people bled away.

The waitress returned and placed another pair of glasses on the table.

'Thanks,' Michael said, looking at them.

The waitress smiled.

She was the same girl who had given him his crab so very long ago. The thought was pleasing. It had – lest he forget – been an extraordinary night.

Which reminded him. Hurriedly, he took his phone out and began, with the Notes function, to record as much as he could remember about Gordon's Ramsay's two kitchens. The 'charcoaled' cottage pie that his wife had left behind was particularly choice. Michael had drunk too much to write it down with style, but that could be revised at home. No details about Hugo, though. He was resolved on that. And he would explain as much to Sally in the morning – assuming he could convince her without proof that they had met. The uncomfortable suggestion that he should have asked for a photograph, like those girls did, started scratching at his thoughts. That would have been a thing to show around. Yet it had almost seemed – it really did almost seem – as if, in their talk, Hugo had left the matter of his famousness behind and become, in some transitory way, his friend. The memory would have to be his souvenir.

boom boom boom boom boom boom boom boom boom
boom boom boom boom boom boom boom boom boom
boom boom boom boom boom boom boom boom boom
boom boom boom boom boom boom boom boom boom
boom boom boom boom boom boom boom particular about
his knives boom boom shade of indigo in the other boom boom
boom boom boom boom boom boom boom boom boom
boom boom boom boom boom boom boom boom boom
boom boom boom boom boom boom of entry boom boom
boom boom boom boom boom boom boom boom boom
boom boom boom boom boom boom boom boom boom
boom green and pornographic boom boom boom boom boom
spume spilled half boom boom boom boom boom boom
boom boom boom boom boom boom boom boom boom
boom boom boom boom boom boom boom boom boom
boom boom boom boom boom boom boom boom boom
boom boom boom boom boom boom boom boom boom
boom boom boom boom radio? '. . . suspected boom boom
boom boom boom boom boom boom boom boom boom
boom boom boom boom boom boom boom boom boom
boom to stop exactly. boom boom boom boom boom boom
boom boom boom boom boom boom boom boom boom
boom quarters, a quarter into boom boom boom boom boom
garden? She hoped he boom boom boom boom boom boom
boom boom boom boom boom boom boom boom boom
boom boom boom boom boom boom boom boom boom
boom boom boom boom *Amassakoul* boom boom boom boom
boom boom boom too late. At fifteen, twenty maybe boom
boom boom boom boom to the 4, and then reversed boom
boom boom pphhhhucccckk boom boom boom boom boom
encased in a padded orange boom boom boom boom boom
boom boom boom boom boom boom ambulance? Before?
boom boom slush was lovely boom boom boom boom boom

Wheeling feeling. boom boom Empty space a room of air. sound off Mute . . . Jesus fucking . . . boom boom boom boom boom boom boom boom boom boom boom . . . sssssssssssssssssit down. bloof. Aahhh. Ppphhhucking K man. rolling boom twist boom boom wayayay boom man boom boom yes. Chair boom. Grip boom boom. Ketamine Giles. Boom boom boom things up. Intended. Boom yess boom squat squat squat boom The squat party. Jeeeeeeezus.

boom

Thath was a *heavy* line.

Whoo.

Jusssht a dash of ketamine. A little sprrrritz. Ha ha ha. Mellody had overdone it a bit. *Ha ha ha.*

She was in a chair. A window sill beside. Specks of white glowed UV blue.

Dab.

Blah! Cigarette ash. Blah!

Ha ha ha.

Gripping weakly sides of chair, she levered herself to her feet. Tried to walk too quickly, found only air where her legs had been and crumpled gracelessly to floor.

Ha ha ha.

What a silly time. She made no effort to get up.

Heavy beats from downstairs hammered upwards through her body. Rapid and regular. Hidden industry. Somewhere near her face, a crushed beer can. Aimless gazing.

Gradually, people and objects. In the middle distance, a cluster of huddled smokers discussing the world, nodding. Now and then a lighter conjured up three faces in a snap of yellow. Elsewhere, chairs. Orange plastic scoops with tubular and pronging legs. And nearby, nearly not visible in the darkness, a discarded little rumple, a body lying where its mind had left it.

Calvin.

With a memory smack.

Calvin.

He curled comfortably around her bag as if it were a favored toy.

There were *things* in her bag.

Mellody sent test signals to her legs. They moved with more control. In earnest then, she crawled across, and Calvin offered no resistance as she plucked the bag away. Why did he have it, anyway? She remembered racking up two lines of K on the window ledge, handing him a note . . . Then she remembered nothing.

The contents of her bag, she was pleased to see, were untouched: Kleenex, mascara, a mirror, seven or eight bank notes, a lighter, Marlboro Lights (she lit one), her phone (two texts, four missed calls) and, in the little pocket at the side, a wrap of coke, a bag of ketamine and a little brown bottle of *opium tincture* (God bless Giles!). She checked her texts. One was from Hugo, predictably, which she did not read. The other was from Pete. 'Where r u?' it said. 'time 2 scarper.' *Scarper*? Mellody did not know what the word meant. Probably a British sex thing. With fumbling fingers, she deleted the message.

Calvin stirred at her feet. He looked *so* adorable, so *new*. It made Mellody feel powerful and protective, kind of horny in a wrong way. Balancing her cigarette on the window sill, she tipped a heap of Giles's coke on to the space beside it. Some probable grains of ketamine remained, so she gathered them in too.

Calvin stirred again, and now his eyes opened. He looked confused.

A wave of tenderness urged Mellody to kneel and kiss him. And in her mind, some part of her did. What was she *doing* with this beautiful young man, she wondered? Whose talk in the car was all about ambition and his new cellphone? In whose eyes she saw herself reflected back the dreamed infatuation of a boy? What was she *doing*, her mind wondered, as her body split the coke in two and snorted up its half.

Calvin murmured something unintelligible.

'How are you feeling?' she asked. 'I think maybe I gave us a bit too much.'

He murmured again.

'I've made you a pick-me-up,' she added.

'Hanks,' he said, and his feet began to scuffle on the floor, legs frogging helplessly in the search for purchase.

Mellody offered him a hand, which he took. But instead of pulling him up, she found herself yanked down. A giggling collapse. She liked that boys were heavy. And this time she did kiss him, in a friendly way.

'Let's have another go,' she said, looking into his eyes.

Calvin reached over to a nearby chair and levered himself on to his feet.

'Spetter,' he said.

Mellody handed him the spiralled twenty, but he just looked dumbly at his portion.

'I durn't w-want any more,' he managed to say.

'That's OK, sweetie. This one's just coke.'

'Hm,' he nodded, and waveringly hunched himself to snort.

His shirt was dirty from the floor. Mellody was stroking it clean with the palm of her hand when a voice startled her.

'*There* you are,' Pete said. 'Shall we get going then, Miss Mellody?'

He was carrying a plastic bag, and had his chimney sweep persona on, but she detected the energy of irritation in it.

'Just give me a couple of minutes.' She answered coldly, out of principle.

Malcolm drew up beside them. Even *he* looked a bit twitchy. For Malcolm.

'Sean and Sashar've run into some mates downstairs,' Pete continued without acknowledging him. 'They might meet up with us later, but for now we'd better shoot.' He paused, and an excited shine began to graduate into his face.

He had found himself a scheme, Mellody presumed, but she would not be suckered into giving a damn. Sure enough, when she said nothing, Pete decided he could wait no longer.

'We got a fucking big score tonight, Mell,' he whispered.

'Fook yeah,' Malcolm agreed.

Again she said nothing.

So Pete held up the bag for her to look at. In it was a gigantic fragment of something pale, enclosed in silvering layers of Saran Wrap, drawn neurotically tight. 'It's a gak attack!' he screeched as quietly as possible.

'Coke?' was all Mellody could say at first.

Pete nodded.

'How much is in there?'

'It's a quarter key,' he whispered. 'Straight off the boat. Me and Malc just had some. It's fucking pure as fuck.'

'Roasting,' Malcolm nodded.

'See that horse's head?' With his finger, Pete described a vague indentation on the surface that could have been anything. 'That's the stamp of the Cali cartel, that is.' He sounded like a child with a new video game.

Calvin was beside her now. And for a moment, they all just stared in silence at the bag.

Despite herself – and she hated to acknowledge it – Mellody was impressed.

'Are you out of your fucking *mind*?' she scolded in the end, unconvincingly she knew. 'Why d'you have to buy so much?'

'Sir Giles wanted to get rid of it,' Pete shrugged. 'We're a little light on cash just now, so me, Sean and Malc went thirds on this. It's worth four times our price, Mell.'

'So, like, what?' She slapped him with a sarcastic glare. 'You're fucking drug dealers now?'

'Maybe for a week or two,' Pete grinned. 'Or . . .' He and Malcolm both started laughing. '. . . or we'll all just have a fucking good time!'

Mellody looked at Calvin's face beside her, so attentive, so unsure.

Soon she was laughing too.

'So there's some people down at K West,' Pete broke in, closing up the bag, checking his phone, looking at his watch. 'Fancy it?'

'No. Let's go back to mine.'

Until then she had not realised that this was what she planned to do.

'You're welcome, Natalie,' said Hugo, sliding a casual finger around the phone in his pocket, feeling the keypad for the 5 and its accessibility bump. The speed-dial for Renée.

'No, seriously . . .'

Found it.

'. . . It was wonderful.'

Hugo held the button down.

'We've all had . . .'

Natalie paused. Eyes slithering about, just gone completely. One could only guess at what had been administered to the brain behind. She looked the way you're only meant to look at 7 a.m., when everybody else around you looks the same.

'. . . such a wonderful time at your birthday . . .' said Natalie in the end.

Hugo waited several seconds for the call to definitely connect. Then he cut it off.

The girl reminded him of Mellody a little, in those old deluded days. The busy eyes, the exerted mind, as she gripped still tighter to normality's disintegrating ledge. Very soon, he knew – everybody knew – they would be watching her descent.

'. . . Really. It just has had, you know, a lovely atmosphere about it . . .'

One of Natalie's friends opened his mouth to interrupt, spotting a break in the flow. But she saw him and was too quick, determined not to be dislodged.

'. . . A sense of *occasion*!' she added hurriedly. 'That's what most parties *don't* have, isn't it? Like people coming and going and nobody cares about all the amazing things you've done for us. But you *have*!'

Hugo's phone was ringing finally.

'Excuse me, sorry,' he said, and answered it. 'Renée, hi!'

'What's up Hugo?' Renée said.

Instead of responding, he covered the mouthpiece with his hand and said, 'I'd better take this.' With a flurry of mimed apologies, they agreed. 'It's been great to see you,' Hugo added, hustling himself away towards the piano.

'Thanks,' he breathed into the phone when he got there.

'Who'd you get stuck with?' Renée asked wearily. She knew him so well.

'Natalie,' he whispered. 'Jesus Christ. Why did we invite her?'

'Mmm,' Renée said. 'Well she's good pap food, with all the shit she does. I thought she might draw some fire if Mellody misbehaved.'

'Yes, I meant to mention that . . .'

'Don't worry about it, Hugo.' Her reassurance rolled across

him like a tank. 'I saw Mell's speech. And actually – I've gotta say – I thought she did a pretty good job. Is she with you now? I'm on my way back to the house, but I should congratulate her while I'm feeling well disposed.'

'No, that's the thing,' Hugo said. 'She left about an hour ago.'

Renée's silence was faithfully transmitted to his phone.

'She left?' she said eventually.

'Yes.'

'Where did she leave to? Where is she going?'

'I don't know. Some music business thing, she said, with her friends.'

'Sheen?'

'I think he was one of them, yes.'

In a large grey overcoat, on the other side of the room, Warshak was talking with his daughter. He spotted Hugo, smiled, and waved a cheerful goodbye. Hugo waved back, examining the seams in the old man's face for irony, or the ore of something darker.

'Fuck, Hugo!' Renée was nearly shouting. 'And you didn't stop her?'

'How am I supposed to stop her, Renée? There were people with us.' He pushed through a door marked PRIVATE, hoping that it was. 'Look, she says she won't be long, and that she'll see us back at the house afterwards. What harm can it do?'

The corridor was empty, and his words sounded louder in it.

'Your own wife walking out of your birthday party early with another guy? Are you serious?'

'They went out the back, I think.'

'It doesn't matter, Hugo. She won't be leaving with *you*, will she? And if the papers saw her . . .'

'OK, enough!' The dank echo of his voice was angry, but not as angry as he felt. 'There was nothing I could do about this, OK? It's bad, but it's not my fault. And I'd appreciate it if you could put your energy into managing the situation instead of bollocking me.'

'You're right. You're right, you're right.' She took a moment to calm herself down. 'Have you called her?'

'No.'

'Well call her. Be nice, and try to get her back to the house as early as you can.'

Hugo said nothing.

'When do you expect to leave?'

He sighed. 'I don't know really. Are many people coming back?'

'Not a huge number, but a few. All friendly faces. Theresa says some are already there. You've talked to Warshak, though, right?'

'Yes. They're just off. It went well, I thought. I saw his daughter, too, who was sweet.'

'Great. OK, well just enjoy yourself now. And don't forget: lots of smiles when you leave.'

'OK. I won't be long.'

'Take as long as you need. And sorry for losing it just now. If Mellody got out quietly, we'll be fine.'

'I know.'

'All right. See you later.'

'See you.'

See you, said the corridor walls.

Hugo looked at his phone and considered things.

Was there any point in calling his wife, he wondered? Even in their tightest days, when the relationship was ripe, even then he could not guide her actions. Indeed, he only made things worse by trying. Mellody so loved a fight. She would feel confronted by his calling now, and delight in having something to defy. Yet she could be up to anything out there . . . His need to know scraped with its familiar itch.

He decided to send a text. Businesslike. No big thing.

Renée loved your singing so much she's hassling me about when we'll see you back home. What should I tell her? x

It was still his little habit, that x, and the extra effort that it took to make it lower case.

He pressed send and pushed back into the room. The party was thinning. Patches of floor were becoming visible again and, in many places, coats were on. Natalie, thank God, had left, though Mike still sat loyally in place, doing something with his phone. Two fresh whiskies were on the table beside him, and beside that Hugo's absence in a chair.

'You're not leaving, are you?' he asked, with genuine concern, as Mike stood up to greet him.

'Oh . . .' Mike hesitated. His mouth and eyes made three big circles of suspense. 'It just seemed like everything was wrapping up, and . . .'

'Nonsense!' Hugo blazed enthusiastically. 'There's plenty of people sticking around. And we can't just walk out on scotch like this.' Listen to him. He was such an old lush!

'No sure, absolutely.'

The clean delight on Mike's face was humbling. Hugo masked the tender moment in the act of flinging himself, with an aged sigh, back into his chair.

'That was my manager,' he explained through the heat from an oversip of whisky. 'She'd kill me if she knew I was talking to you.'

'Oh yeah?'

'Definitely. Press have been tightly managed on this thing. I don't know how you got in.'

He laughed. And actually that was right. He didn't know.

Yet neither was he very interested. Mike just seemed so nice, and too timid not to trust. Besides, after finally fulfilling all his duties, he felt entitled to a spell of boozy laissez-faire.

'Well,' Mike said. 'Actually, I used someone else's invite.'

'Oh yeah? Whose?'

'Camille McLeish.'

'*Camille McLeish?*'

'Yes.'

'She's a bitch and a half,' Hugo said, paying another visit to his glass.

'Mmm.' Mike laughed cautiously, as though no one had ever admitted this before.

'So how did you end up with her invite?'

'Some problem with her kids, I think. She couldn't come. So she gave it to me.'

'Yeah right,' Hugo scoffed. 'She bottled it is what happened. She's spread so much nasty stuff about me and Mellody over the years that she didn't want to face us.'

'Mmm,' Mike said again. 'Maybe. And, she said I should try to get some gossip for her.'

'Oh really?'

'Yes. But I'm not going to tell her anything about you. Honestly. It doesn't . . .'

Hugo raised his hands and snipped him short.

'Don't worry, you can give her anything you like,' he said.

'No, but I don't want to. *Really*. I've jotted down some harmless things about other guests, but I'm leaving you out of it. I promise.'

A quaintly moving word. Why had people ceased to *promise* things? Were they less sincere now? Or had they merely stopped expecting their sincerity to be believed?

Above the chatter, a Gil Scott-Heron sermon struggled

to its feet. Something about Ronald Reagan, the tired voice intoned. It swung with melancholy hip.

The room was emptying at speed.

'So Mike,' Hugo said. 'What are you doing later?'

Calvin shook his head. Ketamine was pretty mad. A real hammer, to be fair. Though he remembered little. The caustic shock of chemistry in his sinuses, much fierier than coke . . . holding a bag . . . sitting down . . . and then . . . Not sleep, but something – it really felt like some*where* – other. A lonely zone of mind loss where some giant bafflement had taken him into its shade and, once there, interfered with him.

Cool.

He took a good deep pick at his right nostril, and tried the coke again. This time it whistled through.

More memories now began to skate across his consciousness, like fingertips cutting streaks of vision through a foggy pane. Cuddling that bag. Flashing lights. Mellody kissing him. *Fuck*. Had *that* happened? Or had he dreamt it? The memory seemed real, but like it happened years ago.

And now she was standing behind him. He could hear her, talking with a man.

'See that horse's head?' The man's voice sounded proud about something. 'That's the stamp of the Carly cartel, that is.'

Pete. And Malcolm.

Calvin stepped weakly into range. He was thirsty.

'Are you out of your fucking *mind*?' Mellody sounded angry, but not with him. 'Why did you have to buy so much?'

For the first time, Calvin noticed the bag in Pete's hand. Just a cheap plastic one, from Costcutter maybe. He couldn't see the logo. Inside was what looked like a crumbly chunk of plaster.

'So, like, what? You're fucking drug dealers now?'

It couldn't be more coke. A piece that size would be worth . . .

'Maybe for a week or two. Or we'll all just have a fucking good time!'

Now everyone was laughing.

Calvin was confused, but excited, but scared. This was like being in a movie.

'So there's some people down at K West,' Pete said, when the laugh was over. 'Fancy it?'

Calvin did. He had not been to K West before.

'No.' Mellody disagreed. 'Let's go back to mine.'

'Come on Mell,' Pete hassled her. 'The night is yet young.'

'Don't worry.' She placed an including hand on Calvin's arm. 'There'll be some people there too. I promised I'd make an appearance.'

'Oh well, if you *promised* . . .' Sarcastic at first, Pete's voice drifted limply into acceptance.

'Doesn't bother me,' Malcolm shrugged, stuffing the bag into his pocket. 'K West's a fucking twatwalk.'

'Let's go then,' said Mellody, with a secret glance at Calvin. 'OK?'

'Yeah,' he said.

And now they were walking back, past the strange bar and over to the staircase, where the air pumped louder than ever. Hard trance, at desperation pace.

Calvin sniffed away the fringe of his last line.

Had he hooked up with Mellody? And now he was going back to her place? Was that what was happening?

It was dangerous. But he wanted it. He needed a girl – no, a woman – like her. Someone he could respect. No more lady-children, with their chewing-gum bodies and their ice-cream eyes. He wanted someone he could talk to, and who could talk to him. Somebody who understood. Calvin wanted it.

He stroked Mellody's arm as they neared the final flight of stairs. But it was crowded, and she was on the phone, which explained why she took no notice.

Then suddenly flashes. Shouts and flashes.

A horde of photographers held back by the doorman's bulk.

'Mell! Mell!' they shouted.

'This way!' they shouted.

A hoarse chorus of competition.

Pete and Malcolm just pushed grimly through, the bag of coke clutched tightly in Pete's hand.

'Over here!' the men shouted, walking alongside. 'Oi! Over here!'

The rippled burst of flashguns was hot on Calvin's skin. He tried to grin. They would leave you alone sometimes if you stopped and posed; he had learned that from his own encounters. But this was different. Never had he seen such frenzy.

'Are you with Mell now, Pete?' asked one, like he was your mate.

'Need a lift, Mell?' said another, in a cheeky tone.

'No thank you,' Mellody replied. Her voice was soft as if, among the chaos, she walked within her own courteous enclosure.

One of the men knocked against Calvin's ankle. There was no apology.

Another tapped on Pete's shoulder. Instinctively, he looked round into a *flash! flash-flash!*

Calvin poured himself a smile. These idiots thought they smelled the scandal of Mellody and Pete. But he knew better.

One photographer, running backwards, stumbled and fell into a puddle. Everybody laughed, riling up a fresh assault of clicks and flashes.

'Wet cunt,' Malcolm said.

They reached the car and climbed inside, while Paul the driver shielded the door.

Pete and Malcolm occupied the front seats. Mellody and Calvin climbed into the back. Everyone was breathing hard.

Mellody wound down the window and leaned out.

'Fuck off, gentlemen,' she said sweetly, before the vehicle's departing thrust put her down in Calvin's lap. Laughing, she kissed him on the cheek.

'That one's nearly as bad as you, Malc.' Pete nodded in their direction with studied unconcern. 'She can't wait ten fucking minutes.'

Mellody said nothing. She had her chin on Calvin's shoulder and still sat on his lap. Cold night roared through the open window, battering his face with her fragrant hair.

'What's so bad about me?' Malcolm was indignant.

'Not much,' Pete said, closing the window. 'Except you'll screw anything that stands still long enough.'

'Will I fuck!' Malcolm protested.

Mellody's hand settled casually on Calvin's leg. Without giving himself time to think about it, he put his own on top.

'Malcolm!' Pete was laughing ever harder, spilling much of the cocaine that he was trying to arrange on the seat. 'You had sex with Anton's fucking *dog!*'

This made Mellody turn her head.

'You fucked a fucking *dog*, Malcolm?' she shrieked.

'Yeah,' Pete replied. 'Anton's old English sheepdog. At a party in his house last summer.'

Mellody gaped, her attention utterly diverted.

Malcolm shrugged. 'Someone said I wouldn't do it.'

'Is that legal?' Calvin said, and instantly felt very stupid.

'Dunno,' said Malcolm. 'It's not cruel.'

Pete cackled, rolling up a note. Tapered locks of hair hung in fangs around his face.

'It is rape though, Malc,' he managed to say eventually. 'You're a dog-rapist, mate. You can't tell me a dog can consent.'

'Yeah it can,' said Malcolm. 'It just sort of goes along with it.'

Mellody's laughing body shook gently in Calvin's lap. Her other hand, to his delight, relocated to his waist.

'Is that what Anton's did?' Pete sniggered, passing Malcolm the note.

'Yeah. Pretty much.'

'And it was a female dog?'

'Of course it fucking was! I wouldn't fuck a boy dog, man!'

'No, obviously.'

Pete paused.

'But he could lap you off.'

Calvin slid a hand across Mellody's right buttock, which was packaged tightly in a soft, expensive denim.

'So this . . .' Pete started up again, '. . . this encounter, Malcolm. It definitely wasn't up the arse, then?'

'No!' Malcolm answered angrily.

'I mean anyone could make that mistake. You were pretty wasted.'

'It was a female fucking dog, man! Anton said she'd had puppies.'

'How sweet.' Pete said this tenderly. 'Did she have a name?'

'I don't fucking know.'

They stopped at lights beside a crowded patch of pavement. A line of black clubbers was queuing up to enter a tiny shopfront venue. The girls' complicated hairstyles shook in conversation.

'So you think gay sex with dogs is unnatural, Malcolm? Is that what you're saying?'

'Too right.'

And suddenly, 'Come here,' whispered Mellody with a smile, leaning quickly into Calvin until her lips were on his. He kissed back, and now there were no thoughts. The chalky taste of make-up. Alcohol's sweet scent. Urgent breaths, taken haphazardly in gasps between their muddled tongues. Wet sounds. Human insides meeting.

'But sex with girl dogs is OK, is it?'

'It's all right.'

'Don't you think that's homophobic, Malcolm?'

'No.'

'So would you expect a gay guy to fuck male dogs?'

'He can do what he likes.'

Mellody swivelled now to straddle him, breasts pressing with intent. Her hands were round his waist, up his back, under his shirt, sliding desperately across his skin, as if searching for a way inside.

He was stiff as iron. She wriggled avidly on top.

The wild release of so much guessed at and unsaid.

And dimly, as though from somewhere far away, Calvin heard a London accent whooping.

From: **valerie.morrell@nortonmorrell.co.uk**
To: **williammendez75@gmail.com**
Subject: **Re: Rescheduling**
Date: **Wednesday, 16 September 2009 11:31:08**

Certainly. Any time that suits you is fine. It would just be good to put a face to a name! Read the new chap this morning, by the way. Splendid stuff, especially the dog sex. I think that's safely excised you from Richard and Judy's list . . .

Vx

From: williammendez75@gmail.com
To: valerie.morrell@nortonmorrell.co.uk
Subject: Re: Rescheduling
Date: Wednesday, 16 September 2009 15:42:03

Thanks Val – I'll admit I was/am a bit unsure about the ketamine sequence. How on earth do you represent an experience like that? I wanted to do something different to suggest how completely the drug distorts Mell's sense of reality, but I also have mixed feelings about playing typographical games. *The Raw Shark Texts* was bloody pompous about it, I thought. Although a black page in *Tristram Shandy* can be quite fun. Would I be allowed a black page, do you reckon? How much is the ink? Don DeLillo has them everywhere in *Underworld*, just marking chapters if you please. But then he's Don DeLillo. He leaves out words, too, you know. Just plain them out altogether. The clever.

Anyway, I'm in a good mood today, so I don't care. Because I've just had one of my brainwaves! Hugo Marks is . . . wait for it . . . diabetic!!! I just saw this guy Elliot something (or something Elliot?) talking about it on TV, and it's perfect for my story! I'll have to go back and put in an early establishing passage (perhaps Hugo should be injecting himself when Michael first looks up and sees him on the balcony?) but for now I'll just weave some insulin into the re-writes. You'll have to wait a bit while I sort that out in the next section.

Cheerio,

W

From: williammendez75@gmail.com
To: valerie.morrell@nortonmorrell.co.uk
Subject: Why you are waiting
Date: Tuesday, 29 September 2009 19:53:08

Hi Val,

Just wanted to say a quick sorry about how long this next chapter is taking. I'm nearly there, but I've had some problems. And money is a bit tight at the moment, so I'm having to spend all my time working, or looking for work. Bloody credit crunch.

Should be just another week or so.

William

From: valerie.morrell@nortonmorrell.co.uk
To: williammendez75@gmail.com
Subject: Re: Why you are waiting
Date: Wednesday, 30 September 2009 08:17:18

Good to hear from you, William, but pls don't hurry on my account. If money is a problem, you could always give the Arts Council a whirl. They give grants to writers.

Or, of course... Look, I'm breaking a lot of my own rules by saying this, but this is a really fantastic proposition we've got here. Seriously. And the story is clearly coming together now too. So I think that what you've already written should be good enough to sell as a partial. Obviously this does mean more risk; publishers prefer finished books, so if you can wait that's better. But if you need the money now, well, it's worth considering. I'm not promising anything of course, but believe me I wouldn't suggest this if I wasn't confident. (Though we would need to submit the rest of what you have, or at least a synopsis, to explain where the story is going...)

Totally your call of course, but think it over, and let me know if the idea appeals.

Val

From: williammendez75@gmail.com
To: valerie.morrell@nortonmorrell.co.uk
Subject: All right, go for it
Date: Saturday, 3 October 2009 19:42:30

Thanks Val – I've had a look at the Arts Council website, and sadly I don't think I'd qualify for a grant. I do need the money, though, so I have also had a think about your other proposal. And on balance, if you reckon it would work, I am happy for you to try selling the book based on the manuscript as it stands.

I cannot let anyone see the rest in its present state, however, so I suppose I will have to write a synopsis giving the story away. It really is a pity, because I was hoping that you and the publisher would be able to enjoy *Publicity****** properly, especially as the pivotal event is coming up in the chapter after next. But then if I don't get some money soon, the book might never be finished at all. And I suppose that would be worse. Anyway, I'll just work as hard as I can. Then when you're about to send it off (and if you think a synopsis really is necessary) I'll do one. Oh well.

William

From: **valerie.morrell@nortonmorrell.co.uk**
To: **williammendez75@gmail.com**
Subject: **Re: All right, go for it**
Date: **Monday, 5 October 2009 10:11:05**

William, sweetie, please don't make yourself unhappy over this.
Lord knows I wouldn't have the soupiest how to write a book myself,
but listen: I do know when a chap can write, and I also know when
something rather splendid lands on my desk. Otherwise I simply
wouldn't mention showing this around. If you'd like me to sit on it,
then say so, and I'll do it gladly. But if you do need the cash enough
to take a punt, I promise I'll give it everything I've got. Remember, I
will only send your manuscript to a selection of editors, with a back-
up selection in case we need to resubmit the complete book in future.
Yes, a synopsis of some kind will be essential, but write a vague one, if
that makes you any happier, and I'll explain that you're an artist
. . . blah, blah, blah . . . They need good writers, honestly they do, and
they're used to reading bits of books, so when they see _Publicity_*****
I just don't think they'll want you to get away.

How about I buy you lunch sometime soon and we can talk about it? I
can't believe we still haven't met!

Affectionately,

Valerie x

Thank you for your reassurance, Val. Go ahead and submit the book then. I have made up my mind.

I suppose I just lose confidence sometimes. I don't know if you've ever tried writing a novel yourself? One minute you're the best writer in the world and you've got more great ideas than you know what to do with... and then you look back at what you've done and you want to weep. Maybe I just shouldn't look. No one asked me to write this fucking thing, did they? No one actually *wants* it. There's already enough unread literary fiction in the world to keep humanity going until we finally wipe ourselves out. Why can't people just leave their shit on the internet where it belongs? Sometimes I certainly think that's what I should have done.

I will be out of the office from Wednesday October 7 until Monday October 19. If your message is urgent, please contact my assistant Carly McBride at carly.mcbride@nortonmorrell.co.uk. Otherwise I will reply on my return.

The crowd stood in silence, holding candles. There were so many of them, even at this time, that they filled the square with quivering droplets of light. Camera flashes (photographing what exactly?) fired off at intervals like sparks of malfunction in a dying machine.

Then in close-up: the vigil-keepers. A large African family, or small church, singing and swaying. A group of teenage girls bundled round a burning mass of wax that flickered dangerously beside their handmade sign. *Notre Père*, it said, inside a coil of felt-tip decorations, displaying depth of feeling, as the young do, with the proof of hours spent. Seen from the side: a solitary man, casually handsome in the Italian way, gazing through an upward stream of cigarette smoke.

Gaudy effigies of Mary.

Tears being mopped.

Nuns.

And underneath, the sliding flotsam of the news:

SERENE . . . POPE'S CONDITION 'NOTABLY COMPROMISED'

. . . HEART AND KIDNEYS NOW FAILING — VATICAN . . .

FAITHFUL GATHER TO

It was the largest television that Michael had ever seen. Black, and yards across, installed among a suite of minion electronics in the basement wall.

This, then, had been the destination of his journey back from Cuzco. This the reason Hugo sent him, with a minder, through funnelled squads of cheek-kissers and coat-getters, to wait patiently in the big black car out front. He remembered how he sat there, silent, as the hubbub of the paparazzi cooled. And how he took to worrying: had he become a nuisance? And been cruelly despatched? The driver kept the engine running, though, which gave him hope. And then in a redeeming instant Hugo had appeared, apologising, framed inside an aperture of shouts and light. He had brought some others for the ride. Guy, a theatre director, and Someone at the BBC. They talked of 'PFD' and 'crossover' and 'a season at the Court', while Michael watched the driver get them, with a maze route made of halts and thrusts, through brimming clubtime to the other side of Regent Street. Thence, they ground an edge off Grosvenor Square to meet Park Lane, before accelerating up past Speakers' Corner to the open greenside straight of Bayswater Road. There had been a rise and fall of human density through Notting Hill, and then a right. To Hugo's big white house in Holland Park from Soho: fifteen minutes. How much money people paid for buildings so a journey should be short.

And this was Hugo's home. He was in Hugo Marks's *home!* With another busy gang of snappers clamped on to its pavement wall. (They knew where all the big stars lived, of course; everyone but Michael knew.) At the steel front gate, Hugo had paused politely with the theatre man in smiling pose, and then proceeded onwards through the garden to his door. A large thick thing beneath a columned portico it was. Someone swung it in as they arrived, revealing a real old hatstand in a wide, resounding hall. People in front of him, and people on the generously shallow stairs. A long oak rail that terminated in a lustrous swirl. And then, it seemed belatedly, there had been a cheer of welcome, started by four people in the hall and soon augmented by a larger chorus from the distant kitchen. Michael thought that he had spotted Stephen Fry in there, joining loudly. With hands and smiles, Hugo toured them all and offered thanks, while Michael chugged on shamefully behind. The rooms were neither sparsely filled nor crowded, though the grand front salon space sat empty, as was the odd geography of parties. Eventually Hugo led him downwards on a humbler staircase he had missed before – to what was, grinning backwards at him, called 'the media room'. It was a swanky modern hollow, windowless besides its big glass garden wall, where a group of men and women disparately lounged. And there was the television, off, hazing back a rough reflection of the talk. Nothing could prevent Hugo – not the standing smiles, not the congratulating gambits – from powering the mighty portal up. 'Just to check how the Holy Father's doing,' he had said, and then did not stop checking.

Now, having passed through periods of interest, polite interest, other business, silence, all the former occupants had left. New legs sporadically stepped downwards into sight, inquiring where 'Mark' was, or someone else, before shrinking up the stairs again with speed. But Hugo and Michael did not move. Two men slumped quietly around their scotches: it must seem the very picture of a moment on which no one should intrude.

'I can't believe he's still hanging on, though,' Hugo said, despite saying it before. 'The news said he was almost finished when I got up this morning.'

'He's been almost finished all week.' Michael shrugged. Then he added, 'Old people always take longer than you think.'

'Yeah?'

'Mmm.' Pause. 'My gran took five months.'

'What, without kidneys?'

Michael had to think about this. 'I dunno,' he said, mimicking Hugo's slurred and laid-back manner. 'But she had cancer of most things by the end.'

Sky News were back in the studio now. A serious-looking man, who might have been modelling golf equipment on another day, sat next to a young woman, who was beautiful and just as serious, though more studiously ironed. Behind them both, dominating the screen, was a gigantic image of a healthy and avuncular John Paul II, to which somebody had added a glowing yellow perimeter, suggestive both of recent death and supernatural power.

... which began with a urinary tract infection, the man was saying. *Italian media reported that the Pope's cardiograph had flattened, but this was quickly denied by Vatican officials. Although the 84-year-old pontiff is understood to have lost consciousness shortly after asking aides to read him a passage from the Bible describing Christ's body being taken down from the Cross.*

The Vicar of Rome, the woman took over, *described the Pope as 'extremely serene'. 'He has completely left himself in God's hands,' said Cardinal Camillo Ruini, adding that the Holy Father is now 'seeing and touching the Lord'.*

As she spoke, the man glowered fixedly at the camera, confirming everything with sad, agreeing little nods.

'I've got a bet on with Sally.' Michael spoke suddenly. 'Did I tell you?'

From inside his glass, Hugo mumbled that he hadn't.

'She reckons he'll die in the morning: 8:03 a.m., she said.'

'Uh-huh.'

'I said tomorrow lunchtime: 13:13, just for fun.'

'I thought you said he would go on for months?'

'Yeah. But he sort of already has.'

For a time, neither of them said anything.

'What did you bet?'

'Nothing really.' Michael was embarrassed. 'We just sort of *bet* each other.'

'Right then,' Hugo said. 'Make it a tenner, and I'll say he goes tomorrow night.'

'OK.' Michael was thrilled by the suggestion that their acquaintanceship would last at least another day. 'What time shall I put you down for?'

'9:17 p.m.'

He noted this in his phone.

When he looked up, the African family was back on the screen again, still swaying. *Notre Père* followed in the same brightly coloured letters. That handsome cigarette still burned.

And when his passing comes, a correspondent called Sophia Cheung was saying, *there will be grief here. And prayer.*

'Yup,' Hugo told the screen. The moment seemed to rouse him into action. 'Right,' he said. 'Shall we open a good bottle?'

Michael frowned. The whisky they were drinking seemed already pretty good.

'Well . . . ,' he began.

'Excellent!' Hugo said. 'Do you prefer Islay or Highland? I do have a very old Campbeltown, but it's not that good.'

Michael had no idea what he was talking about.

'Islay is the one with, erm . . . ,' he said, hoping to pass off his total ignorance as partial.

'That's the peaty one, yes. Tastes like petrol.'

'Yummy,' Michael ventured, which went down well.

'All right then. Islay. Glad you said that actually. I've just been sent this fancy new Bruichladdich.'

'A what?'

'Bruichladdich.'

'Ah.'

Hugo approached the drinks cabinet and opened up its lower cupboard. The bottle he pulled out, wrapped in a hessian bag, was one of many.

'It's still cask strength,' he said, 'so you do need a little water.'

The commercials had begun. The Fonz was thumbing up a Citroën full of girls.

Hugo passed a glass to Michael, who prepared an appreciative response, with details. But it was not needed. The scotch – with two ice cubes, which he thought would be forbidden – was quite extraordinary. Perhaps a minute after being swallowed, the first delicious sip still lingered in his mouth, doing different things. 'Wow,' was all that he eventually said.

'Mmm,' Hugo agreed. 'That *is* good.' Then, quite calmly, he put his glass down, took hold of what appeared to be a hefty marker pen, and pulled his shirtfront up until it left his trousers. 'My insulin,' he said mechanically, untwisting the back end of the device, ratcheting it outwards with a rapid clicking sound. He took the lid off next, pinched a roll of fat together from his belly, and stuck the needle unhesitatingly in. 'I always need more when I'm drinking,' he explained.

Michael did not know what to say, so he nodded. He had heard that Hugo was diabetic, but forgotten. And there was something disquietingly intimate about the sight of it. Like trying not to watch a woman breastfeed.

'So what do you think the new one should be called?' Hugo asked, as he packed away the needle.

'Sorry?'

'The new Pope.'

'Ah.' Michael remembered a joke he had made that afternoon. 'Well, if this one was John-Paul the second . . .'

'He was.'

'Yes I know that, thank you . . .'

'Don't mention it.'

'Well, if this one was called John-Paul,' Michael struggled on delightedly, 'then the next one should be George-Ringo.'

'Mmm,' Hugo said. 'The first.'

CHERYL BARRYMORE DIES, AGED 56,' said the trickling text. FORMER WIFE AND MANAGER OF MICHAEL BARRYMORE WAS SUFFERING FROM LUNG CANCER.

This was followed by a clip of Prince Charles in skiing gear, a bandana tied rakishly around his neck. He was answering questions from the media.

These bloody people, Charles was saying under his breath to one of his sons, the words subtitled for clarity. *I can't bear that man anyway. He's so awful, he really is.*

Yes absolutely, Prince William said out loud. *As long as I don't lose the rings I'm all right. My one responsibility, I'm bound to do something wrong.*

'Poor bastards,' Hugo murmured. 'They're all right, you know, the royals. No one gets it like they do, all their lives. I'm going to the wedding next week for some reason.'

Michael nodded absently. He was enjoying the whisky with the funny name.

There's a lot of coverage this morning, William, of Kate, a male journalist was now saying. *I don't know how you feel about that, and how she's bearing up under the scrutiny.*

I haven't seen any of it, said William in response. *I'm just gagging to get on the slopes, basically. Simple as that.*

'Evening guys!' A brassy voice rang sudden from the stairs.

Michael turned to see a small middle-aged woman entering the room. She had dark-brown hair, neatened around stoatish little features, and wore a sober cocktail dress that glinted intermittently with jewels. Quite without apology, she stepped in front of the television. There was a determined bustle in her movements, a tamed excess of energy.

'Hi Renée,' Hugo said.

'Can I have a word?' The woman was American. Her arms explained that she wanted him to leave the room with her.

'Fire away!' Hugo applied the mute control, but remained in his seat.

She sighed, and finally said, 'Mell's back.'

'Really?' Hugo sounded surprised, and partly pleased.

'Uh-huh. Anyway, she's brought her friends, so I was wondering – I'm sorry to ask you this again – but could you have a word with her?'

'What were you wondering I might say?'

'Jesus, Hugo.' The woman looked around herself dramatically. 'We've got guests, OK? Although you may not have noticed. I just think it would be best if things went smoothly for a couple of hours. Do you think that would be a good idea, maybe?'

Michael cringed, and wished himself invisible. He had not imagined that anyone could talk this way to Hugo, but the woman's manner, the strong clear voice and the straightness of her stance, left him incapable of doubting that she had the right to.

'Of course,' Hugo said calmly. 'Where is she?'

'Upstairs,' the woman answered. 'She was in the kitchen when I left her.'

'I'll go up and see her in a minute.'

Clearly this was meant to end the matter. But the woman had not finished.

'Warshak rang,' she said.

'Oh good.'

'He seemed happy, in case you were wondering. He was pretty drunk, but we fixed up a brunch in LA. He said he talked to you about it.'

'Yeah, I think he said something.'

'*Lady in Red!*' sang a strained male voice somewhere upstairs.

They all looked, pointlessly, at the ceiling.

'Anyway,' the woman continued, 'I'm putting you on the plane on Sunday morning instead of Monday, so you can have dinner with him that night.'

'OK.'

'I need to meet with the lawyers on Monday, which means I'll have to catch up with you the day after, and we'll go see Independence together. They're getting opening-night nerves so it would soothe them to see your face.'

'OK.'

The woman tried to relent. 'It's been a good party, Hugo,' she said. 'Be happy.'

'Happy? Oh, all right. Shall I smile?'

'I'll leave that up to you, but I'm going to head off. I think me being here just antagonises things, so it's better I get going. It's been a long day anyhow. Hi.' She turned to face Michael for the first time. 'I'm Renée Santos, Hugo's manager.'

'Hi,' Michael said. 'Michael.' He stood gingerly. There was a pleasing unsteadiness about his legs.

'Nice to meet you.' She shook his hand, and left without another word.

'Look!' Hugo shouted, pointing at the silent television 'Now he's "*extraordinarily* serene!"'

They stepped from the bushes into a moonless garden. It sizzled invisibly with rain.

'Fook me,' said Malcolm.

'Witness the wetness,' said Pete.

It had been a while since anyone had spoken, so everybody laughed.

In the darkness, Mellody let go of Calvin's hand.

'Fuck!' she cried, to cover up the moment. 'This stupid weather put my cigarette out!'

And it was true. There in front of her, where once the orange ember was, it wasn't. Just a dead suck and tomorrow morning's smell. She dropped the stub, giggling in her blindness. How much fun it was to creep home round the back like this! The moss-tinged, sticking wooden gate, so ill kept and penetrable that even paparazzi never dared imagine it was hers; the pathless walk at first beneath the rhododendrons then across the chewy lawn; the gradual diminishment of streetlight, the guesswork trudge towards her glowing windows, and in between, the dark, the groping zone, where nobody could prove a thing, where one might as well proceed with eyes closed, and where she sometimes did. Staggering, disgraced by lateness, it was her cherished forfeit. Especially performed in rain. She had sacrificed a shoe this way the week before, plugging it flush into the sodden soil before stepping right ahead, pantyhose on mud, too blasted and amused to stop or look. No doubt Mrs O'Sullivan would have found the thing by now, and returned it to her closet – *cleaned*, of course, and with an icy lack of comment. Hugo's woman, Mrs O was. Never liked his new American.

There was a yelp and a wet smack.

'Fookin ell!'

'You all right, Malc?' Pete asked.

Indistinct growls rose from blackness. It sounded like he had fallen actually quite hard.

'Have you fallen over, Malcolm sweetie?' Mellody asked.

Through a grimace: 'Yes I fookin have.'

'Here, take my hand, just here.' This was Calvin's voice.

'Cheers mate.'

'I think maybe you've found the rockery,' Mellody said.

'That's nice,' Malcolm replied. 'It needs a fookin railing.'

Ahead of them, a warm wash of yellow light flooded through the windows of her hefty kitchen. People were visible inside, but not many. One was Renée, her outline blurred by rain, talking keenly to two men.

'Now you all be good, OK?' said Mellody, as they reached the back door.

With a twist and a shove, she made to step inside, but only shouldered bluntly into the static upper pane. She tried again, working the mechanism as Pete and Malcolm sniggered.

'Shut *up!*' Mellody hissed, laughing now herself.

She hooked her bag on to the handle, and searched inside

it for a key. But already an approaching presence was darkening the glass, and now the door swung inwards, taking her bag with it.

Renée stood before them, backed by the interested faces of half a dozen guests.

On the stereo, Leon Redbone quietly played.

'Hi Mell,' Renée said, nearly friendly. 'Sorry, I think the caterers must have locked it.'

'Hi Renée,' said Mellody. 'Thanks.'

Enjoying the silence, and the eyes upon her, she stepped into the room, removing her bag with regal dignity from its hook.

'Hi,' Calvin offered meekly, following her in.

'A'right,' Malcolm nodded in his turn.

Pete said nothing, and shut the door behind them.

They were all more wet and rosy than the party average. In the light, Mellody could also see that Malcolm's pants were ripped around the knee, and that much of the left side of his body was skimmed with mud.

'Fuck me, Malc!' Pete cried when he noticed it too.

'Malcolm lost his footing in the rockery,' Mellody explained primly to Renée, and loud enough for everybody else to hear.

There was some hesitant amusement.

'Mmm,' Renée said through a tight smile. 'Well if you'd like a wash and some fresh pants, I'm sure we can help you out.' Half of this was offer, half command.

'Oh right,' Malcolm said. 'Ta.'

'You'll find a bathroom on the third floor.' Renée pleasantly persisted. 'Just follow the stairs all the way up, and stop before you get to the roof.'

Malcolm wandered off where he was pointed.

Tentatively, conversations began again, and Mellody felt free to glance around. On a table by the wall, spread across a thick white cloth, lay a display of bottles, glasses, sliced fruit, canapés and sprigs of mint. A large zinc tub sat at one end, filled with ice, wine and bottled German beers. Mellody stepped over and slipped her hand in. The slush was lovely and cold. She allowed her fingers to swim among the bobbing floes. It would have been nice to dunk her face. Instead she fished out a Bollinger, and popped away the cork. A gout of spume spilled half across the glasses and the cloth.

'In future?' Renée was standing quietly beside her. 'Do you think you could give me or Theresa a heads-up about when you'll be getting back? She can always bring a torch or an umbrella to meet you.' The woman was clearly trying to be reasonable and polite. As if Mellody and she were going to have a future.

'Yeah, no problem,' Mellody said, pouring as dismissively as possible. To her disappointment, Renée accepted this and left.

Champagne foam had filled the glasses almost wholly without fluid. Pete helped himself to one and slurped away the excess. Mellody poured in more, then filled the others, easing up each bubble column so it toppled off the brim and slid down, melting, through her fingers. She felt surprisingly sober, on balance, though her movements, she could see, were clumsy and approximate.

Calvin quietly received his drink.

'This party's not the heartiest,' said Pete.

'It's not meant to be.' Mellody shrugged. 'It's a shmoozefest, basically.'

'Ah.' Pause. 'So why are we here?'

Pete was often like this. Grouchy and brattish. She ignored him.

'What have you got going on at the moment then, Calvin?' It was the first thing she could think of saying.

'Oh.' He looked a little startled. 'Well, my new single's coming out in a couple of weeks.'

'Uh-huh. And what single is that?'

'It's dead exciting, actually.' A little spark returned to those clear brown eyes. 'We're doing "Lady in Red".'

'You're shitting me!' Pete spluttered with delight. 'What, Chris de Burgh?'

'Yeah.'

A messy laugh.

'We totally re-interpreted it, though.' Calvin offered this apologetically. 'I wasn't sure to begin with, either, you know. It's not my kind of music normally. But with a light beat, and these awesome strings we've recorded . . .'

This only made Pete laugh harder.

Mellody had had enough.

'What is "Lady in Red"?' she asked.

'It's . . .' Calvin began.

'It's the cheesiest fucking Eighties love ballad of the lot,' Pete butted in, 'by this posh Irish wanker.'

'It was a massive hit,' Calvin countered. 'And a lot of people wanted the rights.'

'And this is coming out in a couple of weeks?' Mellody tried to show that she was interested.

'Yeah.'

'So I'm going to hear it everywhere?'

'Yeah, I hope so. Then I start touring in May.'

Pete began to sing derisively.

'Really? Where are you going?'

'The Far East.' There was little enthusiasm in Calvin's voice.

'Oh, wow! Well, you'll have a great time!' Mellody tried to inject some.

'Is it nice out there, then?'

His crumpled brow. His lovely naked arms. He looked so worried. She wanted to kiss him again.

Instead she said, 'Oh yeah, it's fabulous. A little crazy – and like totally fucking another *planet* – but fabulous. I was in Shanghai and Guangzhou last fall, and I loved it.'

'. . . *LADY IN RE-E-E-E-E-D!*' Pete sang on, ignored.

'Right,' Calvin said. 'I'm off to Seoul first.'

'Oh, Seoul's really great. You'll love it.'

A shaven-headed man appeared. He had been drawn over by Pete's singing.

'Let's go get another bump,' Mellody said quickly into Calvin's ear, while she had the chance.

When she looked at him like that it was as if the world slid away. They were just two people, understanding one another.

'Oh, Seoul's really great. You'll love it.'

And yes, perhaps he would. He made his face a mirror of her wishes, while the rest of him set out to think so.

But then how could he love any city when Mellody would not be in it? Somewhere they could be alone: this was the only place he wanted. And she felt the same. He knew she did.

'Let's go get another bump,' she whispered, proving it, flashing him one of those looks again, and walking off into the hall.

Calvin followed with a rapid pulse, holding himself a few wise yards behind.

Mellody glided past a huge front room where a short man and a tall woman were talking privately, their wine glasses resting on the surface of a large glass case that contained a model boat. Now her little arse reeled him upstairs, to where a door ajar showed glimpses of an Asian man playing snooker in a suit and waving hi as they walked on. Calvin could hear the other players' quiet, grown-up sounds. He noticed photographs of Hugo, in frames that lit the walls with Harrison Ford . . . with David Beckham . . . with P. Diddy . . . with this bearded old guy who Calvin knew was a famous film director, but didn't know which one. And now he was excitedly afraid, as Mellody made contact with the handle on an ancient panelled door. To be in Hugo's house, with his wife, on his birthday . . . It spiked his ready body for the rut. Now she was reaching in to tug the light cord. Now looking quickly round. Now pulling him inside. A stack of Hugo's laundered towels. Two vases full of Hugo's birthday flowers. Calvin didn't care. She put her arms around his waist. He leaned into her space. At last to reunite their angry, hungry mouths. She was so beautiful, so famous. How he wanted this. It was so good for him. He wanted it so much.

And then her phone began to ring.

'Shit,' Mellody laughed, and dropped to snuffle one last kiss into his chest.

She answered it.

'Hi honey,' she said.

Calvin tried not to hear the burr of Hugo's voice.

'We're in the bathroom on the second floor.'

A longer talking noise.

'Well come up here and tell me, OK?'

She put the phone back in her bag, and returned her gaze to Calvin.

'Sorry baby,' with another playful kiss. 'That was Hugo. Don't worry. It's fine. He's just going to come up for a minute, OK?'

Calvin nodded through a wave of dread. With his shoulders, he gave a mime of casualness.

This was not fine. It was very far from fine. Facing Hugo now, and acting natural, when he was zombie high and fiercely turned on . . . How could Mellody do this to him? And just stop everything like that? (But girls could, couldn't they? People who could do this, that was exactly what girls were.) Sourly he unhooked the erection in his trouser leg as she checked herself in the mirror and slid back the bolt from the door. He would manage. Like walking out on stage, he would manage. He might even have some fun.

'So Korea's good then, is it?' he said.

'Yes Calvin,' Mellody replied, pretend-impatient, tipping cocaine on to the tiled counter. 'Korea is good. I mean, do you want to be a rock star or not?'

'Oh yeah, I definitely do.' He leant hard against the sink to hide his lurching fly. 'I've just not done a big international tour before.'

'Oh you'll get used to it. And you'll have people doing everything for you all the time. My one piece of advice...' She looked around briefly.

Fucking gorgeous, in spite of everything. He just wanted to walk right up to her, roll those jeans down . . .

'. . . My one piece of advice is to make use of your support team. If you need something, whatever it is, don't be afraid to ask. Remember: you're the talent. They've all got a job because of you, and your job is to look after yourself as well as you possibly can. You'll perform better because of it, so the show will be better too, and they'll all get more work. If you want a grape soda at three in the morning, remember there are guys whose job it is to go and find you one.'

Then Hugo walked into the room.

'Oh. Hi,' he said.

And was Calvin imagining it, or did his voice arch slightly with surprise?

Hugo pecked his wife on the lips, the lips his own had just left.

'So you want a grape soda, do you Calvin?' he asked next, cool and still.

'. . . better because of it, so the show will be better too . . .'

Mellody's voice – tense, urgent, *painfully* sincere – was clearly audible as Hugo mounted the stairs.

'. . . and they'll all get more work . . .'

He had heard this rousing little speech *so* many times before. Be selfish. Be the star. Be the cash machine, the publicity pump. Self-gratify and never stop. Let anyone who doesn't like it try to do your fucking job.

'. . . If you want a grape soda at three in the morning,

remember there are guys whose job it is to go and find you one.'

'Oh. Hi.'

Right in front of him, inches away: the face of Calvin Vance, paler now and wet with sweat, arranged in simpleton anxiety. The boy scratched his forehead, displaying a purple insignia smudged across the tendons on the back of his hand.

Hugo had thought. Well, he had assumed.

Calvin had left with her, of course. He had forgotten that. But surely Pete?

'We're in the bathroom,' she had said on the phone, assembling a large cast of accomplices in his mind.

But no. *'We're in the bathroom.'* Calvin and I are. *We.*

Even by her standards.

That jolt of dread again, not long lost.

Hugo gave his wife a kiss.

'So you want a grape soda, do you Calvin?' he said. It was meant to sound dry and chummy, an ice-breaker. It came out steely, challenging.

'No.' Calvin did a laugh. 'Mellody was just telling me about the Far East. You know, Korea and that. I'm going there on tour, but I've never been before.'

'You want a bump, Hugo?'

His wife, with a pile of powder, blithely grinding it into the tiles. Forbidden powder, by strict principles of rehab, though she showed no shame about it. And how typical of her – how absolutely *Mell* – to offer him a share. The defiant courtesy that said, *Your move.*

'No thanks,' was all Hugo could face right now.

Mell shrugged and carried on.

Perhaps she and Calvin were remnants from a larger group? Perhaps they had come up here with others who had bled away?

'Yeah, so it's my first big tour,' Calvin said.

Just not Calvin. Please not Calvin.

'Uh-huh.'

Heat raced through Hugo's skin. Fear again. His stalking need, his *problem*. And nausea, stretching at his stomach with insistent little tugs. Mellody was talking, but he could not understand her. Something bad was going to happen.

'So anyway. I meant to say.'

He butted the words, with effort, into the middle of her flow.

'Oh yes.' She was preparing a note. 'So what was this message you came up here to give me?'

'It's not my message,' he mouthed, between recovery breaths. 'It's Renée's.'

Could he do this? Was he up to it?

'OK,' Mellody said, handing the tube to Calvin. 'Don't tell me: stop acting like a bitch, don't spoil my party, be nice to everyone, comb your hair, stand up straight, and go downstairs and bake some cookies. Is that about it?'

Could she not see that he was falling apart?

'Yes,' Hugo said, trying a smile. 'About.' He guzzled air in tight half-breaths that never seemed to land. His brow was scrunching his eyes almost shut.

Calvin smiled back.

'Well tell Renée to fucking relax – if that's *possible*.' Mell snorted with laughter. 'Because we are not here to ruin her party. I just wanted to bring some friends back to my own fucking home.'

We, thought Hugo. *We*.

Then the door opened.

'*Here* you are.' It was Pete Sheen, a look of sheepish amusement on his face. '*Whooah!* Hope I'm not interrupting anything.'

'You're not,' Mell snapped.

'OK, OK. Keep cosy.' A leering look at Hugo. 'It's just that I'm off, basically. Some guys are on their way to a thing at Olympic, and I said I'd tag along. You could all come if you like? You too, Hugo.'

Everybody shook their head, and Pete looked pleased.

'The thing is, Mell,' he continued, edging further into the room. 'I can't exactly take this with me. Or not most of it.'

Hugo noticed a carrier bag that Pete was holding close to his body, the handles twisted tightly into wrinkled strings.

'Jesus.' Mell's shoulders fell, and her hair flicked sideways with impatience. 'Just give it to Bonzo. He'll look after it.'

'Wooah! Access denied!' Pete squawked. 'No offence, but the guy's hardly going to leave it alone, is he? And I can't find Malcolm anywhere.'

'OK, whatever,' Mell sighed. 'I'll take it.'

'Somewhere safe, yeah?'

Here you are!

'It's going in a fucking closet, OK? If that's not good enough, you can take it yourself.'

Here you are.

'All right. You all be good. Happy birthday, Hugo.'

Here you are!

It was the first thing Pete had said. Like he didn't know where Mellody and Calvin were. Like no one did.

With Hugo's wife's encouragement, the boy bent down to snort his share.

If Michael was not sober, then he was a funny kind of drunk. Because where the regretted weight of booze would usually be dragging at his thoughts at this point on a Friday night, that scotch instead had blended in a comfortable pliancy, as though readying his brain for sport. He just felt better, he would have said, rather than intoxicated. More relevant to the world. And still utterly himself – perhaps more himself than ever. And confidence: good God, he had *that* going on. He felt its mass pulling him to others, and them to him, by force of human gravity. It had simply been no effort, on being left by Hugo, for him to amble upstairs to the kitchen, latch on to somebody he did not know (a giant in what appeared to be his early forties) and start a conversation. The act just flowed from him undesigned. And now he spoke with executive ease, marvelling at his skill. Machine-tooled *bon mots* and finely calibrated questions marched whole and sequential from his brilliant lips, each phrase glossy with the sheen of manufacture. He just did not feel tired at all. Even though – he looked at his watch – fuck, it was 2:31 a.m.!

'Not that bad.' It was the giant's turn to speak. 'The worst are the Italians.'

They were discussing Hugo's fans, a subject on which the man clearly held himself an expert. Indeed it seemed to Michael that this clenched and beefy character took such a jealous interest in Hugo's affairs that asserting it became a form of physical work, two triangles of shoulder muscle leaping up to buttress his neck on each important word, raising in the process, and then lowering, the collar of his giant shirt. Michael longed to find a way – an amiable way – to make it known precisely which of them had just spent an hour alone with Hugo, drinking whisky from a newly opened presentation sack.

'Ah yes, the Latin temperament,' he agreed knowingly.

'*Exactly*,' said the giant and his shirt.

Could it also be the cockney accent that made him seem so territorial? When the speech of London's working classes entered Michael's ears, it always did so with a burly swagger, as though cheerfully elbowing a prime position at the bar.

'So what do they actually do?' he asked, allowing himself to be ingenuous, for now.

'They think it's all a facking game is what it is, the Italians. They'll camp outside his hotel, singing songs, chanting *You-go! You-go! You-go!* Sixteen years old most of them, like a facking school trip. I wish *they* would facking *go*.'

Surprising himself with this joke, the giant laughed.

A thought occurred to Michael: was he talking to an employee?

'And if I go out and tell them to fack off, it don't make no difference. They just walk round the block and come back. And if Hugo does it, they facking *love* it. Start cheering like mad and crowding round for autographs. Hugo won't do promotion work in Italy no more. They all have to come over here to interview him now.' He shook his head, momentarily subdued.

'Are you Hugo's bodyguard then?' Michael asked.

'Head of security. That's right.'

'I see. I'm Michael. Nice to meet you.'

'Bonzo,' the giant said, taking his hand and inflicting friendly pain.

Had this been the man who led him out of Cuzco to the car? Michael could not honestly remember. And was it *done* to talk to staff? He did not know. And, graciously, decided not to care. To him, all men were equal.

'So does Hugo get a lot of aggro from fans?' he asked, pleased with himself. *Aggro* was a bodyguard's word.

'Just a *bit*,' Bonzo nodded, with a breathy little parody of awe. But then nothing further followed.

And in the pause, Michael noticed for the first time that the room they stood in had been abandoned by all but one last patch of guests. Visible instead, where the bodies had been, were three deep shelves that edged the room with an audience of copper-bottomed pans, arranged by increment like a Russian doll unpacked. Why anybody needed such a choice of pans, Michael could not think, though scorch marks attested to their use. He imagined Hugo in attendance at the hotplate, overhung by tongs, prodding them with wooden spoons.

The final group, three men, at last made up its mind. Collecting their belongings, they began to leave. Michael saw that one of them, again, was Mark Wahlberg.

'See you Bonzo,' one of the group said. 'Say thanks to Hugo for us, will ya?'

'Sure thing,' Bonzo obediently answered. 'I'll let you out.'

As they passed, Wahlberg smiled goodbye. Then he was gone. Michael was alone.

Quickly, in search of occupation, he walked towards a corner table, still well stocked with drinks, where three sorrowful blinis had quietly begun to curl. Despite a perfect absence of appetite, he put one in his mouth, and lost a minute to desireless chewing. A formidable Illy coffee machine watched him from the counter, its roof a foam of chubby upturned cups.

Perhaps now, finally, it was time to go. It had been a wonderful night. He did not want it to end, of course. But of course it would. Better not to spoil the memory by clinging desperately on.

I should be heading off now.

To say it to Hugo, and to leave. To take his final steps past paparazzi, and then address the night bus home.

I should be heading off now.

Bonzo shut the Wahlberg entourage outside. And here was Hugo, rounding the bottom of the stairs. He said something sharp in Bonzo's ear, and with a look of mild protest, the big man left the house himself.

I should be heading off now.

This party was over. He should say it before Hugo reached him. Make it look like the decision had already been taken. Which it had.

I should be heading off now.

Michael swallowed the last of his blini and . . .

'Hi,' said Hugo. 'Whisky, Mike?' The words were heavy, effortful, dumped on the ground as if at the end of a long trip. He looked pale, and was he trembling?

I should be heading off now.

Michael could still have said it.

'Certainly,' he did say. 'Good idea.'

From: **valerie.morrell@nortonmorrell.co.uk**
To: **williammendez75@gmail.com**
Subject: **Out of Office Autoreply: Re:**
Date: **Saturday, 10 October 2009 03:22:20**

I will be out of the office from Wednesday October 7 until Monday October 19. If your message is urgent, please contact my assistant Carly McBride at carly.mcbride@nortonmorrell.co.uk. Otherwise I will reply on my return.

From: **valerie.morrell@nortonmorrell.co.uk**
To: **williammendez75@gmail.com**
Subject: **Publicity*******
Date: **Monday, 19 October 2009 09:09:01**

Dear William,

Very sorry to have missed your messages. I was away in Andalucia. I hope you're feeling more chipper now? If not, it might console you to know that every writer I have ever worked with goes through the same thing now and again – even the ones who've sold millions! Perseverance is the tonic. Perseverance.

Just to let you know, I have a couple of urgent things to catch up on, but then I will begin submitting your novel. Have faith.

Val x

From: williammendez75@gmail.com
To: valerie.morrell@nortonmorrell.co.uk
Subject: Re: Publicity*****
Date: Monday, 19 October 2009 15:38:19

Thanks Val – yes, I was in a funny mood that day, but I am feeling much more positive about things now. I haven't started on the synopsis yet, but I was thinking I could maybe write you a paragraph or two of sales copy, which would flesh things out without giving away the ending – like the blurbs that go on the back of a book. Would that be any use?

William

From: valerie.morrell@nortonmorrell.co.uk
To: williammendez75@gmail.com
Subject: Publicity*****
Date: Monday, 19 October 2009 16:02:59

We can but try. Just give me what you can spare and I'll dip my toe into the market. Cape, Picador, Canongate, Bloomsbury and Viking, I think, would be a good list for now, while still holding some cards back. If you could get your blurb to me by Friday that would be jolly helpful.

And we must finally meet! How are you fixed over the next week? Breakfast, lunch, dinner, tea, elevenses, tiffin... I can do them all.

Vx

From: williammendez75@gmail.com
To: valerie.morrell@nortonmorrell.co.uk
Subject: Is this allowed?
Date: Thursday, 22 October 2009 04:30:38
▶ 🔗 Publicity***** blurb

So I was putting together this synopsis, when the idea hit me: if this book gets published, why don't I actually write the real blurb that goes on the back? Otherwise they tend to be so direly pious, about how the book is a 'meditation' or a 'tour de force' or some other sewage. Bleurgh! (Puts finger down throat.) If I don't know the author, at least by reputation, then none of that is going to lure me to the till. Worse: they give away the plot half the time! Like my paperback copy of *Waterland*, a proper masterpiece which suffers terribly from the indiscretions of its jacket. And another thing...

No. Enough whingeing. That is my idea, and I've put this together. I'm not adamant about every word, but it would be nice to do something like it. Let me know what you think.

William

This book is different. You've really never read a book like this before.

It tells the story of an April night, when a nervous nerdy journalist takes his boss's invitation to an A-list party and meets a reclusive film star, his junkie supermodel wife, and a wide-eyed young pop singer. Soon, his life and theirs become tangled in a web of drugs and decadence.

Yet not one of them sees the real crisis coming, the moment that will engulf them all in a scandal they can't control . . .

From: **valerie.morrell@nortonmorrell.co.uk**
To: **williammendez75@gmail.com**
Subject: **Re: Is this allowed?**
Date: **Tuesday, 3 November 2009 09:12:24**

Sorry for the delay on this – I was totally wiped out by that flu thing last week (not swine, thankfully) and yesterday was a day of frantic catch-up... but anyway, I think this is great. Why the bloody hell not, I say! It's no synopsis, of course, but it shows you are a man with a plan. Will waft it in front of our editors next Monday and see what gives. And have you thought about a date for that lunch? Let's just get something in the diary. Next Weds would be good for me.

Valerie x

PS 'The real crisis' eh? I'm looking forward to it!

From: williammendez75@gmail.com
To: valerie.morrell@nortonmorrell.co.uk
Subject: For your publishers...
Date: Friday, 6 November 2009 14:45:14
▶ 🖉 Chapter 6 – The Real Crisis

Hi Val – I hope this reaches you in time to include in our submission. God, I'm suddenly *really* excited! And I've started to have loads of ideas about how we might publicise the book. Is it too early to bring that up? I've been waiting for this for so long...

Oh, and yes, next Wednesday is fine. See you then.

William

Saturday, April 2 2005

03:09

Why were boys like Calvin *always* in a hurry? Mellody had forgotten the fevered lip-to-lip assault; the fist up blouse on bra clasp; metal tooth levered into human spine; fine underwear, not always replaceable, twisted and desperately stretched for access. Was such lack of skill supposed to demonstrate his passion? The fulfillment of a screen-learned dream of culminating lust? If it was, then Calvin had met her too late. At fifteen, twenty maybe, Mellody might have succumbed to ravishment. Back then it thrilled her, men's ragged hunger for her flesh – back when it still surprised. Though even then . . . Yes, even then it had not chiefly been with sexual delight that she beheld her boyfriend devouring the adolescent proto-breasts her friends had always recommended that she be ashamed of. It had been with pride. A sense of technical accomplishment, almost, that she could cause desire.

Now Calvin was burgling a hand down the front of her jeans. Extending a finger, which straightaway began to loop insistently through the same short cycle on her clitoris, as if in battle with a stubborn stain. Mellody was embarrassed for him. Had he operated a woman before?

And yet.

Well, she didn't want him to stop exactly.

She pushed him away and began to unbutton her blouse herself. She could remove it quickly if she wanted – catwalk work had given her that at least. Instead she chose to do it slow. Instructively slow. But Calvin was too busy taking off his own clothes, fast, to be instructed.

Fear was at home in Hugo's body. A regular guest. It knew how the dishwasher worked. Mostly it dozed in the conservatory, or read a book. But right now it was doing none of these. Right now it was tearing at the wallpaper with shattered fingernails. It was spitting and pissing and shitting on the floor. It was screaming through the letterbox until its throat was just vibrating strands of flesh.

It was happening. The thing that he had never thought about before was happening at last. *That* thing.

He was losing his mind.

Gripping hard, he lowered himself down the stairs, Mike obedient behind.

He had come loose from the world. A piece of him – something so fundamental to the mechanism of consciousness that sane people could not notice it – had broken. He saw the banister rail, and felt it, and smelled the smoky depths of the media room rising up to meet him. But what *were* these things? How did they work? He used to know. Used to think they were easy.

Perhaps he had had a stroke? Some cerebral rill had swollen through its toleration point.

Fear opened its mouth and howled despair. Bars of spit stretched and snapped between its teeth.

He should say something. A bit of safe, normal talking. One of those things that normal people say to each other all the time. If he could just do that then he would feel better. Normal. That would prove he had not had a stroke.

In a minute. He'd do it in a minute. As soon as he remembered what other people were and how he could communicate with them.

At the bottom of the stairs. A large screen. He remembered having it installed. (Very expensive.) Pope. Men and talk of death. Could he make it go away? He did not know how to find the remote control, or how to work it, or what it was.

He sat on the sofa.

'Shall I pour it?' Mike said.

Hugo was not frightened of him. That was good. He nodded.

'Mellody OK?' Sloshing whisky into glass.

'Erm,' Hugo said.

'Most people seem to have gone home by now anyway. I don't think there's many left for her to make a scene *for*.' Mike chuckled.

That was happy chat. That was joking. Hugo had seen it done before.

'Erm,' he said.

Urinary tract infection, went the television. *Renal failure.*

'Are you OK?' Mike asked, placing a glass in Hugo's hand.

He sipped. This was his chance to share. He saw a self-indulgent movie star, the luckiest man alive, complaining about his excess of attention, his money tower, his paid-for friends. He saw that movie star, droning on about his artificial feelings when there were people out there with real ones. But then Mike had *asked*. Was he OK?

'Oh you know . . .' he began casually. 'You know when you just get really nervous? Lot of pressure?' The words were jagged and uneven, but Hugo was pleased to hear them. They gave him sense and comfort. If he was having a stroke, then surely he would not be able to speak.

'Mmm,' Mike agreed.

'I've just, you know, got a bit of that now.'

It was a footstep.

Fear hid behind the door with a sharpened screwdriver.

'Right. Oh, I'm sorry to hear that.'

'Do you know,' Hugo roused himself to manage, 'for years I've had this thing – loads of actors do – that I can use to make myself cry.'

'Oh yeah?' Mike's voice was interested.

'Yeah.' Calmer. Keep going. Stay in the words. 'There's different schools on this. Some people say that if you're just in the character, really living through his feelings, you know, then you'll cry when it's time to cry. And if your character doesn't want to cry, you don't.' This was good. This was helping.

'Uh-huh.'

'But that's not always what the director wants. I mean, male leads don't do a lot of crying, so if the script says I cry at some big moment, then I cry. You can't talk them out of that one.' He even smiled.

'So what do you do?'

'I cheat. Some people use onions, or they've got a machine that'll blow cold air in your eyes – I was offered that on a movie once. But it's kind of old hat now. I think we're just supposed to cry on cue. When you pay someone $5 million a movie you don't expect him to bring his own onions. Anyway . . .' He swilled his ice cubes in a circle, watching. 'Anyway. So what most people do is they keep some memory in the back of their mind that they know will make them cry – like when their dog died, or when they won the Oscar or something. And that's what I do. I used to think about my old dog, but I'm not that sad about him any more. So I always think about this other story instead. I don't know why it works.'

'What's the story?'

'What's the story?'

Everything was just so great for Michael. An adventure, a new friend, a story, a wonderful whisky, and soon, when he found an opening, perhaps the chance to try another?

'Well,' Hugo said, 'when *Little Steve* came out it changed everything. People – casting agents, waiters, other actors, journalists, everybody really – started treating me like a star. I mean they talked to me as if that was what I'd always been, but it was still new to me. I was sharing a flat in Kensal Rise, for fuck's sake. Anyway, so Ben Kingsley, like, *summoned* me to go and have lunch with him in this restaurant in LA. My agent got a call from his agent, and I was in town, so I went. I didn't know you could do that if you were a star, just pick out interesting people you'd never met and arrange to meet them. But it was really nice, you know. He said he thought I'd been great in the film, gave me a couple of pointers, not on acting, but on dealing with people in Hollywood, choosing roles, stuff like that. It was actually really helpful, and I was just glad to be asked. So anyway, I'd always felt pretty grateful about it. And a couple of years later I was doing well, and I saw this really brilliant little movie at the London Film Festival by this new English film-maker I'd never heard of. David Neighbour, his name was. And I thought, why don't I get Renée to set up lunch with him? Why not just ask? It might even help his career, like Ben helped me. I only wanted a relaxed chat, you know, and to talk about his film.'

There might have been a tremor in Hugo's voice just then. Michael was not certain.

'So yeah,' Hugo said abruptly, as if wrenching back his mind from something else, 'I liked his film and I just hoped we would get o-on.'

That was definitely a wobble.

Hugo paused.

Calvin snatched the second roll of denim from his foot and tossed it sideways hard. His belt buckle streaked across the floor and cracked against the pedestal of a basin. Left foot, right foot: socks torn off like sticking plasters and discarded with the same disdain.

He was naked.

He advanced on Mellody, as she fiddled with her jeans and boots. He took hold of a breast and sucked its little nipple. Wonderful. But not enough. He went for the other, did the same.

More!

At last!

More!

With an unsteady, one-legged tug, her jeans and pants came off together. Staggering, she gripped at him for balance. Her bush pressed soft against his thigh.

(Blonde too. Fancy.)

Calvin pushed a finger in.

Hot US princess breath gasped upon his back.

And another. More! More! More!

She staggered again, bobbing back into the corner on her heel flesh. Flat palms smacked for purchase on the walls. She looked smaller now. Not like in her pictures. The under-Mellody. The real thing. What he always wanted. Now it was his.

David Neighbour was late.

Hugo looked at his ice cubes and remembered.

On his own at the table. The jilted diner. Studying the menu for half an hour. Artichoke, monkfish, Montrachet.

The waiter approached. Smiling. Embarrassment by proxy. Would Hugo care for another drink while he waited for his guest?

Why not? He would take the Montrachet now.

Still no messages on his phone. He should not check too often. People were looking. Hugo would have looked. That's why stars were always late, because they could not risk being early. Perhaps the young film-maker knew this and had delayed himself nearby. Or he could just have been terribly unlucky. Hugo remembered his early days: struggling from audition to audition on broken buses and suspended tubes. The sweat, the stress. He was going to tell the young film-maker all about it, with a big smile, when he arrived. 'Seriously, do not worry about it,' was what he was going to say, deflecting all apologies with flattened hands, meaning every word.

And then the film-maker did arrive. And he wasn't young at all. At first, in fact, Hugo did not realise that the crumpled fiftysomething who approached him was the man he had been waiting for. But that was the only explanation that remained when the waiter offered him the empty chair and relieved him of his overflowing bag.

'Hi,' Neighbour said.

'Seriously,' Hugo said, shaking his hand, 'do not worry about it.'

Neighbour gave no suggestion that he was worried about anything. He was dressed without ceremony and not entirely shaven. Hugo did not want to be deferred to — that was the first thing he did not want — but in his imagination this man had been at least as excited by the lunch as he was, if only for the food.

'It's good to meet you at last,' Hugo added with a smile. 'I loved your movie.'

How had he got the idea that the man was going to be twenty-six? The film had been so bold and vivid. Somehow he had just assumed . . .

'Yeah,' said Neighbour. 'I saw you at the screening.'

Not 'Thank you' or 'It's good to meet you too.'

'Oh right,' said Hugo. 'I wanted to come and find you afterwards, but I had to dash off.' This was true, though of course it sounded like a lie.

'That's OK.'

'Anyway.' Hugo pressed on. 'I did love the film. I honestly have not seen anything so original in years.'

'Thanks,' said Neighbour. 'I just wish someone would buy it.'

It was clear now that he was in an irritable mood. No one Hugo asked had ever heard of the guy, so perhaps he was always this way. Directors often were.

'Having distribution problems?' Hugo was matey, a colleague.

'If no distribution at all can be called a problem, yes.'

'I see.' Bad thoughts, unhappy feelings, had begun to form an orderly queue. For some reason, he now realised, this lunch had been very important to him. He had been looking forward to it since it was booked, and it had never occurred to him that he would not have a wonderful time.

The man was looking at his menu.

He ordered the steak.

They ate in silence, punctuated by Neighbour's complaints about the film industry. The lack of opportunities, the closed elites, the institutional dullness.

Hugo had planned to ask humbly to be considered for any future roles that might suit him. He had toyed with mentioning some names, good producers and sympathetic investors that he knew. Instead he simply ate, and said none of these things.

And there it was.

He paid the bill without pudding.

A shadow through the frosted pane. Tears were at the door.

Mike placed a hand on his shoulder, and something inside Hugo burst.

Fear fell to its knees.

Ah.

Actually, she could go for some of this.

Mmm.

Lots of energy. Got to give him that.

Aaa-ah.

A good cock, despite the coke. Stiff and springy, like a sapling stripped of bark.

Lovely . . .

And he was working hard. Pete never worked this hard on anything.

Jesus!

A swift smack on her ass. Sure, why not?

Yeah.

Or Hugo.

Ah, yeah!

He hadn't touched her for . . .

Fuck, YEAH!

. . . she did not know how long.

Aa-AAah!

She would be surprised if he even jerked off these days.

'Uh!'

Calvin leaning towards her face. The scent of candy from his hair.

'Uh!'

What was that smell?

'U-uh!'

Caramel! That was it.

'Oh Mellody!'

Erm . . .

'Oh, Mellody!'

He was talking to her.

'Oh yes!'

Was she supposed to say something back?

'Oh yes!'

This was so embarrassing. Did he think he was at a soccer game?

'Oh Mellody! Oh Mellody!'

She wished he was.

'Oh God, Mellody!'

He was just a dumb kid.

'Oo-oh!'

What was she doing?

'Oooo-oh!'

What was she doing?

'Ah!'

Nearly over. Come on.

'Oh!'

Nearly there.

'You . . .'

There was drama behind his eyes.

'You are the only . . .'

Oh God. Breathe.

'. . . person . . .'

Walls shaking. Cracks appearing.

'You are the only person . . .'

His mum and dad. He kept picturing his mum and dad at home.

Please let him be able to get the words out.

'. . . I have . . . been able . . .'

By force. He would get there by force.

'. . . to . . . talk . . . to . . .'

Tears streamed welcome channels across his skin.

Hugo knew that he was drunk. He didn't care.

Blindly, he reached out a hand. Mike took it, squeezed formally, let go.

'My fucking wife . . .' Did he dare to say the rest? 'She's upstairs right now . . . with your mate. That kid from fucking *X-Factor*!'

He prayed for Mike to say something.

'He's not my mate,' came in the end. 'I only met him tonight.'

'I just . . .'

And again.

'. . . can't . . .'

Boiling up.

'. . . any more . . . And . . .'

'Uh-huh?' Mike said, sipping his drink.

'It's just. I've been . . . having a er . . .'

Waters mounting.

'. . . I've been having . . .'

Meniscus slipping across the brim.

'. . . a really hard time recently.'

A howl that Hugo did not recognise. Grief-taut sinews curling up his body to an S.

Mike's hand upon his shoulder.

He fell forwards on the sofa, shaking.

Fear had left.

Sorrow had arrived.

Relief. Relief. Relief.

'Give me a minute, will you Calvin?' Mellody said.

'Sure,' he said back.

Good idea, actually. He could use a moment's rest himself. Still out of breath. He packed himself back inside his trousers and sat down heavily in a leather seat. The surface gripped his naked back. The skin across his stomach folded to resemble the roll of fat that he knew was not there. Where were his cigarettes? He was so happy.

'No, I mean could you let me use the bathroom?'

'Oh right. Yeah. Sorry.'

He unglued himself from the chair and bent to retrieve his vest.

Girls were funny. You'd strip them naked, do everything you could think of to them, get more familiar with their privates than they would ever be, and still they were ashamed to have a piss in front of you. (Calvin preferred not to go in front them either, but that was different. It was different when you could see the pee.) The point was, girls had rules. Girls always had their funny little rules. Even Mellody, who he guessed might be a little tougher. Perhaps as he and she grew closer things would change.

'It's stopped raining,' she said, glancing at the window even though the blinds were drawn. 'Why don't you go up on the roof terrace and I'll join you in a minute? There should be some beers there.'

She stood in front of him, one impatient arm propped, teapot-style, upon her hip. No clothes. Not even any effort yet to put them on. She looked amazing. Calvin wanted to do it again.

'You know the way?' Mellody added, brisk and businesslike.

'Yeah, I think so.' He had no idea. 'You just go up. Right?'

'Pretty much.'

'Right. OK then.' He just could not stop staring. She was more wonderful than...

Fucking hell. *Mellody*. He had just had sex with . . . *Mellody*! Mrs Hugo Marks.

Get in!

Hugo lay in a bridge from seat and sofa, hands screening out his face, continuously weeping. His back heaved its jacket tight, lengthening the stitches in the central seam, where Michael's hand still sat. He had placed it there so naturally. Tough luck, know the feeling. Just a pal's remark. Men did that, didn't they, for mates? Yet Hugo had collapsed under the contact. Now Michael dared neither to remove his touch, nor smear it tenderly into a stroke. Instead, he held still and wondered: when would be polite to pull away?

In the patio doors he watched his reflection, monochrome and slicing sharp. A man, sipping whisky, staring sideways, one arm resting awkwardly on the shoulder of a movie star. And behind this layer, a universe of night. To anyone standing in the garden, they would be lit up like an advert. God knows what for. Not whisky anyway.

Hugo's sobs intensified. They shrieked and swelled, gathering shoves of emotion until the force of his distress was overwhelming and he just shook silently, as if all his living air had been garrotted out. There was a drowning sound, then a redoubled wail. Michael wanted to get down among the furniture and hug his host. But of course he couldn't.

'. . . *refused pleas from Vatican doctors that he should return to hospital . . .*'

He wished that he could turn the sound back down.

'. . . *which does suggest that he is preparing himself for the final journey . . .*'

At last he took his hand away, and Hugo slumped forwards across the sofa, forcing his face into a brown suede cushion.

'. . . *The chances of an elderly person in this condition with septic shock surviving twenty-four to forty-eight hours are 10 to 20 per cent. But that would be with very aggressive treatment. Without intensive care, the chances of his surviving are nil – unless there is a miracle . . .*'

Michael leaned back as far as he could without standing, and peered up the empty stairs. Where were the rest of Hugo's friends? Was he all the man had left in such a moment? Pity, shame and pride alloyed themselves inside him.

And now a face, blotched with red and shining damply, was rising from its burrow. The mouth opened, it seemed about to speak, then new convulsions overtook it. Hands returned to cover its disgrace.

The howls continued. He was almost screaming now.

'It's OK, Hugo,' Michael said instinctively. 'We'll sort it out.' He did not know quite what this meant, but it felt good.

The empty cushion lay beside Hugo's head, still trenched with the indentation of his nose. At the bottom, Michael could not fail to notice where tears and mucus had flowed together into the suede, darkening it. So real, that damp little patch. It made him want to weep another of his own. The feeling passed.

Mellody waited for the door to close, then locked it. She tottered over to her bag, took out and lit a cigarette, and placed herself delicately on the toilet seat, taking a long deep draw. Her mouth full, she inhaled, and a grey tongue of smoke flickered in and out of her lips. Below, the first dollop of Calvin's mess slipped into the water.

What a fucking idiot she was. What a total fucking moron. Pete was a waste of time. Hugo was a waste of time. But this kid . . . Jesus.

And without a rubber.

She steadied herself with another sip of smoke.

She could actually now be pregnant with a child's child. (Though she was early in her cycle. Somewhere.) And a baby – like *that*, with *him* . . . Mothers like her did not deserve to live. She belonged on Ricki fucking Lake. She was so stupid. She was selfish and stupid.

A larger drip leaked out.

Plap.

Her lilac blouse, a particular favorite, lay on the floor in front of her. She stared at it for a while. One sleeve was stuck down by a spot of fluid, and a boot stood up beside it, her panties hanging like a damsel from its brim.

Slop.

She never carried rubbers in her bag, of course, for fear of what that said. Besides, the counselors in rehab told her frequently that heroin, with time, could damage her fertility. She hoped it had. It suited her, to be a seedless grape.

Slap.

A human sound, something muffled, floated through the floor.

And there was Pete's plastic bag, crumpled up against the wall where she had left it. The thought of flushing away its contents entered and exited her mind. Or consuming it herself. But coke was no drug to devour alone. Really, it was no drug at all.

Perhaps Malcolm was still around?

Mellody sat up, leaving two neat discs where her elbows had pressed into her legs. First white, then reddening as the blood returned.

Twenty-six minutes. That was how long Hugo had been crying. Michael could not prevent himself from working it out. Twenty-six minutes since Sky's squat little clock said *03:31* and he had stared at the digits with his focus locked as if he hoped to hide himself between the pixels. Meanwhile he had asked himself the same repeated question: whom could he tell about all this? Camille? Never. No. That would be plain betrayal. Sally then? She would be rapt. He could see her gleaming as he gave her every detail of the night. Indeed, it would be a kind of lying not to. But could she hold the information in? Was that reasonable? The alternative was telling nobody. To live with heavy memories, to become a secret stranger to his friends . . . Michael really was not sure if he could handle that. He was a private person. Among his intimates he needed to be truly known.

And now at last the howls were fading.

Twenty-six minutes was a long time.

'Sorry, Mike.' Hugo said it very quietly.

'That's OK. You've done nothing to be sorry for.'

What else could he say? It was Calvin who should be sorry,

that priapic little rodent. At first sight he had seemed too young and stupid to be trouble. But then it was the young and stupid that you had to worry about, wasn't it? Like immature rattlesnakes, Michael had once been told; more dangerous because they don't know what they're doing yet. And Calvin had been on *X-Factor*, too, it seemed, which made sense. There was a yearning, prime-time emptiness about the kid. But going back with a married woman, to her husband's own home, at his birthday party . . . It took a very nasty kind of child to gratify himself like that.

'I just don't know where all this has come from.' Hugo was shaking his head, avoiding Michael's eye.

'Don't worry about it.' He noticed, with a flinch, that he was patting the shoulder again.

'Thanks.' Hugo attempted a laugh. 'This must be so embarrassing for you.'

Was it? Michael was not sure any more. He was loyal. He was bored. He had finished his drink. He wanted another. He was angry at that half-grown little shit . . .

'Honestly, it's fine,' he said. 'I'm just glad you don't have to cope with this on your own.' That was a nice thing to say. He was normally not much good in the consoling role. 'I'm sure it must be difficult,' he ventured further, 'you know, being famous. With all the pressure and photographers and everything.'

'It's a fucking bitch,' Hugo agreed. 'I spend half my time terrified of losing everything, and the other half feeling guilty about having it.' He returned to his whisky, two salivary islands floating where the ice had been.

'But you shouldn't feel guilty,' Michael said. 'You worked for it.'

'Yeah.' Hugo blew his nose, and did not sound convinced. 'I did. But I'm supposed to feel lucky, too. You know, like I'm living everybody else's dream. Those people,' he gesticulated at the outside world, 'they think they own you. Like it's, "We are the ones who put you where you are today!" Yes you are, guys! Thanks a lot!' He expelled a single puff of bitter laughter, sounding drunker than before.

'Slike.' Hugo had momentum. 'It's like they consume me. And it's like that gives them rights. That means they can camp outside my house, and send me shit in the post, and take pictures everywhere I go, and I've got to fucking smile about it! And they *interpret* everything I do. People think everything is part of a conspiracy, that it's all about making them like me, or hate Mellody, or buy stuff, or whatever.'

'They just need to feel important,' Michael suggested. 'They'd rather be manipulated by the rich and famous than ignored.'

'*Exactly!*'

Hugo clapped his hands together.

Michael was emboldened. 'You guys . . .' He swigged his empty scotch with feeling. He had never thought this through before. '. . . you guys are special because you are *the unignored.*' He felt dizzy. Flushed. As needed, perhaps, as he had ever been.

And Hugo nodded. 'But I wish I wasn't. Sometimes I just think about giving it all up. Fucking off somewhere with a bag of cash. Grow a beard, buy a bar. I know where I'd go as well.' He looked very serious.

'Where?'

'Peru.'

'Why Peru?'

'My movies always bomb in Peru. Sometimes they bomb in loads of places.' He laughed. 'But I've never had one do well in Peru. They just don't fucking like me over there. Sounds like my kind of place.'

Michael glanced over at the television again. The cut-out Pope still hovered above Sky's sleek and indefatigable anchorpeople.

And still he wasn't tired.

'I know it's rude,' he said to Hugo. 'But is there any chance we could try one of the other . . . ?'

He meant it too. Everyone thought he was joking, or dreaming, when he talked about Peru, but he'd picked up the phone on more than one occasion, seriously intending to make the booking. One ticket, one way. Taxi from Lima Airport up the coast, through Ancash, and into the region of La Libertad. Stop in Trujillo, city of eternal spring, spiritual home of the asparagus. Then busk it. He'd picked up a little Spanish over the years – enough to know that he could pick up plenty more. Then all this would be over.

'I know it's rude,' Mike said. 'But is there any chance we could try one of the other . . . ?'

Hugo laughed loudly.

'Another malt?' he asked, knowing the answer.

'If that's OK?'

'Of course it is. My pleasure. Glad you're enjoying it.'

He lumbered over to the cabinet, and stopped in an inspecting crouch. A Speyside this time. The Glenfarclas?

He felt much better now.

The bastard blue ball pinged off an indestructible brick, slipped past the right-hand edge of Calvin's bat and disappeared into virtual oblivion. A jingle taunted him with sympathy code. Game over.

For the fourth time in succession, he had failed to get beyond the second level. A sorry showing, even in his state.

Fuck it.

He slipped his phone back into his pocket. A murmur of light had slunk into the sky. Greyly he examined his surroundings. A large wood-decked roof garden, bounded by brickwork on two sides, front and right, with a low guard rail offering token safety around the rest of the perimeter. Furniture, plants, a folded-up sunshade and some heavy-looking sculptures casually populated the space.

It was a miracle, Calvin realised, puffing wryly on a fag, that he had not had a serious accident when he first came up here. To think he had been stumbling around, in search of beers, the dithering flame of his lighter illuminating nothing but the hand that held it . . . It must have been those sculptures that had blocked his path repeatedly, announcing their existence with solid interruptions on his toes. His gut lurched at the thought – too easy to conjure up – of himself steering close to that edge, the rail invisible, the chasm on the other side not known . . .

Then he noticed something. In the middle of the floor: two trapdoors with brass handles, like you might expect to find on a well-appointed pirate ship.

He pulled the left one.

Fucking *result*!

A sunken fridge, filled with wine, champagne, and perhaps a dozen bottles of Budvar. No wonder he had missed it!

He put down his cigarette, reached in and withdrew a beer. Its neighbours tittered musically around his hand.

And yes! Set into the underside of the trapdoor, there was even a bottle opener. With an effervescent wrench, it opened Calvin's bottle.

Beneath the other door were glasses, and a stack of towels. He took one and wrapped it around his shoulders for warmth.

This, Calvin reflected as he strolled, was just about the coolest thing of all time. He made a vow on the spot: one day *he* would own a sunken roof fridge. Perhaps one day soon. This, after all, was his world now. The thought daunted him a little, but pleased him more. If he started seeing Mellody, even for a just a few weeks . . . He lingered on the prospect.

It would have to be done secretly, of course, for Hugo. At least until he left on tour. Though secrets were never kept perfectly. There would be speculation, as there was with Pete. He'd be in the papers every day. No question. Sienna Miller was. Pete Doherty was.

Rich and everyone at Warehouse would be delighted.

Though his brother Jason still would not believe it.

Calvin sucked on his cigarette, which delivered just a draught of stale air. The shaft was wet, from an ashtray full of rainwater. He stood up. The lights of London lay before him like a mixing desk. Its levels rose and fell. Small, precise adjustments to the city's pitch. When you were bored of this place . . . What was it?

That's right.

'When you're bored of London, you're bored of life.'

Classic.

Calvin hugged the towel around him and flicked at the trapdoor handles with the tip of his shoe, seeing if he had the skill to lift them.

He wanted to talk to someone. He wanted to talk to someone about the night he'd had. He wanted to talk to someone about the night he'd had so much that he could not stand still.

He took his phone back out.

Jason would no doubt still be going strong. Up to something, somewhere. Calvin could text him. He didn't text him enough.

Ur not gonna beleve this bro, he typed, his fingertips scampering intuitively across the glowing interface. *im on roof at hugo marks n mellody house in ldn!*

He paused for a moment, and lit another fag. He did not want Jason to think he was showing off.

Then, *i cant beleve it ither!!* he added. *theyv got a beer frij hidn in the flor!*

But fuck. Let us not forget that he had just had *sex* with *Mellody*. He did very much want to show off about that.

n that is just the start ;-) Calvin chuckled. *talk soon m8. amazing scenes! cal*

Send.

He sauntered to the front wall and gazed out over it.

Jesus!

He ducked down fast.

There were paparazzi in the street. Maybe ten or twelve of them. They could easily have seen him. But had they? No, he didn't think they had.

Calvin breathed.

Why were they still here? Surely they knew that the party was all but over? Could they be keeping track of who was still inside? It often amazed him what those guys found out. An underpaid waitress, perhaps, had tipped them off for cash.

'Mellody's still in there,' she could have said, pocketing a fifty. 'Calvin too. But Sheen left a while ago.'

Or Hugo could have done it. That did happen. Calvin knew this. Though Hugo did not seem the type.

But Pete did.

(And he knew, didn't he, what Mellody and Calvin were up to in the bathroom? Yes he knew.)

'Where's Mell, Pete?' the paps would have asked him as he left.

'Still in there,' Pete would have said with a wink. 'Having a chin-wag with Calvin Vance.'

And now they were waiting. For the story of the night. Something for the Sundays, at a price.

He shuddered with fantastic panic. How would he escape unseen? Through the back garden again? That might hide him.

Or in daylight it might not.

Jason really *never* would believe this. Not unless they caught him, anyway. Not without seeing his brother's picture. The papers' stolen proof.

Unless.

Here was a thought: unless *he* took a photograph of *them*?

Calvin peered round the side of the wall, his head beneath the guard rail. Yes, he could see the men still. But could they see him? It was too risky.

He tried a new position at the back of the roof. Here, if he lay down beneath the railing on his towel, his shoulders off the edge, holding his phone out just a little, would it see round the side of the house?

He tried it.

Nearly. Six more shuffled inches over, stretching out his toes for balance.

He tried again. The device whirred and snapped.

And there they were. Dim shapes between trees. It was still too dark to see them clearly. But it was getting lighter.

Calvin lay and waited.

This would be brilliant.

He waited.

Blood rushed through his ears.

He waited.

He waited. Fuck it. He dialled his brother's number.

It rang.

Jason would believe him.

It rang.

Jason would believe him.

It rang.

Where was Mellody anyway?

The final track of Tinariwen's *Amassakoul* was still playing to an empty lounge. Mellody could see the CD case lying open on the floor.

No sign of Malcolm in the kitchen, either. (Which the caterers and Renée, thank God, had abandoned too.)

The games room was empty.

And the gym.

Hugo was not yet in bed. The covers were still rectangularly tucked and turned. He would be downstairs, of course, drinking and watching TV. But surely Malcolm was not with him? More likely he had left. Or perhaps found Calvin on the roof?

She checked the spare bedrooms, and Mrs O'Sullivan's utility area.

Deserted. Deserted. Deserted.

Then she tried the door to the second bathroom. It gave way. And a sweet, burnt, vinegary smell – the sweet, burnt vinegary smell – came wafting out to greet her. The light was off, the drapes drawn, but she knew Malcolm was inside. And a sloshing from the tub confirmed it.

Technically this was funny. Malcolm taking a bath. But, 'Malcolm?' Mellody said, seriously.

'Mmmm . . .' A long, relaxed acknowledgement.

'You got any spare?'

The red tip of a smoke glowed yellower, lighting up the smiling contours of a face in steam.

'S'on the side,' he said. 'Weird sticky stuff. S'all I could get. Good though.'

Pulling shut the door behind her, Mellody flicked on her cigarette lighter and advanced into the room. A sheet of foil, charred, lay on the counter behind Malcolm's back. It flapped and tinkled in a gust of air. And there, nestling in cellophane, was what she was looking for: a glistening chunk. Black tar, like they had in LA. *Plenty*.

With her thumb and forefinger, she pinched a piece. It stuck like hard candy to her nail. With one end of the foil, she plucked it off, and sniffed her fingertip instinctively.

'Could you hold this for me?' she asked.

Malcolm reached out and took a corner of the sheet, tipping it very slightly down towards her. Holding her lighter underneath, Mellody watched the dot of matter as it sizzled and melted and began to drip along the slope, emitting as it went a teasing strand of smoke, which she sucked greedily through his discarded tube. A sour lash cracked the back of her palate, but she held on, resisting the urge to cough. The pain passed.

Mellody waited . . . and then exhaled a large and satisfying cloud. The kind that genies came from.

That was the thing about Malcolm. They had a special understanding. Stuff most other people did not *get*.

'Pete's fooked off somewhere,' he said, as if reading her thoughts.

'He went to a party someplace,' she whispered hoarsely.

'Right.'

Malcolm was great. With just one word, he could say everything.

Gently, gently, Mellody eased herself through the blackness and into the armchair that she knew was waiting in the corner of the room.

It would be good to put *Amassakoul* back on. She could go and get it. There was a CD player in here, installed beside the tub.

But then staying here, not moving. That would be great too.

Her knees. Her knees felt . . . mmm. Warm.

The friendly ember floated towards her face.

She reached out and took it. The length of her straightened arm was exactly right.

Finally, things were looking up.

'. . . what it's like,' Hugo said, and stopped, looking at him.

Michael realised that he had not been listening. Outside, the dawn was phasing up, dissolving their reflections in the window. Somehow his busy mind had lost itself entirely in the appearing scene. The long bright lawn, cold and vigorous with dew, waisted at the limit of his vision by two intruding beds of bush. The rockery on the right, gently heaping up its alpine bric-a-brac like muesli in a bowl. A handsomely maintained brick wall, ivy-smothered and spiked, where necessary, with deterrent fleurs-de-lys. How professionally beautiful it was.

'Mmm,' he said.

'Anyway . . .' Transparently aware of Michael's inattention, Hugo raised his hands to call the subject closed, whatever it had been.

5:34, the muted television said. The room was thick and foetid.

Hugo stood, and deeply breathed. 'Thank you so much. For everything,' he said, arching out his back into a stretch.

It sounded like an ending. Michael did not want an ending. He wanted this thing to carry on and on. Fresh air? A change of scene? Might those pick them up again? They sounded in his head like wholesome, practical suggestions, the sort one heard from men of wisdom. The kind of men, on Sunday afternoons, who make their recumbent friends go walking. Yes, fresh air was what they needed. Fresh air and coffee maybe.

'Could we go outside for some fresh air?' he said. 'A change of scene?'

'Sure,' Hugo smiled. 'Good idea,' and seemed to mean it.

Michael stepped over to the doors.

'How do these open?' he said when he got there.

'Let's go on the roof,' was Hugo's answer. 'It's lovely up there in the morning.'

Upstairs? Michael felt a flickering of fear. Wasn't Mellody up there? Calvin? Maybe others? Sleeping or awake? He had not heard anybody leave, but then you wouldn't, would you, in a massive place like this? Suddenly, he loved the safety of the basement. Hugo seemed ready, though. And what objection could there be? So they climbed the narrow stairs together.

'Really Mike, I can't tell you how much this means to me,' Hugo said again as they drew level in the hall. 'I mean, in my business I'm always surrounded by people, you know?'

'Uh huh.'

'But they just agree with everything I say, right? They laugh at all your jokes, tell you you're brilliant whatever you do . . .'

'Yeah,' Michael puffed. 'I bet.'

'Mellody gets it too. Everybody does. It's just totally impossible to live a normal life – with the paparazzi and the public and the travelling all the time. So you have to rely on other people to do things for you. I mean, I haven't actually *bought* a tube of toothpaste in years!'

They hauled themselves on to the horizontal of the first-floor landing. It was darker here, and the doors were mostly closed. But furtively, Michael peered inside the open ones. At a disconcerting Diane Arbus grinner on the wall; at a model sailing boat, glass-cased and rakishly displayed on painted seas like something wild stuffed; at CDs scattered; at a thoughtful roll of toilet paper on the cistern's lid; at a lonely pinball machine, infinitely ready, strobing idly to itself. Mellody and Calvin could be anywhere. Righteously now, he almost willed a confrontation.

'Mmm,' he said, a little late.

'There's just so many people out there on the make, you know?' Hugo still strode ever upwards. 'You can't trust anyone. And – ha – do you know what they always say?'

Michael didn't.

'They warn you about how there are lots of people out there who are on the make, and that you can't trust anyone!'

They both laughed.

'Is it really that bad?' Michael asked soothingly, scaffolding his friend's complaints.

'Yes. It really is that bad.'

They were mounting the final, steeper staircase now, up into a plate-glass chamber full of sky. Summiting first, Hugo swung open the door and held it for Michael, who stepped out on to the damp-stained bevelled boards, and panted with arrival. Ahead of him, slants of heatless sunshine stencilled his shadow long across the wood. At its apex, on the far edge of the roof, he was surprised to notice a pair of jeans, capped at the cuffs by two boldly coloured rubber soles, one orange, the other green. The wearer, one could only suppose, was leaning carefully over the side to vomit.

Then Michael saw cream fabric. And a smooth brown arm extended from it, seeking anchorage on the interior.

It was Calvin. TV boy.

He had had his fun with Mellody, and now this battered whelp had come up here to be discreetly sick. He had even brought a towel. It was such a delightful comment on the night, such delicious justice. A divine joke, above all, that Hugo must not miss. And what a blessing, Michael realised, that he had seen it first and now could introduce it as his own.

The footsteps stopped.

Mellody wondered whose they were.

She looked up at the ceiling – how cool it would be if she could see through it! – and whistled out a long, thin stream of weed fumes which spread into a ghostly stalactite above her head.

Arhythmic clattering. A masculine stomp. What could she deduce? Like those Apache trackers on TV when she was a kid. The guys who could listen to the ground and tell you when the wagons passed.

'White men,' she said into the darkness, in her Injun voice. 'Headed up on roof.'

'Mmm...' the darkness grunted back.

Mellody slid further down into her seat and stretched her legs out straight, allowing them to balance on the boots' hard heels. Somewhere in the movement, the joint came back to her attention. It was still in her hand, and just lit. She drew on it gently, pulling in the bright red pip another quarter-inch.

'Pass the peace pipe when yer ready, Sitting Bull.' The darkness splashed sarcastically.

A wheezing laugh began in Mellody's chest, and she fought to control it, exhaling steadily, before coughing out the tailing chugs of smoke.

'How?' she spluttered, before disintegrating into giggles once again.

The darkness chuckled too.

Maybe it was Calvin on the stairs above? And he'd found a friend. Good old Calvin.

She would go up and see him in a minute.

After one more hit. Maybe put on *Amassakoul*.

'Shhh . . .'

Mike's latex face was gleeful in the sunlight. His lips puckered with suppressed amusement underneath a sealing finger. On secret toes, dark shirt tails half-untucked, he crept out into the air.

Great guy, thought Hugo, but not a pretty sight.

And then he saw what Mike was going to show him. Somebody was lying on a towel, right over the edge. A casualty whose nose had proven bigger than his stomach.

But it was Calvin.

Shit.

Not Calvin.

Hugo grasped about for options. He wanted to stop Mike where he stood, to turn him quietly around and send him back downstairs.

'Mike.'

Voicelessly, he mouthed the word, carving it from breath, which disappeared in a flash of vapour when it met the day.

Mike had reached the railings. He bent down close to Calvin's shoulder. Still the boy did not stir.

Hugo made a final study of the situation. Treetops, strangely near, swaying with a hefty elasticity. His neighbour's roof, patched by newer slate. And on the wind, the arguments of weekend cars. None of these could help.

'CALVIN!' Mike said, loudly in the morning.

'CALVIN!'

Disgrace! Up!

CLANG!

The clean, insolent note of a bell. Calvin could not tell if it was railings or his head that rang.

And he was tired.

His lovely phone slipped from his hand.

Jason?

Was he slipping, Jason?

It felt as if he was. Perhaps he ought to grab something so he would not, er . . .

Missed it. Somebody was playing with his feet.

All gone.

Shit.

This was so embarrassing. What about the tour? Rich would be in so much trouble . . .

Air roaring past his ears.

Shouldn't he have landed by now?

Bollocks. He just *knew* that this would happen.

From: **valerie.morrell@nortonmorrell.co.uk**
To: **williammendez75@gmail.com**
Subject:
Date: **Friday, 6 November 2009 18:08:55**

Fantastic! Both the 'crisis', and the fact that we are finally going to meet! Don't worry about marketing ideas for now, I think it's more important not to confuse people at this stage. (Do write it all down though.) Will submit what I have to publishers on Monday.
In haste,
Vx

From: **valerie.morrell@nortonmorrell.co.uk**
To: **williammendez75@gmail.com**
Subject: **And they're off!**
Date: **Monday, 9 November 2009 18:08:55**

All out! Exhilarating feeling after all your hard work. Now we wait... try not to fret.
x
PS We won't hear anything for at least a week whatever happens, so you can relax a bit for now.

From: valerie.morrell@nortonmorrell.co.uk
To: williammendez75@gmail.com
Subject: Tomorrow
Date: Tuesday, 10 November 2009 11:04:41

Hi William – Just checking we're still on for lunch tomorrow? Come to
my office at one, and we'll scuttle off to the Greek round the corner.
I'm on 07700 900412 if you need me.
Vx
PS No news yet, obviously...

From: valerie.morrell@nortonmorrell.co.uk
To: williammendez75@gmail.com
Subject:
Date: Wednesday, 11 November 2009 15:08:22

Sorry to miss you today, William. We did say the 11th, didn't we?
I trust all is well? Let's reschedule at your earliest. Persistence will
prevail!

From: **valerie.morrell@nortonmorrell.co.uk**

To: **williammendez75@gmail.com**

Subject:

Date: **Tuesday, 17 November 2009 11:14:37**

Hi William

Viking have passed, I'm afraid. I don't think they got very far into it.
Just decided the style wasn't for them. I will forward the email on if
you would like to see. It's important that you don't make too much of
this. There are always people who say no.

x

From: **valerie.morrell@nortonmorrell.co.uk**

To: **williammendez75@gmail.com**

Subject: **Picador**

Date: **Wednesday, 25 November 2009 17:55:12**

Hi William

Picador have said no. They liked the tone and the ingenious plotting
but didn't feel the subject matter felt quite fresh enough to make it
work. It's very disappointing obviously but it simply does not mean
others will feel the same. No other responses so far.

I'm around tomorrow if you'd like to chat? My mobile's 07700 900412.

VX

From: valerie.morrell@nortonmorrell.co.uk
To: williammendez75@gmail.com
Subject: INTEREST FROM CAPE!!!
Date: Monday, 30 November 2009 12:17:43

Jane Jones at Cape is 'interested'. She 'adores' the way you write, she says, and loves the story so far. But 'in the current climate' (blah, blah, blah...) she says she is 'not sure' if they can make you an offer on a partial. Long and short of it is: they want to meet you (as do I!) and find out a bit more about what you have in mind. It's not an offer, but believe me, they would not do this if they were not very close.

So, what are your movements over the next week? It feels like a while since I heard from you. Please check in just so I know you're OK.

All the best,

Val x

PS No word yet from others, but when I pass on news of a bite from Jane that might speed things up...

William dear, I hope you are well and haven't had your computer stolen or something? No doubt you are very busy... I really do need to get your response to Cape asap.

In other news, Canongate have passed, I'm afraid. Loved the book, but no partials at all right now, they say.

Best,

Valerie x

From: valerie.morrell@nortonmorrell.co.uk
To: williammendez75@gmail.com
Subject: **STOP PRESS! BLOOMSBURY INTERESTED!**
Date: **Monday, 7 December 2009 17:08:31**

This should get your attention: Matthew from Bloomsbury just phoned me out of the blue to say he thinks *Publicity****** is 'brilliantly roguish' and all his colleagues found it 'great fun', adding that he has 'just about seen enough' to back you and is 'dying' to see the rest. How much he'll pay, I couldn't say, but he does sound keen. And Bloomsbury and Cape are a great pair to have fighting over your book!

This means I really do need you to get back to me now, William. Matthew and Jane both want to meet you next week, and it will look very strange indeed if I don't tell them something from you soon.

Vx

PS I did smile when Matthew also pointed out the parallel between Petes Doherty and Sheen, as well as – of course – between Calvin Vance and that poor boy Alfie Marsh. The moment Calvin went up on to the roof, he says he was thinking of Marsh and what happened to him. And so it proved. Naturally I explained your purpose (to invite parallels of all kinds with real celebrities) and he seemed to understand. You would have been proud of me.

Hi Val – just got your emails. Wow! This is all very exciting! After years
of working on this book, I am just so thrilled that someone might want to
publish it! This really could be a dream come true for me, and I will always be
incredibly grateful to you for your help. I don't have my diary with me at the
moment, but I'll write back soon to work out the best way to meet up.

What you say about Alfie Marsh does intrigue me too. I really don't think he
was such a 'poor boy', actually. He is often portrayed that way now, like he was
a kind of saint, but I think he knew what he was doing at that party – and was
generally quite a careerist little shit, by all accounts. (Like I say, the media
always take real people and repackage them to their audience's taste.) Marsh
didn't deserve to fall off a roof, of course, but... well... I can think of others
who'd deserve it less. Like Calvin in fact, who, yes, is partly based on Marsh,
but I've made him a bit younger and more naive – almost a victim of celebrity
culture, rather than one of its proponents. That's the idea anyway.

Sorry I've been out of contact, by the way. It's complicated. But at least it
hasn't stopped me writing! Here's the next bit.

W

The noise took so long to arrive that it briefly seemed as though it might not come at all. Then it did. A heavy thud – not loud, heavy. And textured, like a box of books. Mike stared down after it for a while, making little gasps.

Then, 'Oh my God,' he said finally. 'Oh my God.'

There was a passing bluster from the wind.

'He just fell,' said Mike's mouth, dangling from gazing eyes. 'Hugo,' gesticulating now, 'you understand, don't you? He just fell.'

But Hugo had already turned away.

'He just fell,' said Mike behind him, as their feet rattled down the stairs. 'He just fell, you've got to believe me.'

Landing. Banister.

'You've got to believe me, Hugo. I just said his name and he fell.'

Staircase. Kitchen. Door handle.

'I tried to get his legs, but he was kicking around.'

Garden. Lawn. Rockery.

'Hugo!'

And oh my God there he was.

But it was no longer a he. It was an it. Lying on its back, arms by its sides, legs at crazy angles – one folded under, another twisted round an ornamental basalt. No real person could lie in that position, it just was not convincing, like poorly executed sculpture.

And there appeared to be some blood on its neck.

Mike pounded over.

'I believe you,' Hugo said. He thought he did.

There was another little gust of wind. Birdsong even.

'Calvin, are you OK?' Mike asked the thing.

It gave no reply. Not a twitch.

'He just fell,' he added. 'Is it serious?'

'Yes,' Hugo said.

'I mean, how can you tell . . .?' Mike began, approaching closer.

'Don't touch it!' Hugo screamed, startling himself. 'Wait!'

He ran across the lawn to the glass doors and tried the handle. Locked. He ran back past Mike towards the kitchen, adding 'Wait!' again, as if to a dog.

To the hall. Up the stairs. Into the empty first-floor bathroom. Little finger smears upon the tiles. Just a trace of errant powder. Shit. Guests' coke everywhere. He'd have to clean it all away. If the police came . . . Well, Mellody was certainly screwed. And she'd just bought that massive . . . Fuck.

In the cupboard a large washbag. In the washbag – yes – a mirror.

Downstairs with it.

Fuck.

Media room. Still warm.

Fuck. Fuck. Fuck.

5:59, said the TV. *EXTRAORDINARILY SERENE*.

Hugo turned it off. Unlocked the double doors.

Sorry, he wanted to say to someone. *There's been a terrible mistake. I was just in here. I only went up for a beer. This isn't supposed to be happening to me. I'm in someone else's scene. Could we just wind back a page and go again? I'm fine to go again. Sorry everyone. Ready? Ready to go again?*

'Did you call an ambulance?' Mike asked, following in fretful attendance.

Hugo ignored him and knelt down carefully, crushing a

cluster of spring buds into the earth. He wiped the mirror and held it in front of the thing's nose and mouth, trying not to touch the skin.

Condensation. That was what he was searching for, like they did in old movies. *Condensation*. He needed Calvin to breathe, and then get up and be OK. *Condensation*. No, wait a minute. *Condensation*. That wasn't going to happen. This thing was not getting up. This thing had plans to lie here waiting for the world to come and ransack Hugo's house. *Condensation*. They would find everything. *Condensation*. He needed something else. *Condensation*. He needed Calvin to be dead.

The mirror was perfectly clean.

A yellow trickle eased its way through the child-pink gulleys of the ear.

So this was what it was like, Hugo reflected calmly, to be the villain.

'*Hugo*? Did you call an ambulance?'

Michael struggled to speak clearly.

Still Hugo did not answer. Perhaps he was in shock.

'Did you call an *ambulance*, Hugo?'

What the fuck was he doing? Just standing there! Wake up!

'I think he's dead, Mike.'

Oh.

A tide of perfect terror rolled through Michael's gut. This was it. The stall on take-off, the call from the hospital, the test results, the word in private, the shooting pain down the left arm . . . He felt dizzy. All of this was so familiar, and yet misplaced. Surely *his life* was not where all of this belonged?

He could still feel Calvin's trouser legs in his hands.

And was he about to vomit?

The urge subsided. He sat down in a baffled heap.

'Shouldn't . . .' He was shaking. 'Call an ambulance anyway? Supposed to do.'

He reached for the phone in his jacket pocket but found that he was not wearing his jacket.

'It's pointless, Mike.'

'But,' he said. 'No.'

'It is.'

'Let me call. I'll call. My phone's inside.' Michael stood up to get it.

'Look.' Hugo stopped him. 'He fell three fucking storeys on to some rocks! He's not breathing. That is a corpse. We will call, but it won't make any difference, so let's tidy first.'

'Tidy?'

'There's been an accident, Mike, so when the ambulance gets here, they will bring police.' Hugo was a natural authority. 'And when the police get here, they will see the mess from people's drugs everywhere, and we will be arrested.'

'*Arrested?*'

The word did not sound real in Michael's ears, so he said it again.

'Arrested? But it was an accident! I haven't taken any drugs!'

'I saw what happened, Mike.'

And Hugo looked at him with steady eyes.

And was there something in his voice just then? Something intended? Something not so friendly? It seemed that way to Michael, and startled him, but perhaps he was being paranoid? Stress did that, didn't it? Made you paranoid? He had to calm himself immediately. He couldn't. Oh God, he was freaking out . . .

'Jesus, sorry Hugo . . .' His voice teetered unevenly, almost a yodel. 'I'm freaking out a bit. What do you mean you *saw what happened?*'

He was shivering. He wanted to cry.

'Don't worry, Mike.' A warm hand settled on his shoulder. 'Let's just clear up for two minutes and then we'll call an ambulance. OK? Everything will be fine.' Hugo's face was kind. 'But we're not going to save him, Mike. Do you understand? Calvin is dead. Yes? You start in there.' He pointed to the television room. 'Pick up any paper or bags or anything you think might be drug-related. Then check the kitchen and work your way upstairs. Flush whatever will go down and give the rest to me. Yes? There's a loo in the hall, and two bathrooms upstairs. I'll start on the roof and work down.'

What was he doing here? Why was he not asleep at home? This could not be happening.

'It was an accident, Hugo.' The desperation. 'You saw.'

'Yes, Mike. I saw. I think we should be quick.'

'Where did you put all that coke?'

The door banged in against the skirting board. A swipe of air burst across Mellody's face. She felt it on her eyes.

'Hey sweetheart.' She blinked. 'How are you?'

'Jesus Mellody,' he said, sniffing the air.

'Mmm.' Sulking schoolgirl face.

'Listen. Where did you put Pete's coke? It was coke, right? In that bag?'

'You want some coke, honey?'

'No, Mell. Christ. We've got to get rid of it.'

'Hmm?'

Hugo was being all serious. Even more than usual. And trying to make her serious too. Why did he have to get so *stressed* about everything?

'We've got to get rid of that coke, Mell. Everything else too. Now.'

'But . . .' She had flushed away her drugs *so* many times. It

just seemed *wrong*. And it was so *boring* having to go score again
. . . 'OK, OK,' she sighed eventually, to get him off her back.

'Where *is it* then?' So impatient.

'That's *my* fookin coke,' growled Malcolm from the bathtub.

Hugo jumped. Literally jumped.

'Fuck, Malcolm!'

'And it's my smack and all.'

'Jesus. OK. Well either you flush it, or you get out of the
bath and take it home. Make your choice, and do it now.'

'For fook's sake.' Malcolm rose up naked from the water,
dripping like a solemn Poseidon.

Mellody erupted with laughter, which evolved into a
coughing spell.

'Here's a towel.' Hugo tossed one over from the rail.

'I'll have one last hit while you get dressed,' she said quietly,
recovering. 'All right, Malkie?'

'Fill your boots.'

But her practised hands were already at work. Kind of a
shame Hugo had to see it. Though if he must burst in on people
like that.

'So what is the big drama?' she asked nonchalantly, without
looking up.

'Jesus Mell.' Hugo really was exasperated. 'Calvin's had an
accident, OK? Either get your shit together or go to bed. You
look like fucking Terri Schiavo.'

Mellody stopped. Malcolm left off toweling himself for a
moment. His eyes were back to double brown.

'What kind of accident?' she said.

The foil quivered in her fingers.

'A bad one. As soon as that coke is gone I'm calling an
ambulance. So be quick.'

'An ambulance?' She was confused. Tried to lift the blanket
off her brain. 'What's happened?'

'He's in the garden. He fell.'

What was Calvin doing in the *garden*? She hoped he was OK.

With the towel around his waist, Malcolm hitched the drape aside and peered round it.

'I can't see him,' he said.

Mellody nodded, and gently crushed the tube between her lips. Heated, the dose acquired a melting roundness, then leapt off into a trickle, filling up her chest with rich and comfortable smoke.

Hugo was saying something to Malcolm. He liked to take charge. Mellody remembered that time when they went sailing with her parents in East Hampton and he . . .

'Mellody!'

Oops, now he was talking to her.

'Mm?'

'Where did you put the coke?'

'Mmm-mm . . .' She would not release her breath before its time.

'I'll go *get* it, if you'll just fucking *tell* . . .'

The bathroom door flew open once again, chopping off his anger at the stump. Odd. It was that weird guy from Cuzco, Hugo's pal. He looked around, pale and desperate, then rushed in, flung up the toilet seat, and vomited mostly in the bowl.

Though at other times he might have, Hugo did not laugh at all. Not now. Not while thoughts of *Sinbad*, Renée, Warshak, prison, tears and paparazzi assailed in rapid waves his tenuous calm. And questions: about tomorrow, about last night, about any minute now. Questions about questions about questions. With no time. Which simplified. It made him powerful and sane.

'Fucking hell,' was all Malcolm was saying, tangling with his jeans, as Mellody grimaced, ping-pong eyed, and strained to regulate her exhalation.

Finally she succumbed to a cackle of fumes.

'Ha ha ha . . .' she coughed. 'Ha ha . . . ha!'

Hugo held his face strictly to attention. He would defend the perimeter.

'Are you all right, Mike?' he asked, as the heaves subsided.

'I'm so sorry Hugo.' The reply was almost tearful. 'I'll clean everything up. I'm so sorry.' As Mike spoke, he offered up a fist, unclenching slowly for inspection. At first Hugo did not understand, but then he saw that he was being shown a crumpled cast of napkins, cocktail sticks and bits of fluff that Mike had evidently taken to be drug-related.

'Thanks,' he said, and stuffed them quickly in his pocket. They made him sad.

'So where's the coke, Mell?' Malcolm asked, now fully dressed, and almost businesslike.

'Oh. Ummm . . .' Her voice rose heavily from the deep. 'I think it's, um . . .' A smiling face gazed. 'Maybe in the other bathroom?'

'Right,' he said. 'Bye all.' And left.

Mike was drinking water from the tap.

'You're Matt, right?' Mell said.

'Michael,' said Mike. 'We met at the club. I'm . . . I'm so sorry.'

'*Enchanté*.' She proffered her hand obliviously, fingers extended to be kissed. But Mike just waved back and tried to smile.

Hugo looked at his wife, pupils like full stops, scratching at her arm.

'Hey baby,' she said, noticing his glance. 'This . . . It's just a smoke, you know? For tonight.'

'Sure.'

'To get through it.'

'Uh-huh.'

He made his voice sound cold. Agreeing words, spoken with scorn, denying equally the relief of absolution or the satisfaction of a fight.

'Is little Calvin OK?' she said.

'I don't know.' He gathered up the scraps of foil around her, preferring not to talk about it now.

Spontaneously, though, he held her head and kissed it. The hair smelled of smoke, and of her own perfume.

'Got it!' Malcolm bellowed from the floor beneath them.

His heavy footsteps faded downwards.

'OK,' Hugo said after a deep breath. 'I'm going to make the call.'

He descended to the first-floor living room and picked up the phone.

His ears thudded. His intestines pumped.

Outside the window now, Malcolm could be seen wading placidly through paps. The plastic bag swung from his fingers with the careless ease of morning Jaffa Cakes and milk. He stopped to light a cigarette, puffed benignly at his audience, and set off slowly towards Notting Hill Gate.

The receiver droned in Hugo's hand. Veins bounced with excitement in his wrist.

Do it do it do it, his blood impelled him.

At the brim of the moment.

On the verge of the stage.

'999 emergency,' said a bored female voice. 'Which service do you require?'

'I need an ambulance!' Hugo opened up the gate and let some panic out.

'Connecting you now.'

'Ambulance emergency.' This time it was a man who was bored. 'What number you are calling from?'

'020 7946 3342.'

The plastic rattle of a keyboard.

'Can you confirm that number in case we get cut off?'

'020 7946 3342.'

'And can you tell me the address of the emergency?' Lines recited with the sing-song cadences of habit.

'Number 8, Cobalt Street, London WII 8AE.'

'Can you just confirm that address, sir, to make sure I've got it correct?'

'Number 8, Cobalt Street, London WII 8AE.'

'And are you calling for yourself or someone else?'

'Someone else.'

'And what's the problem?'

'He just fell off my roof.' Hugo ventured a gulp. 'I think he might be badly hurt.'

'Somebody's fallen off your roof.'

'Yes. We have a terrace up there, and he was lying down, and then I think he slipped off.'

'OK. I'm just going to ask you some questions now, sir, but it's not delaying any help. OK?'

'OK.'

'Is your friend conscious?'

'No, erm . . .' And with a tremor of uncertainty: 'I don't think so.'

'Can you tell if he is breathing at all?'

'I tried but . . . Fuck, I'm sorry. I just don't know. Sorry.'

Flustered. That sounded good.

'That's all right, sir. Can you tell me the patient's age?'

'Er, about twenty-one maybe? I don't know him very well. Young.'

'And just to confirm: the patient is male.'

'Yes.'

'And are you with the patient now?'

'No.'

Hugo made to go downstairs until he noticed the telephone cord tethering him in place.

'OK. Did you see if your friend had suffered any specific wounds or injuries?'

'Erm, his head is bleeding, I think, and his legs are at funny angles. I don't know. I thought it was best not to touch him?'

'So can I confirm: his head appears to be bleeding and you think both his right leg and his left leg might be broken?'

'I think so, but I don't know.' Hugo added a dash of exasperation. A little stiffener.

'And do you know if your friend has taken any drugs or prescription medications in the past forty-eight hours?'

'He's had a few drinks, I think, but I haven't been with him.'

'Have you ever received any first-aid training, sir?'

'None. I mean, I think maybe I did once, but I can't remember any of it.'

'Don't worry, sir. That's . . .'

'Are the *ambulance* people on their way?'

A frightened interruption.

'Yes, sir. They should be with you in just a few minutes . . .'

'I mean,' with flailing urgency, 'is there anything I can do? I don't know what to do!'

'You've done the right thing calling us, sir. Help is on its way. The best thing you can do would be to stand by the door and let the ambulance crew in as soon as they arrive.'

'Yes. OK. I'll go and do that. Yes, of course. Thank you.'

'That's OK.'

'OK. Bye.'

'Goodbye.'

But Michael's life could not be cleaned up. Once alone with Mellody, to give himself a reason not to look at her or speak, he had started to apply himself with pages of a toilet roll to soaking up his warm, mid-processed porridges of blini, scotch and crab. And it was frustrating work. Double, even treble, thicknesses rapidly grew limp as seaweed in his hand, stirring up the poisonous tang of vomit, which (alone among the body's excrements) offered no proprietary savour to his nose. After tolerating this for longer than expected, Mellody left the room. But still Michael continued cleaning – now with the help of some Cillit Bang and sponges that his explorations found beneath an artful tiling flap. His work completed, he flushed the mess away, sluicing out the solutes from his sponge inside the stagnant bath. Which committed him, he felt, to cleaning that out too. So he released the plug and watched it drain while wiping round the rim. Grey suds and smoker's jetsam drifted almost imperceptibly at first, then joined each other in collapsing orbits down towards the hole. When the gurgles finished, just four drowned homemade butts remained, clinging to a raft of hair. Cannabis, Michael supposed; the air was steeped, besides his vomit, in another pungent smell. He wadded each in tissue and dropped them in the toilet, before firing a destroying cord of urine through the mash. Then as the cistern filled itself again, he washed his hands and raised the blinds and Hugo's second bathroom blazed with virtuous day. But Michael's life could not be cleaned up. Because now he remembered:

He had killed someone.

Oh fuck! Oh Jesus! Help me *please!*

No. He had killed two.

For not only had he ended Calvin's life ('by accident' meant nothing), he had just as surely finished off the Michael that he once had been. The one who watched bad films and nit-picked grammar. The timid failure whose story ended, likewise, with a moment of high spirits on a roof. And to replace him, a new

Michael had been born. The killer. The Michael who ends. In place of Sally and the happy faces of his past, his fellows now were West and Shipman, the bonded boy teams of the Congo, the excruciation officers in Syria and Myanmar. That unassuming garden thud had stamped his entrance to their league. Name: Date: Victim: Method: His authorising signature in blood. And no remorse. Not for Calvin anyway. If anything, he felt resentment at the intimacy now that joined him always to that ignoramus. And fear, yes, of what would follow. Paramedics soon, then police, then press.

Though it *was* an accident. Hugo saw. He said he saw.

The cistern's silence meant it had reloaded. Michael flushed, and quickly went downstairs.

'I mean . . .' The urgent whimper reached him from the drawing room. 'Is there anything I can do? I don't know what to do!'

Michael halted six steps high, his weary gait suspended in a tension jelly.

'Yes,' Hugo said meekly, to silence. 'OK. I'll go and do that. Yes, of course. Thank you.'

Silence replied.

'OK. Bye.'

An object touched another. And then there was no sound at all.

Michael stood paralysed with interest. Was there some hidden importance in what he'd heard? Had Hugo betrayed him? Had they been caught?

No. He yanked back his thoughts. He was being paranoid. He needed to calm down. Information gained in secret always wore a sheen of intrigue. This was the overhearing spell, the intimacy hack. He sniffed with self-contempt, and the action seemed to produce Hugo, standing in the doorway.

'You all right, Mike?'

'Yeah, OK,' Michael said. 'Is the ambulance coming?'

'Yes. They said I should wait by the door.'

'Right.'

'What did they say about Calvin?' Michael asked, as they walked downstairs. 'Did you say . . .' *he was dead?* was meant to follow, but the words would not come. 'Did you say . . . what happened?'

'Yes. They just asked me a lot of questions and I answered them.'

Michael watched the back of Hugo's head as it bobbed purposefully down into the hall.

He could not help saying: 'Did you tell them it was an accident?'

'They didn't ask. They just said to wait by the door for the paramedics.'

He did his best to appear satisfied with this. Once the ambulance arrived, he would have to start saying it was an accident quite often.

They had reached the door.

Beside it, Michael noticed two small screens, relaying video of the paparazzi who remained outside, a pale and tattered band, grimly established in the intervening crevices of cars and urban furniture. One young man, taking his ease beside a monstrous zoom, was reclined across an elbow on the garden wall, two white filaments of flex converging from his ears into the upholstered interior of his coat. Behind him, another, older, sat smoking in a silver Mercedes, lens wedged into the crook of window and door, as two wasp-toned parking tickets flapped beneath its heavy windscreen mono-wipe. On the bonnet, with or without permission, another man loomed above the morning's *Sun*, which he had weighed securely open with a flashgun and a Starbucks tub. Breaking off from the group, absorbed in a phone call, one of their fellows ambled into the road, gesticulating angrily.

An old red-wine-coloured taxi rolled lazily around him, for hire.

Michael heard footsteps.

'I, um,' Mellody said behind him. 'I think Calvin's really hurt.'

She was leaning on the banisters with just a few too many degrees.

'Yeah,' Hugo said after a moment. 'Well the ambulance will be here any second.'

'Mmm . . .' A crunch of puzzlement in her brow, and then nothing, as if she had forgotten what she wanted to say.

Everybody looked at everybody else.

'I know CPR,' she strenuously announced.

'Listen, Mell, darling.' Hugo approached her slowly, depositing a gentle hand on the junction of her waist and hip. 'Seriously, why don't you just go to bed? It's going to get pretty hectic when the paramedics arrive.'

'But he's just lying there.'

'I know. I've called 999. Help is on its way.'

'Why didn't you call before?'

The question was posed as a child would ask it – curious, unaccusing, ready for the reasonable explanation that would surely come. Michael returned to the door, trying to arrange his back like that of a man who was not listening.

'You know that, Mell.' Hugo was adult calm. 'We had to tidy up. We couldn't let people in with all that coke in the house.'

'But, um . . . I think Calvin is really hurt.'

Michael stared at the screens.

'Let's wait and see what the paramedics think. OK?'

A transmitted ruffle of excitement swept across the faces of the men. Through a blue strobe fanfare, the ambulance appeared, a speeding block of purpose, liveried in yellow bright enough to disinfect.

'I just think, in this situation . . .'

It hurtled to a halt, unmistakably in front of Hugo's house.

'. . . that you might find it less stressful upstairs.'

First one, then all of the photographers hurried with their equipment to the far pavement – inexplicably, it seemed to Michael, until he realised that they were positioning themselves to frame both ambulance and house together. Two impassive paramedics stepped out into a fusillade of light.

'Hugo,' Michael said, not turning.

They were a man and a woman. They wore moss-green boiler suits and carried bags. They jogged towards the gate.

'I think the ambulance is here.'

The doorbell was ringing.

Hugo snatched a slim zinc handset from its mount.

'Come in,' he said, and buzzed them through.

Everybody looked at everybody else.

Something was being shared. Relief? Conspiracy? Fear?

Hugo broke the moment and opened the door.

'Hi!' he called down the path, untroubled by a hail of shouts and flashes. 'He's at the back!'

'Please show us,' said the woman, running in with equipment.

And now Hugo was leading them down the hall. Michael hurried in attendance.

'What's his name?' the woman was asking, as Hugo swung open the back door.

'Calvin,' he said, entering the garden.

'And tell me what happened?' She was middle-aged, maternal, her accent delicately Londonised.

'I don't know exactly.' Hugo sounded desperate again. 'We went up on the roof. He was lying down by the edge. And he just – I don't know – slipped off.'

And there Calvin still was. Some part of Michael had been hoping he might have vanished. Or that he would be sitting up now, rubbing his head, perhaps, and wincing through a fag. But no. That crumpled shirt. Those same mistaken legs.

He felt sick again. He did not want to look.

'The *roof*?!' said Mellody.

Everyone ignored her.

'Kelvin? Can you hear me, Kelvin?'

The woman could have been talking to an aged resident. The man passed her something. A torch. She shone it into the boy's eyes, lifting the lids roughly with a grey-gloved thumb.

'Kelvin? Just blink if you can hear me, Kelvin.'

'The roof?' said Mellody again.

Michael hung back. Neither paramedic had looked at him yet. Perhaps, if he went inside, he could avoid being noticed altogether?

'Had he been drinking before he fell?'

Hugo was gazing vacantly at the patient. He said nothing.

'Sir,' the man took over while the woman worked, 'do you know if he had been drinking?' His cockney tones were harder and his face was thin, with glasses, and the geek-gone-wrong demeanour of a tabloid perv.

'Oh, er, maybe,' Hugo's voice was hollow, a withered thing. 'Yes, probably.'

'How about drugs?' the man continued. 'Any prescription medicines? Heroin? Amphetamines? Cocaine?'

'I don't know.' Hugo turned to Mellody.

'Coke,' she said. 'I think. Ketamine maybe. No heroin.'

Hugo was pale.

'And it's *Calv*in,' Mellody added.

'Sorry?' If the man was excited about meeting Mellody and Hugo Marks, he gave no sign of it.

'*Calv*in. Not Kelvin.'

'Thanks.'

'Pupils are fixed and dilated,' the woman said.

'Is he OK?' Mellody asked.

'We're trying to find that out,' said the man. 'Thanks for your help. We can take it from here.'

Hugo was staring straight at Michael – had been staring, Michael realised, for a while. And the stare was loaded, delivering significance. It *meant* something.

Michael looked hopelessly back.

The famous eyes jerked downwards, and returned. Jerked downwards, and returned.

Michael did not understand. He tried to look sympathetic. He wanted to go home.

Frustration gripped Hugo's face.

Something about Calvin. Something about Calvin was important.

Michael did not want to look.

The gaze congealed.

Michael did not want to see. The blood, the death, the consequences of his actions, the walls of his eternal cell.

He stepped forward.

There was more blood on the earth, but not much. A bump was forming where the boy's head had met the railing. How touching it was that a corpse might still be busying itself with minor matters. And now the paramedic woman was fitting a clear mask and bag over Calvin's mouth. Did that mean . . . ? No. Michael saw no breath or movement. Masks, no doubt, were regulation optimism.

He aimed a glance at Hugo, formulating sorrowful and resigned.

Unsatisfied, the famous eyes jerked downwards, and returned. Jerked downwards, and returned.

Had Michael missed something?

He leaned over the male paramedic's head.

On Calvin's shirt. That was funny.

A garden snail and its sparkling scar of mucus were stranded in a dash across the silk.

The woman brushed it off with her sleeve.

'Can you give us some room, please!' she said.

From: **valerie.morrell@nortonmorrell.co.uk**
To: **williammendez75@gmail.com**
Subject: **Re: STOP PRESS! BLOOMSBURY INTERESTED!**
Date: **Wednesday, 9 December 2009 09:22:56**

Morning William – mightily relieved that you're OK! I just got an email from Jane as well, pressing for a meeting with you at their offices, so I think we do need to fix a date today. You don't have to be a charmer or a genius, just turn up and show her you're a chap she can do business with. (And Cape's sales and marketing people may want to say hello too.) So: please name the day. I need one for Bloomsbury too. I have a cattle prod in one hand, and a bullwhip in the other. Don't make me use them…

Now I think about it, your book does have quite a strong foundation in the Alfie Marsh/Harvey Green case, doesn't it? I remember Green also talking about Marsh's legs being 'at funny angles' in his 999 recording. Perhaps you're right about Marsh, in retrospect. He has been canonised somewhat.

Valerie x
PS I'm off out later this morning, but I'll be on my BlackBerry all day. Why not give me a call on 07700 900412?

From: williammendez75@gmail.com
To: valerie.morrell@nortonmorrell.co.uk
Subject: Re: STOP PRESS! BLOOMSBURY INTERESTED!
Date: Wednesday, 9 December 2009 10:54:04

Morning Val – very promising stuff all this, and do tell Jane how excited I am, but I have my diary in front of me, and work is simply torrential just now. I really don't see a window coming up. Why don't you ask them to email me? I'd love to hear from them, and would be happy to answer any questions.

And yes, for the record, I was partly inspired by the whole Harvey Green affair, although I would not describe it as the foundation of the novel. If anything, Chris Heath's book *Feel,* about Robbie Williams, and *The Insider* by Piers Morgan, have been greater influences.

W

From: valerie.morrell@nortonmorrell.co.uk
To: williammendez75@gmail.com
Subject: Re: STOP PRESS! BLOOMSBURY INTERESTED!
Date: Wednesday, 9 December 2009 10:59:02

Hi William – email won't cut it, I'm afraid. Partial deal is leap of faith for these guys, so you need to show your face. Why not just call in sick tomorrow and meet then? Get it out of the way?
Vx

Sorry Val. This is so frustrating. I do desperately want to meet Jane and Matthew to talk about this – I'd do it today if I could. But I can't. I've thought about it, and I just can't. Maybe we could ask them to make their offer first? Or see if they can wait a few weeks? I should have foreseen this situation; it was stupid of me to let things get this far. But I'm working like crazy right now. Surely both of them will still love it in a few months?

From: valerie.morrell@nortonmorrell.co.uk
To: williammendez75@gmail.com
Subject: Re: STOP PRESS! BLOOMSBURY INTERESTED!
Date: Wednesday, 09 December 2009 11:58:56

Doubt they'll be so keen, to be honest. Want this deal now, to pre-empt competition. And you will look v flaky if you back out. Any publisher will expect to meet you anyway. Why not swap a few hours' work on the book for 2 meetings with adoring editors? We are on the pot, I'm afraid, and it is time either to relieve ourselves or disembark. Which? V

Sent from my BlackBerry wireless device.

From: valerie.morrell@nortonmorrell.co.uk
To: williammendez75@gmail.com
Subject: **Need that decision**
Date: **Wednesday, 09 December 2009 13:20:21**

Just got a call from Jane. I said was not sure on meeting yet. Need date asap pls. Vx

Sent from my BlackBerry wireless device.

Morning Val,

I've been thinking about it, and I might be able to arrange for someone I know to go along and represent me. If so, it would probably be next week. Could you check with Jane/Matthew if that's OK?

Thanks,

William

Not a hope, William. Sorry. Why can't this bloody fellow come himself, they will want to know. And, to be honest, I do too.... Though I'll admit I have a theory.

I may well be brandishing the wrong end of this stick, but are you, by any chance, working under an assumed name? People do. The thought occurred to me a couple of weeks ago, when you were away and I was trying to get in touch quite urgently. I called the *Times* to see if they had a phone number for a William Mendez, but they said you didn't work there. I explained you were freelance, and someone went through a list to check, but there was no Mendez of any variety. Then my assistant called round the other major papers (she gets bored and tries to impress me), and none of them said they knew you either. A bit of a mystery, you will agree...

But look, here's my view on all this: piffle! I've got most of a splendid book in front of me. The author's neither dead nor loopy. Who cares if he masquerades as a subeditor called William Mendez in his spare time? I'm sure he has his reasons. Trouble is, I need the author of this book, whatever his name actually is, to meet a publisher, smile and take their money. Otherwise no book deal, no funny blurb on the jacket, no 15% for Valerie. People don't swap contracts with invisible men.

So tell me, is your real name William Mendez? Because if it isn't, and you own up, then we can still save this. I'll tell Jane you're writing under a pseudonym; she'll say, 'Oh, how exciting!'; you'll turn up to meet her incognito; then we all get rich off your talent. And no one need find out who you really are. Please think it over. I'd hate for this to fall through.

Yours, as ever,

Val x

From: williammendez75@gmail.com
To: valerie.morrell@nortonmorrell.co.uk
Subject: Re: Need that decision
Date: Sunday, 13 December 2009 00:40:23

Dear Valerie,

What can I say? First of all: congratulations, you're right. William Mendez is not my real name. And it is a great relief to say so. Secondly, yes, I do have my reasons. Nothing dramatic or exciting, I fear, but sufficient to prevent me from meeting you, or the publishers, for the moment. I would love to be more open, but, for now, I can't.

If this means you can't represent me either, of course, then there will be no hard feelings. But I do still desperately want to make a deal, so if you or Jane or Bloomsbury or anyone can find a way around the problem I would love to hear it. Not just for the money, though that would help, but because your comments and support have only proved to me how much I do want people to read this book when I finish it. Which – honestly – won't be long now.

Please consider what I've said and let me know what you think.

Yours,

'William'

Thank you for your honesty, whoever you are. And sorry to have badgered you so. I may be batty, but it's nice to know I'm not completely paranoid. Will talk to Jane and Matthew to see if a solution can be found. Please do not let this raise your hopes, however. They would already be going out on a limb in buying an incomplete book, so this added complication, I expect, will snap it. Do keep the chapters coming, if you can, but do also be prepared for disappointment...

Vx

From: williammendez75@gmail.com
To: valerie.morrell@nortonmorrell.co.uk
Subject: Chapter 8
Date: Monday, 14 December 2009 22:14:21

▶ 📎 <u>Chapter 8 – Medics</u>

Fingers crossed...

A fucking snail.

Hugo looked around for something to destroy.

A fucking, fucking, fucking . . . *snail.*

He glared at the tousled silk, ruffled now by wind that hid the creature's trail within its folds. And for a dead moment, he allowed himself to wonder if he had imagined it. That tight brown curl of crust perched upon its rain-grey muscle, straining forward through a skirt of slime. Had these been the weavings of exhaustion? The paramedic's demolition arm, a frustrated gesture: could it have been aimed at empty air? Hugo *was* tired.

He looked again. But it was obvious. Obvious if you knew. No shell, no. But there, where two soft ripples ought to billow separately, they didn't. Inside that space was something sticky. It was obvious if you knew.

The paramedics worked fast, bulleting letters and numbers to each other, and jotting them with ballpoint pens on to their gloves.

They knew.

And behind them, Mike stood looking on, holding his arms with an unnatural stillness, like a volunteer dragged up on stage. On the sternum of his shirt a small cream speck of puke had stuck, from where it leached a dark surrounding blot. He glanced back up at Hugo. He knew.

And now he was silently mouthing something, repeating it overtly with his clumsy rubber lips.

Mumble mumble . . . *at a snail?*

Hugo nodded very slightly just to make him stop. And noticed, as his eyes slid round in doing so, that Mellody – perhaps – was watching.

He stopped nodding.

Stopped too quickly maybe?

He was panicking. Making mistakes.

He needed Renée. Her tyranny was called for. Could he ring her now? Would that be seen as callous? Would that be seen? He needed action, some steady line of purpose from which to hang his thoughts. Then he almost – dear God, *almost* – found himself offering the paramedics each a cup of tea.

Or, *'Is he dead?'*

He could say that. That surely was the most important question.

And yet he did not trust himself to ask it. The words would come out wrinkled with anxiety, yes – but it must be the right kind. Not the eager panic that he felt, a restive vulture hopping on its claws. He must be the brave spectator, watching, iterating his rosary of regret. If only . . . if only . . . if only . . . if only . . . Oh yes indeed, he almost smiled, he could count off a few of those.

'Is he dead?' he said.

The paramedics worked fast, said nothing.

Hugo did not find encouragement in their faces.

Perhaps – and this was a promising possibility – perhaps they had not really noticed the snail at all? Perhaps that brushing-off had been an act of instinct, already half-forgotten, lost within the matters at hand. The implications, at any rate, surely could not yet have been assembled.

How fast were snails anyway?

Slow. Famous for it.

But fast enough to slither, what, at least two feet, before the ambulance arrived?

Whatever. No medic with so young a corpse beside them could be considering such matters. They would surely for the moment still be on his side. Yet the man and woman's concentrated faces did not look like those of friends. In itself, this was not uncommon: the proud, the practical, the underpaid, such people often liked to flaunt their lack of reverence in Hugo's company. It can't have been a pleasure wading through those rancid paps at such an early time of day. But still he thought he smelled distrust. And it did not help that Mike kept such a guilty distance, or that Mellody was loitering beside him with her droopy girl concern. Could the paramedics read her pinprick eyes? The signs looked parodically obvious to Hugo in the morning sun. It was all so humiliating. As if these sensible professionals had been summoned here not principally to clear up their mess, but more to shame them all for making it. What once had been his garden now had become their place to work and tut. The site of one more wasted life. One more misadventure.

'Is he dead?' Mellody asked it this time.

'Is he dead?' Hugo said.

. . . yes, Calvin did look kind of dead. Made of death. Like that stuff Steve Klein used to do. Beautiful but sad.

No: beautiful *because* sad.

Broken. Eyes closed and vanquished. Unfluttering lids of skin shielding a victim's wisdom.

Sometimes she envied the dead.

'Is he dead?' she said.

'It's very serious,' the man said, after a pause. 'We're doing everything we can. Is he married? Are any of you family?'

'No,' Mellody said.

Calvin's family. Hugo had not thought of them before.

'Do any of you know where to reach them?'

Mellody, Mike and Hugo all shook their heads.

'Does he have a mobile phone?' The man was at work. He knew what to do.

'He did . . .' Mellody began slowly, her words drifting idly downstream. 'I mean, I don't know where he put it.'

'Renée,' Hugo almost shouted, hurrying with relief towards the basement doors. 'She'll have the number for his record label.'

He went in, scooped up his own phone, held down 5 and listened to the familiar numeric chirrup as it dialled.

The skin on his neck was cold.

Ringing.

What time was it?

Ringing.

Usually it was Renée who woke him up at dawn.

Ringing.

. . . Surely she would pick up?

Ringing.

She *must* pick up.

'Hugo!' Renée's voice. An overmeasure of alertness in it, an attempt to hide the fact she'd been asleep.

'Hi,' he said, not knowing how to begin.

'What's up?'

Once before, reshooting *Sinbad*, Hugo had known a now like this. Drinking out a long weather delay with the director, he had flippantly suggested that he leap in person from the pirate ship's high mast if the moment ever came to film that scene. Two days later, he was taken at his word. The thirty-foot fall, they told him, had been sanctioned by the film's insurers, and everyone was waiting eagerly. Immediately, he knew the deed was just too frightening to be done, yet he agreed to climb up for confirmation with the stunt co-ordinator. And when he got there, and gazed out across the quiet waves that stretched as far as he could see behind his crash mat, the knowledge struck him. His standing on this picture – perhaps across the industry forever – now teetered on a point in time. This one. Now.

'Erm,' he said. 'Something terrible has happened.'

'Calvin? Blink if you can hear me Calvin?'
    They had done that already. Why were they doing it again?
    'Try wriggling your fingers or toes, Calvin.'
    Stillness.
    The purple crescent moon of entry inked upon his hand.
    There was one on her hand too.
    Mellody looked at it.

'OK,' said Renée. 'Something terrible has happened.' It was just a calm restatement.

    'You know Calvin Vance?' Hugo began. 'Mellody brought him back to the house.'

    'Yes. What's he done?'

    'Nothing . . . I don't know . . . Anyway, I mean, he's had an accident. He hit his head and fell off the roof. Mike tried to grab his legs and . . .' There was only one important word, and Hugo nearly could not bear to use it. '. . . I think maybe he's dead.'

    Silence.

    'This is the young guy, right? *X-Factor*?'

    'Yes.'

Silence.

'When did this happen?'

'Just now.' Hugo scratched his neck and leaned awkwardly against the thick French doors. 'The ambulance guys are outside with him.'

'Ambulance guys?'

'Yes.'

'Why didn't you call me before?'

'Jesus, Renée! I'm calling you now.'

'OK. OK.'

'Anyway, look, they said we should get in touch with his family. And none of us know who they are. Could you call his record label and get them on to it?'

Some gasps and exertions indicated that Renée was getting out of bed.

'I'm coming over,' she said.

'OK. But you'll call his label, right? I think,' Hugo sought the right words, 'you know, that we should make sure we do the right thing.'

'Yes. And I'm coming over.'

'OK.'

'Just wait there. Be helpful. Don't say anything to anyone until I arrive, OK?'

'OK.'

Mike was sidling towards him.

'Oh, but Renée!' Hugo shouted urgently into the phone.

'Yes?' She was still there.

'What if the police come? I mean, I can't exactly refuse to talk to them. Wouldn't that look suspicious?'

'Of course you should talk to the police, Hugo. Have you called them?'

'No. It was an accident, and . . .'

'Fine. Well, if they show up, just co-operate, be nice, and

wait for me to get there. But don't go calling anyone else, OK? And make sure none of the others do either.'

'It's only me, Mellody and Mike here.'

'Good. OK. See you in twenty minutes.'

'See you then.'

Mike stood before the open door, gaze on the ground, shoulders pinched forward and narrow, arms digging deep into his trouser pockets. He looked up when Hugo finished the call, saying nothing. Then his eyes burrowed back into the grass for cover.

'Renée is going to talk to Calvin's people,' Hugo said.

'What are we going to do?'

'What do you mean?'

This was getting irritating. Would this guy ever pull himself together?

'I want to tell the truth,' Mike said.

'What do you mean you want to tell the truth? We have told the truth. Don't close the door!'

Mike's hand sprang away from the handle. Behind him, the garden quietly breathed.

'Hugo . . . ,' he began.

'Look.' Hugo did not want to listen or explain. 'Renée will be here soon. Let's just sit tight until then.' If he was a hypocrite, then it was Mike that made him so.

In the distance, Mellody appeared to be bending down over the body. Speaking, it appeared. And the male paramedic was speaking to her.

'You're going to be OK.'

She wasn't supposed to touch, but she could say it.

'Don't worry, everything's going to be OK. The doctors are here, and they'll look after you. Just, you know . . .'

She was going to say relax. But was that right? Perhaps it was a battle in there? You couldn't see with the tubes and stuff all over him. Maybe he was tired and ready to give up? So tired. Like in films. Maybe to relax meant to surrender? And it made a big difference that stuff, in the mind. Her grandfather had had a stroke nine months after retiring, when Mellody was starting out. *Just didn't want the freedom, I guess*, Grandma had said, not with sympathy, at the funeral.

'. . . just . . . stay,' she said.

Poor boy.

The medics hoisted hard at each end of the stretcher. Hoisted kind of roughly, Mellody thought.

'Where are you taking him?' she asked.

'Trauma unit.'

The woman was holding up a bag of fluid with her teeth and backing rapidly towards the kitchen.

'I'd like to come.'

'It's better if you stay here, madam,' the man replied. 'He's in good hands.'

'Could you open the door for us, please?' the woman said, interrupting any protests.

Mellody stepped round to take the handle and scuttled inwards with it, crushing herself into the wall. Through the pane, she saw Calvin's head flicker past into the kitchen, encased in a padded orange box. An hour or so ago, she and that broken boy were having sex. She could still feel the trace of him.

'What is Calvin's surname?' the man asked.

Mellody realised that she didn't know.

'Um . . . I can find out?' she said.

'That's OK. When you find his family, just tell them to call Charing Cross Hospital.'

'OK.'

'You've got that, yeah? Charing Cross Hospital.'

'I got it.'

They had reached the front door. Mellody opened it.

Photographers clustered round the ambulance. Flashes and shouts.

The crew stepped briskly down the path.

Mellody watched Calvin's disappearing body.

She closed the door.

'Uh . . . we need to find Calvin's family!' she shouted to the house.

And again, stumbling across the hall: 'We need to find *his family!*'

With a dreamy determination, she tried to supervise her feet, which swayed and sped regardless, bouncing her against the banisters, the wall, and finally into her husband's large, unloving hold.

'Where are they?' she demanded of his face.

'Jesus, Mell. Calm down,' it said. 'Renée is on her way. She's calling Calvin's label so they can call his family.'

'What . . .' breathlessly, 'the fuck happened?'

Hugo sighed, as though bored by the question.

'*What the fuck happened?*' she repeated. Such effort it took.

'We went up on to the roof . . .' Mike began, but Hugo spoke over him:

'He was wasted, Mellody, OK? He was lying over the edge of the roof when we got up there. Mike went over to see if he was OK, and he just fell off. I doubt he could even walk, to be honest. What the fuck had you given him?'

'Why . . .' She was beginning to crumble. She knew the signs, little shifts and settlings, a burning building's intimations of collapse. 'Why didn't you call the ambulance? Before?'

'It would have made no difference. You saw him.'

A gloomy acquiescence held.

'He might die,' Mellody managed to say.

'Mm?' said Hugo. He seemed not to have heard.

'They think he might die, Hugo. He's got spinal damage, um, ineffective breathing . . . um . . .' What had that woman said into her radio? '. . . suspected subjural . . . heema . . .'

'But he's not *dead*?' Mike's eyes were wide. His and Hugo's faces looked kind of blue.

'No,' she reassured them. 'There is . . . um . . . . ineffective breathing, and . . .'

'Oh,' said Hugo. 'Good.'

They were blue. Everything was blue, flashing blue.

'It's the police,' Mike said.

For a moment, Michael heard nothing. He was deafened by a pressure wave of joy. Innocent: a word for children and for passers-by. And now he knew it as a feeling. He was *innocent.* Calvin was alive. And he was innocent.

'But he's not *dead*?' he asked.

'No,' said Mellody. 'There is . . .' she hesitated, unsteady on her feet, 'ineffective breathing, and . . .'

'Oh good,' said Hugo.

Trying to be so cool about it. Like he cared. Like Calvin was what mattered here. The too-calm tone. Those tightened cords of brow. Michael saw it all. Oh yes. Very good. The lizardly relief. There had been no such signs of sympathy before.

From the street, an urgent perforating light.

'It's the police,' Michael said, referring quickly to the screens.

And even now, as he looked back at Mellody and Hugo, he saw that they were beautiful. Blonde and brown; she quite tall, he taller. Her powdered slenderness, though gripped there, fitting in his torso's groove. His negligently dashing grade of beard. Such specimenship, never better seen than in its mussing up.

For a while, they just stood looking as he looked at them.

But from outside, and rising, a jostled hum was leaking in, broken through with shouts that burst like bubbles of excitement on the surface.

'It sounds like there's a lot of media out there,' Hugo said eventually. 'Mike, when the bell goes could you answer it?'

Michael did not know what to say, so he said, 'OK.'

Then the bell did ring, loud and shrill and real. So he lifted up the handset from its cradle, did not listen, and applied his finger to the buzzer.

And it was strange, but when Michael opened the door it was not the two policemen marching up the path that took his attention, nor the sleek and gleaming silver car they had left cooling at the kerb. It was the sudden memory – surging so strongly to his mind that the first officer had to say, 'Good morning, sir' twice in order to be heard – of Monty Python's *Life of Brian*. It was that scene, when Graham Chapman gets up in the morning after having sex with Sue Jones-Davies, and he opens the shutters and he looks out on to the street below, and there, tucked doggedly into every point of vantage . . . It was the mob.

Michael actually looked down, to check he was not naked.

Dear William,

Bad news, I'm afraid. Jane and I met earlier today, and though she remains mustard keen on your book, she says she cannot approve a deal without an author. I've checked with Bloomsbury, and they said (with some surprise) that they assumed they were going to meet you too. (Frankly, we all did.) On people's minds are the following: the legal problems of an anonymous contract, the question of your reliability in finishing the novel, the difficulty your absence might present in the editing and production process, and most of all, I fancy, the fact that they would have no author to promote *Publicity****** in person. I also detect some anxiety from both of them about where the story is now going, especially in the last two chapters. Virtually everyone who has read them cannot escape the similarities between what is happening to Calvin/Hugo and the story of Alfie Marsh and Harvey Green. I actually knew very little about the case until they mentioned it to me, but after a bit of Googling I have to say that I do see their point. Nor is it much of a stretch to see Michael as a version of that creepy advertising guy Daniel O'Nolan, while Mellody is very obviously a reimagined Vesta Green. Real-life 'inspirations' are fine, of course, but this looks like someone advancing a theory about what really happened, the families might argue, and at times I'll admit that it does come across that way to me. With the matter still under police investigation, I fear that you might have to make substantial changes to the story if you are going to avoid legal problems.

For various reasons then, I think we have to consider the whole thing belly-up. I am so, so sorry to be saying this, but we have talked about little else over here, and nobody can see a way out. I know this will leave you badly short of money, but if you can somehow find a way to finish the book (and perhaps distance it a little from the Green/O'Nolan case) then I would be delighted to resubmit it – and I would do so with great optimism. Do keep sending me your chapters, if you can face it. It is a pleasure to read them.

Affectionately,

Valerie x

Dear Valerie,

That is very sad to hear, and of course I'm bitterly disappointed. If Jane and Matthew have to meet me, and I can't come, then plainly we are at an impasse.

Though on the legal point, for what it's worth, I must admit I cannot see the problem. Yes, I have already said that the book is influenced by the Alfie Marsh case, but that does not mean that I am writing specifically about it. Besides, in the coming chapters I've dramatically accelerated the aftermath of 'Alfie's' fall anyway, so that the whole story now plays out in a completely different timeframe. There are also so many precedents for this sort of thing that it seems perverse to single me out. *Robinson Crusoe* was based on the case of Alexander Selkirk; *Kavalier and Clay* is a patchwork of true stories; even Basil Fawlty originated with some real Torquay hotelier, didn't he? So why shouldn't I put real things in my book? If I invented a new character in the next chapter, a tabloid editor called 'Rebekah Wade', say, and completely fabricated everything she did, that would not in any way purport to be a picture of the things that the real Rebekah Brooks/Wade has done, or would do, because it would be obvious that I'd made it all up. And the parallels you mention seem far slighter.

But then of course this counts for nothing if we can't do a deal. And I suppose we can't, which does leave me short of money. Still, 'something will turn up', I imagine. Dickens's dad used to say that, didn't he?

W

PS By the way, I'm also intrigued by your impression that Daniel O'Nolan was a 'creepy advertising guy'. This idea, much like Marsh's canonisation, has always struck me as a media concoction. Having decided that Marsh was an innocent victim after his fall, the papers needed a perpetrator to blame for it, and O'Nolan, who was not on the original guest list and had no influential friends, was the obvious candidate. By criticising journalists for hassling him, moreover, he only incited further abuse. Just look at how they subtly stitch him up:

- 'Ever since that night [Green's party], O'Nolan **has insisted** that journalists hounded him **"incessantly"**.' (BBC website)
- 'The 35-year-old former advertising copywriter, who has been **on the run** since 2006, is **wanted by police**...' (Telegraph)
- 'O'Nolan, **described by colleagues as "an oddball"**, has not been seen since ...' (Mirror)
- '...**lone gatecrasher**, twice arrested and released, before **bungling officers lost track of him**...' (Sun)

Is this *really* evidence of him being creepy? Or does it merely demonstrate that it is fun to paint him that way? Michael's naive awkwardness, in my story, shows that there are always other explanations.

From: **valerie.morrell@nortonmorrell.co.uk**

To: **williammendez75@gmail.com**

Subject: **Re:**

Date: **Friday, 18 December 2009 08:18:55**

Understand your frustration, but publishers can only go on the advice their lawyers give them. Sorry. Will be in touch if anything changes.

V

From: williammendez75@gmail.com
To: valerie.morrell@nortonmorrell.co.uk
Subject: An idea
Date: Monday, 21 December 2009 22:17:02

Look, I've thought of something. I can't believe I didn't think of it before, actually. It's a bit sneaky and unusual, I'll admit, but it works – and everyone would win in the end.

How about I suddenly relent and agree to meet the publishers? Then they make their offers, I sign a contract, take the cash, and perform all their promotional capering? Fantastic, right? But what if, actually, the person who turns up and does all this is someone else – another writer probably, anyone who can talk the talk. It's my book, after all, so I can give the copyright to whoever I like. (Joe Klein did something similar with *Primary Colors*, you'll recall, and, lawyers aside, the JT Leroy stunt worked beautifully too.) The only deception is that the volunteer would have to say that they wrote all these emails to you, which is irrelevant. Surely some impoverished hack can be found who would be willing to do that in exchange for a cut of the proceeds and a bit of exposure?

And think about it: either we never get found out (which is, I suppose, possible); or we do, in which case I confess everything and we leak it, generating lots of publicity for the book. And *then* what is the publisher going to do? They'll feel deceived, of course, but they're not exactly going to go round every Waterstone's pulling copies off the shelves, are they? And if you're worried about your reputation you can always delete this email and claim that the impostor and I cooked up the deal without your knowledge. I won't tell.

It's brilliant, isn't it? A bit mad, I know. But think about it. If you're not keen, I'll totally understand, of course. Although in that case I think it would be best we call it quits. I've been working on this book incessantly for months, and I really can't carry on much longer without more cash. So if you don't want to help me choose a surrogate, I think I'd better down tools, find some paying work, and then make a fresh start with another agent when I can finish the book.

So... Know any writers who are going hungry this Christmas?

William

From: **valerie.morrell@nortonmorrell.co.uk**
To: **williammendez75@gmail.com**
Subject: **Re: An idea**
Date: **Tuesday, 22 December 2009 09:02:47**

Hi William

Let me think about this over the holidays and get back to you.

Regards

Val x

OK William, I'll probably regret this one day, but let's do it. I can't bear to see you penniless, and you're right: as long as the book sells, your publisher will forgive you. To protect my own livelihood, however, I will want to disassociate myself from the scheme before anybody rumbles it. And, if you are ever asked, you must obviously say that I knew nothing.

When it comes to choosing an impostor, clearly this means I can't suggest any of my clients either. (It would be too obvious that you met them through me.) This complicates things, but I do know someone who might be suitable. His name (it has to be a 'he'; your book is incurably male) is Leo Benedictus. Leo is a freelance feature writer with the *Guardian*, late 20s or early 30s I think, who I met through a friend at the Edinburgh festival and still bump into occasionally. He has been working on a sort of post-postmodern novel for several years, but he and his wife also have a baby boy now, and Leo was telling me just the other day that the writing has ground to something of a halt. He is a merry sort of cove, however, with a taste for provocation, so he might be game for your scheme. I don't think he has an agent, so I could take him on briefly, as long as he swiftly 'decides' to abandon me for someone at a bigger agency once we have an offer in writing. If we do this, however, I'd need to take my commission out of your royalties in cash.

If you're happy with all that, let me know, and I'll speak to Leo straight away.

Best,

Val x

Oh Val... I honestly could not *be* more excited! Leo sounds perfect! I'm actually punching the air with my left hand and typing this with my right. (A tough trick. Try it.) I've had a look at his stuff online – immigration, theatre, interviews, television... bits and bobs, right? He's a different type of writer from me, in some ways, but not too different to be believed. I see he's done stuff for the *London Review of Books* too, which can only help, can't it? Do you think he knows anyone on the books pages of the newspapers? It would be very useful if he did. So yes, do approach Leo in a dark alley and make him see things our way!

Meanwhile here's the next chapter for you to have a look at. (I'm moving really quickly now!) FYI, I've decided to ditch the opium tincture plotline since Mellody's on the junk again. It felt bohemian and exciting when I put it in, but now it just gets in the way...

Yours cheerfully,

The Elusive 'William'!

Here!

'Sir.'

Here! Over here!!

Michael made a sort of noise.

'We've had reports of a serious accident at this address, sir. May we come in?'

He, 'Er yes, sorry, yes,' stood back into the hall.

What happened? shouted from the street.

Who killed him? looked for a reaction.

And *Me-elllll!!!!* with fresh impetus from one cluster. Then *Mell! Mell! Over here, Mell!* craved the rest, fearful she had been spotted, but not by them. Or, like chicks, straining to produce her with their force of need.

'Sorry to trouble you this early, sir, and with all that going on,' said the policeman, back-nodding as he shut the door. 'Are you the householder here?'

He was young, black and polite, like policemen were supposed to be. Michael could imagine him being badgered constantly to do recruitment posters, or stand guard at televised events. Not so his colleague, who was white and older – a little too old, in fact, to be a beat copper with a future. This man, by the sagging look of him, preferred a life of modest torpor, with its locker-room authority and regulation paunch.

'No,' Michael said, as soon as he understood that the question was serious.

'Could we speak to the householder please?'

But Hugo, and to a certain extent Mellody, were already approaching.

'Morning, officer,' Hugo said, offering a handshake which the policemen accepted. 'I live here.'

'Morning, sir. Do you have anywhere we could talk? My colleague and I will need to ask you a few questions.'

'Sure. Let's go into the kitchen.'

Hugo led them through, taking calm control of things. His composure was a parent's hand that Michael longed, despite himself, to clasp.

'Can I ask, did any of you see what happened?'

Like the ambulance crew, the policemen gave no hint of excitement.

'Yes,' Hugo said. 'Mike and I did.' He gestured to the kitchen table and its chairs, but the men declined to sit.

'Mike . . . ?' the policeman asked, pencil poised.

'Knight,' said Michael, yawning to disguise a shiver. No policeman had ever taken his name before.

'And your full name, sir?'

'Hugo Marks.'

'M-A-R-K-S?'

'Yes.' He was filling up a tall and shiny metal kettle at the sink.

'And Miss?'

Mellody had arranged herself with lopsided equilibrium on the surface of a stool. Her eyes were closed and her chin rested in the cup of one hand.

'Miss?'

'Mellody,' she faintly said.

'Mellody Marks,' Hugo confirmed. 'My wife.'

Surely the policeman knew?

But, 'Thank you,' he said routinely. 'And I believe you've been having a party. Is that right?'

'Yes.' Hugo took over. 'My birthday.'

'I see. Congratulations. And did anybody else witness the accident?'

'I don't think so.'

The policeman nodded and made more jottings in his notebook while his colleague's eyes reconnoitred the kitchen and its dressings with suspicion.

'So can you tell me what happened?'

'Well, about half an hour ago . . .' Hugo began. Michael did not flinch. '. . . me and Mike went up on to the roof, and saw Calvin lying there. He didn't look very well, and he was leaning right over the edge, almost off the edge in fact.'

'I see.'

'And Mike went up to him to check he was all right. That was it, wasn't it?'

Michael croaked up an assent. Its smallness sounded shifty and reluctant, so he said 'Yes' afterwards, for clarity.

'And then he . . . Well, it looked like he just slipped off. I don't really know what happened, to be honest.'

The kettle had begun to mutter.

'Do you remember touching him in any way?' the policeman asked, turning to look Michael directly in the face.

'I, er,' Michael said. His breathing ceased. 'I did sort of try to catch hold of him when he fell.'

I didn't knock him off or anything. The words bellowed for permission to be spoken. But he overruled them. Too suspicious. Would most men say that? He began the experimental transposition of his thoughts, trying to imagine, but found the task too difficult, like chess.

'How could you see he didn't look well?' the older policeman asked pleasantly, but without warning.

'Sorry?'

'I mean, if he was leaning over the edge and you couldn't see his face.'

237

'Oh, right.' Michael felt sick again. How could he have seen? Did he see? It was Hugo who had said they saw. 'Well, I think I just sort of assumed . . .'

'It's a party, late at night, people have a little too much of whatever . . .' A drone of reassurance from the fat man, feeding him relief.

'Exactly.' Michael swallowed.

'I thought he was being sick, too, to be honest.' Hugo helped him.

A funnel of steam bullied at the window pane, causing it to run with drops.

'And after he fell, you came down and called 999?'

'Yes,' Hugo said. 'Tea?'

'No thank you, sir.' The young policeman answered for them both. 'Could we just have a look at where all this happened? Starting with the roof if we may?'

'Sure.'

And Hugo had put down his cup and started walking.

'He was leaning off here.'

The side of Hugo's house veered out to meet his downward gaze, a swaying plane of brick perspective. He had never really noticed the drop before. It was substantial.

'Bent over the railing?' the younger officer asked helpfully.

'No, he was on the ground, where that towel is.' A further shake of the head and a solemn 'Jesus' conveyed Hugo's concern.

'So he had already crawled under the railing when you arrived on the roof?'

This seemed to be stating the obvious. Hugo wondered if he had missed something.

'Yes, I think so. Although Mike saw him first, didn't you Mike?'

'Yeah,' Mike said, but hanging back. 'He was just lying there.'

'I see. Had he seemed unhappy or depressed to you at all?'

This thought had not occurred to Hugo before. And it tempted him. Worried about his work, humiliated probably by Mellody, too much to drink . . . Young men often did commit suicide. Or think about it on roofs. Would Calvin's suicide be better for him than an accident, or worse?

Mike just shrugged and looked unhappy.

'Well,' Hugo said. 'He seemed fine to me, but I didn't really see much of him, and I suppose you can never tell. He mentioned he was quite anxious about going on tour to Korea, I think. But we'd only met once before tonight.'

'Oh, all right. Famous is he?'

'Yes. Quite. He was on *The X-Factor*. I don't think he won.'

'*The X-Factor*, eh?' The older officer seemed to think this was important.

'Yes,' Hugo said.

'He'd been hanging out more with Mellody,' Mike added, in answer to an older question.

'I see.' A mild inflection was just detectable in the black officer's voice. The most delicate pointedness. And was that, as he noted down Mike's answer, was that also an eyebrow being raised?

'My wife did spend quite a lot of time with him tonight, I think,' Hugo agreed. 'I don't know what they talked about.'

Near the front of the roof, the older officer was distastefully examining a Marc Quinn bronze.

'Sorry, would it be OK if you came a bit further back?'

Hugo beckoned him away. 'I think we can be seen from the street over there.'

It was true. You had to go close to the edge, but if you did, and somebody was looking, then they couldn't miss you. Hugo and Mellody had half-heartedly applied to raise the wall, but then the 'fucking British planners' got involved and began objecting by the inch.

'Calvin . . . *Vance*, was it?' The black officer snapped a page back in his notebook, hunting for a surname.

'Yes,' Hugo said.

'I think I remember him actually. And have his family been informed?'

'Someone's working on that now.'

'I see. I see.'

For a time – it seemed a long time – the officer said nothing and made notes.

'And at what time exactly would you estimate that Mr Vance fell?'

'Oh, I don't know,' Hugo said, and he didn't. 'Maybe half an hour ago? It feels like longer.'

The officer looked at Mike, who was slow to notice.

'Sorry, yes, something like that,' he scrambled out eventually.

'But after he fell you went straight down to call 999?'

'Uh-huh. I think so.'

'Well, we ran down to check on him first,' Hugo supplemented this, 'and then I went back inside and called the ambulance.'

The time of the call would be recorded, of course. As would the call itself. *Someone has fallen off my roof.* Was that what he'd said? He could not remember exactly. Or was it 'just'? *Someone has just fallen off my roof?* He should have taped the call. The villain would have taped the call.

'Thank you, sir. Could we take a look in the garden now, please?'

'By all means,' Hugo said, with too much courtesy in retrospect.

Through the open kitchen door, as they marched along the hall, Michael could see that Mellody had gone. Just the jilted kettle now put life into the room, a thermal of declining wisps curling from its spout. He did not want to go back into the garden again, to talk it through again, and feel his cheeks betray his lies. Though Hugo, naturally, seemed unconcerned. He led them briskly down the stairs into the media room, where the extinguished television glowered silently and grey. On the drinks cabinet an almost empty whisky bottle sat, and on the floor beside the table, two glasses, unnaturally abutting, as Michael had arranged them while he wiped the surface clean. Suspiciously clean, he guessed now, glancing at it nervously, if one was experienced and looking. But suspicious of what? If Calvin died through their delay, was that a criminal matter? Or Michael's silent creeping and his sudden shout, were these already crimes? He had meant no harm by them. Not physical, at any rate. In his mind, the crime was *this.* The ambulance not called, the police deceived. Obstructing justice, or perverting its course. It was not right. Of that he was quite sure. Yet he had done nothing to prevent it. Was *still doing nothing.* Besides trying not to lie.

He stooped to pick up his jacket, which had somehow wrapped itself around a chair leg. A familiar density bumped against his chest as he swung the left sleeve on. His phone in the pocket. And he had a text.

It was from Sally, sent at 1:41 a.m.

Ah, well we're all self-indulgent bores deep-down, it said. *Say hi back to him from me if you ever ACTUALLY meet. x*

If he let himself, Michael knew that he would cry.

'Excuse me, sir.'

He wanted to go home.

'Mr Knight?'

'Yes?'

The older policeman was peering at him from outside.

'Just a couple more questions.'

'Sorry, of course.'

Standing sideways with his arms outstretched, the man was indicating that he was expected to join them.

'. . . that he was really badly hurt,' Hugo was saying. 'Isn't that right, Mike?'

His tone was friendly, cheerful even.

'Hm?'

'The officers want to know what happened when we saw him, so I was just saying that we thought he was badly hurt and needed an ambulance. We were a bit stunned for a while, though, weren't we?'

The rocks were coated darkly with a liquid skin that pooled down from an overlap of footprints in the earth. Only in one or two places, where sunlight nicked the surface, did Michael spy luxurious glints of red. It bothered him, for some reason, more than Calvin's body had.

The whole thing was an accident, he would say. *I might have startled him*, the words would be indelible once said to the police, *and I panicked. You don't know what it's like. Until it's you, you don't know what it's like. We were going to call the ambulance straight away, but when we came down and saw him . . . it was such a big fall. And Hugo was worried about Mellody. She was upstairs, with old friends. People who might have drugs.* There, he would have said it. *With everything she's been through, we just didn't want her to get into trouble. Her friends left and we called 999. It must have been five or ten minutes. If you'd seen his body.* Michael was trembling. Now was his chance. *If you'd seen him lying there* . . . He opened his mouth.

'Yeah, it was a big shock,' he said, and because the policemen seemed to wait for more: 'He was lying in a really, sort of, unnatural position.'

'I see.' The older man seemed to be in charge now. 'And was he conscious? Moving around at all?'

'No, that's why we were worried.'

'Did you attempt to revive him?'

'I . . .' Was this what he should have done? Was this a test? 'No, I mean, he looked really hurt. I didn't want to move him. I think I said his name a few times.' It sounded so feeble now. And had he even done that?

'Did you try to establish a pulse?'

A raw synthetic rasp cut through the radio on the young policeman's shoulder. 'Roger that,' he said, having somehow understood it. 'I'm just making the assessment now.'

'*I* will make the final assessment,' his colleague corrected him, with weight and age. Then, 'Sorry, sir, can you remember if you tried to establish a pulse?'

'No,' Michael said. He was becoming upset. 'I don't know how to do it. I just thought we should call an ambulance as quickly as possible. And Hugo said he wasn't breathing.'

'Did you *examine* his breathing?' The man turned to Hugo.

Had Michael said too much? He didn't care.

'Yes, I forgot that,' Hugo said, extending a placating palm. 'When we found him I ran inside to get a mirror, but I couldn't see any breath on it when I held it against his mouth. Is that the right thing to do?'

The policeman ignored the question.

'And that's when you called 999?'

'Yes.'

A door – it seemed the front door – slammed inside the house, jerking all heads in its direction.

Mellody? This was Michael's worried thought. She had looked exhausted, so getting up to leave implied a sudden sense of purpose. And she would be seen, of course, and photographed and questioned.

'We'll need to seal off this area,' the young policeman said to Hugo. 'And the roof as well.'

'Fine.'

'And I'll need to ask that you both remain here until the investigation team and the SOCOs arrive. They will probably be a few hours, so you may want to get some sleep in the meantime.'

'Sorry, the sockos? I don't know what a socko is.' Hugo's voice was tauter.

'Scene-of-crime officers. They collect forensic evidence. Please don't touch anything until they get here.'

'I see.' Now it was buttery. 'And they'll search the whole house will they?'

'Oh no, sir!' The policemen shared a laugh at the very idea. 'Just the immediate vicinity of the incident, to gather evidence for the investigating team. It is standard procedure in cases of unexplained serious injury for...'

'*Unexplained?*' A momentary loss of Hugo's cool squeaked out. 'We just explained it to you.'

'I understand that, sir, but for the purposes of an inquest or any future criminal investigation we need to collect all the evidence at the scene of the incident.'

Now it was the kitchen door that opened and shut. A twice-reflected sting of sunshine from its window caught Michael in the eye. And emerging, as his sight recovered: a figure. A woman, not Mellody, in heels and a business suit, stabbing rapidly across the lawn.

'Good morning, officers,' Renée said.

'Good morning, madam,' they replied together, like class-mates.

'I'm Renée Santos, Mr Marks's business manager. I hope you've been given everything you need?'

'Thank you madam, yes.' The older policeman sounded keen to please.

'I don't wish to interrupt your work, but I'm sure you understand that we have a developing situation out front with the gentlemen of the press. Your superintendent has kindly agreed to set up a security cordon on the pavement and to station officers at the gate, but I need a few minutes with Hugo so we can work out how best to control things, if that's OK? Nobody wants this to get out of hand.'

She had taken out a notebook of her own, and made ready to write in it.

'No, madam,' the policeman agreed, gulping something down.

'So with your permission, I'd just like to talk to these guys inside for a few minutes. Is that OK?'

'That's fine. We need to tape off the scene of the incident anyway.'

'Excellent.' Renée wrote this down. 'This is my card. Call me if you or your men need anything at all.'

She gave them one smile each, and turned back towards the house.

Michael followed, gratefully.

'Hi Renée,' Hugo said, as they approached the kitchen door. 'Thanks for coming. And that was really nicely done. I think we need to get in touch with LA, pronto. Someone should still be awake. This is no big deal, but you know what jittery fuckers they are, and we need to make sure they hear about it from us before . . .'

'What the living *fuck* is going on?'

She shut the door and stared at them both.

A pristine slap of newspapers lay across the table.

'Hullo?'

Mellody had picked up her cellphone and said the word before she knew what was happening.

'Mellody, hi. It's Rebekah Wade. From the *Sun*. Is everything OK?'

'Mmmm?'

She must have fallen asleep. The kitchen counter rolled solidly beneath her.

'Rebekah from the *Sun*. Sorry, did I wake you?'

'Yeah.'

'God, I'm sorry about that. It's just that I'm hearing stuff about an accident at your place. Are you OK?'

Calvin! Calvin!

'Is everything OK, Mell?'

The ambulance guys had taken him away. The cops. Where had everybody gone?

'Is Calvin dead?' Mellody said.

There was silence on the line.

'That's not what I'm hearing at the moment.' Rebekah's voice was quiet, not encouraging. 'It is head injuries, they say. Are you at home?'

'Yeah.'

'OK. I've had to send some guys down to cover this, of course. I'm sorry about that. But they're going to behave themselves. The other papers . . . I don't know.'

'Mmm.'

Mellody remembered Rebekah's big red hair. She trusted her slightly.

She stood up.

She sat back down.

'You're going to have TV down there all day, I'm afraid, until something happens. If you like, I can have a word with Rupert about Fox and Sky's coverage when New York wakes up, but I doubt we'll get much joy on that, and the BBC will still give it everything, of course. As will everyone else, I expect. Are you and Hugo going to do a statement, or . . . ?'

Mellody stood up again, steadier. The skin on her arms was dimpled by the cold.

'I don't know,' she said. Rebekah's questions were floating around her. 'Er . . . I don't know.'

'OK. It doesn't matter. Listen, I was calling to make a suggestion. Tell me to get lost if you want, but we keep this very quiet cottage for people to use in emergencies. And I thought, maybe you already have your own plan, but if you want it for the next few days, it's yours.'

'A cottage?' Why were they talking about *a cottage*?

'Yes. It's totally discreet, in Kent somewhere – even *I* don't know exactly where it is.

'Kent? Like the cigarettes.'

'Yes.' There was an amused width on the word, but Rebekah did not laugh. 'It's yours if you want it. I also have a great driver who is brilliant at getting out of situations like this. I mean, I know you have your own guy, but if it's easier, we could have you out of there in ten minutes, before the TV people arrive. Then you could take the weekend, or as long as you need, and see how you want to handle things. The police can come and speak to you if they insist, of course. But no one else will find you. You have my word.'

There was no mention of Hugo.

'Um . . .'

'This doesn't have to be for a story. You don't have to talk to anybody. You can just owe me one, OK?'

Mellody could not *deal* with this now. She needed another hit, just to settle things. Perhaps Giles would be able to bike some over, if he could get it through the paps.

'It's totally up to you, Mell, of course. I'm just here if you need us. You've got my number, right?'

She crept into the hall.

Noise from the street.

A sudden shadow on the front door. The sharpened slot of a key.

Mellody swerved into the dining room just as the door began to open, scraping her shoulder on the corner of a case containing one of Hugo's dumbfuck model boats. At first it didn't hurt and then it did.

The front door slammed.

'Mell?' Rebekah said.

Renée's footsteps, loudly unmistakable, battered down the hall.

'Mell?' the phone said. 'Are you there?'

In the kitchen: the smacking down of stuff, the opening and shutting of the garden door.

'I'm here,' Mellody said quietly.

'Thank God. You had me worried for a moment!'

'Listen, um, I just don't know what's going on right now.' She watched her ghost, reflected in the glass, shrugging at its injured skin. 'I just want Calvin to be OK . . . We're kind of trying to get in touch with his family, and . . .'

'Do you have their number?'

'No. I mean, I don't think . . .'

'I'll find it and get it to you within half an hour.'

The kindness. The motivated kindness. She heard it all day long. And yet today it did not mean nothing.

'Thanks.' The word emerged a little croakish.

'And listen, don't worry about the safe house. Call me if you need it, ignore me if you don't.'

When Mellody had been in rehab, reporters offered vodka

at the compound fence to any patients who would talk about her progress.

'But if things start getting too much, remember I can have that car over there in ten minutes.'

They had found a dealer she did not remember who said she fucked him for a $100 bag and printed it the week her grandma died.

'I'll have the driver park round the corner just in case.'

You never get out of bed with the press, Karl, her agent, always said. The trick was choosing when to get in.

A wrenching of the kitchen door gave way to Hugo's voice.

'. . . in touch with LA, pronto,' it was saying, just like Hugo would. 'Someone should still be awake. This is no big deal, but you know what jittery fuckers they are, and we need to make sure they hear about it from us before . . .'

'What the living *fuck* is going on?' Renée interrupted him. She did not sound happy.

'OK,' Mellody said quietly. 'I'll, er . . . I mean, I have your number.'

From:	leobenedictus@yahoo.co.uk
To:	williammendez75@gmail.com
Subject:	Hello
Date:	Wednesday, 30 December 2009 10:02:40

Hi William, this is Leo Benedictus. I believe we share an acquaintance in Valerie Morrell? And unless what she told me is an extravagant wind-up, you will know why I am writing.

When Val first put your proposition to me, I ruled it out immediately. Then I decided that the least I could do was read your book. To be honest, I think I was hoping it would be so bad that I couldn't possibly put my name to it. (And I usually do hate things, so that seemed a safe bet.) But from what I've seen so far, I must admit I like it a lot – even though you have the audacity, at times, to write better than I do. So anyway, then I changed my mind and decided to come on board. Then I thought carefully about what I was doing and changed my mind back again. It has been a real case of how I used to be indecisive, but now I'm not so sure... Meanwhile, time has passed, so I thought I ought to write and say something. And now here I am, just playing for time as I try to work out what.

Let's just say I'm tempted, but there are things that worry me. For instance, the whole point of this scheme, from where I sit, would be to pay for me to finish my own novel, and yet I don't know what effect the deception would have on my chances of selling it. The story of our ruse would be bound to gather some attention, but would readers and publishers ever forgive me? For this reason, I confess, I am also rather worried about who you might turn out to be. Anonymity is fine, I think, if that's what you're into. But if I am about to get into bed with a convicted child molester then I, like most people, would like to know about it. And I'm only a freelancer, remember, so the *Guardian* can drop me like a hot falafel if they need to. Is there anything you can say to put my mind at ease on this?

The other thing – and I hope this doesn't sound too mercenary – is that the size of my cut is important. Val seems to think that the best case scenario right now would be if Cape and Bloomsbury bid the price up to around £70,000 for a one-book deal. Minus her commission that would leave £59,500. So if I got involved, taking that figure as a guide, how would you feel about a split that gave you the £50,000 and me the £9,500? Payment usually comes in four equal instalments – on signing contracts, delivering MS, first publication, and paperback release – but because of the continuing risks to me, I would need to take my share up front in one go. I would then pass on all future payments to you in their entirety. The 500:95 split, I suggest, should stay the same no matter what size of advance Val can secure, as long as I am guaranteed a minimum of £8,000 (in multiple instalments if necessary) which should be enough to subsidise a final decisive surge towards the conclusion of my own book. For that, I would be prepared to take a few risks.

I seem to be talking myself into this. Let me know what you think.

All the best, and have a good New Year,
Leo

From: williammendez75@gmail.com
To: leobenedictus@yahoo.co.uk
Subject: Re: Hello
Date: Friday, 1 January 2010 13:56:10

Dear Leo,

Happy New Year to you too! And triple thanks: for writing, for your kind words, and for thinking so carefully about my proposal. I know what a huge favour I am asking, and I understand how risky it must seem.

Unfortunately, I can't tell you anything more about who I am, but I do doubt that the *Guardian* would consider me toxic company, so you're probably safe there. (And I can promise, at the very least, that I am not a child molester, convicted or otherwise!) Financially, however, everything you suggest sounds fine. So if you are prepared to take a gamble, and Val can make the deal, then I would be delighted to have your help. I won't try to talk you into it, because I want you to feel free to decide. My only request is that you tell *nobody* about our plans, even if you choose not to go ahead with them. Otherwise we could soon find ourselves in a situation that is impossible to control.

One other thing, that I scarcely dare ask, is what else you think of my book? No one besides you, Val and a handful of publishers has read it yet, so I have been starved of feedback. Do you find the overlapping scenes work well, for instance? I wonder sometimes if it seems a bit laboured. Did it get in the way of the paramedic stuff? And is the whole book subtly misogynistic? All the major women seem to be harridans or strumpets. I worry about that too. And the style? Good? Bad? Indifferent? Mixed? I put a lot of work into it, I don't mind admitting, but then often I look back at a paragraph that took half a day to write and simply *hate* it. And then there's this Harvey Green business. You've probably noticed some parallels between the book and that case from a few years ago. (Val certainly never stops going on about them.) Do you think it's too much? Or in bad taste? Does it seem to you as if I am trying to explain what I think really happened with Marsh and Green and the rest of it? Would you care if I was? Sorry to pester you, but I never get to talk about this stuff with anyone.

Anyway, just let me know what you want to do about our proposal, and don't worry too much about my insecurities.

Yours,

William

PS I confess I just Googled you, and read your recent piece for the *Observer*, reviewing the book about penises. Sounds hilarious! I'm going straight out to buy a copy.

From: leobenedictus@yahoo.co.uk
To: williammendez75@gmail.com
Cc: valerie.morrell@nortonmorrell.co.uk
Subject: Re: Hello
Date: Thursday, 7 January 2010 10:00:54

Hi William,

In life, you only regret the things you don't do, right?

So yes, we have a deal. I'll meet the Cape and Bloomsbury
people, unmask myself as the real William Mendez (explaining my
reclusiveness as a mixture of shyness and slyness), and submit to
whatever they can think up. I'm quite looking forward to it actually.
Nor is it burdensome to add that I love the book – honestly. I think the
overlaps work well, and it doesn't seem misogynistic to me. Male, but
not misogynistic. The Harvey Green/Hugo Marks stuff is obvious, yes,
but not in a bad way. There are so many other clear references to real
celebrities and situations that I just took it all in as part of the fiction.

Regarding our pact, there is one small issue I should quickly
mention. I know you want me to keep completely quiet about your
involvement, but I can't lie to my wife Sarah about it. Partly for the
good of our relationship, and my sanity, but mostly because I really
can't: she knows all about the book I've been working on, and that
Publicity***** isn't it. If possible, we should also put in a dedication
to her. This is something I'd always promised to do with my first novel
– repeatedly and in front of people – so it might look rather odd if I
didn't. But if you're OK with that, William, well... then I'm ready when
you are.

All the best,

Leo

From: williammendez75@gmail.com
To: leobenedictus@yahoo.co.uk
Subject: Re: Hello
Date: Thursday, 7 January 2010 15:14:44

That's great news, Leo! I'm fine for you to tell your wife (and only your wife), and would be honoured to have her name on the book. I'm really relieved, too, that you don't think the real-life comparisons are overdone. As a journalist, you must often have to think about the legal implications of your work, I suppose?

Anyway, utterly thrilled to have you on board. You won't regret this!
William

From: williammendez75@gmail.com
To: valerie.morrell@nortonmorrell.co.uk
Cc: leobenedictus@yahoo.co.uk
Subject: All systems go!!!!
Date: Thursday, 7 January 2010 15:19:21

Hi Val

Just to let you know, Leo and I have been in contact and he has agreed to go ahead with our plan. Great news, I'm sure you will agree.

So... over to you two!

W

From: valerie.morrell@nortonmorrell.co.uk
To: williammendez75@gmail.com
Cc: leobenedictus@yahoo.co.uk
Subject: Re: All systems go!!!!
Date: Friday, 8 January 2010 14:08:15

Splendid news, chaps! I've been in touch with Bloomsbury and Cape, both of whom are prepared to give this one last try.

Leo, are there any dates over the next fortnight you absolutely could not do?

William, I'll let you imagine my reaction when 'Rebekah Wade' actually did turn up. Touché.

Best,
Vx

From: leobenedictus@yahoo.co.uk
To: williammendez75@gmail.com
Subject: Re: Hello
Date: Monday, 11 January 2010 15:07:30

Thanks William – glad to be on the team! And yes, I think about the real-world consequences of my articles almost constantly. Most things are read by lawyers before publication, but it would still be seriously ungood if I let something through that got us sued. To me, however, *Publicity****** looks fine. Publishers are prob just being cautious.
Best
L

From: williammendez75@gmail.com
To: leobenedictus@yahoo.co.uk
Subject: Re: Hello
Date: Thursday, 14 January 2010 02:04:49

You're so right! I've been getting no end of grief about the legal stuff from Val, who says this book might cause us problems from the police or the Green/Marsh families. But when I emailed her a detailed rebuttal, with quotes, explaining my case, she didn't even reply! (Tiring of me, doubtless, when there no longer seemed to be a deal in prospect.) But that's agents, I suppose...
W

From: williammendez75@gmail.com
To: valerie.morrell@nortonmorrell.co.uk
Subject: Leo
Date: Thursday, 14 January 2010 03:14:34

Hi Val,

I just want to say thank you for setting up this arrangement with Leo. He seems really nice (if a little money-oriented), and I feel pleased now, actually, that we are doing things this way. I am aware that you have risked a lot to make it happen too, so as soon as Leo 'abandons' you for another agent, I promise not to email you any more, and to delete all your past messages so that nobody can link you to the scheme. (Your cash will have to be sent by post, I'm afraid, but I'll make sure it gets there safely.)

Before we wind things up, I want to ask you one last favour. Obviously it's great that Leo writes for the Guardian, but he is hardly a household name (I think he has about 50 Twitter followers), and with literary debuts at the moment... well, no one gives a shit, do they? So I think it's going to be really important to come up with some innovative (read 'inexpensive') ways to publicise the book. One idea I have is that we might launch the first edition with various competitions, offering inclusion in the paperback for the winners, à la Fay Weldon.

- One prize would be for readers. We could encourage them to send in a brief outline (up to 200w?) of a character who might appear at the Cuzco party. Leo would then choose the best one and write it in somewhere, giving the character the winner's name.

- There could also be a reviewing competition – encourage readers to visit the book's page on Amazon or waterstones.com, or wherever, and post their reviews, then two good ones – positive or negative (depending on what we get) – would be quoted on the jacket of the paperback. Obviously we may have to contact reviewers directly if we can't get permission from the websites their remarks appear on.

- Finally, anyone, whether they have read the book or not, should be allowed to get their name and a message in print by simply tweeting it, along with an appropriate hashtag (#afterpartybook perhaps?). The complete list of tweeters and their messages (where legal) would then be printed as an appendix in the back of the paperback. Seems a good shot at generating awareness. Worst Case Scenario 1: we have to print a lot of tweets because it was an online sensation. Worst Case Scenario 2: we print an embarrassingly small list. Oh well.

A central website (facebook.com/afterpartybook and www.leobenedictus.com seem to be free) would be useful to coordinate all this. And if Leo's new agent can sell any foreign rights, the same competitions could easily be adapted for those territories. If people think it's a gimmick, that's fine. The book is all about the things people do for fame/anonymity, and the gap between their private and public selves.

So, could you raise all this with Leo when you see him? I think it should be done face to face, and I don't want to risk offending him by implying he's not famous enough. But I do stress that a scheme like this will be *essential* if we are going to generate interest in the book, so we do need him to be on board. Just say I'd been discussing these ideas for ages, and encourage him to talk them up when he meets the publishers. Would that be OK?

Yours,
William

From: williammendez75@gmail.com
To: valerie.morrell@nortonmorrell.co.uk
Cc: leobenedictus@yahoo.co.uk
Subject: Next instalment
Date: Thursday, 14 January 2010 04:01:44

▶ 📎 <u>Chapter 10 – Crisis</u>

Hi guys. Here's the next chapter. (So you can see what you've been writing, Leo!) They're getting short and fast now, so I should be able to get the last ones to you soon.

And Val, do let me know about these meetings as soon as you have anything concrete. I'm on tenterhooks over here!

W

'Honestly, Renée. It's no big deal.'

Her face flattened with disgust.

'No, seriously.' Hugo insisted. His eyebrow was flickering again. 'Me and Mike went up on to the roof and Calvin was leaning over the edge. I was on the stairs,' *flick, flick,* 'and Mike walked up to him and tried to grab hold of him, but he fell off. It was an accident, we think, but no one's to blame. And the police . . .'

'Are you high?'

'What?'

'What have you had?'

The discomfiting non sequitur. The conversational hand-brake turn. He had seen her use the tactic many times before to ruffle hotel managers, or part lawyers from their poise.

Flick, fli–ick, fli–ick.

'Just some drinks. Nothing. It's fine, Renée. The party went well. Warshak's happy. There's been an accident, but nobody's to blame.'

'Are you *serious*?'

Mike was watching.

'That!' Renée's finger quivered towards the street encampment. 'Is not fine! You think Warshak's going to be happy when he sees *that*? Or Independence? You're fucking right they're gonna be jittery! Their big family movie of the year . . . a 200-million-dollar marketing budget . . . and a storm like this? *Un-fucking-believable!*'

The table gave a startled bounce beneath the flat of her hand. The *Guardian* spun skittering for refuge beneath a chair.

Mike picked it up.

'And have you *seen* the late editions?' Renée's voice breached a new octave of recrimination.

Hugo looked at them.

'*The Pope of Popes,*' said the *Times*, which also offered a sixteen-page 'appreciation' of the dying man. '*IN GOD'S HANDS,*' preferred the *Sun*, superimposing it in red over a picture of the young John-Paul II mid-benediction. A smiling family and a Porsche Cayenne dominated the *Daily Mail*, restricting '*POPE SLIPS AWAY*' to half a page. While the *Mirror* lunged alone for '*FACIAL ATTRACTION: Michael Douglas's agonising face op*'.

Hugo did not understand.

Renée made an exasperated grasp for the *Mirror* and flipped through the pages until she reached the '3am' gossip spread.

'Look!' she said. 'They held it back for us. And look!'

There, in full-page cut-out, staggering in collision with a margarita glass, was Mellody. She looked surprised and, one had to say, not fully in control. Not her youngest either.

'*MELLY'S DRUNKEN HUGO BLAST,*' read the fat, black capitals. It was the *Mirror*'s name for her, though it had not caught on. '*Whoops!*' the text continued. '*Astonished guests watched in horror last night as Mrs Hugo Marks, clearly somewhat the worse for wear, climbed on to a table to deliver a shocking snub to her husband at HIS OWN BIRTHDAY PARTY.*

'*After calling for silence at the £80,000 bash in exclusive Soho members' club Cuzco, Mellody delivered a bizarre speech that had some of London's most expensively pedicured toes curling in their Jimmy Choos. Guests including ELTON JOHN, Mark Wahlberg and Gordon Ramsay could only laugh nervously as first she climbed up on to a table, then tripped over the cocktails of bewildered drinkers, and finally announced that husband Hugo was "31 today". (It was last week, sweetie.)*

'Then, when the embarrassed crowd tried to drown her out with a chorus of Happy Birthday, she angrily refused to join them, yelling, "I HATE HAPPY BIRTHDAY!" Old friend Elton did his best to cover Melly's outburst with a hasty solo on the piano. But she would not be silenced. "Poor Hugo was gazing at her, speechless," said one startled onlooker. "It seemed as if he wished the ground would swallow him up."

'Fans of the celebrity couple, who left the party separately, will hope to see them patch things up soon. But after last night's performance, we think their marriage looks about as steady as that table. Watch out!'

Hugo opened his mouth, but did not speak.

'And now *this!*'

Renée was shaking.

'OK, but . . .'

'No! This is a *disaster*, and we need to fix it. Sit down. And you – Mike – sit down. Tell me what happened.'

She picked her notebook up again. There was a shuffle as they took their seats.

'All right,' Hugo began.

Immediately he was interrupted by the back door opening.

'Excuse me, madam?' asked the black officer, apprehensively. 'Does someone have a key to the gate at the side? Some of my colleagues need a point of access for their equipment.'

'Certainly. Take the bunch,' Renée said, her voice quite changed, plucking three pieces from inside the jangle. 'Use these two little ones top and bottom, and then the square brass one in the middle.'

'Thank you madam.'

'So?' She closed the door behind him.

A nervous dew crept across Hugo's body. It brought with

it something familiar, an old and unbeloved friend, the icky unease of elevated glucose. Like cheese in the sun.

'Well.' He took the syringe from his pocket and twisted out a few more clicks of insulin, not bothering to analyse his blood. 'I mean, I was coming up the stairs when it happened. Mike saw Calvin lying there. He was already hanging over the edge, wasn't he, Mike?' In went the needle, a feeble thread of pain through abdominal fat.

'Yes,' Mike said, and nothing else. Clearly he did not want to play narrator either.

Renée noted everything, superfine nib scratching audibly on pad.

'And you went up to him,' she asked, 'and said hi?'

'Yes,' Mike said again.

Hugo remembered it all. The gawdy soles of Calvin's shoes. Mike's mischievous delight, that pantomime creep towards the edge. And his own paralysis, as if in a dream – one of *those* dreams – where one strained to act, almost *retched* with desire, and nothing came.

'And then he hit his head and slipped off?'

Hugo had forgotten about Calvin banging his head. Though he had, hadn't he? He had banged his head. Could it still be suicide if he banged his head?

'Yes.' Mike was being minimal.

'Right. Then what?'

She looked at Hugo, like she was waiting to find out what to blame him for.

'Then we rushed downstairs,' Hugo said. 'I got hold of a mirror to see if he was breathing, but it didn't look like he was. And I didn't want to start giving him CPR, because he looked pretty broken up already. I thought I might make things worse. So we called 999.'

'We didn't call straight away,' Mike said.

And Hugo looked at him.

'Hugo wanted to get all the drugs out of the way first. I helped tidy up.'

Mike had a face like a certificate. Or a fucking church.

'How long did that take?' Renée did not seem angry.

'Twenty minutes.'

'Ten,' said Hugo.

Her pen was in her mouth and she was thinking.

Michael saw his own surprise written on Hugo's face. Neither of them had expected him to say that.

But he had. He had said that. Just by saying it. He tingled with power. If it was that easy just to say things then, well, he could do it again.

'Hugo wanted to get all of the drugs out of the way first,' he said. 'I helped tidy up.'

'How long did that take?' Renée asked, showing no surprise, but lowering her voice a little.

'Twenty minutes.'

'Ten.' Hugo tried to contradict him.

But it wasn't ten. It was twenty. Or more.

There was a long pause. And timidly, in the silence, the idea of sleep announced itself to Michael for the first time. Just a gentle softening at his core. Going home must be his next decision.

'Did you get rid of everything? If there's a search will they find any drugs?' Renée asked the question parenthetically, bracketing this admin from her prime concern.

'I don't know,' Hugo said. 'I can't see anything. But we've just had a party. People leave stuff behind.'

'And where is Mellody?'

'She was in here a minute ago. I think she must have gone to bed. But I did tell her to get rid of everything.'

Renée pulled a BlackBerry from her bag, nodding. It amazed Michael how calm she was. That they had misled the police. That they could have cost Calvin his life. These facts barely seemed to trouble her at all.

'There was one thing we were worried about,' he added, while he had his chance. 'You were worried, weren't you Hugo?' Trying to keep co-operation in his voice. 'When we got down there with the paramedics, there was this snail on Calvin's body. I think they noticed it too. If they did, they might know we took longer than Hugo said to call the ambulance.'

Renée put the phone down.

'I mean, I couldn't tell,' Michael added hurriedly. 'They were busy, so maybe they didn't notice.'

'A snail?' Her forehead wrinkled, winding on another notch of tension to the retracted hair. 'There was . . . a snail on Calvin's body?'

Michael nodded.

'Halfway across,' he said.

'And they saw it?'

'One of the ambulance people wiped it off with her arm.'

'Were you going to mention this, Hugo?'

'I didn't think it was important.'

And the way he said it. So cool. So well. Michael's fury was set free.

'You thought it was pretty fucking important at the time!' he spluttered. 'You were doing everything you could to get me to look at it!'

'It was a shock. I admit that,' Hugo spoke with slow and elaborate patience. 'But it doesn't prove anything. How fast are snails? Could one travel eighteen inches, across earth and silk, in ten minutes or whatever it was? And do you really think that the speed of snails is going to convict us in court? If we've done anything illegal. And I doubt that we have.'

'Jesus, Hugo! Who cares if it's illegal? Calvin could be dead because of what you did – what you made *me* do. *You* pushed me into this. *You* were the one who wanted to clear up all the fucking drugs first, not me.'

'Fine, Mike. You can remember it that way if you want. All I know is I didn't make this happen. I tried to tell you to leave Calvin alone, but you wouldn't listen. I was nowhere near him when he fell. And who the fuck *are* you anyway? Why are you here? I don't know a fucking thing about you!'

Even though this comment had manifestly been designed to hurt him, it did. The stiffening charge of anger slipped out of Michael's body, and with it went his strength. He did not reply. He felt instantly alone.

Then a noise. The rigid thrum of Renée's phone on the kitchen table, and the opening bass chops of 'My Sharona'. It was not a choice of ringtone that Michael ever would have guessed.

'Hi Hamish,' she said, after checking the caller. 'Yes, yes, I did. Have you seen the news? . . . What are they saying? . . . Uh-huh . . .'

Michael refused to look at Hugo. The air sat between them, full of lumps.

'OK . . . Sure,' said Renée. 'Absolutely . . . Well, he's been through it all once with the police. He fell off the roof when he was drunk or high or something, and then Hugo and this other guy Mike went down to check on him before calling the medics . . . No, they were up there with him . . . I don't think so . . . They're with me now . . . OK . . . OK, sure . . . OK.'

She tossed the phone down.

'Calvin's in a critical condition,' she said. 'Head injuries. BBC News have just picked it up. Hamish is still in London, Hugo, you're in luck. Don't say another word to the police until he gets here, he says. Don't even repeat all the stuff you've already said. Be nice, and just say it's lawyer's orders. You too, Mike. And thanks for bringing up the snail. We need to know everything if we're going to be able to help you. You understand that, don't you Hugo?'

'Yes Renée. I do actually understand that.'

'Good. Hamish is going to be here in an hour. I think both of you should get some sleep. I'm going to work out a statement with him, and we need to have that out by lunchtime. So I want you both awake again at noon.'

'Actually.' Michael was confused. 'I thought maybe I would just go back to my flat. I'm tired. I need to go home.'

It took some time for Renée to understand.

'Sorry, Mike,' she said eventually. 'I don't think that's a good idea. For any of us. We should all work together until we've moved this situation on.'

'And the police told us to stay here, remember? Until the "sockos" arrive.' Hugo spoke it drily. In the sunlight, his averted eyes glowed caramel brown.

'Do you have a lawyer, Mike?' Renée followed up.

Michael shook his head.

'Well Hugo has a good one. We can make sure you're properly represented. And I don't know if you've seen the press out there?' She paused, but not for an answer. 'They are not going to leave you alone, I'm afraid. Not until this story's over. Hugo, we can get you to your place in the Quantocks perhaps, or off to LA on an earlier plane. But Mike, do you want them all hanging round your apartment?'

His 'No' sounded meek and superfluous.

'Well, we'll see what we can do to stop that happening. You're lucky: at the moment, they probably don't know who you are. But you'll need to be ready when they find out. Don't worry.' She placed a hand on his arm. 'I know this is all pretty crazy right now, but we'll handle it, and then you'll have a story to tell your grandchildren.' She attempted a laugh. 'Do you need a change of clothes? Is that the problem? I guess Hugo's going to be a bit too big . . .'

'Um, well . . .'

'It's done. I'll have Theresa pick something up.'

And to his shame, in spite of everything, Michael found he was excited by the thought of what the clothes might be.

A bossy lady from the seat in front was standing over him with a see-through handbag full of water. The strap muddled about his face. Why did other passengers have to fuss around so much with the overhead lockers when they could just jam their stuff under the seat?

'I wonder what the film will be?' Mum said excitedly. 'BP still falling.'

It had been a while since she flew. Probably she didn't know that good planes always had a choice of films these days. Calvin did not say anything. It would be more fun for her to find out by herself.

Mellody was not eavesdropping, though she had tried to, lying listening by the foot of the radiator wrapped in a Berber throw that she had never previously liked. '. . . editions,' she heard, and 'this'. But however hard she concentrated, the meanings of the sentences slipped past like mice. (Or rats, or roaches, or electric eels. She could not, in truth, grasp any of them for long enough to find out what their slipping past resembled.) And she was distracted by memories of Rebekah. The thought of getting into that car: it did not revolt her altogether. She found herself considering the sunglazed sanctuary of tinted windows, the clean embracing scents of leather and escape. Taking her somewhere not too far away, but quiet. Maybe Giles could come visit. Another advantage, that, against the prospect of lying low with Hugo. And then there was the feeling – a clownlike impostor of a feeling, to be sure, but real to her – that Rebekah did actually care. This was all business, Mellody knew it. She *knew* it. But the woman's damn *kindness*, her concern for how all this affected *her* . . . She had needed so desperately to hear it. And now she could not forget.

'. . . cares! . . .' someone shouted from the kitchen. A sharp British spike, not Hugo's, jutting from the muddy stream. Then '. . . you . . .' and '. . . *you* . . .' again, but louder.

Disputes were under way. Battle plans.

It was cold. The throw clung harsh.

Her mind returned to Calvin. His graceless fucking, and now his wrong-way legs. Was it her fault? She refused the thought.

'. . . fuck! . . .' said Hugo's voice this time, then 'thing'. It wore the nasty, snooty tone he always used when he wanted you to be unhappy.

Her phone buzzed once beside her on the floor.

A text.

Calvin mum: Judy Vance 0113 496 7614. But she already knows, is on way to London. Am on this number. Rx.

To be rescued, thought Mellody. To call Giles. To sleep. To be taken care of for a change.

His bedroom curtains were easily large enough, but no matter how much care he took to drape them, Hugo could not extract the final shades of day, nor the disapproving glower of his furniture. Meanwhile, noise simmered on regardless in the street. And behind the curtains on the opposite window, he knew from drawing them before, a forensic shrine was being erected. He had watched as a different policeman, taller and younger than the others, began sinking metal stakes into the earth, taking care to avoid all obvious plants. After this, the man had set about sanctifying the interior with blue and white tape, which he supported at each corner with a double winding that pinched its width into a bud. Calvin, of course, would have passed by this window on the way down. But Hugo decided not to think about it.

And now a vertiginous little twinkle in his gut informed him that the sugar in his blood was dipping low. Whooah . . . really quite low. He must have overjudged the insulin a bit. Quickly, he opened the cupboard of his bedside table and took out a can of Dr Pepper – his last – finishing it as he gradually removed his clothes.

Rebalanced, he slid naked into the envelope of his bed. The sheets were cold, as they always were without his wife. She would be slumped elsewhere about the house as usual. Often Hugo came down at morning time to find her garnishing a cushion pudding, or unconscious in the basement, snoring gently in the pastel kiss of daytime television.

Why had she not been on the roof with Calvin? The thought nudged him for the first time. Had she upset the boy? Or lost interest in him? Both were likely. His mind ambled down the paths of possibility. His wife had humiliated her new lover. Sexually, or otherwise. Maybe he had been too wasted to perform – sex with Mellody was always a performance – so she had dismissed him. The idea even stirred something close to sympathy. Or, feeling queasy from his intake, perhaps the boy had gone upstairs for air and lain down across the building's edge to vomit. This had been Hugo's first assumption. But he had neither smelled nor seen the evidence, so it might be that the moment passed. And then as the boy lay there, perhaps a blacker notion had come upon him? A plan for closure and revenge. Did that happen? Expedited maybe by Mike's sudden interruption? Could anybody reach capriciously for such decisive suicide? There was nothing penultimate about easing oneself off a roof. Was that how unhappy people acted? And did they go to parties first to have it off with people's wives?

Hugo took a bottle of Ambien from the bedside table. Without the strength to get himself some water, he gulped one down dry. He would sleep. He always did. It was getting up that might be difficult.

He closed his eyes.

Flick, went the brow. *Flick, fli-ick, flick, flick.*

And Calvin probably would die. A subdural haematoma, if that was the diagnosis Mellody had heard, was definitely bad. And, honestly, if the boy desired death, then Hugo hoped that he would get it. There would follow inquests, drug tests, a reverberating scandal, of course, but nothing that the world had not survived before.

Or Calvin might live, and after days of dreaming wake inside his treatment nest and speak. Then what would he reveal? Truths about Mellody, the party, about the price of fame? Or nothing? Would his brain not recover the few faculties it had? Would it hoard its stories in a living corpse? Drooling Beauty. A motorised parable for the drug war, trundling towards its long-prepared obituary.

Flick, flick.

It made no difference in the end. And Hugo felt no sorrow. His mind seethed quietly in a fervent and unhealthy fizz. Wandering unpurposed.

Fli-ick, went his eyebrow. *Fli-ick.*

Then there was a knock on the door. He sat up to see that it was already opening.

'Listen, I need to talk to you.' Renée's voice, for her, was soft.

Hugo said nothing at all.

'Is Mellody in here?'

He shook his head.

And finally, 'Asleep somewhere,' he said.

'OK. Well, anyway, we'll need to get you both to a safe house after the statement goes out. I'll square it with the police. Bonzo and his guys are coming over. I'm not happy that you sent him home, by the way. But I think it's going to be too hectic for them to handle long term.'

'What about Mike?'

'Yes,' she said. 'That's what I wanted to talk about. Sorry I was a bit rough with you downstairs, but it's important he feels we're on his side.'

Hugo shrugged.

'Listen.' She took up a sympathetic perch on the corner of his bed. 'You did the right thing. You were right to get rid of all the drugs, and you were right not to lie. But I'm worried about Mike's role in this. How much did you actually see?'

'Of the accident?'

She nodded.

Hugo raised himself into a sitting position, not bothering to conceal his naked chest.

'Not much,' he said.

'OK. But what do you *think* happened?'

'I don't know,' he said. 'I really don't know. The police were asking if Calvin was depressed, and I was wondering why he might have crawled under the barrier . . .'

'Uh-huh.'

'I mean I don't know the guy. But maybe he was trying to top himself?' He sounded hopeful. He could hear that he sounded hopeful.

'I see.'

'I mean I don't know. I'm just saying.'

Renée nodded again, with slow understanding.

'The only thing is,' she said, 'that with the situation so

unclear right now, we need to consider all the possibilities. The cops certainly will. Like, say it was an accident, OK? Maybe he got dizzy because he was really high. He'd been taking stuff, right?'

'I don't know. Probably. He had some coke with Mell, I think.'

'And did anyone else give him anything?'

'Jesus, Renée! I don't know. The guy's old enough to find his own . . .'

'I know, I know. But we have to think about these things now. Or, take another example: what if Mike nudged him off by mistake?' She looked directly into Hugo's eyes. 'If that's what happened, Hugo, then we have to make sure we're not protecting him unfairly. If Calvin recovers and says Mike knocked him over the edge then how will it look if you've been saying he didn't? And we also have to think about what Mike might do.'

'What do you mean?'

'Well, if he feels guilty, he'll probably try to blame other people. He may even convince himself that it's all someone else's fault. Yours probably. It would be a natural reaction. I mean I don't want to suggest that Mike *is* responsible – I wasn't there, after all – but you say he tried to grab Calvin's legs when he was falling?'

'Yes. He kind of grappled with them.'

'So if you were Mike you probably would blame yourself a bit. And we just saw how he tends to focus that anger outwards, on you.'

'Mmm,' Hugo said, in the fair spirit of experiment, to imagine that Renée was right. And indeed her way of seeing things did not seem obviously wrong. 'After all,' he added, on reflection. 'I think maybe Mike *was* trying to creep up on him. It could be Calvin was startled, and that's why he fell.'

'Creep up on him?'

She had wandered towards the larger curtains on the street side of the room. She tugged at one edge to release a splinter of light, and peered through it absent-mindedly.

'I think it was a joke or something.'

'A *joke*? The guy's on the edge of a fucking *roof*!'

'I know. I tried to stop him.'

It was Renée who paused to think this time. Leaning with her left hand on the sill, she ran her right across the tightened surface of her hair, as a bald man after shaving might caress his scalp.

'I don't like this at all, Hugo,' she said eventually. 'Seriously. We know nothing about this guy. He wasn't invited to the party . . .'

'I know. He used Camille McLeish's card.'

Renée raised both palms towards the ceiling as if now everything had been explained.

'Exactly!' she said. 'He's a fucking journalist! And he snuck in.'

'He's a subeditor.'

'Whatever, Hugo. He's press. The point is: can you trust him? He's snuck into your party, fucking clung to you all night, and now look at the mess he's made!'

'I don't think Mike meant any harm,' Hugo said, in a little voice. He felt he had to.

'No, sure. It's not like he had a grudge or anything, but he played a pretty stupid joke, and now he's in trouble and he needs to cover his ass. I think we should consider telling the cops about it before you get in trouble too.'

Neither of them spoke. Hugo found that he was buttoning and unbuttoning the entrance to the duvet cover that Mrs O'Sullivan (quite unlike her, really) had placed at the head end.

'Look, just think about it. Ah!' Renée was gazing through the curtains once again. 'I think that's Hamish's car.'

She started to leave, but there was something else.

'One more thing . . .' Hugo said.

She had reached the door.

'Yes?' *Knock, knock*, went her feet, on the old oak floor.

Awkward.

'Well . . .'

Embarrassing.

'. . . I think maybe Mellody might have been with Calvin tonight. They were in the bathroom together a long time. I was quite upset, actually.'

Renée took this in.

'Mike was really good to me at the time, and he was very protective. I think it made him angry that they had come back to the house.'

The room waited.

'OK.' Renee fortified her calmness with a dose of effort. 'You realise this means that both you and Mike had a motive to hurt Calvin?'

Hugo nodded and was about to speak, but a rising hand blocked his protests off.

'I know you didn't go near him,' Renée said, 'but that is how the police will see it. Have you told them this yet?'

'No. But Jesus, Renée, why bring it up?'

'Because it is going to come up.'

'How?'

'If he dies there will be an autopsy, Hugo. There might be . . . residues.' She was back at the window, peering through. 'Look, if it's true, then people are going to find out. Mellody might tell them. We've got to accept that and manage it. And if we tell the police straight away then we'll have a better chance of keeping it back until after *Sinbad* opens. *If* it's true.'

'It's true, Renée. OK? You know what Mell's like.'

And now his voice was starting to crack. His frantic fingers let the duvet go.

'It's OK, Hugo,' Renée said. 'It's OK. When the police talk to Mellody we just have to make sure she tells them everything. Her friends can say what they like. We're used to rumours.'

'I don't know . . . I mean . . .' His thoughts dived wildly around their cage, checking and re-checking every corner for a hatch. He just wanted this to end.

'We'll try the best we can.' She sounded impatient, though clearly she was hoping to console him.

'But . . .'

'Listen . . . *fuck!*' Her face stared through the window, gripped rigid.

'What?' Hugo said.

'Fucking shit! . . . Fuck!'

'*What?*'

'She's fucking *leaving*!' Renée flung herself towards the door. 'Mellody's getting into that car!'

And stumbling through his sheets. And ripping duvet round his chest. And staggering out of bed towards the window frame to see if it was true despite the boiling swell of noise that told him surely that it was. There, his wife from above. Emerging from the shade of their magnolia tree into a blazing slab of sun. Saying nothing, though buffeted by shouts and flashes and the mics that jutted at her on the supplicating ends of arms. A black van in the centre of the road. Two big men, tearing out a path. His quiet wife, stepping unhurriedly inside. Turning to present a solemn smile for the record. So beautiful and gracious. Almost royal.

For what reason had this woman ever married him?

The van reversed away, at speed. And for a while, Hugo watched its wake.

He thought about things.
Then he returned to their bed.

'Flying time to Seoul today is approximately ninety minutes ago from the fourth floor,' said the posh pilot, 'I'll be back to you once we're in the air. In the meantime, just sit back, relax and please listen carefully to the cabin crew as they take you through to theatre straight away.'

It was the kind of voice that Calvin liked to hear.

The doors were levered closed, cutting out the engines. He bathed pleasantly in the hiss of severed noise.

'How long did he say it would be, Cal? Eleven hours? I don't know I've ever done eleven hours before!'

Mum was a nervous flyer. She liked to keep talking.

'Florida was eight.' She laughed, unconvincingly. 'And that was the furthest I've been.'

The air conditioners were working hard. Adding more air or taking it away? Calvin knew it was one of the two.

Mum said, 'How far's Turkey? That was a long one.'

The engines flared, and faded, heaving the plane forward into a dozy lumber. Sunlight flooded the cabin, bright as pain. The wingtips flexed and waddled on their frame.

'It was an acute subdural haemorrhage. Remember?'

No, actually. Calvin did not remember.

In fact it was strange, now he thought about it, that his mum was coming with him at all. Would she be there at every gig? He was a little embarrassed, if that was allowed. But perhaps they saw things differently in the East.

Ping, ping, went the intercom. *Ping, ping.*

'They gave us all a blanket,' Mum said.

Taking air away. Definitely. Already he could feel a drunken lightness. And he had a headache.

'Cabin crew, I need him prepped up fast. OK? *Fast.*'

He was full of energy, the captain, but in control.

The plane wheeled on to the runway and stopped.

To the East. Time to go.

Waiting. Mum's hand on his.

Waiting. Time to go.

Time to go.

And then the thrust was in his back.

Time to go.

The heavy roar.

The ground became a stripe of speed.

Time to go.

To the East, where he was loved.

Hi William – yes, happy to raise all that with Leo. They sound like great plans. Really good way to generate buzz around the book.

Vx

From:	leobenedictus@yahoo.co.uk
To:	williammendez75@gmail.com
Subject:	Re: Hello
Date:	Thursday, 14 January 2010 11:02:38

Ah, agents... Authors may be driven to their art because they crave attention – indeed I'm sure they often are – but only the sincerest book-lover would work in publishing to get rich. (Which probably explains why they have all been sensible enough to refuse my novel...)

Anyway, love the new chapter, which I read first thing this morning. Val and I will be meeting both Cape and Bloomsbury on Monday – I only hope I can convince them that I wrote it! Obviously the connection with the Green/O'Nolan case is there to see, especially now that Hugo and Michael are beginning to fall out. But to me, their characters, and this situation, are clearly archetypes. That's the point, isn't it? Michael is the nerdy ingénu (a classic comic hero in the Portnoy/Woody Allen mould); Hugo is the prince in thrall to his advisors (Tolkien, Macbeth, passim...). They get on, then they fall out. Just because the crisis concerns a young man and a roof terrace does not mean everything must therefore be 'based on a true story'. And I don't think that most readers, while acknowledging the echoes, will see it that way either. Keep it up, I say, and damn the lawyers!
Leo

From: williammendez75@gmail.com
To: leobenedictus@yahoo.co.uk
Subject: Re: Hello
Date: Thursday, 14 January 2010 20:41:23

Finally, someone who understands what I am trying to do! Honestly Leo, I can't tell you how relieved I am to hear you say that. This is fiction influenced by fact: why is that so hard for people to understand? If you actually go back and look at how Daniel O'Nolan and Harvey Green were portrayed at the time, you can see how the media fictionalised them too.

Take this, from the beginning of an interview O'Nolan did with the *Observer* shortly after Marsh's fall:

"I don't want to talk about that," Daniel O'Nolan says irritably. "I thought we were here to discuss the consequences of the accident, not rake over everything again." He scratches distractedly at the crown of his head. And for a moment, almost before we have begun, I am worried that he is about to walk out.

Yet if he did, I admit that I would have some sympathy. Just three months in the public eye have turned this mild-mannered copywriter into somebody so anxious about being misrepresented that he has brought his own dictation machine along to our interview. It is sitting on the table in front of me now, newer and sleeker than my own. Naturally, he would not be photographed either.

Now look at this Liz Jones column on Green, from the *Mail on Sunday* at around the same time:

"...What happened to the cheeky twinkle that no one could resist when he first burst on the scene? Back then I'll confess that I even had my own older-woman crush on little Harvey-Lumps, as I used to think of him. These days I'd rather French-kiss a scorpion.

Understandably, the search for Green's lost mojo has focused mostly on the early hours of February 8th. But it has been obvious to anyone with half an ounce of sense that the real problems started long ago.

This is a man, remember, whose hatred of publicity was well known in celebrity circles long before the gossips turned against him. Did he plan to be a movie star and hope nobody would notice?

Even when he married Vesta? Was that really going to help him lead a quiet life? Sure, it did his career some good, but it was about as convincing as a homemade nose-job."

Just one question: Where is their evidence?!!! The *Observer* makes O'Nolan out to be some kind of paranoid obsessive ('a creepy advertising guy' Val called him, clearly believing every word), while Jones implies that both Green's shyness and his marriage were elaborate deceptions aimed at enhancing his career. Where is the evidence? Hopefully – with your help! – this book can make people ask that question just a bit more often.

From: valerie.morrell@nortonmorrell.co.uk
To: williammendez75@gmail.com
Cc: leobenedictus@yahoo.co.uk
Subject: The Unveiling
Date: Monday, 18 January 2010 14:02:49

Just a quickie, William, to say that we have met both publishers now, and Leo was superb. Everyone obviously impressed, and your marketing ideas went down well, I thought. Jane at Cape confirmed that they will be making an offer by the end of the week. Matthew at Bloomsbury seems delighted that we can move forward, but has not produced their figure yet. Naturally the invisible-author hoo-ha is not forgotten. (I think it created quite a stir in Cape Towers, especially, though we might yet turn that to our advantage.) Will report when I hear more.

Vx

From: williammendez75@gmail.com
To: valerie.morrell@nortonmorrell.co.uk
Cc: leobenedictus@yahoo.co.uk
Subject: Re: The Unveiling
Date: Monday, 18 January 2010 14:11:41

Thanks Val – and well done Leo! In fact, great job both of you! Did they agree to use the blurb I wrote? I think it would work well with a very strong, eye-catching cover. Commercial but clever. Something with a snail or a whisky glass perhaps?
W

From: leobenedictus@yahoo.co.uk
To: williammendez75@gmail.com
Cc: valerie.morrell@nortonmorrell.co.uk
Subject: Re: The Unveiling
Date: Tuesday, 19 January 2010 08:48:20

Thanks William,

Actually (and why does this feel like a confession?) the truth is that I really *enjoyed* myself. It felt very natural being there somehow, and much easier to go through with than I was expecting. Like I just flicked a switch, and I was you. The fact that everyone was so nice at both Bloomsbury and Cape did help, I suppose. And they loved your blurb and marketing ideas, by the way, which I'm definitely up for.

Fingers crossed on the offers...

L

From: **valerie.morrell@nortonmorrell.co.uk**
To: **williammendez75@gmail.com;**
leobenedictus@yahoo.co.uk
Subject: **V URGENT!! - OFFERS IN!!! – NEED DECISION**
TODAY!!!
Date: **Thursday, 21 January 2010 16:14:50**

Afternoon chaps. I bring news.

At about 3pm, Cape formally offered a £20,000 advance for the UK
and Commonwealth rights to *Publicity******. Jane sounded very
keen, and I was literally typing up an email about it when Matthew
rang. Naturally I told him the news, and he said straight away that
Bloomsbury would go to £60,000 but that we'd need to accept
BEFORE 6pm TODAY. I've just called Jane back, and she has now
gone to £70,000, which Matthew says he will not match. So it's make
your mind up time: £70k from Cape or £60k from Bloomsbury? Both
would publish next March, which is a great time for a literary debut,
and both are large publishers with prestigious lists, which would give
Publicity***** an excellent chance in bookshops. As I see it, there are
two issues in play: money, and which group of people you would prefer
to work with, based on Leo's experience of meeting them. Please could
you each let me know ASAP what you would like to do, so I can relay
the decision.

Best,

Valerie

Hi Val, Leo

£70,000 from Cape sounds good to me. (Just as you predicted, Val!)

Leo, are you OK with that?

W

From: leobenedictus@yahoo.co.uk
To: williammendez75@gmail.com;
valerie.morrell@nortonmorrell.co.uk
Subject: Re: V URGENT!! - OFFERS IN!!! – NEED DECISION TODAY!!!
Date: Thursday, 21 January 2010 16:38:04

It's hard to say who I prefer from such a short encounter. But both seemed really nice to me, so yes, I'm very happy to go with Cape.

L

From: valerie.morrell@nortonmorrell.co.uk
To: leobenedictus@yahoo.co.uk;
williammendez75@gmail.com
Subject: Re: V URGENT!! - OFFERS IN!!! – NEED DECISION
TODAY!!!
Date: Thursday, 21 January 2010 16:41:09

Fantastic. Thanks guys. I'm calling Jane and Matthew now.

From: valerie.morrell@nortonmorrell.co.uk
To: leobenedictus@yahoo.co.uk;
williammendez75@gmail.com
Subject: Cape Confirmation – deal done!
Date: Thursday, 21 January 2010 17:03:21

So there we have it! Matthew is disappointed, Jane is delighted, and I now have Cape's offer in writing. Well done, everyone! William, you are slightly rich!

Leo, I don't wish to rush you, but I expect to receive the contract in the next few days, so if you could begin your search for a new agent straight away, I would be very grateful.

William, I'm absolutely thrilled that you have finally got the deal you deserve, and I hope the book will go on to great success. We've had some sticky patches, you and I, and there were days when I thought we would never get here, but I just want to let you know what a pleasure it has been to represent you. I am sad that we must part company – very sad. But I know you understand why I have to walk away, and I hope that circumstances will permit us to meet one day, so I can tell you all this in person.

Affectionately and always,

Valerie x

From: williammendez75@gmail.com
To: valerie.morrell@nortonmorrell.co.uk;
leobenedictus@yahoo.co.uk
Subject: Re: Cape Confirmation – deal done!
Date: Friday, 22 January 2010 01:13:44
▶ 🔗 Chapter 11 – Bed

Thanks Val – I can't believe it! I'm going to be a published author! I really am so grateful. I realise what a risk you've taken on my behalf, and you can be sure I'll never forget it. If you're still interested, I enclose the next chapter, a short one, which I've finally polished off this week.

Yours,

William x

PS Leo, do you think you could find out how long it is likely to be before the money comes through? I enclose my bank details, and whatever you can do to expedite things would be much appreciated. (Needless to say, Val, I'll send your cut as soon as I have mine.)

70,000 (fee) – 12,337.50 (commission + VAT) = 57,662.50
57,662.50/4 = 14,415.63 (first instalment)
14,415.63 – 9,500 (agreed Leo fee) = **£4,915.62**
Could you wire this £4,915.62, plus future payments, to account number 8914954 at the Cayman National Bank. You need to do this through:
Citibank, London, PO BOX 78, 336 Strand, London WC2R 1HB
swift code CITIGB2L
sort 18-50-08
IBAN#GB54CITI18500808914954

A noise, and Michael sat up in bed, breathing fast.

Where was he?

He remembered. And in the instant of its being observed, a terrible new universe constructed itself around him. The accident. The ambulance. The police. Was he still in Hugo Marks's house? There was muffled daylight in the room. Oh God, he was. What time was it? How long had he been asleep? It seemed like he had lain in this large bed for hours trying to pass out, experimenting restlessly with styles of pillow-shape and posture as his thoughts whirred on and on.

11:24, said the dial on his fumbled phone. Still early. He could not have been out more than two hours. Almost certainly less. Too soon to get up. Yet he was far from drowsy. And the discovery of a missed call drew him further in, especially as no number had registered, which was what happened when work rang. He dialled his voicemail. Some contact with the usual was what he wanted. Was what he wanted badly.

'You have . . . one . . . new message,' the computer lady said, her words inelegantly distanced, their human smoothness given corners where the slopes of stress mismet. Michael found it comforting, this steady calm, this mechanical unpanic.

'BEEP . . . Hi Michael, this is Andrea Coles on the home desk at the *Standard on Sunday*. I'm really sorry to bother you on a Saturday morning, but Camille McLeish tells me that you were at this Mellody/Hugo Marks party last night? If you were, I was wondering if you could give me a call on 7946 4320. We are all hoping we might get you to write something about what it was like, especially in the light of what's been going on this morning.'

To write something! A skip hit Michael's heart. In the midst of everything, he had not thought of this.

'Who was there,' the message continued, 'what the mood was, whether you saw Calvin Vance anywhere, that sort of thing. So that's 7946 4320. If you could call me when you get this message I'd be very grateful. I'll also try your landline. Thanks a lot. Bye.'

Michael whispered the number to himself. *7946 4320.*

They wanted him to *write* something! A real story with his byline on it. They *all* did.

020 7946 4320. He entered the code.

But what to say? He hesitated.

He knew Andrea a little, and she'd always seemed nice. It couldn't hurt to talk to her about it.

02079464320, the screen displayed expectantly.

Michael pressed green, and did not wait long.

'Hello, home desk.'

'Er, hi.' His voice popped and crackled drily. He cleared his throat. 'Sorry, could I speak to Andrea please?'

'Speaking.'

'Hi, it's Michael Knight. I just got your message.'

'Michael, hi!' She sounded very pleased. 'Thanks for calling back.'

'No problem.'

'So yeah. Is it right that you were there last night?'

'Yes, and . . .'

'I thought so. Camille said she gave you her invite. And we've actually got a couple of pictures just come through, showing you with Mr Marks himself. Is that right?'

'Really?' He reached for an air of nonchalance. 'Pictures from the party?'

'Yes. You're standing next to him while Mellody gives some speech. They've used it online, but I think they cropped you out.'

'Oh.'

'So what was it like?'

'Fine, you know. Fun actually. But . . .'

'Did you talk to Hugo at all?'

'Yes, I did. But . . .' Even his quietest voice rang loud in the bare bedroom. '. . . I was going to say, I also went back to the house afterwards.' He looked around desperately for some way to keep the noise down.

'No *way!*' gasped Andrea.

'Uh-huh.'

'That's fantastic! You mean you were actually at the house?'

'Yes.' Half-whispered.

'You're joking.'

'No, and . . .'

'And did you see Calvin Vance? Was he pretty wasted?'

'Yeah. Well, I think a few people were.'

'I just can't believe you managed that, Michael! Hang on for one second, OK?'

A fidgeting sound, and then the line went silent.

Should he shove himself beneath the duvet? Behind the curtains? Would that smother this conversation? It would certainly seem odd to anyone that found him. But then – how could he have been so stupid? – he saw the en-suite bathroom. Tearing away the bedclothes, he dived inside, tugging at the light cord, which, a bonus, also activated the extractor. *Perfect.* He felt very clever in the buzz, like a spy reporting to his people. And still he had not told them half of what he'd done.

'Hello, Michael? You still there?'

'Yes, hi.' Now his voice could properly express his pride.

'I think there's a good chance we may be going with this story on the cover tomorrow. Any other week it would be definite, but it kind of depends on the Pope situation. Though even if he dies today, I think this will still make something downpage. Would you be able to file by four-thirty at the latest? Twelve hundred words. Or as much detail as you can remember really?'

'Well that's the thing. I've been trying to say, I'm actually still at the house.'

Pause.

Towels lay around him, folded fat and square as shop-made cakes, attending to a shower stall or 'wet room', as they called it on TV.

'Sorry, which house?' Andrea said.

'Hugo Marks's house.'

'You are *kidding* me?' She was whispering now.

'No.'

'The big mansion in Holland Park with all the cameras in front of it, you're inside there right now?'

'Yes.'

'. . . oh my God . . .'

'So the problem is the police say I'm not supposed to leave yet. But if I'm going to write something I can't do it here.'

'How come you're there? Are lots of people still inside?'

'No. I mean, I don't know. I've been asleep. I'm not sure if I should talk about it, but I was here when Calvin fell off the roof. I saw it. And the police have been. They say some detectives and forensics people will be along later.'

'Oh my God. What happened? Wasn't it an accident?'

'No definitely. It was. He slipped. They're *saying* it was an accident, right?'

Tension tightened Michael's body like a hose turned on.

'Yes, I think so. Hang on, I've got the police statement in my email.' Hurried keystroke chunks came clattering along the line. 'Yeah, OK. Here we are: "A twenty-year-old man has died of his injuries after falling from the roof of a house in the Holland Park area of London. The man, who has yet to be formally identified, was taken from the scene by ambulance at approximately 7 a.m., but died later in Charing Cross Hospital. Officers are interviewing eye-witnesses, and are keeping an open mind about events, but at this stage they do not suspect foul play." I suppose you're one of the eye-witnesses, are you?'

The air was dense. The extractor fan whirred louder in it, struggling through.

'Michael?'

'He's dead?' was all he could say.

'Sorry?'

He looked at himself in the mirror. He was naked except for his boxer shorts, which were covered with pictures of Homer Simpson eating a doughnut.

'Did you say Calvin died?' he said.

'Yes. They announced it a few minutes ago. Oh God, didn't you know?'

Michael sat down heavily on the toilet.

'I'll call you back, OK Andrea?'

'Michael, God, I'm so sorry. Do you want to take a moment and . . .'

'I'll call you back.'

'Hugo, are you awake?'

He did not move.

'You need to wake up, Hugo. I've brought you a coffee.'

A soft thunk near his ear.

'We have some news.'

He lifted himself on to his elbows, and then up against the headboard, dredging limbs through cotton stodge. He sipped some coffee – hot – and rubbed his eyes. Renée was at the end of his bed again. She did not have a good news face on.

'Mmm?' he said, following sip two.

When he put the cup down, she told him.

'Calvin is dead.'

Nothing happened for a bit.

'He died in the operating theatre,' she said. 'I guess we were prepared for this.'

Hugo nodded. He did not feel sorrow. Just tiredness, and the fact that he liked coffee.

'It's very sad,' he said, not meaning it. The world was filled with sadder things, in his opinion; indeed it consisted mainly of them.

'The cops have just announced there'll be a news conference in about an hour.' Renée stood, and put her hands on her hips. 'Nothing big, they tell me, just nailing down some details to stop the bullshit taking off. When they're done, I think we should put our statement out. Hamish is here, and we've drafted something that I'll go and read to the mob if you're OK with it. I hoped we might get Mellody involved too, but nobody can reach her. She hasn't rung you, I guess?'

Hugo shook his head.

'OK. Obviously that's not helpful, but we mustn't jump to conclusions. She could be anywhere. But she'll only make things worse for herself if she tries to run off. And her people will tell her that. But if you can get hold of her, that would be good.'

A nod or a grunt or an 'OK' felt expected here, so Hugo did one.

'Oh, and I called Caspar,' Renée added, brightening. 'He says he has some footage of Calvin from Cuzco last night – dancing or something, I haven't seen it yet. But I'm offering that to the networks in the hope that they'll go easy on the drug stuff for now.'

The drab weight of Ambien still squatted obdurately in his

head, though he could feel the coffee start to needle through. Hopefully Renée would leave him soon.

'So look,' she added. 'I know you haven't had much rest. You must be wiped out. But we need you to look over this statement. I also think you should talk with Independence personally as soon as New York wakes up. Do you need a modafinil?'

He shook his head.

'I'll fix this, Hugo.' She looked over with a face that hoped to find him reassured. 'We just have to keep not fucking up until the world gets bored.'

And now again: her 'My Sharona' ringtone. Neither the handset nor its noise had changed for years.

'I'm talking to Hugo, Theresa,' Renée began irritably. Then she frowned and listened. There was an 'Uh-huh,' and then a 'Right, OK.' Again, 'Uh-huh.' She looked at him once more, not reassuring this time. 'I'll be right out.' Then she hung up.

'I'll be back in a minute,' she said.

Mopping his eyes with a fist of toilet paper, Michael climbed back into bed. He gathered his body, and drew the duvet over in a single sweep, repelling the world. Inside, he was alone with his heat.

What was he going to do?

He thought of Calvin. Poor boy. And of his family. And of himself.

He had done so little wrong, yet this was all his fault. It frightened him.

Fresh drops, fat as ladybirds, wriggled down his cheeks. Michael heard them pat on to the sheet.

He wanted yesterday back, with its companionable dullness.

The late commute, lunch in the canteen, the email repartee – these domesticities seemed edged with sacredness in the light of recollection. And then the invitation, the taxi ride, the fretful stabs at talk. Oh, he would give anything to untake those blithe decisions, all so out of character, and break the chain of consequence that hauled him up on to the roof. It wasn't me, he wanted to scream. *It wasn't me!* But there was nobody to hear it.

And now what was he going to do?

Was he under suspicion? Had he committed a crime? To give Calvin a shock was all he had intended, but it had been enough to kill him. And Hugo knew this. He knew he knew. But would he tell? Yes. In the end, he would.

Outside his tent, the bathroom fan had stopped, leaving just the heavy up and down of Michael's breathing.

He had said he would call Andrea back.

What was he going to say? Would it be wrong of him, now, to write something? Or the opposite? Was this, instead, what writing was about? Or was he just another Fleet Street casuist, trying to believe so? Was he searching only for the viewpoint that would print his name? And make some money. Perhaps a lot of money . . . He was trembling. He needed advice. But there was nobody to advise him.

Sally. *Sally.*

And quickly pulling back the cover, he returned to the dim grey cool. Noisily, he blew his nose, and blinked.

A fresh suit, a shirt, and even shoes and underwear, had carefully been laid out on the chair by the door.

Had all that been there when he awoke? Or just now, when he left the bathroom?

He shrugged, and picked up the phone.

Hugo dressed smartly, for a spring calamity. He chose a mid-grey suit, almost invisibly plain, and left its waistcoat on the hanger. The trousers zipped, he added socks, and then some rich brown brogues he liked. A scan along his shirt rail found an apt companion at light blue. As he buttoned, he approached the window on the garden side, and made a peephole in the curtains wide enough to see that the policeman still stood vigilant beside his dirty rocks. They would be Calvin's rocks forever now. That boy's memory would colonise his house. He drained his cup of coffee and, though it was still hot, placed it on the folded cherrywood of the card table by his bed. Mellody used to make him wince by doing that. They used to play cards too.

'OK,' was what Renée said as she walked in without knocking. Then, when she had Hugo's full attention, 'I think we have a serious problem with Mike.'

'Yes, you said that. But I don't think . . .' It was a feeble attempt to stall her, begun with little hope against such a determined start.

'No, this is something else. Theresa just heard him talking to his editor.'

Now Hugo was confused. Mike had *promised*.

'What?' he said.

'She went up to give him his clothes, knocked on the door, and he didn't answer. When she went in he wasn't in bed, but she could hear him in the bathroom talking about writing something, and how he had to get out of here.'

Renée's face was covered in concern for Hugo's feelings.

'How do you know it was his editor?'

'We don't, I guess. But he was talking about writing an article, and not being able to discuss things on the phone . . .'

'What did he actually say?' Hugo could hear how desperate he sounded.

'Let me get Theresa.'

But Theresa was already coming in. She had obviously been waiting by the door until her cue. Like this was a little presentation they had organised. Like they thought he was unreasonable. Hugo Marks: a pleasure prince too drunk on self-regard to tell sycophants from friends. Like he needed cornering with proof before he could believe that he had been betrayed. And maybe they were right.

'. . . wouldn't have listened. Only I wasn't sure if I'd got his room, so I had a look around, and I heard a voice in the bathroom,' Theresa was saying.

She was a smart young woman. Immaculately organised, intelligent, tireless and quick, yet blessed by some invaluable defect of her character that made her servile, and a treat to bully. Not once, as far as Hugo knew, had Renée ever found a task too unreasonable for Theresa to perform. Even such an outrageous instruction as lying now, to her employer, would have been met, he realised, with meek compliance. She would have come in to see him and stood, as she stood now, talking, talking, talking about 'going to write something' and 'when Calvin fell off the roof'. The words would have been planned, and well delivered. And yet they would not have convinced. Not like the loyally trembling lip before him and the doleful shoe-stare did. Usually he felt sorry for Theresa. He hated her now.

'All right!' he shouted. 'Shut up!' And dipped his brow into his hand.

'Listen Hugo,' Renée said, when a respectful pause had passed. 'You wanted my help, and now I'm giving it to you: Mike is a liability. You have to turn him in.'

'OK.'

'Or else he could make it look like Calvin got so wasted at your party that he died. Do you think he's not going to tell his paper about all the sex and drugs round at Mell and Hugo's place? Maybe he'll say you didn't call an ambulance because you were too busy clearing up?' She spoke in torrid bursts, like she was throwing up words, stopping, and then throwing up some more. 'To be honest, if he's desperate, Mike could say you pushed Calvin yourself because he screwed your wife.'

'I said *OK*!'

Theresa looked close to tears.

'All right,' Renée said. 'Just call the case detective – I have his number – and tell him what you really saw. If you wait until after Mike gets his story out, it will be too late. Anything you say then will sound like some bullshit excuse you've just made up. I only want you to tell the truth, and be believed.'

'Just give me a fucking phone!'

But his own was right beside him on the bed, so he dialled the number that Renée recited.

'CID,' said the voice of someone happy.

'Good morning. Hi,' he said. 'This is Hugo Marks.'

He looked back at his manager. She was mouthing something.

Tell. Him. What. You. Saw.

From: leobenedictus@yahoo.co.uk
To: williammendez75@gmail.com
Subject: Paperwork
Date: Monday, 25 January 2010 09:18:15

Hi William,

Thanks for sending me your bank details. I have now approached another agent (probably best if you don't know which) who has agreed to handle contract negotiations on the deal with Cape. Val was not quite up to the job, I explained. I also filled my new agent in on the whole 'William Mendez' saga, though of course I said nothing about our arrangement. (It all felt a bit caddish, to tell you the truth, but I suppose we're not actually hurting anyone.) Just to warn you, I did ask about the money, too, and she said that contract wrangles can take a while. I'll make it as quick as possible, of course, but you may have to wait a few weeks to get paid.

All the best,

Leo

From: williammendez75@gmail.com
To: leobenedictus@yahoo.co.uk
Subject: Re: Paperwork
Date: Monday, 25 January 2010 11:52:30

Thanks Leo – sounds good. And yes, as quick as you can would be great. When you next meet Cape, I'd also be grateful if you could mention a couple of other thoughts I've had.

- Can we get *Publicity****** into the hands of some celebs for them to pass it around/comment? Wd be good to get word-of-mouth going that the book shows 'what it's really like' to be famous. Strong appeal for readers. (Either way, the proof copies will be important – we really need to emphasise that this is "a new kind of novel", with lots of references to its unique marketing strategy. Perhaps we could coin the term "hyperfiction" for it?)

- On the same point, do you think it might add mystery if you do no press interviews at all when the book comes out? I don't know if you ever actually go to the kind of parties that *Publicity****** describes, but I'm sure that if you say nothing people will enjoy presuming that you do.

- If Cape insist you do interviews, however, it is obviously important that you talk and behave exactly as if you had written the book yourself. Perhaps take a bit of time to work out a story about why you wrote it, how long it took, how the idea developed etc. I don't know what you have already told people about your own novel, but I suppose you can claim this changed along the way? It would also help if you could be as controversial as possible. Maybe write some provocative articles? Or slag off some big-name authors and hope they retaliate? Amis, McEwan, Rushdie, Barnes are all Cape too, so that might intensify the scandal. Amis, especially, seems to enjoy a scuffle. In any case, do please write as much about books and celebrities as you possibly can.

- For the paperback edition, I wonder if some deleted scenes, like on a DVD, might be fun? I have reluctantly cut quite a few good bits, which I still have stored on my computer. You or I could choose some favourites and introduce them with a line or two explaining why they had to go. If I were a reader, I'd be interested in that. And it gives real fans a reason to buy the book twice. Why is this never done?

All the best, and well done once again! I really am very excited. With luck, we can make something rather special out of this.

Best, William

From: leobenedictus@yahoo.co.uk
To: williammendez75@gmail.com
Subject: Re: Paperwork
Date: Monday, 25 January 2010 17:02:39

Hi William – thanks for that. V useful notes. I had a sketchy chat with Jane about it all yesterday, and she was fully behind your ideas in principle.

As it happens, I'm writing an article about creative writing courses for *Prospect* magazine, which I could probably postpone until the autumn. Things may get a bit hectic around then, however, as Sarah and I are expecting another baby. Should be easier by March, when I'll start telling everyone I know to buy the book. I'll email everyone I've interviewed (who doesn't hate me) too.

You'll also be pleased to know that I've just had the contract through. There are some slightly sticky patches where I'm supposed to 'covenant' things (that I am 'the sole Author of said work', that it is 'original' to me, and what have you...) but I think we should be able to find a way round this if I change some parts of the novel myself and we add a line in the contract about my extensive use of quotation (which is true, after all). I can't quite believe Cape would sue me, in any case. What loss could they show?

Anyway, watch this space, and the money should be with you in another week or two.

L

PS Thought this line from the contract would amuse you: 'The Publishers undertake that the Author's name shall appear prominently on the title page front cover and binding of all copies of the said work.' Prominently, eh? Shall I push for gold embossed?

From: williammendez75@gmail.com
To: leobenedictus@yahoo.co.uk
Subject: Re: Paperwork
Date: Monday, 25 January 2010 17:32:01

Ha ha! Insist on three inches tall at least!

Keep up the good work. And big congratulations to you and Sarah on the baby!

W

From: williammendez75@gmail.com
To: leobenedictus@yahoo.co.uk
Subject: Any news?
Date: Monday, 8 February 2010 14:32:01

Hi Leo

Just wondering... It's been a couple of weeks... Any movement on the dosh? I've had to sell my computer, so I'm now working from printouts before typing everything up in this shitty cybercafé. It is slowing me down and making life very difficult. Would welcome some good news...
W

From: leobenedictus@yahoo.co.uk
To: williammendez75@gmail.com
Subject: Re: Any news?
Date: Monday, 8 February 2010 15:19:05

Hi William – sorry no, nothing yet. We have now sorted out the contract, but it still needs to be rubber-stamped by Cape's legal department, and then my agent has to invoice. Not long. Promise. Leo

OK Leo, I admit I'm losing patience. Where is this money?

'Hello?' she said tentatively, as if it might not be him.

'Hi Sally. It's Michael.'. He sealed himself back inside the safety of the bathroom. The light clicked on, the fan resumed.

'*Hi!*'

And there was such happiness in her voice, such relief, that already a stab of sweet self-pity was threatening to take him over. Michael blocked it. He had cried too much.

'Is it true?' she said. 'Are you there right now?' A breathy rhythm told him she was walking briskly to a place, he guessed, where she, too, would not be overheard.

'Yes. How did you know?'

'Are you kidding? Everyone knows. We were just talking about you. I showed them your texts. I hope that's OK?'

'Are you at work?'

'Yes. I'm on Sport today, remember?'

Michael didn't, actually.

'And are you going to write something then?'

It was impossible, from the neutrality of her tone, to tell what Sally thought of the idea. Which meant she did not approve.

'I don't know,' he said. 'I'd like to.'

'OK.'

'What do you think?'

'About you writing something?'

'Yes.'

'I think it depends.'

'On what?'

'On a lot of things. Like, does Hugo know? . . . This is mental!'

Her excitement burst out once more. 'I can't believe we're talking about you and *Hugo Marks*! Did you really, seriously, spend the whole evening with him?'

'Pretty much. Yes.'

'And Mellody too?'

'Less so, but she's been around.'

Michael picked up a bottle of moisturiser and looked at it.

'Jesus, Michael! Fucking *how*?'

'I don't know really.' He pressed the pump, and a quick white string of lotion hit his foot. 'I just got talking to these people – Calvin was one of them, actually – and they introduced us.'

'Calvin? The guy who died?'

'Yes.' He rubbed it in.

'Oh my God. And he just fell off the roof like they're saying?'

'Yes.'

Pause.

'So what do you think?' he said.

'What about?'

'About me *writing* something.'

There was an echo in here.

Michael found that he had paced into the wet room.

'Oh right. Well, what do *you* think?'

'I think I'd like to.'

'Uh-huh . . .'

'It seems like a once-in-a-lifetime thing.'

'OK.'

'If I just write truthfully about what's happened, then what's wrong with that?'

'Nothing. I suppose.'

'You're not being very supportive.'

They were arguing already. Why were they arguing?

'Sorry,' Sally said. But he could tell she wasn't.

That stab again. 'I just thought you'd be on my side,' he said.

'Of course I'm on your side, Michael.'

'You don't sound it.'

He sat down on the toilet. It made a hollow *bock*.

'Well I'm sorry about how I sound. And I do think if you want to write something for the paper then you should go ahead.'

'Even though you don't approve.'

'Jesus! Did I say that?'

'Oh come on, Sal.'

'I said it depends. Like, would your new friend be happy about what you'd have to say?'

Michael tried to find a way of imagining that he would.

'Probably not,' he admitted.

'Well, there you go. If it's all true, then I suppose it's legally OK. But it does feel a bit funny to go to some guy's party, be invited back to his house, and then tell the world about it without his knowledge.'

'I was supposed to find gossip, wasn't I?'

'This is different'.

'He's no fucking saint, you know.'

'Well who *is*?'

For a long time, neither of them spoke.

'Look,' Sally said, 'why don't you just hold fire for a few days? You must be shattered. And I can't imagine what it's like in there with all the paparazzi and everything.'

'Surreal.'

'I bet. So why not wait until you've had a chance to think it over?'

'Andrea says they want something today.'

Outside, there was a rap at the bedroom door. A timid knuckle triplet, quiet but distinct.

'Just a second!' Michael shouted, as cheerfully as he could. 'I'll talk to you later,' he whispered down the phone.

'OK. Good luck. I'm thinking of . . .'

He hung up, and left the bathroom.

'Morning, Mike. It's me!'

Hugo's voice filtered through the door.

His shadow crept down the stairs ahead of him, zigzag. The villain, like all villains, just doing what had to be done.

He knocked on Mike's door.

'Just a second!'

The shout came out cheerfully and too loud.

'Morning, Mike!' Hugo shouted. 'It's me!' He tried to seem light and airy. He thought he managed it.

'I'm just putting some clothes on!'

Hugo waited.

There were noises. The sat-on creaking of a chair. The sullen clump of shoes.

Finally, the door swung back. Mike stood the other side of it, fully dressed and haste-flushed, hair a flattened skew. He looked different in these better clothes. Smarter, yes, and older, yet more innocent. Behind him lurked the rumple from a failed night.

'Hi,' Mike said.

'Hello there. I hope you managed to get some sleep?'

'A bit.'

Something almost pleasant passed between them, a wry nostalgia. As if their rest had sectioned off the panic of the morning, and framed it safely in the past. They were companions in disaster now. No words were needed to acknowledge this.

'Good,' Hugo said. It was time to perform. 'Look, erm, I've got some news.'

He allowed himself to be ushered inside, into Mike's warm smell. Neither man sat down.

'Calvin has died,' he said.

'OK.'

Mike already knew. You could see he knew.

'I'm sorry.' And for his friend, Hugo truly was. 'I think maybe we always guessed.'

'I got a call.' Mike was looking at his new shoes. 'A mate told me.'

'Right.'

'It's terrible.'

'Awful. He was twenty.'

'Fuck.'

'I know.'

'Anyway.' Hugo stroked his chin and watched Mike's former clothes. 'The police are holding a press conference in a moment, and Renée has prepared a statement. She wants you to have a look at it too.'

'Me?'

'Because you were there.'

'I see.'

The bed looked desolate.

'Are the clothes OK?' Hugo had to say something.

'They're great.' Mike looked down at himself. 'No, yeah, they're really nice. Perfect. I'll have them cleaned when I get home and then send them back to you.'

'Don't be silly. Just keep them.' Hugo wished that he could buy him more.

'Seriously?'

'Sure. Renée'll put them on my tax bill.'

Mike smiled.

'Wow, thanks,' he said. 'Are you sure?'

'Positive.'

They stood together, not sitting, not closing the door, but not leaving either.

'Any word on when the detectives will be here?' Mike said. 'I've got some stuff to do at home, so I do need to get back soon.'

'Oh yes, someone from the police called, actually. He said that, under the circumstances, he thought it would be better to interview us here tomorrow. But he's happy for you to go home in the meantime.' There was a chilly satisfaction in how naturally these words elapsed.

'Really? That's great. I'm dreading having to wade through that lot.' Mike nodded at the street. 'But I've got to go back some time, so I think I'd rather just get on with it.'

'No, definitely. I understand. Although quite a lot of them will probably clear off once we've done our statement. Shall we go and have a quick chat with Renée about it? Then we'll get you a car. How's that?'

Mike looked relieved.

'That would be great,' he said.

A policeman, another young one, was coming down towards them from the roof.

'Yes, sir,' he said, looking up the stairs behind him to a superior, unheard and unseen.

Michael looked up also, surreptitiously, then felt worried about looking, then fearful about looking worried. He put his hands in his new pockets. Then he took them out again. No one noticed.

Approaching from the lower flight, a young woman stopped beside them at the banisters. She had a large sad nose, going-on proboscis, and a pristine bob of walnut hair.

'Hugo,' she said, an open laptop grinning in her elbow's crook.

She looked at Michael for a moment. Then she looked away.

'Theresa!' was Hugo's bright response.

'I've cleared your diary for today, and . . .'

'What did I have?'

The policeman had reached them now, and squeezed past on his way downstairs.

'Nothing much. *Batman Begins* screening at two. Vikram at six.'

'Let's keep Vikram,' Hugo said. 'I can't just put my whole life on hold.'

There was a special heartiness in his bonhomie. Like he had made a decision about it.

'Of course, fine.' The woman tapped something into her precarious computer. 'Also, there's been lots of calls. Renée's dealing with them for now. And Elton has sent over a fruit basket and some Alka-Seltzer. There's a note about having lunch tomorrow? I don't think he's heard about the situation.'

'No, I suppose not.' Hugo laughed, unconvincingly. 'Sure. Tell him I'd love to if I'm not in prison. Book us somewhere private though.'

'Got it.'

'And have you met Mike?'

'No.' The woman offered him a hand, which still had a pen in it. 'Hi.'

'Theresa picked out your clothes.' Hugo looked at her almost with paternal pride.

'Oh right!' Michael said. 'Thank you!'

'Are they OK?' She asked nervously. 'Renée had to guess your size.' She was still reluctant to meet his eye, perhaps embarrassed by the intimacy of dressing him.

'Perfect. Thank you.'

Guiltily, it pleased him, having staff.

'Come on,' Hugo said. 'Let's go find Renée.'

They all set off downstairs.

And soon '. . . *Excuse* me?' Renée's voice, itchy with disdain, was travelling up to meet them. 'No, I've got a question for *you*,' it continued. 'How do you think it makes *him* look if he *doesn't* attend?'

As they reached the landing, Michael could see that she was leaning against the wall in the first-floor living room, a mobile phone held tightly to her ear. On the sideboard behind her, two anchormen, BBC and Sky, prattled silently on a pair of muted televisions. There was a man in the room, too, dressed with casual expense in chinos and an open-necked shirt. He was reading a sheaf of papers and did not look up.

'Yeah. You're not kidding!' Renée was saying.

A pause, while the person on the other end replied.

'Fine,' she answered crossly. 'No, no, no . . . *Fine*.'

She hung up.

'Trouble?' Hugo said.

'Some stupid royal equerry butler-in-waiting *fuck*.' A burst of anger thundered out. 'Morning, Mike.'

Michael waved.

'*His Royal Highness*,' Renée recited, in simulated aristocrat, '*considers that* under the circumstances, *it would be better if Mr and Mrs Marks did not attend the wedding on Saturday.* Don't waste any time, do they?'

'Obviously not. Doesn't matter, though, does it?'

'No. No. Completely meaningless. Independence aren't going to like it too much, that's all.'

Michael stood and read the headlines as they scrolled across the screens.

BREAKING NEWS: MARKS STATEMENT 'IMMINENT' and VANCE POLICE 'RULING NOTHING IN OR OUT'.

'Anyway. The police have had their press conference,' Renée said. 'No surprises. Someone asked if any drugs had been found.

They didn't comment. Post-mortem's tomorrow, though, so I think we should prepare ourselves.'

'Sure.' Hugo seemed strangely uninterested. 'Mike and I were just talking. What do you think about him going home?'

'I've got to go back some time,' Michael chorused weakly, 'so I might as well get on with it.'

Theresa edged into the room, and had a quiet word with the man in chinos.

'Totally agree,' Renée said. 'My only thought is that you should wait until we've got this statement out. Once they've had something from us, most of the media will go. Not everyone, but I do promise you'll have an easier time in an hour or so. The caterers are coming to collect everything, in . . . Teri, when are the caterers coming?'

'Two p.m.,' Theresa replied without looking up. She was cross-legged on the sofa now, with the laptop on her knee.

'Fine. So, if you leave when they leave, you'll definitely get less attention.'

Renée smiled and took a bite of a banana. She seemed almost to be enjoying herself.

Michael made some calculations. Even if he was home at 2.30, that would still give him just two hours to write his piece. And to embrace such pressure, with so little time, and so little sleep . . . perhaps it was a sign that he should say no to Andrea. At least for now.

'OK,' he said.

'Good.' Renée took a swig of coffee. 'So anyway, I want you to have a look at the statement Hamish and I have prepared. Hugo, you're OK with it, right?'

'Yes.'

'And have you called Mellody?'

'Yes.' Hugo was leaning against the door jamb, watching the two TVs.

'And?'

'No answer.'

'Could you try her again? We need to coordinate with her if we can.'

'She is not going to coordinate, Renée.' He sighed.

'Humour me.'

Fuck! Were they dwarfs, the people who built these tiny cottages? *Seriously?* She rubbed her head with anger, and stooped into the kitchen beneath its enemy beam. Stunted British goblin folk. Like being quaint was just their permanent excuse. Though they had tried to make it nice for her, the *Sun* men, with flowers and this week's magazines (no papers) and a yapping little fire back there in the hearth. There were chocolates in the kitchen, too, and cakes and croissants laid out on the counter, with a spread of different coffees if she wanted one. If she didn't, there was champagne in the fridge, plus beer, water, sushi, salads, pesto, strawberries, cheese and mango slices, stacked up in hasty plastic packages. There was even ice cream in the freezer. Fucking *ice cream*, when she was shivering with cold.

Mellody searched the coffees for a black one, and tore off half a croissant as she scanned the dozen missed calls on her cell. Hugo and Renée and voicemail, and some random numbers. They could wait. Renée had also sent an SMS, which Mellody deleted on the inbox page, before opening another from her agent.

glad ur ok hun, it said. *tv is playing pretty big here, so I guess london sun not worst friends we cd have right now. am taking many calls too – theres a lot of people care about you back home remember! have told them ur being v strong. call again if you need me. love karl*

She smiled fondly, then walked back into the lounge. The

fire had reached its showy yellow phase, sending up the kind of flames that scorch nearby objects instantly but never warm a room. She toured the walls, visiting each little window to jerk its drape shut, wafting up the cosy ghost of woodsmoke. Outside the last, she glimpsed the shaven stern of her driver's head working through a bacon roll. On his nearside ear, a Bluetooth receiver was still clipped.

She lay down on the couch. Scratched her elbow. Scratched her calf. Too annoyed to sleep. Scratched her elbow again.

Beyond her feet there was a bookcase full of volumes – bought to fill it, by the ancient look of them. Old red boards with tissue pages, cloth-hinged at the spine. No one seriously expected her to read anything like that, of course. (No one ever did.)

Now there was a nasty drumming on the table at her head. It was her phone again, vibrating acrid in her ears.

Rebekah's number.

'Mell, hi.' The voice was serious and loud.

'Hi Rebekah.'

'Is the cottage OK?'

'Yeah. Fine.'

'Listen, I'm sorry to bother you . . .'

'Calvin is dead. I know.'

'Sorry. I wasn't sure . . .'

'My agent told me.'

Her neck was stiff from sleeping in the wrong position in the car.

'I'm so sorry,' Rebekah said. 'Twenty years old. It's absolutely awful.'

Twenty. Mellody had never thought to put a number on it. Twenty. Terrible.

Yet she was past sad now. Past even guilt. Though people would do their best to make guilt for her out of blame.

'Were you close?' Rebekah asked.

Calvin's battles were concluded. Now she had her own.

'No, not really. We only met last night.'

'I see. Well look, I thought I ought to call, because – I don't know what you've heard – but there really are a lot of rumours flying around.'

'I bet.'

'Most of it is rubbish, of course. But I thought I should tell you, we've been approached with one particular story about you and Calvin.'

Mellody scratched her leg.

'They're saying you were getting pretty close all night, that you were kissing at some party . . .'

'Excuse me?'

She made her eyes wide, as was her habit when indignant.

Rebekah pushed on. 'This person is saying that you and Calvin got together last night, that loads of people saw you kissing, and that later you performed a sex act on him in your car.'

'*What?* Jesus! Who's saying this?'

'Well it's come to us through a publicist, and . . .'

'It's Sean, isn't it? It's Sean from the band.'

But she already knew.

'It's Pete, Mell.'

She scratched her arm.

'He's claiming he dumped you, and you did it to get back at him.'

'I *bet* he is! Ha!'

She laughed, and the fire spat out a sympathetic pellet.

'So look. I'm really sorry. But I thought you ought to know that this is out there. They have no idea that you're staying with us, of course, or that I've told you any of this.'

Mellody's eyes stayed tightly focused on the orange ember as it seared itself a nest among the fibers.

A beep informed her that another call was waiting. It was Hugo.

'So what do you want to do?' Rebekah's voice was still at work.

'What do you mean? No one's going to print that garbage.' But even as she said it, she knew this was a hollow hope.

'Our lawyers have checked it out, Mell. They say it's OK. As long as something did go on between you and Calvin. And there are some shots of you going round . . .'

'What shots?'

Hugo's beeps continued.

'On the floor in some club. It looks sort of like you're cuddling. And then again outside. It's definitely you, Mell.'

'But nothing happened in any fucking car!'

A moment's silence, then, 'Would you sue?'

'Print it! You'll find out!'

'No-oo!' Rebekah gave the word two syllables, like a person actually insulted. 'No, no, no! This is not about us running it, Mell. I'm just telling you it's out there. You'd rather know than not know, right?'

'Oh yeah. Sorry. I forgot to say how incredibly fucking grateful I am.' That was childish, and too much, but she did not care.

The beeps had stopped.

'Listen Mell. I totally understand that you're not happy. And I feel completely rotten about doing this to you now, with everything you're going through. If it could wait, I would leave you alone, believe me. But you have to understand that if I don't buy this story, someone else will. Maybe you can live with that, in which case, fine. But if you can't live with that, and if your lawyers can't stop it, then I might be able to help.' The voice paused here for breath. 'We are not going to run Pete's story, OK? But if you like, we could buy it as an exclusive, and then sit on it. The details will probably come out eventually, of course, but you'll have time to get your version in first.'

'It's not my *version*!' Mellody interrupted shrilly. 'It's what happened!'

'OK. I understand that. But my opinion – and you may completely disagree with this – is that you need to act quickly so people hear you.'

And now Mellody got it.

'What do you want?' she said.

'It's about what *you* want. As I say, I can buy this story and shut it down, but that will be expensive to do – like, six figures – so I would need something to show for all that money. Obviously, if you chose the *Sun* as the place to go public, that would be perfect. We'd give you the cover, copy-approval, everything. And you'd have the biggest possible readership for what you have to say.'

'Lucky me.'

Mellody was angry. It felt good to be wronged and to be angry.

'Look, you don't have to make a decision right this second. Talk to your people and get back to me. I've told the publicist I'm thinking about it, and I'll string them along until I hear from you. Garth Spicer, one of our best writers, is just around the corner from where you are. So I'll tell him to be ready in case you need him. I know this is a shitty situation for you, Mell. And I'm sorry. Seriously.'

Again, that sympathetic voice. It touched her, damn it.

'Are you OK, Mell?'

'Whatever. Thanks Rebekah.'

She hung up.

She selected the Contacts menu.

She spooled to K.

Karl would be pleased.

'Engaged,' Hugo said. 'But she's still not answering.'

Renée raised a hand in acknowledgement. The other held her own phone to her ear. Theresa was folded behind her computer. Hamish had given Mike his own machine and was watching him read. Hugo turned to the televisions, which had resumed their commentating on the dying Pope. A little man, hesitantly bearded, was giving his opinions to the BBC anchor. Even in silence, Hugo could read what they were. John-Paul II had defined an era, said the man's wrists. He had touched the hearts of millions, his eyebrows concurred.

'I can't believe he's still alive,' Hugo said.

'What?' Mike glanced up.

'The Pope.'

'Still going, is he?' Hamish cheerfully chipped in.

Hugo liked Hamish. He was dry, urbane, officer class. He knew everything, and had a way of telling it to you that made all other opinions sound hopelessly naive. Mike didn't stand a chance.

'Yes, still going,' Hugo said.

The little man on TV, his time up, was dismissed and thanked.

'That was Warshak,' Renée said when she had finished. 'I asked for his advice – which I do not need, but he sure likes giving. I think he thinks this whole thing is kind of funny, actually. Which is good. For every Matthew Broderick there's a Robert Downey Junior, he said. And he's right. We just have to tough this out and recover. And you've never been Mr Clean-Cut, Hugo, so I think our chances are probably better than 50-50. If *Sinbad* opens well it might all be forgotten.' She looked up from dialling another number. 'If it tanks, well, we've got something to blame besides your shitty acting.' Renée did not frequently make jokes like this, so her smile hardened slightly when Hugo failed to laugh. 'No word from Independence yet,' she added quickly. 'But if we can stabilise the situation before LA wakes up, we might just sell this as a blip.'

'Good,' Hugo said. It seemed like what she wanted him to say.

'Have you seen this?' Theresa cut in, swivelling the laptop on her knee to face him.

It was the classic night-time pap shot. A startled tableau scooped from darkness, figures sheltered in a momentary cave of light. Mellody stared defiantly from the screen. Not sober. Malcolm and someone else behind him. Calvin by Mell's side. How strange it was to see him living.

'There's lots more of this on the wires,' Theresa added.

'It's good,' Renée explained. 'It makes this thing about her, not you. And you've been very lucky with the Pope too. Just pray he dies in time to fill the Sundays. That *would* be a fucking miracle.'

On Sky, the first helicopter shots had appeared. Hugo had never seen his home aerially before. The varnished floor of the roof terrace and its sad diagonal towel stood out brashly in its slate community. At the front, the media encampment looked enormous, scalloping across the road like debris from a landslide.

Now the BBC had come back to the story, too. Simon Cowell was being interviewed on a satellite link from New York. In the studio, his questioner sat before a wall of Calvin's smile. *Calvin Vance 1984–2005* was written underneath it.

Hugo turned the volume up.

. . . *Absolutely,'* Cowell said, nodding. *Calvin had the best energy. You know when you meet somebody and you're very comfortable with them? That's Calvin. I don't know how he did it. You never saw him in a bad mood. Ever. Ever. You just got the feeling that this was a guy with the talent, and the attitude, to go a long, long way. I still can't believe he's gone.*

As Cowell spoke, the screen began to show recorded footage. A young black man in white and yellow uniform was creeping up the path to Hugo's house beneath a flashgun monsoon. Encircled in his arms was a giant basket full of fruit.

'Hey! Have you seen this?' Hugo looked around.

'They've been showing it all morning.' Renée said, covering the mouthpiece as she stood on hold.

Theresa was on screen now, opening the door and taking in the fruit.

'So where's this basket?' Hugo asked.

'In the kitchen.' Theresa did not meet his glance.

'I'm going to take a peek.'

He drifted downstairs.

At the front door, Bonzo was standing guard again. 'Morning, boss,' he said, and nothing else. It looked as if he'd had a ticking off.

'All right, Bonzo.'

Hugo didn't dawdle.

The kitchen was immaculate. A stack of hired crockery sat packed away in boxes, waiting for its next affair. And there behind it, in the middle of the table, was Elton's basket, gigantically untelevised. Peaches and pears, rare-variety apples, black grapes in a reclining cone.

Fruit's good for a hangover, said the ballpoint scrawl. *And you can keep the basket. Still on for lunch tomorrow? E*

Hugo plucked a pear from the stack and bit it, noting its perfection.

Outside, he saw the vigil round his rockery went on. The young officer, the same one, looked cold and bored now, scanning hopefully for intruders.

Somewhere up above, a stationary helicopter knifed thumps out of the sky. Quite loud. Had it been there all along?

Hugo idled into the sitting room. His Berber throw sat up in a crumpled peak on the floor. Stepping round it, he approached the curtains and tweaked one in a glint. Still more police had shut the road and were keeping everybody off the pavement with a line of tape. Satellite vans. The backs of journalists. Cameras mounted on pneumatic struts. They looked calmer and more ordered than on Sky's recording, but also more entrenched. Hugo watched them while he finished his pear. Then he went back upstairs.

'I think –' he began, and stopped.

Everyone was looking at him.

No, they were looking at him *now*.

Before that they had been looking at the nearside television.

BREAKING NEWS, it said. It kept saying. Because periodically the letters reannounced themselves by falling from the foreground, as if out of his own eyes, and cratering the surface of the screen.

'*VANCE'S LAST MESSAGE*' REVEALED, was written next to this, beneath the same smiling picture of the boy.

And there was talking too, now Hugo listened.

. . . his voicemail when he got up this morning. It appears to be a recording of Vance's last moments on the roof, and then the conversation of horrified partygoers after his mobile phone fell with him into the garden below. We can now exclusively bring you this recording, in full.

Nobody said anything.

Calvin's photograph shrank into a sombre graphic. The icon of a mobile phone rose helpfully beside it.

All right, Jase. It's Cal. Words slushy, but fast, but clear. *You're not going to believe this, man. I'm on me own, up on Hugo Marks an (beep) Mellody's roof at their party and there's paparazzi and that everywhere. It's (beep) mental. Hold on. Hold on. I'm gonna a take a picture. Hold on.*

Shuffling sounds. Loud. Birdsong. A long, long wait. Birdsong.

Then: *'Calvin!'* Mike's voice. Shouted.

A shortlived scratching sound.

Hugo looked at Mike. So did Hamish, Theresa and Renée.

Experts, the Sky anchor said gravely, *believe this to be the moment that Vance fell. You can clearly hear what seems to be another partygoer calling out in shock.*

Birdsong.

Shortly afterwards, at least two male voices can be heard apparently discussing his injuries.

Silence, then:

View. Muffled and approaching.

. . . *believe you,* stark white subtitles suggested.

Calvin? Are you OK? Mike's voice again. Frightened. *He just fell.* Pause. *Is it serious?*

Mike was pale.

Yes. And this time it was clearly Hugo speaking.

I mean how . . .

But Mike's voice was cut off.

Don't touch it! Wait!

Hugo sounded quite out of control, which was not how he remembered it at all.

At this point, the anchor's voiceover continued, *it seems as if one or both of the men can be heard leaving the scene.*

Silence.

On three occasions, the first man asks someone called Hugo, believed to be Hugo Marks, if he has called an ambulance.

Silence.

Birdsong.

An unintelligible murmur, subtitled *You call an ambulance?*

Silence.

Hugo? Mike. Loud and clear. *Did you call an ambulance?*

Birdsong and silence.

Did you call an ambulance, Hugo? Angry.

I think he's dead, Mike. That was calmer. A real doctor couldn't do it better.

A noise, identifiably Mike speaking, but faint and muddled.

Shouldn't we call an ambulance? said the subtitles. *You're supposed to.*

And then Hugo remembered something.

How long were voicemail messages these days? Three minutes? Longer? Probably it varied between networks.

He fell three (beep) storeys on to some rocks! He heard himself say. *He's not breathing! That is a corpse!* Angry. Angry. Words covered by the wind, but angry. . . . *let's tidy first.*

Another raging gust.

And the tape went on, and Hugo listened from his life.

. . . the police get here, they will see the mess from people's drugs everywhere, and we will be arrested. Every single word, bright and clean.

This appears to be the voice of Hugo Marks, the anchorman said. As if there could be any doubt.

His career was finished, of course. He and Renée would have to talk about that later.

And still the tape went on.

. . . rested? But it was an accident! I haven't taken any drugs!

A pause. And then:

I saw what happened, Mike.

The menace. The foreboding tone. Got that spot on.

Freaking out, Mike's voice said.

And the recording ended.

And Hugo knew what he was going to do.

According to the time signature, the message was left at 5.58 a.m. this morning. So far police at the house, which Marks shares with his wife, the supermodel Mellody, are refusing to comment on reports that a mobile phone has been recovered from the garden. We'll bring you more on this story, and all the rest of the day's news from Rome and around the world, when we come back.

Michael was such a fool.

'Guys? Is this genuine? Is that what happened?'

Renée looked at both of them.

Nobody was more of a fool, or more publicly a fool, than him.

'I need to *know*! Is *that* what happened?'

'Yes, Renée.' Hugo was calm and quiet. 'That's what happened.'

The way Michael had just forgotten. How he had been exploited. That threatening voice, after all his sympathy and care. And he had timidly forgotten. And *he* was feeling guilty. So *weak*. And such a fool. Just Hugo's voice disgusted him. He could not look at the face.

'Mike?'

Humiliated. So angry. Throbbing with impotent anger. Humiliated on television. His subjugation broadcast. And he had never seen a phone – not in Calvin's hand, not on the grass.

He could not look at Hugo's face.

'*Mike?*'

'That's what happened,' he whispered.

'Renée.' Hamish was shaking his head and almost smiling, trying to calm her down. 'If this ever goes to a criminal trial – which I'd say is unlikely – we'll get that tape ruled inadmissible. There won't be a juror in the country who hasn't heard it by then. That's a good thing,' he added.

'Why would this go to trial?' she said.

'Obstructing justice. Possible perverting-the-course. But as I say, I doubt that will happen. Those are difficult to win. Sky', he pointed at the screen, 'have done you a favour.'

Theresa was watching the commercials.

'How about this statement?' Renée said.

Hamish considered the question.

'Up to you,' he announced finally. 'Hugo did not say they were *his* drugs. Nor was he specific. That's not enough for a prosecution, and the police have left it too late to search the house. They might have to at some point, for appearances, but it won't go anywhere in the end. You cannot avoid a lot of embarrassment, but I don't think that, if you go ahead with the statement, it will change anything, legally.'

The TV still flickered mutely on the sideboard. It was the Crazy Frog, ogling them all with its rapacious eye.

Hugo was a few feet away. Michael could feel his presence.

Could he just walk downstairs? Step out into all that noise and leave these people? Could he? It almost felt as if he could.

'OK,' Renée said. 'OK.' She breathed deeply and closed her eyes. Then she opened them again and said: 'We're fucked. Everybody? OK? We're fucked. But it's better not to delay. This will only be as big as we make it. Just give me a minute to freshen up, and I'll go outside and read the statement.'

'No,' Hugo said. 'I'll do it.'

And Michael looked at him then.

From: onolan.daniel@gmail.com

To: leobenedictus@yahoo.co.uk: valerie.morrell@nortonmorrell.co.uk

Subject:

Date: Tuesday, 16 February 2010 16:19:05

Looking back, it is just so obvious, isn't it? Actually, let's start again: it was probably obvious all along. I just chose to be gullible. That way I could believe I had a book deal. Even so, you should both be very proud of yourselves for convincing me so utterly. I mean that. Well done. *Round of applause*

Greater Manchester Police, on the other hand... dear oh dear. You'd think I was Ayman al-Zawahiri, the number of vans and uniforms they left outside. I mean, I'm just a bloody writer; I'm not going to climb out on the window ledge or crawl through an air vent. But nor am I a total idiot, so when I'm on my way back from the all-night garage (turns out they don't sell notebooks, what an irony!) and I see all those coppers shivering on the pavement, I'm not exactly going to walk right past them, am I? One guy with a taser knocking on my door at lunchtime, that's all it would have taken. Couldn't they see how late at night I often send my emails? I trust someone's been demoted.

You two though, honestly. You really had me thinking that my dreams were coming true. And I'm glad, actually. I've had the experience now, and nobody can take it from me. The feedback has meant a lot too. Being isolated like this makes it very difficult to connect with people, and knowing you two were there has been such a help, even when I've had to disappear at times. Believe me, Val: I don't blame you one bit for turning me in after I behaved so furtively, so please don't deny you did it. And Leo, you were put in an impossible position. Knowing so little about me, it was very brave of you to volunteer. I wish you luck with your own novel (if there is one) and I hope this experience has not been too upsetting for you or your family (if there is one).

My final point is this, and I want you both to pay attention to it: neither of you deserves to feel remorse for what you've done. If someone must be blamed for where we find ourselves today, the only candidate is me.

But then justice, when we judge ourselves, is frequently miscarried. I, of all people, ought to understand that. So if you ever do feel guilty about this whole episode and wish that there was something you could do to mitigate it, take comfort, there is. Please just leave me alone.

Daniel

Dear Daniel,

I know you would prefer to be left alone, so I am very sorry to be writing to you now. I only do this because I believe that it is in your interests to hear what I have to say.

And yes, I do also feel guilty. I took fright, I think, once the thought occurred to me that you might be the person they were looking for. You're right, all the reporting of the case did make you seem like a sinister character, so when I read that second 'incessantly' in your email, echoing the one you quoted, I panicked. I began to worry that I would become an 'accessory', or some such, if you were who I suspected, and I carried on without informing the authorities. These were selfish motives – I was about to call you 'William' – and I can't pretend that justice was much on my mind.

Though once the police got involved, it's true my wrists were bound. They told me that your emails came from the north of England, never Sicily, and that parts of the book corresponded with details of the crime scene which had never been made public. (Detectives will be reading this message, I'm afraid, so I can't tell you any more.) In any case, it was they who insisted that I keep the relationship going while they traced you, and talked as if I were some splendid Miss Marple figure, though I felt more of a Jezebel as I typed. I do appreciate your forgiving words, but I don't think I will ever cease to blame myself for the deception.

Which is why I must now reveal more of it. You ought to know that Leo was never involved. He agreed to let me use his name, and set up an email address, but I wrote those messages, with a detective at my shoulder. Besides advising on a couple of facts, Leo has no knowledge of what I wrote, or your replies. I hope this does not upset you, but I cannot bear for there to be any more dishonesty between us. Though of course I cannot compel you to believe me either; I can only tell you the truth, with hope.

In which spirit, I have another piece of news to relate. Though the emails since Leo's appearance have been fictitious, Cape would still like to publish your book. (Bloomsbury declined in the end, but I kept them in, on police instructions, to simulate the excitement of an auction.) Jane loves what you have written – that was always true – and she wants to go ahead, even now she knows that you are the author. You might not be permitted to profit from it if you are convicted of anything, but I sense that money is not actually the most important thing to you. And I believe that you are innocent anyway.

Which is why, whatever you decide, I do think you should turn yourself in, Daniel. You won't be surprised to hear me say so, of course, but that does not make it bad advice. After all, if you can convince me of your innocence, you can convince others. And, though you have managed it so far, you cannot keep eluding the police indefinitely. It is your decision. Please think about it carefully. And do look after yourself.

All my love,

Val x

Dear Val,

Such a kind email. Thank you so much for sending it, in spite of what I said. The warmth of your concern is obvious, and I do not doubt a word of it. Yet I wonder if your loyal optimism, in the event of my surrender, is what prevents you from seeing things as they are. The truth is that everybody thinks I did it, Val. The story is I did it. I can give in. I can protest my case. But jailed or acquitted, I will never be recast.

It is flattering, of course, that Jane still wants to go ahead with publication. And it is enchanting of you to believe she wants this 'even now she knows' who I am. But search your instincts, Val. This is not an 'even'; this is a 'because'. Take Daniel O'Nolan's book to any publisher and see how many rejections you get. They won't even need to read it. This is the power of fame: always being listened to, never being heard. (We are, as Michael Knight has said, 'the unignored'.) I fear that you'll discover that yourself one day, when the details of our partnership emerge.

Thank you for your message, though. The answer, to all your questions, is that I still have a little work to do. I realise that someone in a uniform will probably compel you to write back, in which case I apologise in advance for the slowness of my reply. It has become rather difficult for me to reach a computer recently.

Affectionately, of course,

Daniel

Dear Daniel,

Just so that you know, no one is compelling me to send this. The final draft will be checked by the detective, but whether I write – and what – has been left to my discretion. So please do not imagine that this is a policeman's voice you're reading. This is Valerie, just as it always was.

Nor am I here to hassle you about giving yourself up. You understand my argument, and I understand your objections. I still think it would be better if you surrendered, but we will leave it at that.

I do want to clarify Cape's intentions, however. Jane would never deny that a book with your name on it will attract a good level of attention (and neither would I), but you should not let this blind you to the sincerity of her admiration for *Publicity******. She wanted to publish this before either of us had any idea of who you really were, remember. And when I spoke to her earlier, she said she was happy for you to have no role in promoting it. She also said you could use a pseudonym if you would like to keep your name off the cover. Jane will do anything she can, in other words, to disassociate you from the finished edition, if that is what you prefer.

Meanwhile, Cape's legal department have also made a suggestion, which, under the circumstances, you might find more appealing anyway. In its current form, they do feel that the book could be actionable. (The whole O.J. fiasco made publishers very wary of 'what-if' books, I think.) If our email correspondence were also included, however, the lawyers feel this would put the chapters of the novel in their proper fictional context. We would have to change your name, my name, everybody's name, and a few details, to avoid direct references to the real case, but in Jane's opinion (and mine) this would add another fascinating dimension. (And she suggests using a different title, such as *The Afterparty*, as the result would essentially be a different book.) It also means you need not make any further revisions. With your consent, one of Jane's colleagues would acquire the book and edit it into a suitable form, inserting the usual 'any resemblance to actual persons, living or dead' disclaimer. For my part, I would be happy for my emails to be published in this way. But the final decision, of course, will always be yours.

Please think it over, and do look after yourself. I'm sorry I called you a 'creepy advertising guy'.

Valerie x

From: onolan.daniel@gmail.com
To: valerie.morrell@nortonmorrell.co.uk
Subject: Re:
Date: Friday, 26 February 2010 21:16:04
▶ 🖇 Chapter 13 – The end

Dear Val,

Thank you for your email. I've thought about your proposal, and I accept. Jane has my permission to publish the book and all my emails, calling it *The Afterparty* if she wishes. I would be grateful if you could take out any mention of my name and email address, and print it under a pseudonym of your choosing. Or perhaps allocate it to Leo Benedictus, if he would still be willing to stand in for me. He is free to play the author and deny my existence if he wants. I would also like to stipulate that my suggestions for promoting the novel should be adopted whenever possible within the limits of a reasonable marketing budget for a book of this type. Please hold any payments due to me in trust until I can collect them. Failing which, please give them to the charity of your choice.

I enclose the penultimate chapter. It was originally intended as the final one, but I have amended it in order to create the opportunity for another, which I am currently writing. It will all be over soon.

Love,

Daniel

The Crazy Frog was on TV again. That bubbling, babbling child machine.

'Do you mind if I turn it off?' Garth asked. He still had his overcoat on, and was being polite. More polite, Mellody suspected, than usual.

She lowered her head in slow assent, just once, and hugged the blanket closer. 'Turn it *down*,' she said.

He reached across his two dictation machines for the remote control, and pressed mute.

The fire rustled softly through its middle age.

'So does this voicemail surprise you?' he asked.

'Not really. If it's genuine.'

'And how would you feel if it was genuine?'

'How would I *feel*?'

'Yes.'

'You're "one of the *Sun*'s best writers" and you're asking *how I feel*?'

'I am.' He smiled, answering both questions.

Mellody lofted her eyes in resignation.

'Sad, I guess.' But sadder for Hugo than for Calvin.

'And do you think it is genuine?'

'I don't know.'

'You weren't there at the time?'

'No. I was asleep.'

'But do you think your husband would be capable of leaving a young man to die?'

Yes. Mellody did think that.

'No,' she said. 'But Hugo's not been himself for a while.'

'Since when?'

She lit a cigarette and exhaled hard.

'I don't know. Two years ago? During all the *Sinbad* reshoots. We were still close. But the pressure . . . I think he began to have issues with it.'

Odd that she was defending him now. The sourness of those days seemed suddenly so faint, diluted by time.

'Did you think about having children together?'

Garth had removed his coat, revealing a suit and tie. He asked the question seriously, like your oldest friend, but the body was wrong. Too much focus. Perching eagerly forward from the armchair's lip, elbows on knees, hands clasped together tripodding the chin, gaze locked. Mellody's addiction counselor had sat a bit like that.

'Nope.' She was firm. 'I'm not going to talk about that.'

'I just think it's something people will want to know. You did say, um . . .' He shuffled through a pack of printouts. '. . . last March that children was something you were thinking about.'

'It doesn't matter what I said. I'll talk about last night, and Hugo. Whatever else you get is a bonus. Call Rebekah if you're not happy about it.'

'No, that's fine Mell. You're in charge here.' His BlackBerry fizzed and murmured. 'So let's talk about last night, then,' he continued, ignoring it. 'When did you and Calvin get together?'

Mellody expelled a little scoff. So *this* was how it would be. No delicacy, no seduction of her secrets into being told. Consent had been granted. The only thing remaining was the act.

'After Cuzco,' she sighed. 'We went to another party, and he kissed me. It just seemed right. Hugo and I have had an open marriage for the past year now. I wouldn't be surprised if he's had his own liaisons, and I know he didn't mind about mine.'

'Who were his liaisons with?'

Irritably: 'Like I said, I don't even know if there were any.'

'How about yours?'

She said nothing. Smoked her cigarette.

'Did Hugo know about your relationship with Pete Sheen?'

'He knew. We didn't talk about it, but he knew.'

Once one violation was survived, how easily the others followed.

'And was Pete there at the squat when you and Calvin kissed?'

'He was. Although Peter and I split up a while ago. We still hung out, but that was it.'

'Why did you and Hugo stay together if you were seeing other people?'

Mellody considered this. The front of her house shimmered silently on TV.

LIVE, the screen said.

'He's been having a hard time recently. A lot of stress – with work, I think, and with personal problems that I'm not going to discuss. If I'd left him I don't know what would have happened. When you're as successful as Hugo, you get surrounded by a lot of people with agendas, not all of whom you can trust. But he knew – he's always known – that I only had his interests at heart, even if it was obvious that we couldn't stay married much longer.'

'So why are you telling your story now?'

'Oh come *on!*' Like he didn't know.

Garth rephrased it. 'What would you like to tell people?' he said.

Mellody considered the question.

'That I just cannot be a part of what happened last night.

I am worried that Hugo may be being badly advised, by people who are exploiting him for their own gain. If that tape was genuine then it can only be because other people have got him all confused and messed up inside himself. Hugo is the sweetest guy I've ever met. He would never harm anyone. The Hugo I know would have done everything he could to help Calvin. I'm sure of it.'

'Do you think the tape was genuine?'

'I don't know. It sounds like him, but I don't know.'

'So what did happen last night, as you experienced it?'

She stubbed out her cigarette. Scratched her knee. Her arm.

'Well, after the party, I went on to this other party. Then I came back home with Calvin and some friends . . . Jesus, I just can't believe he's dead.'

Garth nodded, but said nothing. He was young, and his tie was pink like Turkish delight, suspended from a beefy Double Windsor.

'So anyway, there were still a lot of people at the house who had been at Cuzco. We all kind of hung out for a while – just talking and drinking. Calvin was great company. A lot of people in the music business get pretty cynical, but he was just totally positive about what he was doing. And he had a great sense of humor. We had only just met, and I know he was younger than me, but we really clicked. It's like we had a real connection. I was really looking forward to getting to know him better. I'm devastated about his death, especially for his family. It doesn't seem real.'

'Did you have sex together?'

'Jesus. You really expect me to answer that?'

'I think it's an important question.'

'I bet you do.'

Now her roof was on TV. There was a policeman on her roof

on TV. And one of her towels. *LIVE*. What was her towel doing live on TV?

'Well, people are saying you did have sex.' Garth's voice gave its first hint of irritation. 'If you don't deny it, what do you think that means?'

'You know what?' Mellody leaned forward now. 'I don't give a fuck.'

The guy actually looked hurt. Like he believed he was only trying to help.

'I'm not your enemy, Mell,' he said. 'I'm here to write your story for you.'

'*WINE RADICALS' CLAIM RESPONSIBILTY FOR BOMB ATTACK*, read the tickertape along the bottom of the screen.

'OK, OK,' Mellody said impatiently. 'You're just doing your job. I get it. But the answer is still "no comment".'

'And in your car? Did anything happen?'

'No comment.'

'How about drugs? Did Calvin take any drugs?'

'Possibly. I didn't see him.'

'Were there drugs around, as Hugo says in the recording?'

'If you go to a party, there will be people taking drugs, so sure, there probably were.'

'Did you take anything?'

'No. That time of my life is behind me now. Drugs have destroyed people I was very close to and they nearly destroyed me. I was lucky enough to get help before it was too late. And Hugo was there for me all the way . . .'

It only took a second for the tears to come . . . But no. *No!* Mellody squeezed them back. *Not* in front of this guy. She would not allow it.

'Wait a minute,' she managed. '*Wait!*' And breathed deeply.

Back to her front door again, live on TV.

'No,' she said. 'There probably were drugs around, but I didn't have any.'

'How do you feel about Hugo today?' The guy just kept on coming.

'I'm sad for him. Things are difficult right now, of course, but we'll always be friends. Most of all, I feel so sorry for Calvin's family.'

'Mmm.' The sympathy noise.

And now on screen, her front door was opening.

Hugo was stepping out.

Hugo was stepping out.

He looked OK. His face was calm, though it seemed to shiver in a thousand claps of artificial light.

'*Turn it up!*' Mellody yelled suddenly. 'Turn it *up!*'

Garth released the mute.

Hello, Hugo said. *I hope you all have your equipment ready, because I'm only going to say this once. There will not be any questions.*

Hello, he said. *I hope you all have your equipment ready, because I'm only going to say this once. There will not be any questions.*

Hugo stood in front of the gate. A man arched by dark magnolia leaves above, and steel bars behind. He held the statement low, one white sheet gripped fast in an untrembling hand. There were mixed shouts. Orders and interrogations. *How did Calvin die? Hugo, over here! Is this a cover-up?* All were ignored until all faded.

Renée pressed in close by Michael's side to improve her view of the screen. He edged fractionally away.

A young man, Calvin Vance, died today, Hugo said slowly. *What it is like to be in the shoes of his family and friends right now, the rest of us cannot know. And we should all hope that we never find out.*

'Good,' Renée hummed appreciatively. 'Good.'

HUGO MARKS STATEMENT, crashed on to the screen. LIVE.

Michael felt sick, but could not look away.

I met Calvin only twice, and briefly. But just a few moments in his company was all anybody needed to feel his warmth, and his enthusiasm for life and for his music.

He spoke it very plainly, with authority, giving everybody time to write it down.

I know many people, not just his fans, believed that Calvin was on the brink of achieving something special. It is just one of the many tragedies of his death that now we will never know.

Michael's phone rang, making Theresa jump. Renée looked at him crossly. It was work. He considered answering, then pressed *Reject*.

As the police have already indicated, Calvin's death seems to have been a terrible accident. But while the investigation continues I have been asked not to comment publicly on the events of last night or this morning. And I won't.

Had he? No one had asked the same of Michael.

I understand your interest, and the interest of many people, in finding out about what has happened. But today, and in the coming weeks, Calvin's family must be put first. Events in Rome have made this is a sad time for millions of people around the world, but they also show us that decency and respect are infinitely more powerful forces than gossip and insinuation.

VANCE WAS 'ON BRINK OF SOMETHING SPECIAL', began to roll beneath his knees.

The purr of helicopter blades, rising in pitch, then passing overhead.

As for myself . . .

'What the *fuck*?' Renée yelped suddenly, snatching up her copy of the statement.

. . . if you feel your story needs somebody to blame, blame me.

Michael was transfixed. What was this? It was not in the speech he had read.

The price of success is an obligation to set a good example. I accept that, even though I have not always managed to do it. And it is difficult, you know, when some people prefer to watch the spectacle of failure.

'What is he doing? What is he doing?' Renée offered her palms in open desperation to the room.

This is the audience that I have, however, so I must accept that, too. And more than that . . .

In his pocket, Michael's phone was ringing again.

. . . I would sincerely like to thank all the thousands of people who have taken the trouble to watch my stage and film performances over the years. If my work has pleased you, then I'm glad. Nothing has made me gladder. All I ever wanted was the chance to tell good stories. But I am a real person, and real people fail. Thank you very much.

There was a confused silence.

In the flat centre of the camera's gaze, Hugo folded up his piece of paper, put it in his pocket, walked back through the gate and up the path. A few journalists, jolted from their shock, called out to him – *Why are you to blame? How have you failed?* – but too late.

VANCE FAMILY 'MUST COME FIRST' said the yellow letters.

Michael's phone was still ringing. He slipped out with it.

'Hello?' he said.

'Michael, it's Andrea.'

'Hi there.' Scurrying up the stairs to his room.

'Hello. Look, I've had a word with a few of the top brass about this, and we all really want to hear your story. We can set something up over the phone, send a car, come to your house, whatever, really. And the editor's prepared to pay you quite well, I think.'

'OK.' Shutting the bathroom door. 'That's great. I've been thinking about it too.'

'Well done, boss,' Bonzo said, closing the door.

'Thanks, Bonzo.'

His hall looked different.

'What the *fuck*, Hugo?' Renée was pouring down the stairs at speed. 'What the *fuck*?'

She was very angry. He knew she would be very angry.

'I wanted to explain myself.'

'And you didn't want to tell me about it?'

Hugo shrugged. 'You would have said no.'

'I'm not your fucking boss, Hugo. You can do what you like. But you're damn right I would have said no. That would have been my advice, yeah. Because what you just did . . .' Eyes revolved in their sockets. Hands rose together as if imploring God for a new hyperbole. 'It could kill your career, Hugo. OK? It could kill your career.'

He was so tired.

'They will tear you apart! They will make it look like you've gone crazy. Like some spoiled showbiz brat. If you think you're going to get these guys to blame themselves, then . . .'

'Look,' he said. 'I'm tired. I want some time alone.'

'OK.' She tried to calm herself. 'Good idea. You go upstairs, get some sleep. I'll talk to the police. We'll see how this goes down. Independence will never forgive you, though. This is not exactly . . .'

'No!' Now Hugo was shouting. 'I want to be alone! I want everyone out! *Now!*'

Theresa's face peeped out above the banister rail.

'Hugo.' Renée was gentle. Friendship for a mental patient or a child. 'I know you're under a lot of pressure, but we need to stick together.'

'*Leave!*'

So loud he squeaked it, though he felt no real rage. It

felt like he was watching himself. This was what his tantrums looked like. How interesting.

'There are police, Hugo.' She was trying to calm him now, which was sensible. 'We can't ask *them* to leave. Why don't you take a few minutes, maybe have a nap, and then we'll talk.'

'Just go! All of you! I don't want your help!'

Bonzo looked frightened. Renée sighed.

'OK.' Glancing back over her shoulder. 'Let's go, Theresa. Get our stuff together and call an extra car. We'll go out the back. Hamish, do you need a lift?'

'Thank you,' Hamish said.

'You too, Bonzo.' Hugo tried to sound kinder.

'Boss?'

'I think Bonzo should stay here, Hugo.'

'This is *my house*!' It sounded almost as if he really was upset.

'OK, Bonzo,' Renée said. 'Just wait on the street with the guys. Don't let anybody in.'

Bonzo nodded, and walked out of the door.

Hugo looked at Renée. She seemed smaller, in her pressed white shirt, vibrating even now with energy, blazing out great wavefronts of fear.

And now Theresa was shouting something. Something about bakers.

'What?!' Renée yelled impatiently.

'What about the *caterers*?' she repeated, picking a route down the stairs with three laptop bags.

'Cancel the caterers,' Hugo snapped, and noticed himself accelerating along the hall.

'Erm…' Theresa speaking timidly. 'And Vikram?'

'Cancel Vikram!' he bawled. 'Cancel *everything*!'

He began his descent into the basement.

The curtains were closed, the TV still on. Mute light played upon the walls in coloured alternations.

'BLAME ME' BEGS MARKS IN SPEECH.

EMOTIONAL STAR CONFESSES 'I FAILED'.

He heard the front door shut. After a minute, the back door slammed too.

Hugo knew what he was going to do.

Mellody opened the front door and winced.

'You must be Giles's friend?' she said.

'That's right,' said the man. And then, oafishly, 'Sorry oy took a while getting 'ere.'

He had a weird accent, like a pirate. And as he smiled, two red cheek blemishes, stalled healings from some long-lost wound, stretched lengthways with the skin. Nor were his teeth of the quality that Mellody expected.

'That's right,' she said, standing back. 'Come in.'

Ducking beneath the doorframe, he ambled past her, smile still in progress. A hooded top and boyish face, much too deeply lined, overworked by grimaces and grins. He might equally have been a lively forty or a ruined twenty-four. Mellody eyed the shrivelled backpack hanging off his shoulder.

'Could you just wait in the kitchen for a minute, while I take care of something?' she said politely, as he was about to advance into the lounge.

'Don't mind,' the man said, and did as he was told.

Garth was in the armchair, peering at his BlackBerry.

'Can we take a break for half an hour, Garth?' Mellody said briskly.

'Half an hour?'

'Yup. A friend's arrived and we need some time together. It's

351

been a difficult day. Do you think you could just go for a walk or something?'

'A friend?'

'Uh-huh.'

'OK.' He wasn't happy. 'We still have a lot to cover, though, Mell.'

'Sure.' Picking up his overcoat for him. Ushering him to the door. 'Don't worry. I'm not going anywhere.'

She closed it behind him.

In the kitchen, Giles's man had found some sushi in the fridge and started eating it.

'That's a lot of bubbly you gat in there.' He licked his fingers, and nodded at the line of Moët.

'It is,' Mellody said. 'Open one if you like.'

'Nah. I'm driving, thanks.'

'OK.'

She shut the door and the bottles jangled.

'I had a hell of a time getting here,' the man said, as he unpacked his bag. 'There was an accident on the A28, I think it was. They was diverting us all round Beckley.'

'Mmm.'

He had placed a set of digital scales on the countertop, and was reaching inside what looked like a gent's washbag.

'How much you want then?'

'How good is it?'

She would only get enough for a day or two, that way things could not get out of hand.

'Oh, it's very good. Don't you worry about that.'

Naturally. It always was.

'Just give me a gram.'

The man took out a Saran-wrapped package and worried away the outer layers to reveal a small beige ingot.

'You not got any white? Giles's was always white.'

352

'No-ho.' He laughed the word. 'S'all right, though. I've got some citric if you need it.'

'OK.' She sighed.

He dropped a little morsel on the scales. It landed, and shook off a layer of dust.

0.844 g.

He dipped the corner of a card into the plastic, and slid off another tiny golden helping.

1.096 g.

Holding the package beneath the edge of the scales, he gently scraped a ridge back in.

1.010 g.

'Close enough.' He grinned.

'Thanks.'

Carefully, the man folded a square of paper into an envelope, swept in the heroin, and tucked it closed. After this he rewrapped the block and returned it to the washbag, from which he also produced a handful of citric acid sachets.

'Have you got a needle?' This was so humiliating.

The man raised his eyebrows.

'You not got one?'

'No.'

'All right. I only got one new one left, but you can have that. Giles says you're good for the money. Zat right?'

'Yes.'

'All right, then.'

He looked at her carefully, like something for sale.

'You're married to that Hugo Marks, aren't you?'

'Yes.'

She slipped the goods into her pocket.

'I knew it was you! *Mellody*, right?'

His manner had changed utterly. He was repacking his bag with childish excitement.

'That's right.'

'With two Ls?'

'Yup. Two Ls.'

'Giles said you was one of his important customers, and I thought I recognised you! What you doing down here, then?'

He handed her a syringe. It was long and narrow with a bright orange cap.

'I'm on vacation.'

'Right, OK. Yeah. It's pretty round here.'

'I guess so.'

'Yeah. Yeah.'

He seemed to be searching, with great hopefulness, for some strand of sense in her behavior. Evidently, he had not seen the news.

'Anyway, enjoy that,' the man said, pointing at her pocket with his finger. 'It's good stuff. I better run, but say hello to Giles when you see him.'

'Sure. I will. Thanks.'

She opened the door, and he loped off indifferently into the sun.

OK.

Now back into the kitchen for a spoon. Blood fluttered in her guts. It made her want to pee. She bounded up the stairs to see to it.

And for a tourniquet?

She sat down on the toilet.

No scarf. And her belt was too wide.

Pulling up her jeans, she snatched out a rag of tissue, wiped, and left the bowl unflushed.

Bedrooms: clean smell, no cords on the drapes.

Downstairs: cupboard: just sticks and galoshes.

Kitchen . . . an electric kettle. That so British thing. A chalkish yard of flex from plug to charging base. She picked it up, with some Evian and other items, and struggled to the couch. Using a credit card, she crushed and plowed the powder on the table into guessed-at halves, then one half into quarters, a quarter into eighths, eighths to sixteenths, and a sixteenth into two experimental hits, the babies in a family tree. One chosen share she coaxed into the spoon, and dribbled citric acid gently on it. Now the needle's cap came off – nicely, with a *puck*. She plunged its point into the Evian bottle, drawing water to the 4, and then reversed the action, pushing out a hairline jet of drink to take the drug. Lighter next: flicked on, and left to stand upon the table, its flame a ripple round the teaspoon's silver hull, sizzling its contents' edges in an instant, then gradually stirring up the center to a dirty seethe. The smell, the smell, of candied pickled corpses, spread into the air. And by the time Mellody, having forgotten wadding, had picked a piece of filter from a Marlboro Light, her dose was cool. It quenched the fluff on contact, making it dark and emptying the bowl, before she pierced the filter with the needle's tip and sucked it white again. Now finally she had the liquid captured, glimmering a muddy gold beneath the measures in her tube, which she tapped and squirted slightly to squeeze out any air.

With great gentleness, she placed the needle on the table, rolled her left sleeve up and hesitated, staring for an outbreath at the kettle flex, before noosing it at last around her upper arm and pulling tight, soft plastic chewy in her teeth, untethered base and big plug jostling around her breast. Her left fist pumped, her veins bulged green and pornographic. The needle's point slipped easily through soft and ticklish skin, a tiny plunger tug confirming what she knew: a feathering of red inside the tube. Got the blood in one. Mellody released her tourniquet a little. A prod to test and . . . oh . . . plunge home the rest . . . oh, oh . . .

And she was lost.

A reunion to make her cry with joy.

How much she had missed you.

Picked needle out. Mopped weakly smear blood.

The fire was ringing. A pulsing lovely glow of sound.

Oh, it was the telephone in her bag that was ringing.

Ring ring. Ring ring. Hello?

'Hugo,' said the screen. Darling Hugo.

Now you press the green button.

'Zello,' she said.

'Mell.' His voice. 'I'm so glad you answered.'

'Ahhh . . .' How nice. 'I am too.'

'Where are you?'

Clattering in the background. He was doing something.

'Oh . . . a cottage.'

'A *cottage*? Where?'

'No, no, no,' she had remembered. 'Kent! I'm in Kent, baby. Like the cigarettes.'

'What are you doing in Kent?'

'Well . . .' It didn't matter any more. 'I'm talking to a journalist about some things.'

Silence.

Then, 'OK.'

'Are you angry with me, baby?'

'No. I'm not angry with you.'

'You were on TV!' She had just remembered!

'Yes.'

'I thought you were fabulous.'

'Thank you. Look . . .'

It sounded like he wanted to say something.

'Mm-hm?'

'Look. I think, well . . . I think it's over, really. It's right that you should go ahead and look after yourself now. I may be in trouble, and it's not your fault.'

'Did you kill that boy?'

'No. I didn't.'

'But he died.'

'Yes he did.'

There was another ringing. A long ring. *Rrrrrrring!*

'Look, Mell. I just wanted to say, you know, whatever happens, I love you. I always will. I'm sorry things didn't work. It was my fault.'

The door. It was the doorbell.

'Aah. It's not your fault, baby.'

'No, it is, Mell. And I'm sorry. I love you and I'm sorry.'

Rrrrrrrring!

That Garth guy. Maybe Garth was back? Mellody unwrapped the cable from her arm and gathered all the bits under her blanket.

'I love you too,' she said, distracted.

Keys in the lock.

'Do you know what you want to do?' Hugo said.

'Mm?'

'After this. Are you coming home?'

'Yeah, I think I'll go home.'

And here was Garth all grouchy-looking, about to say something until he saw she was on the phone.

'You might want to wait a while. The press are all still here.' Hugo's voice was filled with love again.

'No, no. *Home.*'

'America?'

'Mmm. I think so.'

She sighed happily.

'Yeah, OK,' Hugo said. 'Maybe that's a good idea.'

Garth sat back in his chair. He looked really mad.

'Listen baby, I have to go,' Mellody said.

'Of course. I love you, OK? Just remember that.'

He was so sweet.

'I will. I love you too.'

Now you press the other button.

She pressed the other button.

'I don't want to rush you, Mell,' Garth said, red. 'But we really have to get on with this. Are you OK to continue?'

'Yes I'm OK.'

She lit a cigarette. It had no filter in it.

'Continue,' Mellody said.

Hugo upended the Glenfarclas into his glass, but just a shallow slosh came out. Someone, thoughtfully, had locked the cabinet, removing the key, so he could not help himself to more.

He climbed back up the staircase to the kitchen and found a fresh bottle of everyday Macallan in the far-left corner of the sideboard, where fresh bottles could always be found. His fingernails searched for the weakness in its metal capsule, then stripped it off in one long peel. Outside, the police officer had left his post. Large slow clouds crept undetected through their blue.

Mellody had sounded OK. Tired, which was understandable, but also relieved. Hugo was relieved, too. He knew what he was going to do.

Back in the basement, the BBC man was picking through a stack of foreign newspapers.

'*Ciao, Karol,*' said the front page of *Il Tempo*.

Upstairs footsteps strode along the hall. The back door shutting. Finally, Mike had gone.

And there was the key! He must have simply left it on the table.

Picking it up, he sprung the Bruichladdich, and filled another glass with that instead.

He picked up the phone. There was one more call to make.

The digits sang their sequence.

Connected. Ringing. And continued ringing, until a noisy, tape-recorded silence and a wakened rumble introduced the ancient answering machine. It was a Saturday, of course, so they were out. Going round a garden centre probably.

'Hello,' said a recording of his father's voice, more than ten years old now, and still starchy with performance. 'You've reached the home of Martin and Caroline Marks. We're not in at the moment, but if you'd like to leave your name and number after the beep, we'll get back to you as soon as we can. Thank you. Goodbye.'

Hugo loved the smiling way his dad said 'beep', trying on the word like it was a funny hat. He could see the old man's eyebrows popping up.

Then his cue came.

'Mum, Dad. Hi, it's me,' he said. 'I'm really sorry I haven't called for a while . . . And er . . . I don't know if you've seen the news, but I'm having some problems this morning. I just called to say don't worry, really. It's OK. I know what I'm going to do. Things may be quite hard for you for a while, and I'm sorry about that. But whatever happens, I just want you to know that I love you both very much.'

The whisky was trembling in his hand. His voice splintered.

'So anyway . . .'

He took a gulp. A tear had crawled between his fingers and the plastic handset.

'I just wanted you to know that. And I'm very sorry about the grief you'll get. That's it. Love you. Bye.'

He switched the phone off in a hurry. He did not want to wait any more.

He took a sip of whisky, and looked at his supplies.

There were nineteen pills in the Ambien bottle. Hugo tipped them out on to the table. He had never taken more than three before. And there were still six Valium left too. He burst them from their pack on to the pile.

A Valium first, with whisky.

Then an Ambien, with more.

Then one of each. Quicker.

More whisky, not too much. Must not sick it up.

Two by two.

The bitter dust seeping through his tongue.

Two by two.

That one scraping on his palate.

Two by two.

Two by two.

Whisky. He had no water.

Two by two.

The final one.

As the Pope gazed down from television.

Hugo took his insulin pen, twisting out the ratchet to its largest dose. He had done this many times before and looked at it. Just looked at it.

The needle disappeared into his belly and he eased the button flat. It travelled such a long, long way.

Again he prepared the largest dose. The pleasant, antiseptic whiff of hospitals.

The plunger sighed in deep.

And he could feel it now. A soft, seductive sickness creeping.

One more needleful, pressed until the tank was empty.

He reached for the remote. How heavy his arm already was.

. . . cardio-respiratory and metabolic conditions of the Holy Father are substantially unchanged and therefore are very serious.

The words drifted on the screen, and a voice was reading them.

Outside, the helicopter had returned. Hovering still.

Last evening the Pope probably had in mind the young people whom he has met throughout the world during his pontificate.

Hugo closed his eyes.

In fact, he seemed to be referring to them when, in his words, and repeated several times, he seemed to have said the following sentence: 'I have looked for you. Now you have come to me. And I thank you.'

The helicopter muttered overhead.

That's great news, Daniel! Really pleased to hear it.

Is everything OK? You don't sound quite yourself. Feel free to call me on 07700 900412 if you would like to talk. Any time, including the weekend, is fine.

Wonderful new chapter, by the way.

Val x

Hi Daniel

Just to prove we're on the level, I thought I'd let you know that BookBrunch ran Cape's announcement of the deal last night. Go to www.bookbrunch.co.uk today and it should still be up there.

I note that they call the book 'modern fiction at its very best: a smart and savvy satire, ingeniously plotted, and full of mind-blowing twists and turns'. Not bad, eh? Cape are getting quite excited by the ebook possibilities as well. And Leo's keen to get involved. He has some big ideas of his own he wants to run past you.

Do feel free to call me when you have a minute. It would be so good to hear your voice after all this time. My mobile's 07700 900412. I promise this is not the police making me ask. (Or if you're still uncomfortable, and you want to talk to someone in complete confidence, there is always the Samaritans on 08457 90 90 90. They are really great.)

Hope you're OK!

Val x

Dear Daniel,

I know it's not easy for you to get to a computer at the moment, but if you're receiving any of my messages, do please let me know you're OK.

Love,

Val x
07700 900412

From: onolan.daniel@gmail.com
To: valerie.morrell@nortonmorrell.co.uk
Subject: Re:
Date: Tuesday, 16 March 2010 23:43:30
▶ 📎 Epilogue

Dearest Valerie

Honestly, you can't imagine how many times I didn't send you that first chapter before I did. Writing it, rewriting it, saving it, reading it, rewriting it, deleting it... feverishly scrubbing at each line of prose to fidget out its music. In the end, the only way to free myself was to get drunk and email what I had, regretting it immediately, as I knew I would. What is interesting, however, is that I don't regret it now.

The thing is, Valerie, that what I've done is what I thought I needed to do. We're all going somewhere, even if it's nowhere. To me, this is actually a kind of happy ending, though I realise it may not seem that way to you. In which case, never mind. Remember only that it was the ending that I wanted. I think I always knew what I was going to do.

With love, as always,

Daniel x

Michael danced down the stairs in his new suit. He was a busy man.

Twenty thousand pounds. For twelve hundred words, twenty thousand pounds. For twelve hundred words. And best of all, he haggled for it. They wanted to give him ten thousand. *Is that OK?* Andrea had said. And probably because she said it, Michael had found himself replying, *How about twenty?* Almost as a joke. *How about twenty?* Who would have thought he could haggle? He never haggled.

And now – at last – he was going to write a proper article, with his name on, for a proper paper!

It was quite by accident that I met Hugo Marks, it might begin.

Or, *I knew nobody when I arrived at Hugo Marks's thirty-first.*

Yes. That was better. He could not wait to go home and get to work.

His feet drummed down from step to step like expert fingers on piano keys. The old suit beneath his arm flapped merrily in time, clacking the spoon in its pocket on his trousered phone. He was a busy man in a hurry. It was time to go. And he looked forward to it. He would leave these broken people as their better, buttressed by his deal.

But where were they? The living room was empty, televisions off. Michael stopped and listened for a trace of chatter. Nothing. All those laptops gone, too, and the papers cleaned away.

A flush came from the bathroom.

He hurried to the landing and came face to face with a policeman.

'Just using the toilet, sir,' the man explained unnecessarily on his way out, and lumped off down the stairs. The cistern hissed.

Where were they all? Michael did not want to leave without his great goodbye.

Gingerly, he approached the other rooms and knocked. Each was empty.

Down in the hall, even the security guy had left his post, though the cameramen outside had not. In the front room, a twisted piece of drapery sat up stiffly on the carpet. The air was curtained and crepuscular, smelling old. Michael made his way into the kitchen, creeping softly, though there was nobody to hear him. Just a huge basket of fruit. In the garden, the policeman had retaken his position. A helicopter hovered overhead.

But on the basement steps, Michael faltered. He heard the happy sounds of television advertising. Life. He started to descend.

'Mike! Fuck. Are you still here?'

Hugo sat in slovenly collapse.

'Sorry,' Michael said, stopping on the steps. 'Where is everybody?'

'Oh, they went home. I thought, um, they had got you a car out the back?'

Woozy in his chair. Drunk again perhaps, or still shaking off some slumbers.

'Yeah, they said it would be here at two. It's out the back, is it? I just came down to say goodbye.'

'Oh right. Yeah. They were going to get you a car out the back.'

Definitely drunk.

'I thought your speech was great, by the way. It pissed everybody off.'

'Thanks.' Hugo laughed very slowly.

A moment's sorrow pinched at Michael as he watched the

guy, seven empty chairs around his own. It felt right to sell the story. No guilt there. But the desire for revenge had left him. There was simply nothing in the man to punish. Just whisky and television, and what looked like sleeping pills.

'You shouldn't drink with that stuff,' he said, descending fully, placing his old suit on a chair.

'S'fine.' Hugo slurred him away. 'Don't make a panic. Your car will be waiting. Thanks for everything.'

A jab of unease.

Instead of leaving, Michael stepped further forward, so he could look at Hugo's eyes. They were bored and hazy. And on the table he noticed something else: a plastic blister pack, crinkled to a shallow arch, sixteen shattered exits in its silver skin. He picked it up. Hugo did not try to stop him.

Diazepam Tablets BP 10 mg, read the intermittent letters on the foil.

'Have you had Valium too?' he asked, trying to keep the worry from his voice.

Hugo did not answer. He looked as though he was about to, but then he didn't.

Hot fear surged up Michael's spine. He grabbed the other pill bottle. It was very light, and silent when he shook it.

'Fuck, Hugo! What have you taken?'

'Ss'OK.'

'Hugo, what have you *taken*?'

'Ssh sh sh! S'fine. Don't worry about me, just go your car.'

'I'm getting the police.'

'*Don't!*' Suddenly the vigour in his voice was back. 'Just don't, OK?'

. . . *conditions of the Holy Father are substantially unchanged and therefore are very serious*, the television said.

'You don't have to do anything,' Hugo added. 'Just say goodbye, and get in your cab. After what I've done. Just go.'

'Listen . . .' Michael had to find the answer. 'I know things seem bad right now, but later . . .'

'No. This is not about now. It's about everything.'

'But I can't just leave you!'

Fear and pain.

. . . he seemed to be referring to them when, in his words, and repeated several times . . .

'Yes you can. S'the bess thing you can do.'

. . . *'I have looked for you. Now you have come to me. And I thank you.'* . . .

'Michael. This is what I want. Look at me. *This is what I want.*'

There were tears on Michael's face. 'What about Peru?' he said.

'Hmm?'

'Peru, Hugo. You could go to Peru!'

'Proo?'

'Peru.'

'Mmm . . . asparagus.'

'That's right! You can have lots of asparagus!'

'Oh . . . No. I know what I'm going to do.'

'But Hugo . . .'

'S'what I wan. Juss go. I know what I'm going to do.'

'I'm not going to sell you out, if that's what you're thinking. I'll never sell you out.'

'It duzzn matter.'

Hugo closed his eyes and folded his hands neatly across his stomach.

Michael watched.

He thought.

The man looked almost happy.

He thought.

And now he was walking. Tears and walking. Climbing

through his rain. Go go go. Away from choices. Up through doors and handles, up, and out into the sky. Out into the cool elsewhere. The reverential trees and shushing lawn. On and on. Through wet warm land and clean botanic lives. To leave, and leave for ever. To walk into another day.

'Are you all right, sir?' the policeman asked kindly.

And Michael walked on. He did not want to talk about it.

Deleted Scenes

Don Scarlett's spring collection

In the first draft, Hugo spoke to Don Scarlett in more detail about his out-rageous new designs, which were being worn for the evening by the Italian model Carlotta Bossi. I cut this passage because it felt too similar in tone to Hugo's previous conversation with Brian and Edie. It is also rather silly.

'You awight, Hugo?' Don was half hiding, and half refusing to hide, his irritation at not being listened to.

'Sorry, Don.' Hugo scuttled back into himself. 'I was miles away. You were saying?'

'It's camouflage, innnit?'

In contrast to most younger designers, Don had absorbed his love of fashion through callused hands, assembling, staffing and dismantling his mother's fabric stall in Barking market. His boutique, Smack, had been ignored until the early punks swept in — a noisy vindication Don had never yet recovered from. A recent BBC2 special, in tribute to his three decades in fashion, hadn't helped. He was somebody that Hugo did not wish to tangle with.

'Camouflage?' He presumed he had misheard.

'Yeah, camouflage. I thought you in particular might appreciate it.'

Carlotta Bossi smiled.

Hugo looked at her again. Unbelievable.

At first sight, he had innocently wondered what the letters

UNTC, printed endlessly in black across her lime green gown, might stand for. Some nobly failing cause presumably (the United Nations Tree Charter?) which had got desperate enough to chance it with Carlotta's semi-lingual ambassadressing. Moments later, however, he noticed a horrible and hilarious accident, which, moments after that, he realised was actually Don's horrible design. What was written on Carlotta was the word CUNT, many, many times.

'What do you mean, "camouflage"?' Hugo was irritated by how satisfied Don seemed. He and Carlotta were still glowing from the stir that they had caused outside.

'*Cam-ou-flage*.' Don enunciated it like Hugo was Japanese.

'But I'd say it was quite noticeable.'

'You're missing the point,' Don said testily. 'It's for high-profile people like yourself who get sick of all the aggro. What newspaper's going to print a photograph of you in a shirt with the word "CUNT" written all over it?'

'Cunta!' Carlotta cheered.

'I,' Hugo said slowly, 'see.' He laughed a little. 'It's definitely a great idea, Don. All that repetition almost takes away the meaning of the word.'

'Nope. It still means cunt.'

'No, no, I mean it isn't shocking when you see it written out so many times.'

'Isn't it?' Don sounded disappointed. 'How about "NIGGER" then?'

Several people near them were no longer talking.

'But Don, do you think anyone's going to want to walk around with "nigger" written all over them? Or "cunt" for that matter?'

'They will if they don't want their picture in the paper,' Don said patiently. 'That's the fucking point.'

'OK. Fine.' Why was he arguing? Why did he care? 'So you've foiled the paps. But how about the people you encounter who *aren't* trying to photograph you? Is it worth provoking all of them?'

'It's a concept Hugo, for fuck's sake. Just choose a different word if you don't like those. We can't use "FUCK". French Connection did that. I like "WANK", but it won't work in the States. . .' He chewed on his cigar. 'How about "ANAL"?'

There was a thoughtful waft of smoke.

'People will think it's "ALAN",' Hugo said.

Their neighbours now were very obviously listening. He glanced at them for support, and didn't get any. Mellody was laughing with her friends at the edge of the dance floor. Right now, even she would be a relief.

'"FEESTING"?' said Carlotta.

Mellody's early years

No passage in the novel was deleted more reluctantly than this one. It comes from the scene where Malcolm knocks over a tray of drinks, and tells the story of Mellody's first serious relationship, with an unhappy rock star called Corey Burns. As things panned out, however, she was the last of the four main characters to appear, by which point I was doing everything I could to stop the early chapters being clogged with backstory. That meant wincing, and cutting this.

What was she doing with these kids? No longer one of them herself, Mellody could see their carefree desperation, their synthetic confidence. She'd done the same, and seen it done.

I'm young, I'm wild, I'm free! I'm not afraid of you! It had been the living motto of her youth.

But now she knew what the grown-ups had been thinking. *If that is so, then why do you keep telling me?*

Even when she was fifteen years old, in the infancy of her career, Mellody must unknowingly have known this. The boys in her class back then, well, they seemed so young. So keen to please, yet so inept. Like it was skateboarding that would impress her, or poetry, or general knowledge. Display, display, display. With teenage boys, there was nothing but display. And looking like she did, of course, Mellody saw more displays than most – though fewer, still, than people thought. So marked had her early beauty been, and then so distant did she become with her success, that most boys in the neighbourhood gave up on her. The exceptions, on the whole, were those too mentally restricted to think their chances through. If anything she treated them – the goggling nerds, the dweebs, the drawling bozos

– with more sympathy than their naïve arrogance deserved. She was out of their league; she would not dispute that. Yet she sympathised as well, now that she'd discovered men – men in their twenties, men in bands – who were out of hers.

And though she strained against the tendency, the same men lured her still. Which meant younger men these days – some young enough, she once calculated horrified, to be the sons of her first crushes. Easily too young to know the name of her first boyfriend, Corey Burns. When she met him, Corey had been frighteningly twenty-three. His brains the brains, his voice the voice behind the Jersey grunge band Sling, whose records she and all her friends were smoking to at high school. But 'Hey, nice boots,' he'd said to her in passing at a party. Within three hours they'd be screwing in his car. Mellody's first time, though she hadn't really wanted it to be. Virginity weighed heavily upon her in the adult company she kept, yet the speed of its destruction, the speed of him . . . She hadn't realised. Though nobody, of course, expected twenty-three-year-olds to take you to their car to cop a feel. Still, it hadn't been that bad. Not bad at all, really. And when she walked back to the party with his arm around her shoulders, it was with the feeling, never known to her before, that she belonged there.

Even so it was surprising when, the next day, her mom passed on the covered phone in their big kitchen saying, 'It's somebody called Corey?' His deep voice, uncertain in the daytime, asked if she would come – that is, if she wasn't busy – to a gig that he was playing. She said yes about eight times, and loved him instantly. Two months later she told him her age, which was by then sixteen. Though by then it didn't matter. It didn't even matter when she, the high school girl, found herself responsible for looking after him when he got drunk and started shouting about his dad. It didn't matter when he called at 4am, or sent a taxi to her window charged with bringing her to him.

Despite her homework, his drug use – a shock to her at first – and, eventually, the opposition of her parents, she obliged him willingly. And more than willingly. Though sad, it was exciting, being needed by this wounded star.

Nearly ten years passed between their final break-up and Corey's death. When she heard, Mellody was inconsolable. He had been clean of heroin for more than a year, according to a news report she found online. On being tempted back, however, he had administered to his disaccustomed bloodstream an addict's dose, easily enough to kill him, if he realised or not. (Three weeks of tests were needed, even so, to confirm what finished off his kippered body.) Mellody's grief became extreme. In part, this was because she'd only heard the news so very late: nearly six months after the event, obliquely from a mutual friend who mentioned Corey guessing, as seemed safe, that she already knew. And piecing things together, shaking intermittently with sobs, Mellody realised that she could have made the funeral, if she had known. They had been on holiday in Mexico, she and Hugo – diving probably – at the moment Corey was incinerated. She was even working in New York, not two miles from him, on the day he died. Rouged and lit and grumbling, she sat and smiled while he was pushing in the plunger just a nudge too far. No mystic twinge had warned her. Though it was around that time, coincidentally, that her own illicit needle-play began to build.

Hugo's struggle with fame

It seemed important to relate somewhere a little of what the top stars have to live with. Like the rest of us, however, they lose sympathy if they bang on about their problems. The inclusion of this section, in which Hugo tells Michael of the paranoia and unfairness that regularly visit famous people, risked taking him too far into that territory.

Hugo had momentum.

'It's like I'm a business. They consume me. And it's like that gives them rights. Like that means they can camp outside my house, and send me shit in the post, and take pictures everywhere I go, and I've got to fucking smile about it! There was a guy, this fucking German guy, who showed up when I was on holiday in France – don't know how he knew where I was – and he just demanded to meet me. *"I am driving more than a thousand kilometres!"'*

This was in a crazy German accent.

'*"Five minutes is all I am asking from you!"* I could hear him shouting from the pool. *"I go to see all your movies! Why will you be cruel to me? I buy all your DVDs!"* Well don't!'

Shouted.

'Don't fucking buy them! Just go away and hate me!' The flowers in his jacket twitched with rage.

Michael did not know what to say.

'And whatever I do, everyone always thinks it's part of a big plan. Like it's always about them. I mean,' Hugo lowered his voice slightly, 'there are *times* when you use the media to your advantage. But usually it's just to correct the lies they've already spread about you. Or when someone who worked for me was selling stuff here and there, just little diary stories, tip-offs about where I would be, that sort of thing. That made it really hard to get some peace. We had to get Theresa – that's Renee's assistant – we had to get her to book tables at three different restaurants with 30 minutes' notice, and not with our usual pseudonyms either, but. . .'

'You have pseudonyms?'

'Of course. Everybody does.'

'Like what?'

'Stephen Little is my main one,' Hugo said without hesitating. 'Like the movie. It's just a joke, really. It's also the name of some poet Mellody likes. Anyway. . .' He pressed on. '. . . No, what bothered me wasn't the hassle of booking tables, it was that someone I saw every day was tipping people off behind my back. So do you know what I did?'

'What?'

'I mentioned a few things to different people – totally made up stuff, of course – and waited to see what would happen.'

'What, like stories?'

'Yeah, just little bits and pieces about me that I knew the papers would like. And bang!'

His palms slapped together. He was almost gleeful now.

'*Daily Mirror.* 'Hop-along Hugo. Movie star Hugo Marks has injured his knee horse-riding while researching his role in the new...' Blah, blah fucking blah.'

A dramatic pause.

'It was my reflexologist!'

'Wow!' Michael said. Then, 'What did you do?'

'Fired her. That's what. And it was a fucking pleasure. Told some people why as well. She'll never touch Bowie's feet again. That's certain. I still get all sorts of weird stuff happening to me, mind you; people just know things. But I've never planted another story after that one.'

'No. I believe you.' What else could Michael say?

'Other people don't though. They think everything is part of a conspiracy, that it's all about making them like me, or hate Mellody, or buy stuff, or whatever.'

'They just need to feel important,' Michael suggested. 'They'd rather be manipulated by the rich and famous than ignored.'

'*Exactly!*'

Hugo clapped his hands together.

Michael was emboldened. 'You guys. . .' He swigged his empty scotch with feeling. He had never thought this through before. '. . .you guys are special because you are *the unignored.*'

Tweets

All of the messages below are genuine. The user names of the people who wrote them are in bold, and when a tweet contains an @ address, this means it is intended for the attention of a specific user, or is a reply to another message. If part of a conversation does not contain the #afterpartybook hashtag, however, it has not been included.

To avoid excessive repetition, some retweets (one user's message that has been relayed to the followers of another) are not included. For the same reason, a handful of tweets by the author in which he explained the hashtag to those who asked have also been removed. Where people have mistakenly used the wrong hashtag, but then clarified their intentions, their messages have been included. We've also admitted a small number of late messages. There seemed to be no reason not to.

Tweets

leobenedictus
This is an intriguing test. #afterpartybook

zoelaura
#afterpartybook. There you go

Dempster2000
@leobenedictus Yeah good luck with the 'stealth marketing' ploy. It'll never wor...#afterpartybook #afterpartybook #afterpartybook #afterp

zoelaura
@leobenedictus no god. In that case 'everyone must follow @zoelaura'. #afterpartybook.

Tweets

oilysailor
Van der Vaart's suicide after only six months in the English game was inevitable #afterpartybook

moonjets
superintendant ywenty SKY going to the get a drink #afterpartybook

AnthonyC1988
Just finished the afterparty by leo benedictus, wow like no novel i have and will ever read. A landmark novel! #theafterpartybook

BetaRish
Hell is other people's glamswank parties. #afterpartybook

mpphillips
IT'S BALLS. #afterpartybook

icemark
RT @mpphillips: IT'S BALLS. #afterpartybook

john_self
@leobenedictus @mpphillips "NOW ONLY 99p!" #afterpartybook

leobenedictus
@john_self @mpphillips So very, very droll. #afterpartybook

RobBuckley
I have no idea why I'm retweeting this, but hell, why not? RT @mpphillips: IT'S BALLS. #afterpartybook

JonLeeWriter
@mpphillips I read the first chapter. It's really good. But, for these purposes, IT'S BALLS #afterpartybook

mpphillips
The IT'S BALLS campaign is on fire. There are FOUR of us now, not including the BALLSY cop-out @chriswakling. Join us! #afterpartybook

Tweets

chriswakling
@mpphillips 'Ballsy Cop-Out' = 'So Cool But Play'. That took ages. #afterpartybook

lizfraser1
@chriswakling aha, I like BALLSY. I also like the other stuff you said about it. Your work here is done! @leobenedictus #afterpartybook

lizfraser1
@chriswakling you are SO @leobenedictus's book whore. I can only do hashtags in tweets. You have alphamum book club! *sighs*#afterpartybook

lizfraser1
@leobenedictus @chriswakling we are now all his slaves. We have been captured into the #afterpartybook net! *does it again*

mredwards
Oops, I used the wrong hashtag for my Afterparty tweet. It should have been #afterpartybook. Silly me.

DigitalDanHouse
'Wow', exclaimed R Kelly, 'there's so much great cuisine on offer here it's as if this party was catered.' #afterpartybook

Renegatus
Also signed myself up to moderate and prune the #afterpartybook Twitter entries. Damn you, free wine.

chriswakling
So, bookgroup devoured #afterpartybook: 'Brill-bleak' 'Celeb-clever' 'Drug-sharp' 'The snail!' and ... 'There's a man under the ice cube!'

cognacbrown
If Spike Jonze wrote an airport novel then the Leo Benedictus' 'The Afterparty' would be it #afterpartybook

Tweets

Tiny_Camels
Without postmodern trickery #afterpartybook wld still be a pretty sharp funny & sad media satire. Wout media satire it wld be zip. Go figure

ellijandro
Just finished #theafterpartybook in one go. My inner english geek loved the meta-fiction/post moderness. V funny also. Gd wrk leo/william

FlossieTeacake
Vicki Watson clutching a copy of #afterpartybook. Through happy synchronicity, I am taking notes with my @leobenedictus pen. Marvellous.

mpphillips
@FlossieTeacake A @leobenedictus pen. Would that be a ball(s)point? #afterpartybook

fridayproject
I'd rather be reading 21st Century Dodos by Steve Stack #afterpartybook

firebookswap
Come to the Firestation Book Swap, every third Thursday in Windsor. It's great. #afterpartybook

EmmaB4
Hear, hear RT @firebookswap Come to the Firestation Book Swap, every third Thursday in Windsor. It's great. #afterpartybook

SmartShirtSoc
RT @firebookswap: Come to the Firestation Book Swap, every third Thursday in Windsor. It's great. #afterpartybook

Tweets

leobenedictus
Now THIS is getting into the spirit of things. RT @fridayproject I'd rather be reading 21st Century Dodos by Steve Stack #afterpartybook

meandmybigmouth
Hello Kat x #afterpartybook

katobell
Hello Scott x #afterpartybook

john_self
@Baddiel @leobenedictus If only you'd tagged that #afterpartybook, it would be on the paperback (as this tweet will be).

jesseversed
@leobenedictus just finished #afterpartybook after seeing your first ever reading at review bookshop, Sunny Peckham. page turning enjoyment.

jesseversed
@leobenedictus also, how peculiar to be in a world so recent, yet so pre-twitter... #afterpartybook #2005

JezzaTrev
@leobenedictus Give peas a chance! #afterpartybook

StevieFM
#afterpartybook

charlieplum101
@IamJamieG The Afterparty (possibly by Leo Benedictus) is the book you need dear Giles! It's perfect for Ritalin lovers #afterpartybook

charlieplum101
@IamJamieG harsh giles, i should have told you i'm a personal friend of william mendez #afterpartybook

Tweets

alicemhancock
Read this book; better than an afterparty, morning after effects just as damaging http://t.co/V2p2nq5 #afterpartybook

JuandeFrancisco
@VarsityUK #afterpartybook

condorcet
@VarsityUK Great piece about Leo Benedictus! #afterpartybook

gavinjamesbower
The blurb was right. I really haven't read a book like the #afterpartybook before. Post-Meta-Benedictus-Fiction at its best, @leobenedictus

emmaryoung
#afterpartybook

entropic1
Got my treat for the long weekend: the #afterpartybook by Leo Benedictus finally arrived today. I'm glad. I'm glad.

bookhashtags
The Afterparty, #afterpartybook by Leo Benedictus has been added at http://bookhashtags.com/book?id=146

matthewharvey
Just finished #Afterpartybook by Leo Benedictus. Not only is it AWESOME, it's got fictional versions of Rebekah Wade and Andy Coulson in it!

RosyPosy19
After an amusing twitter convo with author @leobenedictus I def recommend #afterpartybook to anyone! ;)

fechtbuch
At Latitude, a man handed me a piece of paper with cryptic instructions. Perhaps he was a spy. #afterpartybook

mralexcheeseman
Did it really happen or is it a novel or is it both or will I never find out? #afterpartybook – read it in 2 days, relaxing by the pool.

tristanyeoh
Dear Daniel/"William", this tweet idea – like Malc's sheepdog encounter – is fantastic. Leo would be proud. #afterpartybook

adoingword
I hereby nominate @leobenedictus' #afterpartybook as a deserving #fridayreads candidate. There.

Fintalloneword
@bookworm1979 Yep If I'd won, was going to give friend's address. I was gripped. V clever piece of writing by @leobenedictus #afterpartybook

ScottDDixon
Just finished 'The Afterparty' by Leo Benedictus. Never read a book like it, very clever how it mixes reality and fiction #afterpartybook

bookhashtags
The Afterparty, #afterpartybook by Leo Benedictus is the featured book of the day at http://t.co/2IFlmsG

ERMarty
Will definitely be Amazon wishlisting #afterpartybook by (the unbeknownst to me) Leo Benedictus – always interested in the undiscovered :)

sefasaurus_rex
The #afterpartybook is shaping up to be a good read, but I'm a little confused – is it real or not? You know what I mean if you've read it.

CRL_HE
#afterpartybook is taking twists that I didn't see in the beginning. Also enjoying the style of writing! Has gone beyond my expectations!

sefasaurus_rex
@vintagebookclub here's what I thought! :) also check out the comment! http://t.co/dqCAXK3 #afterpartybook

CRL_HE
@vintagebookclub #afterpartybook was great! Much better than I anticipated, great style of writing. Already lent it to someone else! :-)

vintagebookclub
Remember, any tweet with the hashtag #afterpartybook may end up being included in the paperback version!

JonathanCape
any tweet you write with #afterpartybook included can still get included in the @vintagebooks edition of @leobenedictus's book out next yr.

JonathanCape
5 copies of hilarious celeb satire #afterpartybook by @leobenedictus given to first to answer with names of the last 3 Xfactor winners!

sbroadhurst
@JonathanCape joe mceldery, matt cardle and alexanda burke #afterpartybook

JonathanCape
@melspur great work! DM address and will send copy. tweet with hashtag #afterpartybook to get your tweet printed in back of next edition!

phillipjedwards
@JonathanCape Is it too late to win the #afterpartybook? The last 3 X Factor winners were Joe McElderberry, Matt Cardie & Alexanda Burke

phillipjedwards
@JonathanCape So if I spelled the names Joe McElderry, Matt Cardle & Alexandra Burke properly would I win one? The #afterpartybook that is?

Fintalloneword
Self-publishing be damned! Twitter tag fame awaits. All this & a rollicking good read. You're spoiling us, Mr B, so you are. #afterpartybook

AntF
#afterpartybook Very unique book. Fascinating to watch it be created while you read. Feels remarkably realistic. Met the Author at Latitude

Shemadene
I enjoyed the #afterpartybook so much that I'm reading it again & recommending it to friends.

leobenedictus
THANK YOU to the sharp eyes at the Practical Law book club, for pointing out some errors in the novel. (And for reading it.) #afterpartybook

LigaDugdale
@leobenedictus That's what you get from lawyers... Loved the book but as mentioned think you should sort out those fonts! #afterpartybook

andi_t
@leobenedictus Surely if you had you could have just asked the actual author to re-send it to you? #theafterparty

mikegrady87
@leobenedictus I haven't read it yet. But I want to.
#afterbookparty

mikegrady87
@leobenedictus Erm...I meant #afterpartybook, naturally. I lost out to a woman in Waterstone's the other week over the last copy.

Shemadene
In fact "I'm sorry for rubber-stamping your desk, i dont know what came over me" could be a line in #afterpartybook

leobenedictus
ADVERTISEMENT FEATURE. Tweet anything with #afterpartybook and we'll print it in the p/back. Best tweet today wins free copy. Ends midnight.

raygarraty
Why I'm still hangover if I drank only water? #afterpartybook

sarahaxtell1
This book's rather good – I like this Leo Benedictus character's style. Hope he writes another one sometime soon! #afterpartybook

Ziggy_Evitts
#afterpartybook Monday start. A Whygirl in falsetty workskins left Dr Robert with a broken nose, a bag of grey pills and I smiled at her.

leobenedictus
Thanks for some great tweets with #afterpartybook (and variants). JUST ONE HOUR OR SO LEFT TO GO.

leobenedictus
Any messages with #afterpartybook sent now may well end up as the last lines in the paperback....

Tweets

booksellercrow
@leobenedictus #afterpartybook and then, they all lived happily ever after.

clairemaugham
@leobenedictus all I know is what the words know #afterpartybook

autogyro42
It was all the fever dream of a grimly despairing subeditor in a dystopian future. The End. #afterpartybook

natapoupard
@leobenedictus On finishing The Afterparty book I feel it has all the good viral techniques to make it a truly "live" book #afterpartybook

neilcole
If I *had* gone to the Awards after-party last night, I would never've finished reading #afterpartybook today #hyperfiction